MAN ALIVE!

MAN ALIVE!

MARY KAY ZURAVLEFF

FARRAR, STRAUS AND GIROUX   NEW YORK

Farrar, Straus and Giroux
18 West 18th Street, New York 10011

Printed in the United States of America
First edition, 2013

Library of Congress Cataloging-in-Publication Data
Zuravleff, Mary Kay.
    Man alive! / Mary Kay Zuravleff. — First edition.
        pages   cm
    ISBN 978-0-374-20231-6 (alk. paper)
    1. Lightning—Fiction.   2. Life change events—Fiction.   3. Domestic fiction.
I. Title.

PS3576.U54M36 2013
813'.54—dc23
                                                            2012048073

Designed by Jonathan D. Lippincott

www.fsgbooks.com
www.twitter.com/fsgbooks • www.facebook.com/fsgbooks

10 9 8 7 6 5 4 3 2 1

To Eliza Lee Zizka, Theo Matthew Zizka, and Gary Zizka,
for family life as we know it

MAN ALIVE!

INSIDE THE FLASH

Everyone deserves a vacation from himself, Owen Lerner thinks, on the last day of his. He's convinced that spending three weeks at their beach house each summer makes him a better doctor and a better parent, if not a snappier dresser. Early every morning, face flushed with a good night's sleep, the sun lifts itself out of the ocean and travels across the summer sky, hanging out even as it warms the sand. Through such measured leisure, Owen catches up on his medical journals as well as his sleep, but he lets himself go, too, a year's worth of bacon and booze packed into three weeks at the Delaware shore.

This evening he is sporting the baggy shorts and soft rubber sandals he only ever wears at Rehoboth. He's missed a button on his lurid Hawaiian shirt, so that the excess shirttail hangs over his belly like a pennant, catching the wind the way a ship's flag might. Reaching beneath this flap, he fishes in his pants pockets for meter change and comes up with an inch of quarters—*Lucky strike!*—as if he's snagged a tuna from one of those monster fishing boats. First a parking place—on Reho Ave., in August, at dinnertime—and now quarters galore.

Nostalgia triggers the vertigo Owen has come to expect on the last day of vacation, when he's looking to the past and the future. Hard to believe that the twins, who resemble surfers from old beach movies, will be juniors in college or that his baby girl is sixteen. Hard to believe it's 2008. They've been coming here since the boys were born, back when the boardwalk was low-budget, greasy fun. Used to be, he could nickel-and-dime his way through August, springing for a waxed-paper bag of saltwater taffy if Will or Ricky had a loose tooth, or throwing pitches in the arcade (three for a *quarter*—is that possible?) to win Brooke a stuffed dolphin bigger than the dog. He remembers Toni as barely clothed. She wore gauze sundresses that were nearly as insubstantial as their house, which was a mere shack in the sand then, tar paper applauding the ocean breeze.

As Owen looks forward, his fistful of quarters brings to mind the patients waiting for him on the other side of vacation. Try as they may, his kids cannot play well with others, and the only rule they understand is that whatever they enjoy will inevitably be taken away. Owen's pocket change could serve as a lesson in planning ahead. Unfortunately, his patients can't anticipate what might happen in the course of a day; how can they prepare for a future that seems haphazard? Everything catches them by surprise, and predictably, they hate surprises.

His beach reading this summer has included a number of promising drug studies for his practice, and as he counts the meter fare, he's also mentally mixing meds to alleviate anxiety and boost executive functioning. At the same time, he's anticipating sliding into a varnished booth at Dogfish Head and having Axe mix him a drink with the house-made gin. He may even order onion rings. The cumulative effect of his thoughts is a moment of gratitude for the brain's plasticity: onion rings, gin, kin, and meds, all considered within the time it takes to manipulate a handful of coins.

The face of the parking meter is bubbled like a gumball machine, with forty minutes from the last parker showing in the window. Owen still considers time on a meter to be found money, that little bit of grace his wife will never acknowledge. A hundred-dollar goof in their favor in the checking account—Toni can't get excited about it, considering they have mortgages on two houses, two college tuitions, and two cars, as well as insurance out the wazoo. Spare change is all relative, he supposes. A hundred dollars buys thousands of meter minutes, not so many therapy minutes, not even thirty.

Malpractice insurance, therapy minutes. He'd felt the tide changing from vacation to vocation an hour or so earlier, while taking a shower to sluice off the day's sand and sunscreen. Upstairs, between toweling off and getting dressed, he'd lunged for his blinking cell phone in spite of himself. Outgoing message be damned, mothers filled his voice mail with their requests, listing the vegetable soup of disorders ladled out to their children: ADD, ADHD, OCD, ODD, PDD, SID. He was still standing there naked except for his glasses and cell phone when Toni, lovely Toni, strolled in from her bath.

"Stripped to the essentials, I see." She dropped her own towel to the floor and began dressing, unceremoniously stepping into plain cotton underpants as if they shared a locker room rather than an entire life. He admired her softening waist, alluringly belted with a thin stripe of tan, before it disappeared beneath drawstring pants and a crisp linen shirt. Her cheekbones glistened with some cucumber-scented mist she used only at the beach.

Although he clamshelled the phone, she waved him off. "Don't let me get between you and new clients. We're supposed to stay away from the boys' college fund until the market has time to recover."

"But they're in college *now*," he'd said.

"Them's the breaks." She shrugged. "As for us, it's a good thing Dr. Lerner's in demand."

And so he keeps the parking meter credit to himself, pocketing a few quarters and then, *What the hell*, retrieving them, intending to feed the meter as if it were a slot machine, either spending the time out with his family or paying it forward to the next carload of beachgoers. Earlier in the vacation, they would have left the car at home and walked to the restaurant; the boys would have raced each other there. Owen drops a coin into the slot, which adds a paltry seven minutes, and a second coin gives them only another eight, returning him to summers when a quarter bought more.

This last day on the beach has been a pleasant one: overcast but no rain, which makes for easier reading and, in general, a less beaten-down feeling (as if beach life were an ordeal, which it isn't, but after a bleached-white sunny day, occasionally riding the waves with the kids or shoveling sand, the first beer pulls him under). His itchy beard brings to mind the trim he'll get once he's home. Maybe he'll ask for a goatee this time, aiming for the fleshy Freud look. More likely, he'll be mistaken for a slender Santa.

"Behold, people." Brooke points out the roiling clouds that have moved in since they left. "I'm glad we're finished with our *heliolatry*."

"Verily," Will agrees. "And isn't the thunder *vociferous*?"

Owen's not sure if Will, the adoring big brother, is actually helping Brooke with her test prep or if he just enjoys releasing words, like viruses, into his little sister's vocabulary.

"That *language*," Toni complains, but she laughs when Will says, "Yeah, what the flux?" because that's her line. She looks at Owen over the top of her sunglasses and then raises her eyes toward the greenish sky. "We should have made do at home. We threw away so much food."

Ricky says, "We ran out of ketchup," and the rest of them concur. No ketchup, no dinner.

Truckloads of clouds flash their lights across the horizon before ramming into one another, and the resulting collision rumbles across the sky.

Brooke cups her hand around her ear. "It's a total *cacography*." When the boys don't respond, she ventures, "Harsh, awful sound?"

"You mean *cacophony*." Smugness deepens Ricky's dimple. "*Cacography* is awful handwriting."

Will says, "Like Dad's. Right, old man?"

"Occupational hazard," Owen says. Although he should feed the meter and get his family inside already, it's worth spending a few of the minutes he's bought listening to the kids. Maybe he and Will could take a week at the beach alone sometime.

Will says, "To remember *cacography*, think *dadography*. That's your mnemonic, Brooksey."

"Use it in a sentence," Ricky is saying. "Dad's cryptic scrivening, his crapulous scrawl, is cacographic."

Brooke looks sideways to make sure he isn't annoyed. He isn't. Family dynamics fall in a light sprinkle around Owen, who considers it healthy that they've united to mock their father. His motto, which he inherited from his mentor, is "The art of family life is to not take it personally." Judging from his reading stack, the money these days is on brain imaging, which can pinpoint the very nerve cells that tackle the word *cacography*. He wonders what part of the brain recognizes sarcasm—what sector distinguishes laughing at from laughing with?

The sky spasms like a lightbulb on its way to burnout, and that also reminds him of brain scans. An able-bodied head has vivid flashes of yellow, orange, and red as different associations flare up. However, the scans of autistic subjects are remarkably dark. In their brains, the lights are on for a literal translation of what is heard; as for tone of voice or facial expressions, not a flicker. He should resurrect the ear-training therapy he tried to develop twenty years ago. He'll have to ask Toni where she stowed the master tapes; he'd recorded hours of angry exchanges and excited chatter, friendly overtures and meddlesome inquisitions. In those days, the estimate of autism in the population was one in fifteen hundred. The newest numbers are one in one hundred kids—surely he can snag some funding with those burgeoning odds. He glances at Toni, who's focused on their daughter.

"I wish you'd put on more clothes," Toni says to Brooke, tapping her on the rump. Emblazoned across her tiny shorts, for some reason, is *VIXEN*.

"How about more glasses, Mom?"

"Don't tempt me." In addition to the shades Toni is wearing, her regular glasses squat on top of her head, and reading specs, suspended from a chain around her neck, rest on her chest, as if her breasts might be called upon to read fine print. Reaching into her bag, she tugs a fringed corner into an arm-length span of fabric. She pulls a second and third time until she has drawn out a shimmery red square that she wraps around Brooke's slight hips as the wind tries to undo her work, lifting the fringe to reveal their daughter's branded backside. The sarong Toni fashions takes Brooke past jaded teen to alluring island girl.

Owen says, "That's worse. Now she looks like a Tahitian maiden."

So Brooke leaves it on.

The attention she's been attracting this summer is disconcerting. In truth she looks remarkably like the pictures of Toni as a teenager, a little smaller and with darker hair.

Toni is lassoing her own hair into a hybrid bun/ponytail. She says, "I hope it's raining at home. Our yard is probably straw by now."

"Tinder," Brooke pitches.

"Kindling," Will says.

And then Ricky: "Tender kindling. Locofoco."

Owen is oddly satisfied when Will gives his brother's shoulder a shove.

"*You're* locofoco," Will says.

"Locofoco is a safety match," Ricky says. "Obviously, your test scores didn't get you into Penn."

"At least Mom likes me." Will lifts one foot onto a tall bike rack and then effortlessly steps up, climbing the three-foot rise as if it were a single stair. He walks along the rack's steel spine, which is slick and crisscrossed with handlebars, prompting Ricky to get on at the far end. They start horsing around, grown boys still trying to knock each other off-balance.

"Must we?" Toni asks.

Apparently we must. In the morning, they'll close up the beach house, handing bundle after bundle like a fire brigade down the line to Owen, who's in charge of fitting everything into or on top of the van, including what they don't want to leave for renters or lock in the shed. Once home, they'll repeat the drill twice more to return Ricky to Duke, Will to Penn. The scramble ends with all three children tucked in for the fall semester, he and Toni hunkering down to keep everyone in chicken feed.

But first, dinner. A moment ago, as Owen had slipped two quarters into the meter's slot, his fingertips had touched the satiny metal, still sun-toasted despite coming under the thunderhead's shadow. Now he deftly thumbs a coin from his palm to between his thumb and forefinger, a learned skill that has become almost autonomic. With pay phones being phased out or taking only phone cards, with jukeboxes demanding dollar bills, what is left but parking meters to oblige such dexterity? If he gave Brooke a few quarters, would she cup them in her palm, fishing around with her other hand to pluck out individual coins? Are there deft maneuvers she or the boys have developed via mousing or texting that have blazed neurological shortcuts in their brains? Has our internal wiring always been the same, or does the circuitry of playing Guitar Hero differ from that of playing marbles?

Knock off the shoptalk, Owen tells himself. If they've timed this right, families with little kids will be settling their checks about now, and they'll have a twenty-minute wait at most. And if Will's Kyra is their waitress, all the better. He fantasizes for a second how *VIXEN* could rightly be appended to Kyra and posts a mental note to encourage Will to visit her during the upcoming semester. Unless a father's backing of a potential girlfriend scotches that possibility. As Owen thinks about the observer affecting the observed's behavior, he hears a loud buzz, an intensifying hum zeroing in on him. He figures the noise for a beach plane trailing a happy-hour proclamation and questions the wisdom of flying one of those two-seaters through flashing clouds. All of this is happening as he touches serrated edge of quarter to smooth slot of parking meter, the barest of contact, and he is, literally, blown away.

His first reaction is, *That parking meter packs a wallop!* Of course he can't understand, inside the flash, that he's being struck by lightning. It's more like stepping off the high dive—and then plummeting into a hot spotlight of water. Neither inhaling nor exhaling, Owen feels heavy pressure on his ribs and within his sinuses—both his heart and ears yearn to rupture—while his arms and legs flail spasmodically, not in a swimming groove. More like a believer shot full of god, some maniac at a revival compelled to twitch and moan in languages not yet discovered before plunging into the baptismal font. He is white-hot as well as deeply quenched by the singed, syrupy fluid of his surround.

Water magnifies, lubricates, cleanses, and conducts, all of which is the case here. Water flows, and Owen rides the torrent everywhere at once, having been granted infinite perspective: he is looking down at his body, which isn't actually in water but is writhing on the sidewalk, his shirt ripped open and his white underbelly jiggling away; then he is eye to eye with his remaining quarters, which are suspended midair in the unlikely shape of a bell curve until one is picked off by a pair of sunglasses flying or flung through space; then he is somehow staring at his wife's new tooth, her square jaw unhinged to reveal her crown. Next, he is looking to the horizon, across the parking lot, over the board-walk to the beach, all the way to the surf, which has picked up height and mass since they broke camp an hour ago, lugging their umbrella and beach chairs as well as all the sodden, gritty towels back to the house, where he took his last outdoor shower of the season; then he is staring straight up into the sky from some-where up in the sky, shimmering with the crackling clouds and bright static that have knocked him off his feet.

Up among the ether, everything is so fucking clear, as if he's viewing his life through the Hubble telescope. He has never distinguished such vivid shades of gray, from the thundercloud to the sidewalks to the gum stains irregularly blotting the sidewalk beneath Toni's flaking silver sandals. Her chipped red toenails are an eye-popping contrast. He clearly sees Will's tenderness as well as his vulnerability, along with the long dent across the van's sliding door from his run-in with the principal's Prius. Brooke's strawberry birthmark shines forth, as does her skeptical squint, and he can detect the gap returning to Ricky's front teeth be-cause he stopped wearing his retainer. How can there be a light in which his banal life is so complex and invigorating? They are but an urban suburban family who spend money like water— *like water!*—and who each go about doing mostly what is ex-pected of them. And yet they are sublime, and he loves them to the point of pain.

Concern presses on Owen's heart and then releases it like a clutch, so that he shifts into transcendence. From this vantage point he beholds his wife and children as they are, but even more so. Toni is intensely beautiful as well as shockingly old, nearly half a century, and she is fierce with the expectations she harbors for the five of them; Brooke has every reason to be confident, what with her gymnast's poise and her mother's profile, but when had the world begun to bore her so?

With any luck, they will exceed Toni's high hopes as she lives to grow older still, and Brooke will be freshly amazed; such is the tolerance and optimism his height and warmth inspire. Seeing the twins from boys to men, Owen recognizes the danger in Will's dark wit and the sexual ambivalence in Ricky's neediness. He feels honored to know them all so intimately. Owen does not glimpse their future; however, to peer this intricately into the individual cogs, their teeth and their turnings, is to better understand how things might play out.

Time is as warped as space, because there is Will balancing atop the bike rack as Ricky prepares to leap off. Their flares of mutual resentment and competition burn bright, and yet the boys' latest argument only deepens Owen's contentment—don't they have to grow apart to be individuals? On the verge of adulthood, wouldn't an identical twin be the best and safest sparring partner for asserting your very self? He remembers the two of them wrestling in Toni's womb. The obstetrician worried that they'd strangle each other before they were born.

Owen sees now, and he sees then. Distinct life segments have been tossed into a jumble like socks in his dresser drawer, and he lovingly draws them out, the threadbare as well as the warm, and matches them together. An unreachable patient stares at him from the cage of autism, which pairs up with her speaking intelligibly—"Dogs can bite"—a miracle assisted by his pharmacological know-how. He sees himself much earlier and trimmer, getting married in the university chapel and then signing divorce papers in the university's legal clinic, memories set apart from most of the bundle and gingerly nudged aside to get at any segment starring Toni, whom he is eager to hold fast to through all other memories, including their own courthouse wedding.

Brooke bounces into the air off his knee and then back flips off a balance beam, fracturing her wrist in a botched landing. A twin birthday party goes south when the boys, having attacked Batman piñatas, turn the bats on each other; those same boys enter the world from *between Toni's legs*. Lust stirs as voluptuous Kyra whispers in Will's ear, which leads Owen back to a randy episode between himself and Toni.

Like the space telescope, Owen is privileged with a view of our very origins. He is especially riveted by the formation of his family planet. Their connection each to the other, his to them, and his to the universe is mystical and mind-blowing. That he and Toni merged in pleasure, their combined emanations carrying all that was required to make three sentient beings, blows his mind anew.

It is bliss, pure bliss, and though he's aware that he isn't breathing, he has the scent of barbecue in his nostrils—hickory-smoked, well-marbled meat with bourbon-and-mango-spiked sauce caramelized by intense heat.

Ricky brings him back. Ricky and Dogfish's bartender, damn them both. Of course, Owen isn't able to assure them that he is fine where he is. Strapping man-child lifeguard gets right to work, prying open Owen's mouth and sweeping a finger through, then slamming the meaty part of his fist against Owen's bared chest. Owen has had the wind knocked out of him, and Ricky huffs into his lungs, reciting "barbecue spareribs, barbecue spareribs" over Owen's twitching body between breaths.

Brooke must have bolted into the restaurant for help because she is bolting out now, followed full tilt by the bartender with his brand-new defibrillator. Owen doesn't think his heart ever stops; the bloody piston revs itself into the red zone, lurches, and then slams against its bony chassis, preparing to make a break for it. Ricky's rhythmic pounding keeps his heart in its place and gives it something to keep time to until the muscle-bound, shaved-headed Axe, previously prized for titrating drinks, shocks Owen into resuming the lub-dub of the gravity-bound masses.

So much for expansiveness; ditto for infinite perspective. Owen's torso does a little defibrillator dance, and his shoulder blades clatter against the sidewalk. The ecstasy of leaving his body is, in the first few seconds, equal to the excruciating, edifying pain he is beginning to fathom.

No amount of deduction can explain the hot beam that lifted him like a sheet off a clothesline, shook him out a few times, and dropped him near the restaurant in a wrinkled heap. His situation is beyond deduction, and yet he knows all sorts of things without having thought them through: Ricky's touch, for example. Although he's never felt Ricky's palm against his heart, he has a muscle memory of hoisting the boy onto his shoulders and of squeezing his hand to quicken him across a busy street. Nothing remotely recent; even so, Ricky's touch is instantly, and instinctively, familiar. Owen opens his eyes. His son is a silhouette to him, scrub-brush hair, square chin, and the neck muscles of a swimmer.

"I did not see that coming," Owen says.

"Fucking A." Ricky speaks with awe. "You are here."

There is a boyish sincerity in his son's voice that he hasn't heard for years.

"Man alive!" Owen says. His body hurts in distinct layers, from his deepest tissue to the hair standing up on his arms. Meanwhile, a ravenous hunger overwhelms him. He is Rip Van Winkle starving. "A full rack sounds right for tonight."

His son's face clouds over in confusion. Where is Toni? One look at her, and Owen will know how to assess the situation. He longs for her direct gaze—*Are we okay here?*—but he's lost his glasses. He tries slapping at his shirtfront pocket; however, he's lost his shirtfront and slapping, too. You wouldn't think that could inspire such glee. Squinting, he manages to see his wife's willowy torso bend toward the ground like a weeping willow. He opens his mouth to warn her; all that comes out is laughter. "Ha ha," he says. No, that isn't remotely right. "Hee hee hee."

Toni blurs convulsively before falling against the bartender, nearly taking them both down. Impossibly far away in pieces on the ground, Owen manages to think: *My wife has fainted.* He has been with her through natural childbirth (or what passes for natural childbirth) and the children's stitched-up gashes, from Ricky's hernia and Brooke's ear-tube surgeries to the repositioning of Will's elbow from a freakish angle to its rightful crook. He has never seen her faint.

He hears sirens on the left, slowly recognizing that he's hearing everything on the left. He tries to snap his fingers on the right side of his face, but the operator refuses his call. He commands his arm to bend, his hand to make a fist, his thumb to push off his middle finger and click against his index finger. Nothing doing. Euphoria subsides to allow for his first actual moment of fear. Fortunately, the comforting smell of a pig pull lingers: fat on coals and the dusty odor of baking bricks. He can smell flesh tenderizing in the infinitely long cooking time.

Can he lift his head? There is a vast difference, he knows, between the brain being able to tell the body what to do and the body responding. In fact, he can lift his head!

"I think you should be still, Dad." Ricky is grinning as well as scowling.

Owen is seeing double, or possibly past and present. But it's Will and Ricky together looking down at him.

Despite Ricky's admonition, Owen lifts his head, because he can. His shirt has been blown open, but not his shorts, whose metal snap has burned his gut. That would once have been proof of feeling below the waist. He must have feeling down there, because his right foot seems to be on fire. Now he lowers his heavy head, ear to the ground, as if to listen for a stampede; in fact, the siren sound grows louder, abruptly stopping at its highest pitch. A group of pallbearers surrounds him.

"Don't touch his body," the chief pallbearer orders. "Not yet." Except for this one's cap, they're identically dressed in dark short-sleeved shirts, shorts, and rubber gloves.

"He's not *live*, Harold."

Owen's heart tap-dances in his chest, and he sniffs another wave of burning flesh that he hopes isn't his.

"Smell that, genius?" the first guy, Harold, says. "If your gloves touch him, they're liable to stick—you'll lift his skin right off." He brings a sheet to Owen's sternum and then under his chin. Owen puffs out air so they will not be tempted to pull the sheet over his head. "Hyperventilating," he hears, or maybe he thinks, or maybe he should have thought, because the next thing he knows, he's in a flying bed with Toni at his side. He's got his sheet, and she's wrapped in a blanket.

Nasal as a siren, she whines, "His sandal is melted to his heel."

"Yes, ma'am," the pallbearer says. "He got singed something fierce. His other sandal is back there, fused to the sidewalk like grilled cheese." So they're all on a cooking wavelength.

Toni wheezes in and out—does she have to breathe so loudly? Owen is irritated by his pettiness, coming on the heels of his grand tour, until Toni lays her hands over his ears, allowing him to deduce that the siren sounds he's been hearing are from a siren.

The pallbearer is a paramedic, and they are in an ambulance. He gets that now. Owen grins up at his wife, who is cradling his head. He wishes they were alone so he could tell her about the roasted meat that has opened up his sinuses. It seems incredibly personal and not for other people to hear. "The smell," he moans. Then he says, "You fell."

"I know. I'm sorry."

Don't apologize, he wants to tell her. "Everyone falls," he says.

"His neck," the paramedic warns.

"I'm sorry," Toni repeats, and removes her hands. Without her grip, Owen's head wobbles, coming to rest on his right cheek. He sees Toni cocooned in a white blanket, though he knows it to be a hot August night. He manages to ask, "Do you prefer pork or beef barbecue?"

"Owen," she says, as if he's forgotten who he is. She is raining.

"He's got to be pretty scrambled, ma'am."

But isn't that a standard summer beach question? And the scent in his nostrils! As much as he's always been a beef man, this is obviously pork. "The flavor's in the fat," he says.

He practices focusing on Toni. Most of her glasses are gone and her hair is trying to loosen up. Her eyes are the color of tinted windows, and although it's not possible, he considers their reserve a result of her nomadic childhood. In his blurred vision she looks almost the way she did when he espied her in the grad-school library: her hair a haystack resting on her magnificent clavicles; her clavicles an elegant horizon beneath her pale oval face. He was recently divorced and beginning his first residency, and he'd arrive at the library after doing everything in his power to keep a dozen developmentally devastated kids from jumping out a window or digging holes in themselves with a pencil. All he ever wanted for his patients was a fraction of her self-possession.

On the leather reading chair nearest her, he used to lean against the wing, pretending it was her clavicle. How he wishes he could join her inside her white blanket. He says, "You, you, you, you, you."

"Me." Toni points to herself. "What about you?"

A bright aura surrounds her face, its harsh intensity making dark shadows of the wrinkles he noticed in the flash of lightning. But the glow also renders her majestic, a treasure. "Antoinette."

"Owen, I'm here." She surges forward, melting toward him.

"My queen," he says. "My Kyra."

New wrinkles are brought to light. "Kyra? The boys' Kyra?"

"Yes, yes," he says. "We won't have long to wait."

The paramedic taps Toni with his latex glove. "He's not going to make much sense for a while."

"Oh, he's making sense," Toni says. She blows out a long sigh, like a flare from a blowtorch. His face tingles, and after that, the blaze spreads all the way down his body until his toes catch fire, the old hotfoot gag.

Before pain and confusion short him out, he says, "Please, if it's not too late, make it a cheeseburger."

He comes to among strangers in a room whose appliances are as familiar to him as those in his kitchen, yet he can't place them. Dozens of people lift his eyelids to shine a light into his soul, which seems to be a form of greeting. Their word for hello is *lucky*. Everyone says it back and forth.

Owen berates himself for underestimating the beach traffic, because now they are stuck in a jam. Occasionally, the gridlock eases, and he and the jam are on the move. Someone takes his picture or his blood. They measure his impulses. And then a man in blue pajamas drives him and him alone through tunnels and over bridges to meet a young woman in a white hat, who tells him he'll be prepped for surgery. "I don't do surgery," he says. She laughs at him, and then she says, "And I don't do weekends, so what are you and I doing here?" That's apparently as many servings as he'll be getting out of this jar, because as she's driving a spike into his arm, a tubby, scrubbed surgeon appears, wielding what looks to be an electric cheese slicer. He pokes Owen's gut, but he's not happy about it. "Anyone ever told you that you have thick skin?" he asks, and adjusts the impressed blade to cut a denser slice.

Owen awakens on a raft, tethered to a pier. As he floats, he watches drive-in movies projected on his eyelids. Rather than headphones, they've rigged up liquid sound, which hangs in a pouch and drips into his bloodstream. All the movies have the same music, a piercing wail that sounds uncannily like Toni crying. "Let's not buy this sound track," he says to a hologram of his wife. He asks Will to come closer and he *is looking him in the face*, but Brooke says Will isn't here "right now," whatever that means.

Sense and nonsense are interchangeable, and he has a hard time remembering what the world was like when they were separate. His love for Toni is boundless, but he is also the whole world and everything in it, and so Toni is simply the bed or his socks. Pain like at no other time in his life rips through him, simultaneous with a deep, abiding happiness that is impermeable to stab wounds or flaying or whatever the scrubs and whitecoats are doing to his swaddled body. He's been melted down and half-assedly poured into a mold of his old self, which many are trying to patch, deburr, reanimate.

"Lucky," a new one hails the crowded room. "Lucky," the others respond.

2

NUMBER ONE SON

The great chain reaction is set in motion outside Dogfish, waiting for Dad to shake out meter feed enough to last through dessert. Thunderclouds are rolling in so fast that just by staring at one spot, Will can pull off the illusion that the sky is stationary and he is moving, spinning along on planet Earth. Meanwhile, heat waves from the lava-paved parking lot are going up his baggy shorts to his boxers. He climbs the bike rack, followed by Ricky, *of course*, and they start sparring—hook to the chin, left to the gut—mostly in fun, except that everything with his shadow is a competition. Also, there is the Penn jab. Also again, he's amped because he's about to see Kyra.

Will has his back to the rest of the family when this *force* thumps him, the world's strongest drumbeat sounding against the inside of his rib cage, and Ricky blanches pale green, so his face matches his swim-team hair. As Will pivots around, he smells the dusty ozone of electricity—lightning and his father are in the air. His dad's silver hair stands out from his head—he looks like a dandelion with a beer belly—before he crumples to the sidewalk. His exposed white gut ripples with convulsions.

Will studies robotics, and he knows electricity. Ricky does something with heroes and mythology that sounds like comic books. And yet flipper-footed, lap-swimming Ricky is the first responder, leaping from the railing to Dad's twitching body, knocking on his chest and breathing right into his mouth.

Although nobody says it, Ricky is understood to be Mom's

protector and companion, and he, Dad's. Will has always visualized himself and his dad on the same plane, parallel and slightly elevated. And now here is a promotion for the brother he's always thought of as $\leq$. What if this evens the score, if from here on out Will = Ricky, or better yet, if neither has to concern himself with $<$, $>$, or $=$? By the time his dad has been moved from Emergency into Surgery, most of the Beebe Medical Center support staff has congratulated Ricky on saving Dad's life.

The doctors generally agree that his dad would have survived without CPR, which somewhat relieves Will of not having offered it. He wishes the doctors would ask something of him: blood, for example, or his skin. Need a kidney? Cut mine out of my side, *now!*, if it will help Dad. But at this point, the family's only standing by to relieve the vending machines of their salty snacks and endure the litany of his father's good fortune. Evidently, a little more voltage, a harder landing spot, a blow to the x instead of the y, and Dad would be toast. Ergo, lucky, lucky, lucky.

Maybe Will is just rationalizing, but he almost feels as if his inaction is a present he has given his father and brother. Ricky, Dad. Dad, Ricky. Have at each other. Being released from their grips leaves him reckless and a tad manic. If he isn't Number One Son, imagine what he could be doing. He's held himself in check because someone is always looking up to him. Or just looking. Unobserved, there is no telling what might happen, how he might behave. Whenever he thinks about a tattoo, for example, or hang gliding, he pictures Ricky doing it, which changes his mind. He couldn't watch his replica break his neck.

Dad's apparently lucky that in falling from the sky, he didn't break his neck. Many in his circumstances land badly or get pounded by storm debris and die from blunt force trauma. Dad's right hand and left foot, both pierced by lightning, are under wraps. Consequently, the most visible marks on his body are the red lightning-shaped zigzags running the length of his right arm, ruptured capillaries that essentially map the lightning's route from his wrist to his shoulder. All the doctors point the jagged lines out, as if the family hasn't noticed them, and make assurances that they're as harmless as a sunburn and last about as long. Will recognizes the branching lines from freshman arcs and sparks lab, where they created Lichtenberg figures between charged glass plates. He's unsure if he should explain the phenomenon to his mom. Or not.

Despite the luck of heel and palm harboring the body's thickest skin, all 2+ millimeters of it, his dad's heel and hand are in bad shape. Will didn't know burns got as bad as fourth degree—they're talking muscle and bone damage on his heel and a hole through his palm. He's also singed the center of his chest and his left forearm, patches that don't require grafts. Will bites the inside of his cheek in a private display of empathy. He wants to be *stalwart*, a word he mentally bookmarks for Brooke, as if they were in the parking lot before this happened, a scant thirty minutes ago.

Orderlies wheel his dad off and then bring him back, reversing and turning his dad in the bed the way Dad pushes them around in the patio chaise. Or used to—will everything, from now on, be "used to"? The attendant who comes at eight holds the door for them, and they follow in a row down, across, through double doors, up, and over to the surgery wing, where they stand the fuck by for two hours in the waiting room.

Will chews his cheek until it's swollen as a raspberry; soon, he can't avoid biting the pulpy bumps. He wishes he'd been anesthetized along with his dad, who has to have his sandal separated from his foot and then grafts cut from his gut and butt to patch his burns. Will and company endure euphemistic updates amid gale-force air-conditioning.

He admires his mom's binary style. She listens to surgeons talk about "harvesting" and "planting" skin, as well as "opportunistic infections" that can kill a burn victim when the body can't fight its own bacteria. Someone comes out to explain that they've decided to cover his heel with a flap of skin sliced from the arch of his foot. His mom absorbs the updates like a sponge, nodding and asking pointed questions about the prognosis until they leave, and then she wrings herself out on him or Ricky.

"Mommy," Brooke singsongs, stroking Mom's arm for a sec before she rewraps herself in the oversize red scarf and huddles, knees to her chest, like a squaw in a blanket.

Next comes a wave of specialists with nothing special to say. Skin heals well though scars prevail, mutter the dermatologists. Neurologists, including a neurophysiologist and Dr. *Payne*, a neurotraumatist: time will tell. And internists, each waving a different scan: there is no evidence that "the episode" has hardened any organs. Will arches an eyebrow the first time they speak of "the episode," as if his dad's life were a prime-time series. Their lingo eliminates the victimization and freak odds of being struck by lightning, replacing it with someone's idea of regularly scheduled programming.

Another of their understatements is "Some people feel a little discomfort," as in, "The pressure change ruptured Dr. Lerner's right eardrum. Some people feel a little discomfort when that happens." There's also sinister jargon that makes Will want to choke the doctors with their own stethoscopes. "Auditory issues," for example, means that his dad might be deaf in his right ear. And "potential long-term effects" is code for massive brain damage, as in not talking or walking. Their plan is to wait and see. These are the experts? Dr. Sanborn, his father's orthopedic surgeon, has actual information, but his tic is talking about "the patient" as if Dad were a mannequin. Or a cadaver. Will's gut twists into knots like the rubber bands in the cars he and Ricky used to build. When Sanborn says, "The patient's collarbone appears to be fractured," Will speaks up. "*His* collarbone, you mean. Dad's."

"Yes, of course," the surgeon agrees, and then he compounds the fracture: "The patient also has sinistral rib damage, and the coccyx has suffered a severe bruise."

Before Sanborn is completely out of sight, Will says, "I spy a coccyx that's cruising for a severe bruise."

"Willy," Brooke titters, but Ricky says, "Stop it—that's Dad's doctor."

Will cocks his arm and punches his fist into the vinyl cushion of the waiting-room couch.

Their mother says, "Do that again. Give it one for me."

He appreciates her directness. He can see that she's sapped by the whole thing, while he's kinked tight, and he imagines being let loose to career down the slick hospital corridors, unwinding all the way. He knows he should stick around. The clock on the wall says 10, except not really. Really, a short and a long arrow point to the numbers 10 and 12, which we're trained to translate. *We tell time*, Will thinks, and even that's turned around when all Dr. Payne can say to them about his father's trauma is, "Time will tell."

Will says, "I'm pretty hungry."

"Oh, you guys—food?" His mother leans against him, instantly soaking his sweatshirt with tears. So, not yet. He puts his arm around her, and when Brooke sobs, he does his best to comfort his baby sister as well. He blames the doctors for making them cry, which he knows is irrational, but so what? His father has been struck by lightning.

He volunteers for another coffee-and-muffin run—how can a rectangular building have so many ninety-degree turns? Perhaps the maze of hallways and heavy doors keep patients from escaping. Televisions blare in every room and lounge—*phosphorescent therapy*, he thinks, despite knowing that radiation from a year's worth of TV is equal to a single day in the sun. That's the kind of crap he knows. Nearly all the sets are tuned to the Olympics, a cruel joke in light of his father's injuries. U.S. swimmers win another gold medal and bikinied beach volleyball women set and spike through a summer shower in the time it takes Will to retrieve snacks. He offers them orange juice separated from its pulp, muffins with their doughy faces pressed flat against plastic wrap, and coffee, coffee, coffee.

His mother sips from the thin-walled foam cup and says, "This may be the worst coffee I've ever tasted."

Ricky mimes a spit take, which amuses Brooke.

Will asks their mother if she thinks this is a good hospital, and she says, "They've got every specialist I've never wanted."

"Ever wanted?" Ricky clarifies.

"Never," she repeats. She seems to have toughened up while Will was on a food run. "I'd hoped to steer clear of them all. Neurotraumatist, my ass."

"Mommy," Brooke objects. She's got a hank of her hair in her mouth, a habit from when she was little, as is his mother's leaning forward to swoop it behind her ear.

"Seriously, ten years ago, you couldn't find a plastic surgeon in this town," his mother says.

That's for Will, because of his scar; however, as soon as she says that, a doctor with an eerily taut face shows up in their waiting room. "We were just talking about you," she tells the surgeon, who takes it as flattery. They listen to him crow about the "pedicle flap" he's fashioned for the wounded heel, until he gets to the part about Dr. Lerner being out of surgery as well as post-op.

"He's upstairs alone?" Will's mother gasps. She sweeps their wrappers into the trash and, pulling Brooke up by the hand, dashes to the stairwell as if every second counts. He and Ricky run smack into her when she unexpectedly stops just outside Dad's room before leading them all in.

They surround the bed where Dad is laid out, *like a patient etherized upon a table*, Will remembers from Mr. Holt's AP class; in fact, hospital time passes the way it did in that seminar, each syllable agonizingly enunciated and given space. Will and Ricky drag four chairs into a horseshoe around their father. Twenty minutes, thirty, an hour. When the shift changes, a new crew arrives to take Dad's vitals. His left foot and right arm are elevated, and the red tracks on his arm look as if he shot up with lightning.

Will knows his odds for being excused have greatly improved when his mother stretches her spine like a dancer and tugs her shirttail, pulling the creases out. Next, she frees her tricolored hair—simultaneously dark *and* blond—and smooths it into the exact same arrangement, encircling her ponytail with the band she's just removed and then flopping and doubling it into a tasseled bun. *Wait,* he tells himself, and sure enough she reaches into her purse to swipe gloss on her lips. If she does this after lightning, then surely after the apocalypse she would perform her three-part grooming twitch.

"You want me to stay?" he asks.

She sighs but does not slouch. "What time is it?"

"Eleven-thirty." They'd headed to dinner at the beginning of Kyra's shift, practically early bird, and now six hours have passed.

"I'm not going anywhere," his mother says. "And tomorrow's probably more of the same. Why don't you three head home?"

"I'm fine here," Ricky volunteers. "*I'll* stick around."

"You sure?" she asks.

"I want to be with you and Daddy," Brooke says before her head yo-yos down and she's asleep again. Even if it costs her test points, Will hopes she didn't understand "necrotic tissue" or "pedicle flap" or "air-powered dermatome," which he's pretty sure is basically an electric skin peeler.

He tucks the blanket under his sister's chin and tells his mother, "I've got my phone."

"You're going to let him take the van?"

Mom waves Ricky off. "He's got his phone, honey."

Will kisses his mother on the cheek and then comes around to the other side of the bed. His dad's face smells like rum, whose medicinal properties Will would welcome right about now. Although his lids are closed, Dad's eyes are zipping all over the place, ball bearings moving in tandem under their baggy blankets.

"Bye, Dad. I'll see you later. Just tell Mom if you want anything from town." He straightens up. "Can he hear us?"

"Willy, you're asking me? I have no earthly idea."

Will leaves before she cries again. In his twenty-one years, he's spent a total of maybe thirty minutes worrying about his parents' mortality, a lack of concern that is now headed to read-only memory. No amount of new information will be writing over that sector.

Grateful for the tread of his sandals, he speed walks down the slick halls. *Elevator? I don't think so.* He takes the stairs two at a time, and he hears his heart racing as he waits for the sealed glass doors to unsuck before he can launch himself into the humid Delaware night.

After the freezing hospital, the van's door handle is a warm welcome, as is the lightly baked interior. He is happy to break a sweat, buckling himself into the capsule and rocketing out of the sea grass–infested parking lot—Ocean View Drive, you wish. Stages of the night fall away in chunks, allowing him to accelerate beyond the hospital's pull of gravity.

Whatever storm had materialized is over. Light rain responds best to a syncopated wiper beat, with the rear wiper sounding like the foot pedal of his drums. He's been thinking of leaving them at home this fall. None of the snobs at school play his kind of music anyway. He wonders if he's outgrown the drums or if Penn is too tight ass for him. *And speaking of tight asses*, he has the nerve to think, closing the gap between him and Kyra.

A dozen summers their families have been in Rehoboth the same weeks, even after her parents split up. There were other kids his age, but once he and Kyra found each other, no others were necessary. Will would ditch Ricky, basically exchanging one twin for another. Despite his brother's pouting and the weird vibes of getting reacquainted with Kyra, the first day of vacation was always the most thrilling. His brain would perform a version of time-lapse photography, morphing the image he'd been carrying from last summer into the current year's model. Same gap-toothed grin and froggy eyes, but glasses, pierced ears, long black hair, braces, new glasses, taller and faster than him, breasts, blue hair with bangs, contact lenses, then shorter than him and slower, muscular arms and shins of a field hockey player, black hair again, a tiny nose piercing, and then no braces. No froggy eyes, either, just big, wide-set ones as enticing as her big, wide-set breasts and her oval gut as on a belly dancer (complete with the latest piercing, her belly button). A telescoping neck that she calls circus freaky but he finds alluring.

In the bumper-to-bumper midnight traffic of Reho Ave., Will searches for a space near Dogfish. He parks close to a hydrant on a side street and then weaves through ambling drunks along the sidewalks. "Ricky!" someone yells, which annoys him. Looks aside, how could anyone think he's Ricky?

The front door of the restaurant has the same heft as the hospital doors. Inside, Will blows past the hostess to sit at the far end of the bar, and Axe rushes a draft to a sloppy finish so he can get to Will. "What's the story?"

"His vitals are good," Will manages to say. "They're working him over. Thanks, man."

"That's a worthy hospital. The residents come in once in a while, and they're not assholes—I'd tell you if they were. Decent tips; they sketch body parts on the napkins." Axe puts a coaster on the bar and a beer bottle smack in the center. "Listen, I've been dying to use the defibrillator—now I could kick myself for wishing that."

"Don't. You and Ricky saved his ass."

"I get the feeling you didn't come to give me a medal." He points to the ceiling. "Most likely, she's upstairs."

"Thanks," Will says. He can't stop blinking his sandpapery eyelids. He faces the mirrored wall, where beach glass–colored bottles are lined up for duty. Behind him, the restaurant is stuffed with people who miraculously eat and laugh. Their mirror images salt their fries. A fat man waves an empty ketchup bottle in the air and says, "Yoo-hoo."

Will witnesses how life goes on, which of course is really a recognition of how life almost stopped going on. *Potential long-term effects*, for fuck's sake, *burned muscles and bone*. The time-space continuum—let's cut to the chase and call it life—has advanced far beyond his family's cataclysm, happy hour having been covered with strata of hot crab dip, flavored vodka, and the band's first two sets. *A little respect, people!* he wants to scream, but these aren't likely the same people. The crowd may have turned over two or three times since his father was carted away in an ambulance.

Will's skill set is his ability to move forward; in all his projects, to stop time is a failure, a crash. Now he gets it, and he envies history's ability to hang on to a moment, any moment deemed significant, and analyze it to death, thereby giving it lasting value. To dwell, to preserve—until his dad's accident, he didn't have an application for that approach. This restaurant crowd has moved hours beyond what he wants to think about, they've moved on to small talk and yet another round. He chokes beer past the bile rising in his throat. *These people*, he thinks, *are the counterexample to my major*. And then he thinks, *People are the counterexample to my major*.

The crowd faces the stage in the far corner, where the band is plucking through the intro of "I'll Fly Away." A prehistoric bassist stands behind the other three band members, a fiddler, banjo player, and lead singer who all look to be around Will's age. Why is this stuff considered classic and Zappa isn't? He is surprised to hear them overlay the hymn with a cynical vibe: "'*Oh how glad and happy when we meet, I'll fly away.*'" They sing as if they were going to meet their dealer rather than their god. Listening to their version, Will again recognizes the potential for nostalgia to be more than wallowing. Alongside that is the disconcerting notion that everything he is learning will be obsolete by graduation. Watch Ricky's courses on math and mythology, specifically the Life of the Hero, prove uncannily more relevant, like the lifeguard training he put to use earlier tonight.

Will's phone vibrates in his pocket. Ricky can't take a shit on his own, except he certainly acted autonomously when *he saved Dad's life*! His hunch is confirmed. "Dad woke up & axd 4 u," the text reads. "Be me," Will thumbs back. "Or not." But he feels crappy that he wasn't there when his dad's eyes opened.

"'*Just a few more weary days and then, I'll fly away.*'" Now the band seems to be singing about suicide rather than heaven. Fortunately for Will, Kyra comes through the kitchen's swinging door. She is gripping an empty platter, but the instant she sees him, she flings it like a low-flying Frisbee into the restaurant. The large metal disk clatters against a table leg, and in the middle of the song, the tray settles into a wobbly spin before clanging to a stop. Customers in the vicinity applaud while the band plays on.

Kyra lifts her arms, and Will expects her to take a bow. But she has opened her arms to him. In a heartbeat she closes the distance between them. *Lub*—she is a giant step away—*dub!*—she's squeezed between his knees and is pulling his cheek to her aproned chest.

My god, but he needed to get here. Will wishes they were six or even ten years old again and could simply interlace their fingers and run through the sand to the waves, laughing themselves sick. Kyra is summer to him, she is his best. He's fulfilled some homing instinct, returned to familiar waters via internal compass and desire. Although he wants to show the depth of his gratitude, all that comes up is panic. *My dad! Zapped within an inch of his life by a rogue bolt that blistered his flesh and nearly fried his organs. Too early to know what's wrong in his head!* But he can't say any of that; instead, he blubbers in fear. Kyra pets him like a dog, which calms him. Finally, he manages to tell her, "Two hours of surgery! I left before he woke up, *I left!*" With their awkward embrace, he basically weeps into her cleavage. "I left to come here!"

"It's okay," she soothes him. "It was okay to come here." She arches her swan neck so she can talk through the music right into his ear. "Brooke ran in here screaming—I freaked. I thought, *Sharks!* I thought it was you."

When he feels her hot breath blowing inside his head, Will exhales grief and inhales lust. Could he really be wanting to stick his tongue in her mouth amid such dire circumstances? He clamps his lips together, feeling his pulse beat between them as if his heart were actually in his mouth. The lead singer's yodeling solo resembles a gurgled scream, the likes of which Will might make if he tries to speak. *Maybe trauma causes Tourette's*, he thinks, fearful of becoming like his dad's patients who yip and yell out stuff.

"Don't let me overserve you tonight, bro." Axe puts a fresh beer on the bar in front of him, and Kyra takes the first sip.

"Here's to two years in kindergarten," she says.

As a junior, he's legal because his mom started him and Ricky a year late, but the joke is that Kyra flunked kindergarten. To keep himself from wrapping his hands around her waist, he wraps them around the beer bottle, which lifts off the bar with its coaster attached, the way his dad's sandal stuck to the bottom of his foot. Will tugs the square free, concentrating on the circle of condensation embossing the square, and the cocktail napkin brings to mind the hospital residents Axe has served. Will can only hope that an appreciation for microbrewed beer and the consideration to tip well translate into capable health care.

The band sings the last chorus a cappella, and a table of women at the front join in. With their old-fashioned harmonies and unsullied voices, they must have come from choir practice or from heaven. " '*When I die, hallelujah by and by, I'll fly away.*' " They wag righteous fingers at him. All right, already! He has seen about enough tonight, starting with his father flying through the air. He swabs his forehead with the bottom of his shirt as the women clap for the band, who clap for the women.

Kyra unties her Dogfish serving apron, exposing her clingy Dogfish shirt, and hands it over to Abigail, the other waitress their age. The apron's pockets are stuffed with wadded bills.

"You're off duty?" Will asks Kyra.

"Says me. I made it worth her while."

"Don't fork over your tips," Axe says. "She knows what happened."

"Yeah, well, it's Abigail we're talking about." The band starts a raucous rockabilly number, and Kyra drags a stool as close to Will as its splayed legs will allow. When she climbs aboard, their thighs touch. "Two Summer Sizzlers, if you please, Axe. With salt."

And then time is suspended so that Kyra and Will can watch Axe tip tequila into a chrome shaker, pour his trademark mixings from on high. He closes the cocktail shaker and raises it to the left and the right like a prizefighter, his tattooed muscles bulging. Holding the shaker in one hand, he retrieves two long-stemmed glasses from the overhead rack, salts the rims, and twirls them upright to pour in the shaker's contents, as foamy green as the ocean.

Will is lulled by Axe's display, so like the beach shows he and Kyra have shared. Hands clutched around wadded bills and hot change, they've watched kettle corn being mixed in a copper pot, warm caramel drizzled over popcorn. They've stood at the fudge-shop window as women in hairnets and nurse uniforms spilled fudge onto marble slabs and worked it stiff. The treats of beach life could largely be previewed, and anticipation enhanced their pleasure. Toffee pulled from sugar and butter, uniform fries punched out of rough potatoes, cotton candy spun from webs of pink sugar, white balls of dough whirled flat into disks of pizza crust and ladled with sauce: they've witnessed their world made each summer. Huddled against Kyra, Will watches Axe stack lemon and lime slices and wedge two garnishes onto each salt-crusted glass.

Kyra tilts her sizzler toward the bartender in thanks. "Axe to the max," she says. Next, she tilts her glass toward Will before licking the rim and sipping from the froth. For all the years they've been sampling beach treats together, this is the first summer they can sit at the bar.

She says, "Are you totally creeped out? I am. My dad's not around, but at least he's okay."

Oh, yeah, he thinks; *many are down to one parent. Some are orphans.* Every sort of noise is coming off the stage, so Will gathers up his breath to shout, "HIS BUTTONS WERE SHATTERED. THERE'S A HOLE IN HIS RIGHT HAND." Turns out, he's screaming through the finale; after people whoop and clap, the band gives it a rest. "When he fell to the ground," Will finishes, "his foot was smoking."

Kyra's heavy lids raise like a shade. She says, "One second he's your dad and the next"—she shoves him hard with her palm—"Sand Salesman! Oh, my god!"

Will grips the bar, reeling. How could he have forgotten that? Pressed to play with Brooke and Ricky, the four of them pretended all the parents were dead and they were on their own. As the oldest child, he sold sand to support the two families. "Sand Salesman!" he'd sing out for customers. They'd try to say, "She sells seashells, too!" until they fell down laughing. His throat seizes at their careless make-believe, though his dad would say that their playacting was a healthy reaction to something. He is a big believer in playing. And healthy reactions. Who would they be without Dad or without the dad they know? Will can't help but follow a few of the scary paths: his dad a vegetable, his dad a paraplegic, his dad a Republican.

"Poor Will," Kyra says. She kisses him on the cheek, and her caterpillar eyebrows scoot up under her bangs. She's down to the ice in her drink, and Will drains his own in seconds. His phone shudders in his pocket as he follows Kyra's oscillating hips outside, where he instinctively looks left, right, behind him. The clouds have blown over, and the moon's pockmarked face leers knowingly. The hamburger and onion-ring fumes coming from her hair are the dinner Will never had.

Kyra picks up speed as they make their way to the gazebo, where they cross the boardwalk beneath the *Dolles* taffy sign, shining like a rising sun. She pulls him toward the dark side of the dunes, and he begins tasting the yeasty beers on her neck. Tonight is becoming memorable for all the big reasons. A spear of lightning nearly killed his dad—obviously, there is that. Nevertheless, meanwhile, and now. In addition to nearly losing his father, he seems to have lost his shadow, and he may lose his virginity yet. He wants to tell her all that, but she is busy kissing his nipple, which is a sensation he hadn't even *known* about until she touched it off. She unzips his pants, and as much as he wants her, he doesn't want to be rolling around on damp sand at a public beach—on cigarette butts and sand fleas. "My house," he directs her.

They run along the boardwalk and cut over at Hickman. Just past the empty driveway Kyra says, "Wait. How did you get here?"

"I took the van," he says. "Shit." He checks his phone to see if everyone is stranded at the hospital; mercifully, there is a text from Brooke. "G'night" is the whole of it, which he shares with Kyra.

"Brooksey," she says fondly.

Will fishes the key from under the garden gnome, and trained from toddlerhood, they leave their shoes outside before heading upstairs to his and Ricky's room. Sand skitters across the bedroom's vinyl flooring when Kyra drops her shorts. Will wants to savor each second even as he is crazy to rush her. Either of them might grow self-conscious, though from the way things are going, he doesn't think it's going to be Kyra.

He's seen her in bikinis for years—wet bikinis with a seatload of sand, bikinis twisted by a wayward wave, bikinis she's outgrown—and yet Kyra in her string underwear and raggedy bra is an intimacy he's only dreamed of. She gathers his T-shirt up to his ribs, and he lifts his arms like a child. He is desperate to speak to her, their whole relationship based on telling, and this being the biggest damn tell in his life.

"What's wrong?" Kyra asks.

"Everything. But if I'm actually awake and you're actually standing there in your underwear, then I guess nothing."

"You are and I am," she says. She unhooks her bra and, leaning forward, lets gravity do its magnificent work, one of the most natural forces on earth. Then she hooks her thumbs into the ropy string of her underwear, which rolls down her legs. "Except without my underwear."

The room has no curtains, and he's always loved viewing the moon from his top bunk. Moonlight illuminates her tan lines; high along her haunch, stripes embrace her like a pair of arms and modestly protect her crotch. "Mole," he says, tapping the dark dot on her left hip, and "bruise," a purple spot on her butt. He wants to describe her to her. They have played at kissing the same way they've played at scuba diving or castle architects, except in the last couple years he's extended their kisses into his private fantasies, private because if he'd made a move and she'd shut him down, he wasn't sure he could have faced her again. How often he has imagined stroking her waist the way he is doing in real fucking time.

She tugs at his shorts and then reaches inside and fishes for the drawstring. He watches Kyra, *Kyra!, pull down his pants! and his boxers!* His dick bobs up—and she clamps her hands over it. As if he's standing in the surf, the floor sways beneath him, waves of lust and fear, alcohol and hunger rocking his world. He says, "I don't know about you, but I haven't done this before."

"Never? Not even like this?" and she strokes him with a heavy hand.

"Shit." He exhales, and any tension blows over.

Her staged laugh is from their playacting days. She's always been more experienced, and for now he's glad because he's heard it hurts them at first.

"Good thing your dad's okay. Don't you think he wants to live to see you guys grown?"

"I *am* grown." He sounds like a kid, still counting his age in fractions. "Do your parents know?"

"That you're a virgin? Everyone does. Your problem is that school you go to. If you'd aimed a little lower, you'd be fucking your brains out."

"Like you?" he asks.

"Ooh, maybe this is why you're a virgin. Let's hope that was the grief talking."

Grief? He is actually puzzled for a second, thinking that had been jealousy talking. *Oh,* grief! His knees go soft, and his lungs practically collapse: he left his father in a hospital bed, having nearly been melted; he hugged his heartsick mother and made off with the car keys so he could be standing here, naked with a naked Kyra.

Kyra leads him to the bottom bunk, pushing her hand on the top of his head like a cop easing a perp into a squad car. *Ricky's bed*, he thinks, but doesn't say, because he needs to be Will alone. He props himself up on his elbow until Kyra eases his arm out and lays him flat. Then she climbs on top of him, hunched over so she won't snag her hair on the underside of the top bunk. Her warm, soft flesh rests on his ribs, which he spreads with his deep breath. It helps that her hair tickles his armpit, that her muscular thighs are straddling his penis. The idea of her having at it with someone excites him, and he opens his eyes to take in that he's next. His pulse beats fast, a syncopated four-four against her thigh.

"Everyone's rooting for you," she says. "Speaking for the people in your life. Ricky and your mom"—she kisses him with each name—"Brooke, your dad." She kisses the tears leaking out beneath his eyelids and streaming down the sides of his face. "Me." She kisses his ribs, which are buckling with sobs. Crying is as rare for him as being in bed with someone.

Kyra brings her legs together and slides herself toward the bed so she is stretched alongside him. He scoots closer to the wall to keep her from falling out; she is so tight against him, they move like two inchworms. She holds him while he cries, and her acceptance is both his undoing and his salvation. Of course his dad wants to see him grown, have sex, leave home, raise a family. Could they do all that tonight?

When his tears subside, Kyra is staring at him; her eyes have gotten froggy again, bulging with discovery.

"What?" he asks.

She says, "You've been saving yourself for me. For a while. You have, haven't you?"

Is she right? Something had stopped him. Even at Penn, plenty of his classmates made the time to fuck their brains out.

"Even if you haven't, say you have," Kyra says, and lets loose a giggle.

"I have been saving myself for you." Will says it without any teasing, and it rings true, like a tuning fork, like an anthem.

She pivots out of bed to put her feet on the floor. "Which one's Ricky's?" she asks, pointing to the dressers.

"By the window."

He hears the scrape of the drawer and the sound of her sifting through Ricky's stuff. Will can't imagine what she wants in there. He sits up, mindful of the top bunk springs touching his head. The scene in front of him is strangely familiar, like a dream or a dramatization: except for her nakedness, the moonlit girl rummaging through the bureau is right out of the Peter Pan book he'd overread as a child. Here is the page where green-suited Pan, perched along the windowsill in pointy shoes and a triangular cap, spies on Wendy. Surely Kyra isn't looking to pull Will's shadow from Ricky's dresser and sew it to the bottom of his feet.

A streetlight winks off a foil streamer that Kyra tugs free. "Eureka!" she says, an accordion pleat of rubber packets dangling from her hand. "You guys should compare notes more often."

Will has the sick thought that maybe she's already been with Ricky. "How did you know to look for those?"

"Just a hunch. Abigail told me there's been some messing around."

Will's temples pound with the dissonance of his situation. Ricky the lesser has been having sex, or is at least in a better position, protectionwise, than he is. Not that it's a competition. Still, the checks he's put on his own behavior for that randy bastard; even as he is glad to see the condoms, they also infuriate him, insult him. Kyra, the beloved, the naked, the willing, is in his room. Really, the only appropriate response is to thank his stars that they've chosen each other. But what kind of son excuses himself from a family crisis to get laid? He worries about the fallout, knowing that all this selfishness will be taking place while doctors who doodled on Dogfish napkins treat his badly damaged father.

Will can only see Kyra from the ribs down as she rips a tile off the astonishingly long column of condoms. True to his nature, he admires the square foil packet circumscribing the raised circle within, like the imprint of his sweating beer bottle on the bar coaster.

And then Kyra climbs into the bottom bunk just as she had on hundreds of rainy summer days when the bed had been a fort or a raft. Her wide grin lights up her dark face, mischievous and joyful at their cache of shared secrets. They are Will and Kyra alone, enjoying a night at the beach. Clutching each other and learning how to mix, what melts at the touch, what stiffens. A clavicle is foreign and then intimately familiar again, and that goes double for thigh and for neck. Better than kettle corn, better than beer; they sample, they learn. More cotton candy. Another flavor, please! Better than watching, noses pressed against the glass. Pull that slowly. Unroll a new one and don't worry about getting sticky. Here's the souvenir that will make your summer. In bed, on the floor, anywhere you want! They learn all night long.

3

THROWN BY THE BLAST

The luxurious sensation of waking up in the beach-house bedroom is ruined by waking up. Toni's foot touches the bunched elastic corner of the sheet, and the mismade bed and her being alone in it awaken her to her heartsick condition. *Noooo!* She curls up, hugging herself, fear and confusion more painful than her worst cramps. She concentrates on the first comfort that comes to mind, an uphill slog to focus on. *At least the children knew their dad.* She must pace herself—she has to have courage enough for the three of them. Unfortunately, at the end of this deliberate climb, she realizes what is on the other side of the hump. *They're still so young!* She teeters at the top and plunges over, her breath rushing out in a panic. If she weren't in bed, she'd be flailing in terror, screaming down the tracks until she levels herself to try again. *He could have been killed.* This is the next rise, which she bravely ascends; however, there's no getting off the roller coaster as it crests the death-defying hill. *He's burned, broken, and batty!* Anxiety jabs her food-deprived stomach, so inflated with gas it is ready to pop. Here's a curve she can lean into—*He can stay in the hospital as long as he needs to*—but before settling into the spiral, she whipsaws around a hairpin curve: *We have got to get him out of there!*

For the life of her, Toni can't imagine how she'll face the day. Burrowing down in her clammy bed, she presses her mouth against her wrist so that when she screams, the kids won't hear her. She sounds like the blender before it starts smoking. Last night was the first one she didn't sleep at the hospital, but if this is what a little rest gets her, she prefers exhaustion: at least she was numb then.

To be in the beach-house bed is to remember Owen when he has been completely theirs. Waking the boys at dawn to fish in the surf or letting them all sleep in while he makes waffles, winning yet another stuffed animal to crowd into Brooke's bed or flying kites on the dunes before bath and pajama time—he soaks up the children. She loves him at home in Bethesda, but not the way she does here. She falls for him again every August. Whatever they've done in this bed, they've done heartily, lustily: the sun and the kids wear them out *and* rev them up. This is the bed of not holding back, be it snoring, fucking, or talking.

Since Saturday, Owen has been tethered to his hospital bed, where his left hand deftly squeezes his self-administered morphine drip as often as possible. In what feels like one long day on another planet, there's actually been all sorts of progress. The grafts on his heel and hand seem to be taking: both sites have successfully made it through what the doctors call the *plasmatic* stage, all his surgeons too young to remember the 1980s band.

He's not exactly coherent. For one thing, he pipes up with something obscene in the middle of many a sentence. Meanwhile, as he becomes more stable, she's becoming less. He's gotten out of bed twice, to the surprise of Drs. Payne and Sanborn. He's even taken a few steps. What she really needs is for him to look at her as if he means it—*I see you*—her worry being that if he doesn't look at her, she doesn't exist. How unenlightened is that—unless her feelings count as deep, abiding love.

This is how Sparkle used to behave, silently padding into their bedroom to stare Toni awake—the first thing she saw each morning were the retriever's cow eyes. Sparkle would quietly stand there fluttering her lashes until Toni crossed the threshold from awake to aware. Once Toni recognized her, the dog began swishing her tail and panting. She would skip in place, toenails tapping on the bedroom floor like typewriter keys—*Oh, you are alive! And I'm your dog, right? YES!* She'd toss her blond mane from side to side, darting in to lick Toni's nose. Daffy, devoted dog, long dead.

Toni wipes her face with the sheet. "You'll be amazed how fast he'll heal," the dermatologic surgeon had said. *Oh yeah? Amaze me.* Because Dr. Payne had already said, "Best-case scenario, six months before he's himself again."

She can't help returning to the scene of the accident, reviewing Owen's version for hidden messages. When she was a kid and her father brought champagne home, he'd say a celebration is in order, but she knew champagne meant they were moving. And even as her father was cutting some ribbon for a mall's opening or an office complex renovation, her mother had already begun organizing their possessions into piles. They'd leave the day her mother wrapped quilts around the huge oval mirror that tilted within its heavy oak frame.

Likewise, Owen's account dodges the truth. To hear him tell it, he was scooped up, thrown by the blast into the sky; however, what she's learned is that people hit by lightning actually toss themselves through the air. Lightning isn't like a flood or a tornado, both of which can carry people away. Instead, the nervous system gives itself over, muscles contract as never before, and people take a giant leap. She *saw* the bolt enter Owen's thumb and pointer finger, saw him throw his arm out in salute—*Yes, sir!*—and push off against the sidewalk. As the flash traveled through his legs and out his heel, he kicked himself up a notch before plummeting to earth. Ricky and Axe ministered to him a good thirty feet from the meter.

Really, there's not much difference between being carried away and carrying yourself away, but his version is wrong from the get-go, and it makes everything about him seem delusional. It could be that her suspicions about him and Kyra stem from this distinction—was he carried or did he do the carrying? Maybe neither. Is she jealous that he took a trip to heaven without her? Or is it rejection she feels, hurt that he doesn't seem eager to return? She's certainly feeling something, maybe all of the above and lonely, too.

Downstairs, and god knows how Toni gets downstairs, the coffeemaker heaves a wet sigh, as if masking a sob. *You and me both, sister.* The kids are not only already awake but also sitting around the kitchen table, another indication that things are serious. Just seeing the sun-bleached down of their tanned arms makes Toni wobbly in the knees, and then Brooke says, "Good morning, Mommy." With her pillow-matted hair and off-the-shoulder nightshirt, she's more waifish than usual. She's improbably tiny, which is handy for a gymnast, but she won't be a gymnast all her life.

Toni worries that gymnastics stunted her growth. All that stretchiness and flexibility—she's pliable as rubber—might not be conducive to growing taller. Just like a mother, to feel guilty that she'd encouraged a talent at the expense of something else.

Brooke stretches out her fingers and says, "Let me see yours."

Toni obliges. Her hands aren't even her hands; Brooke gave them both French manicures last night while they watched some of the Olympics.

"Mom." Ricky offers her coffee, and Will lifts his rump off his chair to get the milk to her. The boys are shirtless: their shoulder bones protrude so it looks as if their torsos are draped over hangers, and each muscled bulge of their abdominals casts a shadow on the one beneath. She instinctively averts her eyes before she corrects herself. She's their mother, for heaven's sake, and is certainly permitted to admire them, though she doesn't want to gawk the way the girls on the beach do, freshly amazed that not only one but two could look exactly like that. Ricky is actually broader in the shoulders, and Will's thighs, tucked under the table, are more muscular. Both boys have been bare-chested, their boxers riding low, since they hit Rehoboth; they seem naked now because she's seeing them from the waist up, and for the last two days they've been swaddled in the chilly hospital.

The children chitter as anxiously as baby birds in a nest— "Why would his body reject its own skin?" "He called Dr. Sanborn a cunt!" "Did you hear him dis Dr. Payne?"—and Toni moves to fill their gaping mouths. It is habit that has her cracking eggs into a bowl and spilling them into a skillet, rinding cantaloupe slices as the eggs set, and slotting bread into the toaster, which latches on to the bread and won't release. The skillet, too, could use an upgrade; careless cooks have crazed the coating. Although Toni thinks of the beach house as roughing it, she's going to have to adjust her attitude if she wants steady rentals. Despite her determination not to spend money, she adds kitchen supplies to her mental list, as if a new skillet might keep them from financial ruin.

Will says, "Every night he has that weird loop."

"Again with the chorus girls," Ricky agrees.

"I know, right?" Will says. "And he's got plenty to say about barbecue pits and flaming beasties, whatever the hell those are. We should record some of his shit."

"Will!" Brooke objects.

"Did I say *shit*? I meant his *logorrhea*."

Toni divides what she's cooked onto three plates for the children. A burp of coffee bubbles in her throat; she's been practically gargling coffee the last few days. To think that she and Owen used to relax over a mug each morning! Now she takes swigs and slugs of it, all the while running the numbers required to keep them in skillets and college and their houses. What exactly is their place? When she tries to identify their niche, she thinks of a mother-daughter tea she and Brooke once attended. Seeing the infinity pool in the huge backyard, Toni said to one nine-year-old, "Come summer, we should sneak into that pool," and the child replied, "What's wrong with your pool?" What's wrong, indeed.

Because she was raised on the fly, she'd been the one to press for a vacation *home*. Even away, they'd be at home, she'd marveled to Owen, who didn't have the same baggage. Except for vacations, he'd slept in the same bed between crib and college dorm. To him a suitcase was just a suitcase.

"Mom." Ricky gets her attention. "Dad walks the hall again today, if he's up for it."

"What *is* today?" Brooke asks, and her subsequent yawn starts a round-robin of yawning.

"Tuesday, honey—"

"Not anymore," Ricky interrupts. "Today's Wednesday, Mom."

And she's devastated, just as when she was stretching in her splendid bed and her big toe touching bunched fabric reminded her that everything was completely fucked-up. "Good lord." She slumps into the nearest chair, hangs her head in defeat.

Brooke grabs her sleeve. "I'm sorry, Mommy. I'm confused, too."

If Brooke's got her by the sleeve, Toni reasons, then she must be wearing clothes; she peeks down her own blouse to make sure she's wearing a bra. She is. Let's hear it for habit, twenty-three years cooking their breakfasts, twice that many dressing herself! But the mistake of equating routine with stability—we're okay here—sends her into inevitable free fall—we are *so* not okay! In moments like this, Owen's helplessness seems like a dress rehearsal for death. Her head still down, she sees her improbably manicured hand, and then she sees the butter dish slide by, followed by the jelly, which she tracks along the table to Will.

"What?" he says to her. "I'm hungry."

Really, she doesn't want them to stop eating; after all, she cooked breakfast. And now she wonders how that was possible, since she'd emptied and sponged out the refrigerator days ago. "Did someone buy groceries?"

Will smiles. "You're welcome. You owe me forty-five dollars, when you get a chance."

Habit has her say, "Put it on my tab." She's grateful that Will is still who he is. And she's not blind to his frisky happiness, leaking out like a band of bright light beneath their darkened door. She can't avoid imagining what he needed that sent him to the grocery store. *My queen,* she thinks, *my Kyra,* and coffee slops over the sides of her shaky mug.

Toni has lost a day because Toni is lost. When she hasn't been crying, she's been managing Owen's care with the unthreatening authority she feigns when bossing college brass around. Just substitute surgeons for the provosts and presidents she helps place: hospitals are enough like universities that she knows to respect the pecking order and massage the egos. Of course, Owen is not a demanding yet fulfilling career opportunity. He's her burned-out husk of a husband, urgently in need of her immediate attention. As Toni tries to gather the breakfast dishes, the children hunch protectively over their food. Forks clink against rims, and the butter's carved from both ends.

"Mom, *Mom!*" Ricky says, spraying toast crumbs. "Find your purse and stuff, and we'll be ready."

"We need to get moving," she agrees, although she sits down in a stupor. What keeps sandbagging her is not that Owen is hurt, which is horrific, but that he's *gone*. It's the kids who manage to clear the table, somehow changing from their skivvies to sweats, and they get her into the van, where she stares out the window at a town gearing up for the final lap of summer. There are tandem, three-wheel, and reclining bicycles. There are wagons, pedal cars, and Rollerblades. A corgi glides by with his stubby hind legs resting on a shelf between two tires. How many ways can there be to get around? Toni wonders if there is a lesson for her in this display of variety.

"When will they let him go?" Brooke's voice floats into earshot.

"Soon," Ricky answers from the driver's seat at the same time that Will, in the back, says, "Any day."

"If only he'd drone on about sensory integration studies and spectrum disorders—all that stuff," Brooke says, "though it used to bug me when he'd say 'my kids' and he didn't mean us."

"He's always done that," Ricky says.

"I know," Will agrees, "but I'm with her. That shit still throws me every single time."

Will used to ask her if Owen had another family—add that to the list of funny stories from their childhood that turn out to be disturbing. Ricky parks facing the bakery's plate-glass window; already they have a new routine that includes front-loading the interminable hospital day with lavish treats. Will jumps out of the van and leans on Toni's open window. "Let me show you guys what good looks *and* charm can do."

"They'll think you're me," Ricky says.

Toni sighs. "Here we go again. Just be speedy-quick about it, and don't buy anything from yesterday's bin."

Ricky chimes in, "We mustn't give away stale scones."

Will softens his face so that his eyes grow large and lovable. "I'll play the orphan card for an extra ten percent." In a flash of irrational exuberance, he kisses his mother right on the tip of her nose.

"You're such a mother-kisser!" Ricky taunts. "I'm going to tell your girlfriend you're a mother-kisser."

Their antics lift Toni right to the cliff's ledge. Will has always been a mother-kisser, but with the next step, she can't help but ask herself: Is his girlfriend a father-kisser? Her gassy stomach rises into her throat, although even in free fall she manages to locate and surrender her credit card to Will, who swipes it as efficiently as a machine. The bank balances won't cover three months of their expenses, now increasing by a hundred dollars' worth of pastries per day.

Owen's surgeons tell her that he's upper-upper-moderate or perhaps lower-severe among victims of lightning strikes. Just by surviving, he has nearly transcended severe, most of whose members die because their heartbeat or breathing isn't restored quickly enough. The classifications ring in her ears because she's been calculating how long they can stay in their upper-upper-moderate life.

"Let's get some music in here." Ricky punches the button for a CD.

Kettledrums, so it's not one of hers. Swelling strings rise and are crested by a woman's seductive, mournful chanting. The emotional overkill points to one of Owen's sound tracks.

"Dad's," Brooke calls out.

Ricky agrees. "Sounds like *Troy*—the action-hero remake anyway. When we saw this in mythology, everyone harped about what the movie got wrong."

All that tuition to watch Hollywood blockbusters, Toni thinks, which is not Ricky's point. The twins rarely talk about their classes—they're boys—and so she pays attention to his coming-attractions parody.

" 'From a world of epic love and war, when the gods chose whom to favor or torment, comes a new film, lightly based on Hellenic gossip.' " In his regular voice Ricky says, "The movie is this total hybrid of history and myth, and everyone in seminar is bickering over details! I can tell Dr. Clifton's about to pounce— I've been watching her pretty closely—"

How closely? Toni's beginning to understand his attraction to mythology.

"*Wham!* She takes it up a level, scrambling our brains until all movies tell the same story. What changes is *how* we tell the story.

So filmmakers used to hire thousands of extras for crowd and battle scenes, whereas the *Troy* guys used inflatable dolls—she had a field day with that! Basically, she says, our stories tell *us*." When he stops looking out the window, he says, "Oh, Mom," and, pawing through the cup holder, finds a wadded tissue.

Toni is struck by Ricky's other life, but mostly she's moved by his feelings for his professor, who knows about inflatable dolls and how to scramble their brains. With her own runny brain, she admires the woman's flexible thinking. What would Dr. Clifton say about the music they're listening to, this group wail? These singers seem to be mourning their men, lost or deflated, but perhaps that's an example of the story telling her. Toni misses being a part of Owen's story as much as she misses him. Inexplicable sound track aficionado, broad-chested man surprisingly nimble-footed, or he was. Defender of the underdog, her partner—or he was.

Will is at her open window with the platter of baked goods, as if they were at a drive-in. "Jesus, guys. You can hear the Greek army invading from in there. We'll all be crying in a second."

Toni dabs her eyes before accepting the tray, and Ricky wipes his hand under his nose on the way to turning down the volume. The overblown music is still in Toni's head when they pull into the Beebe Medical Center and have to enter the air lock of the double doors separating fresh sea air from the sterile stink. In a world where their struggle is a movie, she'll don a flowing sleeveless number sashed in bright silk and carry offerings to white-robed soothsayers wearing stethoscope amulets. Flanked by her strong, beautiful children, she will square her chin and gather her pluck. And while she intends to rescue her man from the brink, who would stop her from looking to the heavens and ululating her sorrowful song through the temple of the sick?

Thus she ascends to the third floor, east wing, wearing flared yoga pants and a cashmere hoodie, and she takes rocking steps on her toning sport shoes as she enters Owen's room, which reeks pretty strongly of shit.

Nurse Cherise puts her finger to her slight mustache. "Sleeping. He may go on and on about heaven, but that's not where he spent the night."

Owen's cheeks puddle on his flaccid face. Brooke holds her flat palm an inch above his nose and mouth. She says, "He's breathing."

Nurse Cherise is making eye contact with the scones, which Toni tilts in her direction until the top-heavy muffins tumble over the croissants. The nurse carefully chooses a flavor. "It's good you weren't here."

He had a bad night, and she wasn't here—she should never have abandoned him. What's more, having stepped away and returned, she's sickened by the prospect of his recovery or, worse, his lack of recovery. The attendants bathed him—Owen's fluffy hair is slicked down and his sheets are freshly hospital cornered—and Toni can't help but wonder if he's incontinent now. Echoes of the Trojan War beat like a kettledrum through her viscera; she feels the floor tremble. Brooke must sense the shaking as well, for she plants her feet in a wide stance and clutches Owen's bed rails. The very ceiling tiles shudder with the sound of nurse clogs thumping toward the room, gathering staff and momentum as a crowd arrives to take blood pressure and cheese Danishes.

Owen chooses this moment to lift his heavy lids and jerkily move his eyes from point to point. All Toni has wanted since his accident is for him to see her, but not right this minute, when her defenses are down and her reluctance fully exposed. She thinks of his hand on her tailbone as they enter a party, his groan when he eats her grits. She tries to radiate loving thoughts, such as when he aims his camera at her. What lies ahead for him, for them, has her quaking in her sneakers, and she sees that he sees that. As he would say, he sees all that and a plate of muffins.

4

BRAZIERS AND SPITS

Owen spends the better part of his life in a railed bed brilliantly tricked out with a morphine drip and a call button. He is attended by multitudes, many of whom speak with their mouths full. They clutch glossy rolls with topknots and chunky scones; they drink from a box of coffee: evidently, his room has brunch service. When he reaches for Toni, which hurts, she lays down her phone to take his arm, which hurts. It seems to him that she has a different phone than she used to, and that he has a different arm.

He's alternately comforted and undone by the randomness of his experience. At least it wasn't Toni or the kids—that's the comforting part—which is followed by the horrifying: *not only out of the blue was I struck down and nearly killed*, but, worse, *it could have been Brooke holding the quarter; it could have been the boys, jousting along that metal railing; it could have been Toni, three or four pairs of glasses surrounding her face!*

And then he gets stuck at the intersection of arbitrary and singled out: you may already be a winner! Lasered by truth and joy, he has had mystical delight drizzled down the back of his throat, poured into the marrow of his bones. Don't talk about luck to a man who has had the universe cooked up and served to him in a beam of light. He has smelled heaven—mouthwatering, sugar and spice, toothsome heaven.

Everything came together; unfortunately, in the next instant, everything fell apart. It pains him to think that his conscious mind can't reassemble what he understood. Sometimes the feathery burns along his right arm are deeply colored, and some-times they're thin threads. Is that time? Or is it a function of concentration—does he have to keep in his mind's eye what he wants to see? He squeezes his morphine drip like a quiz show con-testant, except that he's eager to get the answer rather than give it.

Owen might need to devote the rest of his life to his electrified moment, which encapsulated his entire life and also made a sense of it he'd never experienced in any of those actual moments. Like now (if there is a now).

Morphine provides visions, albeit with distortions aplenty—the bending light waves add a sinister element. Toni has trained the staff to hear their van's ailing muffler enter the hospital lot; the boys arrive to a hero's welcome as she unpacks goody bags. At night she spoon-feeds him his dinner and then gives her chair over to Ricky, host of the evening's variety show. It's always a re-peat. Toni's texting in the corner, moving forward in time while Owen recedes. Each drip takes him into the epic of a man cast into peril, saved by his quick-thinking offspring. *And away we go.*

Ricky narrates, "We watched the storm building over the ocean, a black anvil of a cloud." And the chorus girls sing, *"Black anvil of a cloud."* They shake their exquisite, thonged butts at the audience, facing forward again when Ricky mentions the quarter, so that each girl can pluck a shimmering coin from her ample cleavage.

The whole scene is not so much enlightenment as it is wish fulfillment: How fucked-up did he have to be to imagine a dozen chesty women singing backup to his hypernarrative son, eager to tell and retell the tale of his near demise?

Ricky's epic is incomplete, seeing as how he can't be in Owen's skin. His description of Owen as "boneless and light" gets close. Owen's extensive injuries seem small payment for the beatific joy that enveloped him, doubling and redoubling as his knowledge infinitely unfolded, until what he knew was writ on an unwrin-kled sheet the size of the universe, which he could clearly see had been flattened and creased by amateurs.

You do not, it turns out, have to be present to win. After all, he was in the moment when lightning took him by the thumb and danced him into the air. He flew, despite the fact that people do not fly! His thoughts performed the same kind of impossible. It didn't last, and it took its toll.

When his fickle partner was done with him, he hit the sidewalk with his full and formidable body weight, tailbone first. As they say around here, some people feel a little discomfort when that happens. His coccyx rammed his entire spine up a notch, snapping two ribs on one side and fracturing his clavicle on the other before disks and ligaments could absorb the shock. He's ever so lucky that he chipped only one vertebra. However many days later today is, every breath pushes against the snaggletooth edges, impeding their efforts to mesh. Pain slices like a shiv through his calf muscles, which compacted into a loaded spring to catapult him through the air and, having sprung, seize with cramps. He has a bad case of road rash down his left haunch; however, rather than spinning a motorcycle out on asphalt, he's had skin sliced from there and moved to his hand, exposing his nerve endings to, let's see, *everything*.

And yet, he is not his body. *He* is fine. He needs time to pass, both so he can have another dose of morphine and to speed his healing so he won't need the morphine. He's terrified that time, like water, will erode and disperse what he's trying to hold on to. To Owen, the most remarkable physical manifestations of his ordeal are not his injuries, but the lightning flowers that traverse his skin like a root system, crawling all the way to his shoulder and behind his neck. They'll be gone by tomorrow, if tomorrow ever comes; again and again, he asks the boys to take pictures of the jagged tendrils.

"Do they hurt?" one of them wants to know.

"They pulsate." Left-handed, which he imagines he'll be for a while, he traces the tributaries, and the trails throb and radiate heat like the full-body sunburn he experienced from the high dose of UV radiation.

"Yesterday I e-mailed photos to my arcs and sparks TA. We made Lichtenberg figures like that in his lab."

Now Owen knows it's Will, although not what all his words mean.

Will says, "They're usually gone in a day or two, so you got a little extra."

"Praise be," he draws forth, as if his son were responsible.

Will dabs a tissue around Owen's eyes. "Mom's right behind me here."

Indeed, there she is, clutching a sandwich so hard the egg salad is trying to escape from between the bread slices. "I just stepped away for a minute," she says.

A minute, an hour, a day—it's all the same to him, as is whether they're here or not. His love for them is separate from their hovering watchfulness. When he wants to move, he experiences the delay of his internal signals having to bounce off satellites before reaching his brain: he tells himself to walk and then patiently waits to witness himself peel the sheets back, sit up, scoot to the edge of the bed, and swing his feet around so they are parallel to the floor. A moment of gratitude is to be observed just then, because *some people* expressed doubt about the future of walking.

He asks that one, "Better than you expected, right?" but it comes out, "Suck on that!"

Then he gets his. Scooting to the edge of the bed is all well and good, but the real fun has yet to begin. Although he knows he's not touching the ground, the sensation is of stepping on hot, sharp gravel (he would have been in better shape wearing shoes, which are often blown off when lightning vaporizes the sweat confined within). And he feels the full thickness and punctate burns on his right hand, where skin from his hip has been grafted. He got away without blood transfusions or massive daily debriding, which turns burn victims into howling monsters. Lucky, lucky, lucky. Even so, he is in a house of hurt.

A longer or more enduring current would have cooked him from the inside out, like a microwaved meal, overwhelming the heart or the lungs' inherent automaticity. Nonsense runs amok in his head, words with the sound of elaborate swearing— *heliolatry* and *locofoco*—coming out of his children's mouths. There are braziers and spits and all things barbecue.

They want him up and around, though he's supposed to keep his left heel off the floor and his right arm elevated—how exactly is he supposed to bear his own weight, balance, and propel himself, all the while wheeling his monitors and fluids along? His body has been divided up among the many specialists, each of whom gets a bodily function, limb, or organ. Some of them get his machines, which give off the green, green graphs of home.

He has newfound respect for Will's robots, who require a semester of team effort to negotiate a crack in the sidewalk. Why can't someone program him?

If walking and talking require all that, sleep requires all that and a plate of muffins. Nights are zig-a-zag with lightning, and there are ten nights a day. He breaks into gales of tears or laughter, like an infant, before finally tumbling down slumber's bottomless well. *Falling* asleep is terrifying, and sleeping isn't all it's cracked up to be, either. He feels deep compassion for his patients, a sizable number of whom never get more than four hours of continuous rest.

He tries not sleeping; when that doesn't work, he attempts to direct his crazy-busy nightmares himself, funneling the multiple burning fires into several barbecue pits, herding the grotesques onto spits turning atop the grayish-red charcoal. To his relief, the pits become both more realistic and fantastical, until he is consulting with vapors about the dimensions and materials necessary, googling his subconscious. How wide a surface, how high above the coals, what type of cover to use, and what doors on the outside of the fire pit. Where has he picked this stuff up? An alien in a cowboy hat advises a naked beast tending the fire, "You're gonna need a rain cap for that smokestack," and he files that information away.

He knows he's awake when he can see his arm, mapped with the side streets and scenic views few are shown. Therein lies his change of heart, from victim to chosen. He offers his temporary tattoo as a sign. The tingling he feels follows the toothed red paths, his circuitry made visible. Hasn't he been marked as special?

Nerve endings that aren't sizzling because of the strike are tickled by the morphine drip; meanwhile, the routine interruptions of hospital rounds border on torture. Maybe fragmentation is to blame for his nested dreams, one within another. Each popping fresh drama is peculiarly fraught, so that just when he is relieved to be out of the frying pan, there he is heading into the fire.

Last night, after he convinced Toni and the kids to sleep at the beach house, his harrowing descent lasted for hours. The dream began innocently enough, with him happily stoking up his barbecue pit: although it's stormy out, he's got a tarp to cover the fire, and he is initially delighted by the sky's show, cracks of light splitting the dark globe. Soon, however, the smell of burning hair permeates his dream with dread, and a mournful howl sounds. There is such woe in that shriek, yet he isn't sure whether he's feeling his own pain or someone else's. Is he on fire and letting loose a primitive, pure cry of anguish? In his dream, he registers what is lost in translation. Gut-wrenching emotions are too sloppy for words. How ineffectual the mapping of language is against the contents of the human heart! He removes his mitten to inspect the pink shine of new skin, which should eventually cover his arm from wrist to fingertip, and then he surveys the burned, corrugated flesh of his shin, knowing with a certain sadness that the scent of his injuries has long ago faded.

If he's not the one howling, who is? Terror spreads like wildfire toward his family, fear tinged with intuition. He is barefoot, and the pavers around his barbecue pit are actually hot, bubbling lava. Frantic, he hops in circles searching for shoes, thinking he'd be better off looking for Toni, who will tell him where his shoes are, and then—marvel of marvels—the sandals pried from his skin that sizzling summer night are *right here*, with enough stickum to adhere to the bottom of his feet. They slap beneath his soles as he runs around in a high-stakes game of hide-and-seek, discovering all three of his children where he started. His beautiful, safe children are screaming their heads off: tongues of fire are trying to lick them, and the air is horribly fouled, more shitty than smoky. Will turns Brooke's head away from the rotisserie so she won't see the squirming roast covered in fur, its black and brown twitching tail trailing from the spit. Here is the source of the unearthly yowling: in his delusional state, he has skewered the family cat and set her turning over the coals.

Moans rise and fall together as the monitor's siren registers Owen's arrhythmic heart. He is bathed in his own sweat and, sure enough, his own shit, which is something, considering the constipating plug of morphine. Is this payment for the rapture he's been allowed to glimpse? How many dips into the underworld before healing begins?

"Nothing wrong with your lungs." Nurse Cherise resets the monitor and takes his vitals before checking under the worn blanket. "Marcella," she calls at the door. "Dr. Lerner has a job for us. And tell Amazu to bring the linen cart."

He's much obliged to the delegation, who expertly strip and remake his bed and him: the overweight southerner, the tiny Filipina, and the West African—although they have to change him, they don't have to be this nice about it. Marcella holds the bendy straw to his mouth so he can sip cool water. Lucky again, and lucky for being in a hospital not his own. Convinced he's been enlightened, he'd have to admit that his dreams reveal another dimension. Really, who kebabs the children's pet?

"Those are tasty scones your wife brings to us," Nurse Cherise says, followed by Marcella's "Almond, yes. Apricot is a little bitter, I thought, and dry."

"I'll tell the boss," he mumbles, vaguely aware that Toni is responsible for brunch and perhaps their charity.

The next thing he knows—and it may be the next day or the next inhalation—here comes marzipan and yeast's funky tang. It is an awake smell, nothing seared or saucy, from which he deduces that he's been recovering from the ordeal of his dream and the drama of his cleanup. Brooke flinches, as if his blanketed body were a hot burner. "Daddy, you're awake!" she lets him know.

He looks upon his wife, whose face is going through the emotions. She tries a little tenderness, followed by terror and then pragmatism. Everyone is looking at her, which he resents. *My Antoinette*, he wants to assert. When she puts forth her tray, it's as if she's strewing chum in the waters, drawing nurses and surgeons into a circle around his bed.

So much for his being an interesting case and the crew inordinately kind.

"Caterer's here," he says meanly. Nurse Cherise takes a croissant, and golden buttery flakes drift down like dandruff.

Toni stands clear of the door as it swings open and staff flock to his room, scuffling like seagulls moving in on french fries at the beach. "Are the orange bits ginger or apricot?" "There aren't any nut-free ones, I suppose." "No coffee?" They split muffins in half and in half again, reaching over, grabbing, and taking flight.

"Shoo," Owen says as forcefully as he's able. "Get the fuck out of here."

Toni is by his bedside with his slippers. She says, "Let's go on that long walk. The sooner you're ambulatory, the sooner you head home. Owen, are you listening?"

Ambulatory sounds like ambulance, which takes you to the hospital, and yet Toni links ambulatory with going home. He looks at his wife, whose tan both ages and unages her. "Ambulatory," he repeats.

Brooke chimes in, "Up and around. Able to amble."

"You." He smiles her way.

Four days and counting is proof that he's badly hurt. No one under seventy spends that long in the hospital anymore. He should be grateful for the way Toni works the staff on his behalf. She begins the complicated tube-and-cord arrangement whereby he can leave his bed but take along a wheeled rack, like a little red wagon. He sits up and pivots so Nurse Cherise can wrap him in the special robe that ingeniously accommodates his IV—there's a zipper along his left shoulder seam! Then he watches Toni's fingers, which have changed since last night. Her shiny nails are tipped in white; for some reason, they've been rendered more nail-like.

"Fresh paint?" he asks.

She looks around. "I don't see a sign."

He moves the way a baby does, prone to folding but also a little looser and groovier than before. He is supposed to keep his heel off the floor: *step ball change*, he remembers from who knows where, and he scuffs his way down the interminable hallway escorted by his wife, whose sweater feels like pebbles against his uninjured palm.

Toni cheers each step: "That's it; much better than yesterday. Lift your foot and put it down—don't just shuffle—stand straight if you can." It's the way she talks to Brooke on the beam, and he wants to please her all the way to the elevator, though it hurts his tailbone to pick up his foot and his ribs to stand straight.

"Dismount," he says. "Going for the gold."

Would that he had a fraction of Brooke's strength and elasticity; he yearns to touch his palms to the slick linoleum and cartwheel down the hall for her. He has quickly become the ward's most popular patient, and he waves to his fans, wagging his tail behind him. A wounded and occasionally foulmouthed MD, a relatively cheerful patient, not to mention a miracle. Who doesn't love a miracle?

On the return trip, however, his eagerness withers. Toni's "one foot after another" sounds like *How hard can walking be?* She says, "It's only a few more steps," and he hears *Any day now.* He swallows a bit of vomit, brought up by the stabbing throb in his heel.

She stretches out her right arm, as if showing him the way through a complicated highway cloverleaf, when they both know he is merely retracing his steps down the hallway tunnel. Walk this way, indeed. Each step pulls on his skinned flank, which seeps, as does he, and the hallway breeze chills his seepage so that he shivers. Just as she's admitted that she has no idea how their lithesome daughter can do a handstand on a four-inch-wide beam, neither can she know what his body is up against, and he wants to throw her patronizing advice in her face. Instead, he picks up the rickety pace for the final run to his room, whose baked goods he can smell down the corridor.

"Good work," Toni says tepidly. She gives him her straight-lipped smile. "You'll be back to normal in no time."

Owen wrestles his arm free of her grip, furious. *That explains it,* he thinks, realizing how low her aim is. He has no intention of returning to normal. How you going to keep them down on the farm after they've had a transcendental experience? He says, "Normal is for pussies."

"Nice," Toni says.

Anger propels him to his bed, and he falls into it as if into water. Tubes and cables arc in the air and snap taut, tethered as they are between the wheeled rack and his body. Toni rolls the rack closer until it clinks against the bed railing. He can feel his mouth straining in a deliberate scowl; tears of betrayal run down the sides of his face and soak into his beard.

"There, there; they're here," Toni says, addling him further: *there there; there here.* But then the whitecoats move in on him with their demands: pull my finger, touch your nose; look up, look down, look all around, look at my thumb. They raise his bed and pose him like a broken action figure. Owen lets them play doctor, watching them provoke a twinge or a full-on reflex out of his body. Unspooling, rewrapping, they are all the while complimenting each other until they return him to his declivity. Tall One smiles down upon him to proudly proclaim his professional prognosis: "You're coming right along."

"Bite me," Owen says, and is stunned silent when they laugh in return. Nonetheless, they shamelessly grab bagels and such before scooting out the door. Is he their patient or a pastry delivery system?

His wife is hunched over, and her eyes have a darker tint than usual. In fact, she's holding the rail of his bed like a raven on a perch and looking at him as if his only two options are to die or get over himself. "Everything must feel pretty raw to you, but there has been progress. Look at your arms, for instance."

Horrified, Owen clenches his fist, reviving his fading lightning flowers. Whatever vanishing road map he has been dealt is his to decipher. Speeding along his internal highways of blood and nerves, the heavens impressed the underside of his skin with dozens of tiny straight segments that together curve into a veritable signature. Owen beholds himself as the human Etch A Sketch, and he needs to make Toni understand that the lightning, which picked him up and shook him clean on that sandy beach day, has both entered and claimed him as its own.

5

RESET MODE

Kyra shows up by Owen's bed in all her fleshy loveliness. "You came to see me," he announces. The family is a little drop-jawed in her presence, which might be because they've been sealed up together for a week. Kyra seems naked compared with Brooke, who's wearing long sleeves, long pants.

Toni has on *two* white sweaters, a hooded one over a pullover. She says, "Your mom told me she was heading home. She left you here by yourself?"

"Sort of." Kyra leans against Will.

"They need her at Dogfish," Will says.

Kyra strums her hand down the front of her shirt, where a dogfish shark careens across her bodacious breasts. Her nipples are the size of gumdrops.

"Is it still summer?" Owen asks.

Toni shivers. "Not in here, it's not. They have you on ice."

Will opens his jacket to Kyra, who wraps both arms around his waist, and then he zips them in together, as if his sweatshirt were a sleeping bag.

"Way to go, Willy!" Owen cheers. His people look pasty and cowed huddled around their dark, spangly visitor—she has a jewel embedded in the side of her nose! "What happened to Denver?" he asks.

"You mean Delaware, Dr. Lerner?"

"Shit, I was this close."

"Oh, yeah," Ricky agrees. "You're practically at the height of your powers."

Brooke pushes his bendy straw toward his chin. "Denver? Delaware. They sound close, but they're across the country."

"Dad's in reset mode," Will says, and Owen sees a great nodding go around the room.

He sucks on the straw, marveling at the accordioned tube. Tasting the stale water, he remembers the kids' kindergarten teacher preaching that all the water that has ever been is the same water. She used to call it dinosaur pee. Rather than reset, he'd say he was in recycling mode. Powered by drugs and dreams, he rides cosmic waves that lift him up to where truth sounds the same as circular logic. Perfect loops or loopy, to find wisdom in "I am what I am" or "nothing needs anything"? He relies on Toni, but she's looking down upon him. Someone has disappointed her, and he doesn't have the wherewithal to figure out who.

"That girl is what we used to call stacked," he thinks, unless he says it out loud.

The next morning—or morning, anyway—he's stationed at his window when his coconspirators come to spring him from the hospital. It's a testament to his healing powers that he's out of bed and dressed. Nurse Cherise has helped him into a pair of thin pajama pants that aren't supposed to stick to anything. He watches as the van catches some air on the first speed hump, which tells him that one of the boys is driving. Do most hospitals have speed bumps or just hospitals near beaches?

When Brooke is spit out like a seed from a watermelon, he assumes that they've piled everything in there willy-nilly. Three of them enter the seashell-etched doors of the hospital lobby. They've left one twin behind, maybe to keep the van from heating up like a coffin; however, the motor running in the getaway car substantiates Owen's suspicion that this is a breakout.

Hasty farewells to the nursing staff, including final parting gifts and a sheaf of papers that Toni scrolls through for his sloppy signature (which he admires as barely affected by the lightning), and then he's wheeled out into the scorching sunlight. Toni says, "Ricky, why don't you drive now?" and Will climbs out of the front seat and through the side door. On the passenger seat there's an inflated tube for him to sit on, what the nurses call his doughnut. His family's thoughtfulness brings a lump to his throat.

Brooke pushes the wheelchair toward the curb as if she were returning a shopping cart at the grocery store.

"What day is it?" he asks out the window.

"Oh, sweetheart," Toni says. She touches his good arm.

"No, I know: August twenty-second; Rehoboth, Delaware; Obama for President! I just don't know if it's Thursday or Friday."

Brooke is already behind him in her seat. *Crap*, Owen thinks, *these people move like lightning.*

"Good job, Daddy. Today is Friday."

So this is what Friday looks like. There are no shadows in the parking lot. "High noon," he says, thinking of gunslingers fighting their duels at noon, so neither would be staring into the sun.

"See? He knows what's what," Brooke says.

Owen studies the boy at the wheel. Although Will is a biker and, when he can find a mountain, a skier, and Ricky is a swimmer and a bookworm, they've arrived at the same muscled intensity. It matches their long, slightly droopy eyes and yellow thatched hair, which stands up identically from their heads. They both have one dimpled cheek. They both have everything. Sometimes, such as now, Ricky wears glasses, but except for that, Owen has not been able to tell his own sons apart since the strike. This is especially troubling because he's so resentful of Ricky. Owen revels in his memory of that crackling joy, looking down upon his nearly independent children and the beauty of the earth, the heavenly scent of a picnic filling up his head. "Why couldn't you have left me there?"

Ricky's eyebrows go up above his sunglasses. "You're kidding, right?" He pats Owen's thigh and says, "Listen, we're going to get you home to your own bed. Are you comfortable, old man? You want to pick music or anything?"

He can't remember if they called him old man before. Owen has a sad sighting of his future: all he needs is a lap quilt. Rocking in his seat, he's indulging in the self-stimming behavior of most of his kids and, come to think of it, his departed mother. "What have we got?"

"Don't let him pick," says his wife, who's getting a tutorial in advanced phone. The kids can't believe what their parents don't know about their phones. She yells, "I'm vetting candidates on this thing!"

"Will got her an upgrade," Ricky says. Then he hands Owen a tiny something or other.

Once, Owen almost knew how to use the device—jukebox? camera? "Ball buster," he says, and Ricky's laugh tells him he got it wrong. But that's how he spent car trips as a kid, solving ball busters. "No, I mean brainteaser," he tells Ricky. He remembers trying to free twisted nails and sliding numbers within a black plastic frame. Were kids that easy to amuse in those days? He abandons the mini-device in the cup holder and leans forward to turn the power switch of the car radio, which yields a satisfying click. "I'm a little out of the loop. How about if we listen to news?"

"*News*. I was hoping you'd ask for that," Ricky answers, saying the opposite of what he means and finally sounding like himself.

They drive past Elmer's Market, where they usually load up on fruit and vegetables, even if Brooke has to rest her feet on a watermelon for the ride home. No one suggests that they stop, and when Brooke announces, "Three miles to Jimmy's Grill," Will says, "Let's just get Sonic and get home, okay?" Burgers all around at the drive-in, filling the car with the smells of hot fries and dill pickles. Toni has Owen wrap napkins around his bad hand so the salt and grease can't get past the bandages. "That dressing has to last a few days," she says. When Owen finally bites into his cheeseburger, the food is a revelation. Grilled onions! Pickle! In the end, he makes a funnel out of the paper wrapper and shakes onion tendrils and a wayward pickle slice into his mouth.

"I'll take your trash," Toni volunteers, which touches him in ways he can't explain. Why is that understood to be her job? Yet it is, and she accepts it.

Soon they're driving around the Bridgeville circle and then the Scrapple billboard. Brooke says, "Scrapple—come for the pork snouts; stay for the eyeballs," and he remembers that she always says that. In fact, each landmark they speed by has the feel of routine, like hand washing. Everything is going by so fast.

Owen says to Ricky, "I should teach you guys how to grill."

"And steal your fire—I don't think so."

Ricky's remark is a tiny dart aimed at Owen's frontal lobe— *thonk*! *Steal your fire*, his son said. After a slight delay Owen replies, "Me, Zeus; you, Prometheus."

"Nailed it, Dad."

Owen thinks about the Greek gods and goddesses freely journeying from realm to realm. Maybe before the earth was covered with antique malls and tanning salons, eighteen-wheelers and discount outlets—maybe before cell phones—the Greeks could see a little beyond themselves. Maybe they mixed it up with the gods. *Or had really good drugs*, he thinks.

"Has school started?" he asks Ricky.

"No, but I should have registered last spring. I've been trying online—it never occurred to me that Sanskrit would fill up."

Owen pictures sand's grit filling up a depression, and then he finds the meaning east of Greece. Sanskrit. He says, "I know people who studied Norse. That would go with mythology."

Ricky turns his whole big head toward his father, visibly impressed at his staying on topic. "I'll take that under consideration."

Rapid-fire radio comes through the central speaker at Owen, who may or may not ever hear on his right side again. The acoustic wave that follows lightning's pressure change—essentially, thunder—ruptured that eardrum, which hasn't yet healed, but no longer hurts. As for the news, the election that's been going on for the last year or two is still going on; the power grid continues to be overextended. And although his entire nervous system has been on a tear and he's enjoyed something of a holiday from the global cycle of cruelty and destruction, his week drifting through the stratosphere doesn't count for much against momentum. To hear the serial commentators tell it, a world in motion will remain in motion: suicide bombers, Hamas, fish-killing algae, twenty-six-car pileup.

Fifty-two-card pickup, Owen thinks.

No new strains of wonder were discovered last week. There are no dispatches on the electrochemical possibilities of scent as a teaching tool or, for that matter, anything at all about the stunning yellow of the day. *Hello, yellow*, Owen thinks, knowing how juvenile that is and trying to do the heavy lifting of globally relevant thoughts.

"Phew!" Brooke exclaims. "We're gagging back here."

The raunchy smell of manure fills Owen's sinuses and burns his throat. Endless red rows of chicken sheds with shiny tin roofs stripe the view out both sides of the van. *Someone should report on that flag of color*, he thinks: green spinach and soybean fields on the bottom, red and silver chicken shacks in the middle, and the cloudless cornflower-colored sky on top.

Ricky pushes a button on the dash for air. "Does that help?"

"I'm fine," Owen says. No shit, no chickens—or is it no chickens, no shit? The road turns away from the sheds, and now the sun is like a heat lamp through the windshield. He unfolds the visor to see in the mirror that he has a canary-eating grin on his face. He hadn't even known he was amused.

"What's so funny, Daddy?" Brooke asks.

"Nothing," he says. "Caught myself smiling."

He winks into the mirror and Brooke winks back, though his peripheral vision registers Toni shaking her head. What, he isn't supposed to smile?

He is unaccustomed to his emotions having a life of their own. They stop for car and passengers to offload liquid and rehydrate, an amusing and primitive loop to Owen, who dutifully pees and receives the bottle of water Toni pushes on him. He thinks they change drivers. If he can still read faces, everyone is exceptionally eager to get going—lips are straight across and pressed together, heads are bobbing, *come on, come on*. They're all leaning forward, too, though his plumb line could be off.

Disability has destabilized him: he remembers the side effects of atypical antipsychotics, but not his eye color. If he's learned anything in his practice, it's that people do best when they're consistent. Average across the board or smart in everything—that level line somehow applies to temperament as well. Large discrepancies throw everything out of whack: his most challenging kids are the ones with too much in one column and not enough in another.

Suddenly Owen has to wipe his face, which is dripping with sympathy. He wonders when his internal clock and compass might reset themselves. Or if he wants them to. Could he exist in several time zones at once, like a news anchor in front of a wall of clocks? He swings the visor up because he doesn't want to see if he's crying rather than sweating, and that gives him a clear view of the Bay Bridge, its slender support inspiring a terror he's heard plenty of patients describe but has never felt before. He's driven over this bridge hundreds of times. Closing his eyes makes it worse, so he looks to the horizon and tries to breathe. Anxiety stretches time like taffy: it takes six hours to cross the bridge. Fifteen minutes after he opens his eyes, they've passed Annapolis, joined up to 495, and exited; he blows his nose, and they're pulling into the driveway.

Limp from ricocheting through time and space in the rocket van, Owen is shelved, put to bed so the productive members of society can take the van apart and put it together. No, you don't disassemble the car, you unload its contents. The moving highway trundles beneath him, just as, at the beach, seesawing waves rock you all night. Is that a factor of the inner ear, that we continue to sense motion in stillness, or might it be a form of nostalgia? He's having some difficulty separating mind from body.

It's still light when he rouses himself from bed to look out the window, relieved to be home. This is his yard all right, aged with weeks' worth of neglect. The van's bench seat is out on the driveway, so maybe you do disassemble the car. There is the expensive marble table they never use because they never eat outside. There is the scummed pond whose filter needs to be changed; a whiskery koi surfaces, scales flashing like reflectors.

Owen remembers when Will was Brooke's age, not really that long ago, and volunteered to clean the pond. "I got to the muck at the bottom," he said proudly. "I got down to the premarital ooze."

Oh Willy, my sage, you don't even know how much you know.

He wonders if he could get Will to take him out for supplies, if he could nonchalantly offer to make dinner. He is itching to light the grill, just beyond the rough. How much meat could fit on that puny grid? His smile widens his beard until it tickles his earlobes. *Whoa there.* He reins himself in, feeling the day take its toll.

For along with the grinning, there is some distress. His collarbone is swollen where the van's shoulder harness crossed it, and road food or morphine is backing him up. The strain of a bowel movement makes him clammy. Staring up at his home ceiling, he misses his self-administered morphine pump the way he used to miss his grandfather, so comforting and nonjudgmental.

Another thing from the hospital that is sorely missed is name tags. The friends who drop by in the next couple days resemble one another—did they always? They speak about him in the third person: "Owen could have been killed!" "Owen looks pretty good, considering." "Owen wants to grill? What the hell, let Owen make dinner, if he's up to it."

He can talk well enough, and hear enough to catch Toni telling some man that Owen isn't making much sense. She just isn't prepared to discuss his new favorite topic—namely, barbecue. Everyone else is sweet and patronizing. That gives him retroactive sympathy for his patients, who complain that "neurotypicals," as they call them, generally vacillate between critical and condescending. Nothing enrages his kids like the slow, loud voice people use on them, even specialists: "DO. YOU. KNOW? YOUR HOME ADDRESS?" Patronizing pricks. And wasn't Dr. Payne surprised when Owen answered, " '*Home is the place where, when you have to go there, they have to take you in.*'" Okay, he was overcompensating, but the line had just bubbled up.

It occurs to Owen that he is no longer neurotypical, and he imagines that he'll be even more help to his clientele once he's ready for them. Not only that, it is his right side that has taken the hit, the side more and more credited with nuance and connotation, the basic deficits facing his patients. See? He remembers that.

Sleep is just as complicated and upsetting at home as it was in the hospital. Fortunately, the Internet is up at all hours, too, and there he finds detailed plans for barbecue pits at every level of do-it-yourself. Also true for making bombs or intricately cabled sweaters, though he isn't sure how he arrived at those sites. The Web is a veritable swap meet of information. Although he sees medical sites per se that are dubious or downright false, like the ones still claiming that vaccinations cause autism, there are also impressive chat rooms and support groups. He's read credible dietary and behavioral tips that are only beginning to enter the medical community.

As for barbecue, devotees have strong opinions about everything from the meat to the mortar in the pit. Their fixations remind him of his Asperger boys. Take bricks in the barbecue pit, for instance. Purists demand that you mix up your own, shape them to optional dimensions, and bake them among the ash of certain trees—or you may as well go to Sonic for your sandwich. As he explains to Will, you wouldn't want your pork butt flavored with the off-gases of a brick factory.

"Yeah, that would be tragic, if my butt had off-gases," Will says. He laughs at Owen, and then he hugs him. "Take it easy, old man. Don't let your meat loaf."

Somehow Will gets himself—including drum set and bike—off to school on Saturday, and on Sunday, Ricky finds a ride to Duke with the Wilmerdings, whose son goes to UNC. Before Ricky pushes off, he stands silently in front of his father. Expecting what? Owen's blessing? A thank-you note? He looks so sweet and confident, Owen almost mistakes him for Will.

"Have a good fall," Owen says.

"I will if you will," his son replies.

In some ways, he holds Ricky responsible for his injuries, though he knows he's being a baby. After Ricky leaves, Owen skulks into the living room, where Brooke is doting on Mittsy. The cat arches her spine beneath Brooke's hand, rounding it to get maximum pettage. Owen takes two wobbly steps toward the cat, who—*me-OW!*—flings herself from Brooke's lap, front paws forward and hind legs stretched behind her, as if leaping off a building.

"She's afraid of you!" Brooke says. "Mittsy, come here, honey."

Was the cat like that before? He thinks she used to rest against his thigh as he read, but that could have been an earlier cat. He wishes they'd gotten a new dog after Sparkle or, rather, that they still had Sparkle. Even if that dog had seen his dreams, she would have wagged her tail and nuzzled under his hand. That dog would have let him skewer and grill her, if that's what he required, and then she would have come when he called and let him roast her again.

Owen joins Brooke on the couch, stretching his better arm around her. He remembers walking Sparkle and Brooke to first grade, when any day now she'll be starting eleventh. A few weeks into the school year is Toni's craziest time—her university clients want to hit the ground running, and it's her job to start rounding up presidential hopefuls for them. For him, September has always been something of a grace period. Who isn't eager for a fresh start? Inside zippered pouches, unsharpened pencils are lined up like a fresh pack of cigarettes; soon enough, his kids are on their last chewed stub, the eraser long ago rubbed down to a bent metal lip. If he's going to see patients, he'll need to be functional by Halloween.

"What?" Brooke says.

"I'm just looking at you." Unlike Toni, his daughter doesn't treat him as if he has an arrow through his head. In fact, she's reverted to being openly affectionate and curious about him.

"Are you planning to remain *barbated*?" she asks, wobbling along on her new words the way she used to teeter on Toni's high heels.

Barbated sounds like barbecue, so maybe he is. "You never know."

"Barbated is bearded, Dad."

He playfully sticks out his chin so she can scratch him there. It feels terrific, and he makes a note to scratch himself there. "What do you think—should I keep it?"

"It's okay. You might consider some pruning."

Toni comes into the living room holding an iced tea to her forehead. "Nobody home but us chickens."

"We've got our chick," Owen says.

"She'll be flying the coop soon enough." Toni coasters her glass, then plops onto the couch, leaving space between herself and the two of them. She's uncharacteristically grimy, and she smells of the garage. "Ricky hadn't touched his boxes since May, but he stuffed every single one into the Wilmerdings' car. Better there than here, I suppose."

Brooke brushes tears off her mother's cheek as casually as if they were crumbs. Because neither she nor Brooke says a word about it, Owen doesn't either, and when she picks up two of the remotes, he follows the women's attention to the TV, where arms and legs move across the pool like windup toys. This is the hospital channel! He'd thought the hairless people in wet bodysuits were part of the chorus-girl phenomena. But this isn't a morphine dream (although it is a montage of sorts). Men bounce off an ultrahigh diving board, somersaulting and twisting through air; bikini-clad women spike volleyballs in teams of two. Intertwined circles fill the screen accompanied by a mountain trumpet call.

"It's the Olympics!" He's proud to have put all the pieces together.

Toni and Brooke lock eyes. Evidently, they've already solved this puzzle.

Toni says, "They're nearly over. Tonight's the closing ceremony."

"Wait, it's Sunday already?" Brooke jumps up. "There's practice at four today—remember?"

"No. I don't have it on the Big Board." Toni points in the direction of the kitchen, where the master calendar hangs.

Brooke says, "It never got on there. Coach sent us an e-mail."

"Coach should send a coach." Toni consults her watch. "Cabin John or Gaithersburg?"

"Gaithersburg. My days are all screwed up, Mom."

"Me, too," Owen chimes in. "Screwed to the fucking wall."

Toni cringes. "I know, it doesn't seem like Sunday. Or Saturday or Monday." She drinks the rest of her tea. "We still have an hour—gather your stuff. All the sport tops are on the dryer, or in it."

She turns her false cheer toward Owen. "We need to change those bandages."

"I'll do it myself," he volunteers. A roll of tape and all the time in the world—it seems the least he can manage.

"Sure you will," Toni says. He means to protest, but she disappears and returns with washcloths and towels, saline, scissors, gauze, tape, a tongue depressor, cream—two handfuls of supplies. She must have scrubbed, because he can smell the iodine, but she hasn't changed her clothes; when she sits down—the greasy garage odor reaches him then—she lays a clean towel over her thighs and pats herself there as a signal for him to put his foot in her lap.

He is having the damnedest time reading her, and he suspects she is hiding her feelings from him. Why is that? She's always been underreactive, but not distant. She unwraps his foot for the second time since his surgery to make sure the exposed open slice is the bloody red of ground beef and there's no swelling or pus around the extensive stitching. She suppresses a gag reflex; however, she quickly irrigates the grotesque wound and swaddles him in fresh gauze. She spreads Silvadene cream on his shin with the tongue depressor, bandaging his leg before easing it off her lap. He pivots so she can get to his haunch, where they peeled him like a potato. No word from Toni on how things look today; no word on anything.

Now, he remembers the flash-card set he has his autistic patients study to become familiar with facial expressions—it has never once occurred to him that people speaking to his kids might set their faces to unreadable or blank. It has never occurred to him that his near and dear might not want her thoughts known. Seeing more tears on her cheek, he hazards a guess. "You seem sad."

"That's because I am," she says, her voice shaking. "I am sad."

And so he hasn't completely lost touch. Smiling warmly at his wife, he tries not to gloat. She is sad, and he figured that out, and there is some satisfaction in the deducing. He used to surprise people by telling them how they seem; they didn't know, and he did. Except that she is sad and already aware of it, which diminishes his insightfulness. Although he can feel his mouth grinning madly, he modestly says, "I'm here if you need me."

6

STOP MAKING SENSE

Preparing Brooke for gymnastics revives the mother hen in Toni, and yet changing Owen's bandages makes her want to fly the coop. Each unwrapping reveals how badly hurt her husband is, possibly befuddled beyond repair. In Rehoboth, she had steeped herself in the ways of the hospital, somehow overlooking that when they released him, he'd still be a mess and his complicated convalescence would be her responsibility. *I'm here if you need me!*

Toni wants to be the kind of partner who radiates compassion even as she could be kinder pulling tape from his rash-pocked hip, which has developed sensitivities to the adhesives. Her behavior doesn't make any sense, she knows that. With the boys leaving, she is happy to do for Brooke. So why not Owen? Tears being sterile, she wonders if she might wash his wounds in them. Although it's only the third time she's changed his foot, hip, and hand bandages, as in most things, she displays no small amount of precision. She has him rewrapped before another plucky Olympian profile wraps up—this one is about the single mother who is on her third medal. As soon as Toni finishes, she scoops up the supplies and takes off for the other end of the house. "Thank you, darling," Owen calls after her. *Now peel me a grape.*

She tells herself she is weepy about Will and Ricky—everything with twins is two for one—and there is some truth to that, but she is also tired of Owen's grin, which she knows isn't voluntary, but it makes her feel like a servant to a fat and happy ruler, a simpleton who is nonetheless in charge. She remembers when the kids were younger and she also took care of his mother. Meanwhile, she has conquered the mother of all to-do lists this weekend. Who knows—she might be crying with relief. She peels off her sweaty shorts and T-shirt, filthy from packing Ricky off. She hangs a thin white linen dress on the bathroom door hook. It's a little treat she bought herself in the last long days at Rehoboth, something to look forward to on a day such as this.

The showerhead has lost its sting—she'll have to unscrew it and soak it in vinegar—and the water comes out as one thick braid rather than dozens of jets, causing Toni to turn the dial farther left of center. Too hot, but one millimeter to the right and it's too cold. She has made every mundane decision in this bathroom by herself, from the pedestal sink to the arc of the spigot to the train rack towel holders. That's not so much significant as simply her role. What strikes her as significant is that a few tiny adjustments can ruin a shower. Such is family life. Just as she gets the stream of water a reasonable temperature, someone—*Owen!*—flushes a toilet in one of the other bathrooms and she is scalded.

Toni rests against the cool horizontal subway tiles she selected and cries in great, heaving sobs. She weeps in loneliness for her two boys, who are supposed to go out into the world without her; she weeps for Brooke, who is pretending with all her might that her father simply has a limp and a new cooking interest; and she weeps for herself. While she's at it, she weeps for Owen, too, who might very well end up sticking a fork into an electrical socket seeking to re-create his experience.

"Mom! I'm ready!" Brooke yells outside the bathroom.

"Be right there," Toni chokes out. She can't even have a crying jag to herself. Will she ever be allowed to finish anything on her own agenda? And then she laughs sardonically: only if she outlives them all.

As Toni and Brooke prepare to leave, Owen is stationed at his laptop at the kitchen table, gorging himself on actual beef jerky and virtual grilling tidbits. He says, "We need an instant-read thermometer, just a simple one."

"You know where we're going?" Toni asks. "Say it back to me."

Owen, annoyed, says, "To practice—she's wearing her grips."

"Good." She puts a cell phone next to him on the table. "Push this button and say 'Toni' and it will dial me. Okay?"

"I'm fine," he insists.

"Me, too. I'm just fine," Toni says. She wonders if there is some product she can use to rinse the mean out of her voice. In her office alcove she paws through her basket of glasses, looking for her distance sunglasses. She owns three pairs of glasses for long distance alone—clear, dark, and "transition" lenses that go from almost clear to almost dark—and she also has middle-distance glasses for working at the computer, four or five pairs of drugstore reading glasses, and several kinds of sunglasses. Like television remotes and chunky chargers dangling tangled cords, everything in the house is proliferating. It's a wonder she can keep track of anything, she thinks, trading the glasses she's wearing for prescription shades.

"Can I drive?" Brooke asks on their way out to the van.

Are you out of your mind? "We're pressed for time," Toni says.

"I'll go fast—I drive better fast than slow."

Toni doesn't know how to respond to that. "I'm nonplussed—do you know that word?"

Her daughter says, "I'm nonsurprised. Will says if it were up to you, I'd never drive."

"Did he mention the four accidents he had before he got his license?"

"He mentioned one."

With her remote, Toni unlocks the passenger side for Brooke. "I don't think I'd be a very good teacher today."

"You could relax and enjoy the ride. When I get my license, you won't have to drive me anymore. Won't that be great?"

Of the two of them, Toni wonders who is more likely to drive off the road. "Let's get you to practice." She wishes she were heading to work. Yesterday alone, 150 e-mails showed up in her in-box. And next week she's going to have to schedule at least one entire day, maybe two, for nonstop conference calls.

Brooke plugs herself into her music and hunches down in her seat. Her earbuds must be set on stun, because Toni can hear the white hip-hop her daughter favors, apparently without irony. Miles from home, as they merge onto I-270, Brooke speaks up loudly: "Daddy only makes sense to me when he's talking about barbecue."

As we get older and stop making sense, Toni's invisible playlist sings in her head. "I hear you," she says.

"You do?" Brooke actually pauses the music. "Well, how long till he's better?"

"Hell if I know," she mumbles, and then, recognizing a chance to practice a little humanity, speaks up. "He's made incredible progress, all the doctors say so."

Brooke worries her cuticles, ragged from her attention. "I mean how long till he's *normal*?"

"A couple months. You'll see, it will go fast. Don't pick your nails."

"It's either that or smoke. Saxy started smoking when her mother got breast cancer."

"Sweet mother of god," Toni says.

"Mom!" Brooke admonishes.

"I mean, what an unwise choice." Toni takes one hand off the steering wheel to lift Brooke's fingers back to her mouth. "Here, pick your nails."

"Mom, the last nine days have been the longest ones of my life."

And mine? Gaithersburg can't come fast enough, though that's nothing new. "We have to get our act together, here," Toni says, trying to show they're on the same team. "School starts Thursday. How many pairs of jeans do you have?"

"Someone should have thought of that while we were in Rehoboth," Brooke says snottily.

"I was a little preoccupied with someone else's life support."

"Mom! I thought you didn't believe in sarcasm."

That is mostly true—she strives mightily to resist it—and she takes Brooke's remark as appreciation. Also, whatever crap teens dish out, they're offended by the mildest slight, as if her daughter's skin is as sensitive as her husband's. Toni says, "Let's shop tomorrow. There should be all sorts of sales."

"Excellent." Brooke immediately brightens. "Can we go to Tysons? Saxy got a lot of stuff there. And they have Yael Style, too." The gym finally rises into view, its ribbed white orb shining in the sun. "Saxy told me we have a Brazilian kid on the team now."

"How's Eleanor?" Toni tries to remember what she's heard about Saxy's mother.

"Fine. Turned out it wasn't really cancer."

Well, bravo for her. The unfairness of it galls Toni, that Eleanor could wake up thinking she'd been living a nightmare and find out it was only a bad dream. Trying to exit off 270, Toni seethes. She should be relieved for Eleanor, who has already survived divorce and Saxy. And yet, if Toni has learned anything in this experience, it's how rarely we can tell ourselves how to feel. Now she feels slighted by every car that does not let her in, which is every car. When there is an opening, she races across four lanes of traffic, and when she finally turns into a parking space at the gym, she scrapes the curb with the van's front bumper, which sounds as if it might not bump back. Heads turn toward the crunch, but Toni ignores the gawkers. She calmly asks, "You think Eleanor can give you a ride home?"

Brooke is staring at her in horror. "I certainly hope so." She doesn't wait for the van to stop idling before jumping ship. "If not, I'll call."

Out in traffic, Toni sees Brooke's phone in the cup holder. Maybe she should have let Brooke drive—certainly her own performance was no example. At sixteen, Brooke seems so much younger than her brothers did. Toni wonders if that's because she's the baby, the only girl.

The twins were more self-reliant at that age, but they had each other. Also, their independence got them into all sorts of trouble—that's what inspired Toni to lecture them on intelligent disobedience, an expression she'd learned when they adopted Sparkle. It's a great pet that reliably sits and stays; however, Sparkle had flunked guide-dog school because she *only* did as she was told.

"They programmed her that way," Will had defended her. "Didn't they want her to obey?" Yes, *but*, Toni had explained. You want a guide dog with enough sense and resourcefulness to protect a blind master from stepping into an open manhole; intelligent disobedience is what they call that ability to ignore the rules (or the mob) when necessary. In her applied version, the twins needed to pay attention, have the courage of their convictions, and be able to defend their decision if they chose to break the rules.

She wonders how well Brooke remembers Sparkle and if a dead dog could keep her daughter out of trouble.

Toni exits at Old Georgetown Road for some company. She loops through neighborhoods of oversize homes and early Bethesda cottages, knowing that mansion and rambler alike hold life-threatening illnesses, precarious finances, or the simple syrup of unhappiness that is part of every family recipe. She runs through the dashboard options looking for her music, and the first song starts in about how when the morning comes, this too shall pass. The strong bass beats beneath her rib cage, and the completely unoriginal message hammers her as well. From Johnny Cash to OK Go, with a million stops in between, people have been moved to sing nearly the same words. She likes that as much as driving.

Her route snakes beneath a clotted 495, and she briefly feels the satisfaction of avoiding a frustrating mess before she drives smack into a mental wall: she has left Owen home alone. There is no one to help him climb the stairs or, far more important, to dissuade him from firing up the grill. She and Brooke hurried to the van almost as if it were July, a mere and impossibly distant month ago. Apparently the limitations of his condition have yet to override a decade-long ritual—this is the way we go to gymnastics—though she had the presence of mind to furnish him with a preprogrammed cell phone. Really, a cell phone? She should have brought him along, she should have called a neighbor, she should have given him his painkillers (with a bonus half) early to knock him out. He is essentially a toddler with a higher reach and a slower reaction time.

There were moments in the last week when Toni wished she'd

been the one struck by lightning. Being brought to life by your own child has a poignant reciprocity to it, especially to a mother. She always suspected Ricky had that in him. Such courage and love he displayed for one so young. Maybe if she'd survived a strike, she'd see how much of life is precious, Owen already being more receptive to grace's little gifts. But she is too practical to sustain that fantasy for long. It's like wanting to be at your own funeral and then realizing afterward that, duh, you're dead.

More often, she fantasizes that Owen, waking to see her face in the ambulance, would have fallen for her the way he had in the library and, of course, spoken only her name or hers and the children's. And there are the times she wishes Ricky hadn't brought him back. Not that Ricky had failed—she wouldn't want her child to have to live with that. Owen is always getting excited about how finding five dollars in his pants pocket is cause for celebration. Big damn deal. But with a five-million-dollar life insurance policy she could be a completely grateful person. She and Brooke could live in Rehoboth, or they could downsize to a two-bedroom apartment and travel during school vacations.

While she is deep in magical thinking, Toni imagines that Owen might be enjoying his time alone. He'd complained about the lack of privacy in the hospital. Maybe he's reading a medical journal; maybe he's watching more of the Olympics. Maybe his heart has stopped. Toni speeds toward the intersection despite the light, and when she sees the white flash of the camera in her rearview mirror, she welcomes documentation that she hurried home. In a day or two, an envelope will arrive bearing the evidence: a photograph of her rear end, license plate in perfect focus, racing through the red light at Wilson Road to get to her husband.

In fact, when she runs into the house, sweaty and anxious all over again, he is on his doughnut in his boxers, exactly as she left him, consulting the laptop at the kitchen table. She approaches him from his deaf side; sunburned and bearded, he's grinning at the screen, and he looks remarkably game. He is sitting with his gut tucked beneath their kitchen table, briefly in no need of assistance, and he exudes the wry confidence of a movie star. He has always been supremely assured, and when she sees him like this, desire juices through her, stunning in its unfamiliarity and its insistence.

No wonder she bursts into tears at a moment's notice: she's just been fantasizing him dead, even as she tormented herself about leaving him alone and in danger. She is going to have to readjust to traveling through time, not to mention space. She is practically felled by her vertiginous thoughts of lust and a life apart. She remembers how they clung to each other when she miscarried, when his mother was found dead, when they spent a weekend alone at their beach shack fucking in every room, what Owen called "breaking it in." Toni kisses him on the top of his fluffy head, and she sees that the creepy red trails have finally faded from his arms.

"Just the woman I've been thinking about," he says, leering. His erection is peeking out of his boxers.

Toni says, "Jesus, are you looking at porn?"

"Pits. I'm going to make one for us. Something in stone, where we can cook all the livelong day. When the wood gets hot enough, the pit ends up doing the cooking. Then we'll have us a pig pull, and you will be happy."

"I will? Tell me how happy I will be." Though rarely alone in the hospital, they'd kissed, and she has to admit he'd become a better kisser in the storm. Once, he cupped her ass when a specialist inquired if he could feel anything.

Toni pulls a chair close to him, and he nuzzles her. His beard at the hollow of her neck makes her tingle and heat up.

"Sauce dribbling down that lovely chin as you crunch through the burnt sugar crusted on the skin," he says.

"I'll eat the skin?"

"You will, and you will love it."

He leans forward for another kiss, one of deep appreciation. Oh, how he appreciates her, softly tasting her lips and in no apparent rush toward the next step. Savoring her, drinking her in with great interest and presence all the way through the end of the kiss, after which she leans away to catch her breath. Owen wears a smile of mischievous delight, like a new lover, but better really, because here is the familiarity of Owen without habit. As if the past were prologue. She feels recognized, known but also separate and fresh. And she eagerly wants him alive and in their bed with her. Owen reaches out his good hand, which in itself is unfamiliar because she's accustomed to holding his other one, to being on his right side. Each time he lifts his right foot, he lightly squeezes her palm, either because of the pain or the effort a single step engenders. He lets go of her so he can clutch the banister to ascend the stairs.

In their bedroom, she undresses herself, her linen shift floating easily up and over her head while Owen wrestles his boxers to the ground. He undresses the bed, chivalrously gesturing for her to climb aboard, and then he strokes regions of her, incanting words he's never uttered over her body. "Baby's back ribs," he says, petting the back side of her ribs, slightly hidden beneath a layer of fat. He caresses the great slope of her hip and says, "Saddle." He is playful and chatty as he stretches across her. "Here is the tender and lean Toni loin." Then he returns to her side and kisses the top half of her breast. "Behold, brisket of wife." He quits speaking of her as a piece of meat and fondles her fondly. His good hand is very good.

She comes before he even reaches for a condom, and then there is more pleasure to be had. Owen is guffawing, and she's mindful of the pain friction may be causing him. Yet when she slows things down, he holds on to her saddle for dear life. "Now we're cooking," he whispers to her.

"Now we're *fucking*," she boldly says, eager to take them out of the pit.

Owen snorts in response, but he also says, "You are gorgeous," which makes her nipples stand up with pride. In the hospital, she could not have envisioned their future as better than the past, and she has a brief understanding of why he considers normal a setback rather than an aspiration. When he rolls off her, she wants nothing more than to start again, and she smiles not only because she hasn't felt this way in five or ten years but also because that much pumping and adrenaline might kill the poor man.

It occurs to her that the future could be something she's never imagined.

Owen is obviously spent by their efforts. Toni pushes the hair off his glistening brow; he turns his head to kiss her palm. "Ah, Antoinette, my queen," he says, and closes his eyes, powering down. Within ten seconds he's fallen asleep, his thin grin gone to blubbery fish lips.

Toni slips from bed, ticking items from the list she relentlessly compiles: get dressed, maybe find Eleanor to see if she's driving Brooke home. Duty calls, but so does memory. Her linen shift is crinkled from where it parachuted to the ground; she thinks *sandals, watch*, to keep her mind on the present. She doesn't want to follow the train wreck of her worst thoughts, reliving what Owen said to her in the ambulance.

Outside the kitchen window, the garden thermometer registers ninety degrees; nonetheless, Toni will make a pot of coffee. *Antoinette, my queen. My Kyra.* Her hands begin to shake with anger and resentment. Beach nights, did Owen ever meet up with her? Having driven Brooke and a few friends to a movie, had he hurried Toni off to the outlets for the afternoon so they could have the house to themselves? In the hospital, Toni's thoughts had run to this brink and skittered away, the way a sandpiper courts and flees the ocean's edge. Ministering to him, she had obsessed about Kyra—had Kyra seen his child-size rump or uncircumcised penis?—but she was always interrupted by one of the dozen hospital procedures that count for care. Now that things are still, a tidal wave is building, coming straight at her. She takes refuge in habit and starts the coffee regimen. The suck of her vacuum-sealed beans, their soft rattling as she pours them into the grinder, the change of pitch as they are transformed from oily beetle shells to aromatic dust—more than habit, this is her toilette, her meditation, and her sacrament.

Owen's feet slap, slap down the stairs, and she literally hunches her shoulders, as if he's pinched a nerve. *What exactly does he take me for?* she thinks, disappointed that the coffee has not given her peace.

He pulls a chair out from the table and settles himself onto his doughnut. "That smells so good." A thin line of drool dangles from the right edge of his mouth, heading toward the kitchen table. She stares until he grows self-conscious enough to realize what's happening and wipes the spittle on his bare arm.

Now we're cooking, she thinks. *Now we're fucked.* There wasn't time in the hospital to think a thought through to completion. Every minute of the day had been claimed by Owen, staff, one or another of his specialists, or the kids, though the kids had certainly gotten the crumbs.

Toni moves toward the coffee, wondering how many months it will be before Owen can serve himself. But that is a different streak of resentment. She takes down one of the mugs that isn't emblazoned with the name of a drug and hands it over.

Owen grips the handle with his right hand, unsteadily, bringing it quickly to the table, while she hovers with the sloshing pitcher of coffee. Reaching toward her face, he presses his thumb in the twitchy flesh beneath her eye. "Hemifacial spasm. Is that new?"

Toni flinches, as if suspicion of his disloyalty is jumping from nerve to nerve. She remembers the summer, years before, when she nearly broke ranks. Fight or flight, the most primal instinct, and every ounce of her is responding to it. She puts the pitcher on the table, smooths down her dress. She deserves to know, and in her shaky voice she asks, "Was there something between you and Kyra?"

He gazes at her with his shorted-out stare. She has confused him. Or maybe that's what being discovered looks like.

"Something *between* us?" he asks, as if Toni will specify a moment when he and Will's girlfriend were on either side of a difficult-to-see object. Was there *something* between him and Kyra?

His wife hoists the coffee pitcher again and unsteadily brings it toward his cup—her squinty attention bounces between the scalding pot and his lap—while the idiom settles into sense. He tries to imagine what prompted that question. Did he lose a few hours between sex and coffee? He remembers Kyra coming to the hospital with Will. And, vaguely, Kyra in the ambulance with them, but that can't be right. They'd known Kevin and Annie since the first or second summer they'd owned the beach house, perhaps inspiring Owen's misplaced pride in the way Kyra has turned out. Did other parents do this?

Kyra's dark bangs an inch above her heavy eyebrows should have been unattractive, and when she wasn't on Dogfish duty, she wore her shirts high and her shorts low, so her mildly fleshy belly always showed. In an effort to keep from staring at her, Owen often watched Will, but there were all sorts of details he'd none-theless noted. When she waited on them, for example, she had this beguiling way of keeping eye contact as she walked away that was equal parts attentive and flirty, as much did-I-forget-anything as I'll-be-back.

He remembers Toni's disgust at Kevin, who showed up post-divorce with a girlfriend who looked a hell of a lot like his daughter. Lucky bastard.

Now that Toni has brought her up, he realizes he thinks pretty highly of Kyra, maybe even has something of a crush on her. And he recalls debating, between leaving the van and feeding the meter that stormy night, whether he should spur Will on in his lackadaisical courtship of her.

Why does Owen think Kyra was in the ambulance—did she run out of the restaurant to help? Or is there something more to it? He is scandalized to think himself a tomcat, and he may have smiled just then. *Merely a passing thought*, he wants to tell Toni, to defend himself, if he did indeed smile. These days, he smiles a lot. The naughty enjoyment at having possibly dallied begins to expand and fill his imagination, unless it is his memory. He can see them alone in the kitchen, frying bologna because it happens to be a shared fetish—the pink disk curls into a cone—and admiring the way mayonnaise makes her lips shine.

Is Toni screwing with him, planting the seed of a false memory? He yearns for her accusation to be true, though his recall has nothing to corroborate pressing his calloused palm to Kyra's soft belly, her hair falling toward his chest as she lifts and lowers herself on top of him.

There was the night that Will's phone danced on the kitchen

table, and seeing Kyra's face appear on the phone, he'd eagerly answered. He might have picked her up at Dogfish and driven her home—or maybe she asked Will to do it, because he cannot for the life of him recall driving there or her hoisting her ass up into the van's front seat. Was that because he hadn't or because he'd done something repressible, something reprehensible, but obviously not out of the realm of his imagining?

Owen is engulfed by sadness and injustice. From one direction, a life of clean living has been undermined by horniness toward his son's girlfriend; from the other direction, there's the dismal realization that if he took part in such a liaison, he can't relish it. Upon being shocked, his brain may have thrown that singular memory overboard—last in, first out—if such a memory existed. And now he's frantic because it's taking him forever to answer a question that requires an immediate and unequivocal denial. *Had there been anything between him and Kyra?*

"No," he answers, far too late.

Toni has been watching his rubbery face, like that of a silent movie star, register confusion, titillation, bewilderment, lust, and resignation. His answer is not an answer. She takes her hair out of its elastic, then regathers it into a thick tail and winds the band around, same as it ever was. She is sitting on the fence between devotion and revulsion, and she could fall either way. His hesitancy is devastating, evidence that he is certainly interested in Kyra and capable of entertaining such an act. Unless he's trying to distinguish between recall error and a fantasy brought to his lips when his poor brain was scrambled. Sometimes, for example, even Toni forgets that Owen had a first wife. As far as she's concerned, his history begins with her.

They have, after all, been married since the Stone Age. Together, Toni and Owen invented the wheel, human reproduction, and at least three ways to serve Thanksgiving leftovers. It's entirely possible that he put his sweaty palm on Kyra's loin, gave her a kiss that lodged in his fantasy lobe. How much does Toni care, really, if a spark flew between them? If he hadn't spoken Kyra's name in the ambulance, if Toni wasn't ministering to him around the clock, *would* she care?

Men his age are worse than college boys, with their leering and elbowing of each other—her friends often remark how their husbands act around a glimpse of thong (and a breast on television gets their full attention). If he lost time when he shorted out, it could be argued that even if something potentially graphic and disgusting had been imagined, it hadn't happened. Worn out from her bedside vigil in the hospital, surely she understands disorientation. He was no doubt identifying her with his favored son's love interest: *My queen, my Kyra*. Reanimated and reintimated, they are something of a clean slate—that's what she wants to think.

Or he could be lying his ass off.

7

FLOATING FREE

To remember Kyra going down on him is to be double-teamed by desire and jealousy. There was no fumbling or embarrassment on her part—she'd obviously been around—which was fine then, but it tortures Will now. Not only that, every memory of her flashes between when they were little and August: he remembers them joking about how she can pooch her belly into a bowling ball of malnourishment, like in the starving-children ads, and then the very thought of her stomach, soft and bejeweled, tents the top sheet.

Kyra's the one who figured out that he'd been waiting for her. She hadn't waited. She'd been part of some Friday-night movie-and-a-fuck tradition since her freshman year. He can't stand the thought of standing in line for her, of there being a line.

Will's left arm is dead to him, trapped under last night's stray. Her name is Cat, he remembers with some amusement. Why do they always want to spend the night? A better question is why does he keep doing all this junk, all this sex? The sheets of his bed are actually crusty. He has a post-weed head-busting-ache and he is badly hung over, too. Despite his useless arm and the stab behind his right eye, he wants to get up and go. To the Schuylkill and around the museums. He imagines pumping his legs through the long incline. Alone and crouched against the wind—fuck the bike path, full of picnic cyclists and their kiddie trailers. He'll use a lane and irk the minivans backing up behind him.

He reaches his good arm toward the ceiling to retrieve a

drumstick impaled in the acoustic tile, and it's all he can do not to rap on this girl's head. *Bap bap bap bap: get up off my little bunk bed.*

He's doomed to spend his life in a bunk. This one is built as a loft so he and his roommate can have some room. However, Will's drum set, his two hulking amplifiers, and his precious LeJeune have left them with about four square feet of floor space. Doesn't take half of that for Henry to do his business, which is just about all he does there. How many weeks before someone catches on to the foot traffic and the fact that Henry has stopped going to classes? Not Will's problem, and isn't that refreshing? No one is his problem anymore.

He wriggles free and drops to the ground, his arm like a chimp's hanging by his side.

"It's Sunday," Cat says. "Where you going so early?"

Away from you. "I got stuff to do. Later, okay?" He grabs his boxers from the floor; as luck would have it, they'd landed on his wadded-up socks, so he doesn't have to look for those either. His phone skitters across the desktop, its intermittent backlighting doesn't display the number.

Sometimes when the phone shakes, it's his mother, and he yearns to teleport himself home and give her a hug—until she starts in. Why doesn't he jump on the train, come for the night? Can't. Just can't. It's as if his dad fell off a mountain and, on the way down, pushed Will off a cliff.

"Is that your girlfriend calling?" Cat asks.

"No, it's my dealer."

Her laugh is kind of sweet, but then she says, "Jesus, how much did we do last night?"

"Junk or sex?"

"You'd think you didn't get either, the way you're being." A drumstick shoots down at him like an arrow. "No wonder you're into robots."

He's surprised she remembers that, considering how many Skittles she ate. He'd been on the brink: messed up *and* still aware he was messed up, as he'd reached into the bowl and let the pills slip through his fingers. The variety of all the meds—shiny ellipsoids and dusty pastel capsules—reminded him of Rehoboth afternoons when he and Ricky and Kyra pooled their parents' pocket change for a candy haul, passing the communal bowl around through an epic Risk battle. As the sugar buzz overtook them, the game would deteriorate to apocalypse and hysteria. His biggest worry then was that he'd suck through the hard shell coating to a chewy fruit center instead of chocolate.

He finds bike shorts on his desk and a jersey over his chair; the only shoes he sees are his Sidis, which are overkill for a Sunday ride. Once he's clamped them on, he grabs his helmet and a water bottle. He says, "Listen, stay as long as you like. I'm gone." He knows he's blaming her for himself, so he adds, "Thanks for last night."

She leans way out over the bunk until her flat hair hangs like fringe, and her shoulder blade blooms with a marijuana leaf tattoo. "You sure know how to make a girl feel special."

Maybe if you were more than a druggy bobblehead. He maneuvers his bike around his drums and makes sure the door doesn't slam behind him. The truth is, she is not special, and she should just be grateful he didn't point that out. She's all right— they'd met in the dinner line when he admired the way she piled food on her tray. But Deirdre is all right, too. And Cheyenne and Rachel and Siobhann, whom he actually met crossing Spruce Street. They're all just fine.

It's as if he can't stop twinning. After Ricky, then Kyra. And after that, apparently, anyone. What happened to the surge he'd felt returning to school, relieved of Ricky and his own virginity? Rather than floating free, his feet off the ground and his head in the clouds, he's like an electron knocked loose from his valence—a lonely negative charge eager to hook up. Last night was some birthday blowout where the honoree faced a lineup of twenty-one shots of tequila. Everybody gathered around a spiked punch bowl, and Will drank the damn Kool-Aid. Why the hell not? Usually, he has an inside track to whatever meds are floating around; in high school, kids got their hands on all sorts of things—he'd heard about one kid who sold scrips signed by Dr. Owen Lerner. But last night's supply was from a *veterinarian*.

The guys made jokes about being able to lick their own balls; the girls meowed and hissed, claws out. Then the bowl of pills came around and things got weird.

Things are still weird. This isn't who he is, and if he were clearer-headed, he'd examine what the flux is going on. Will walks his bike down the dorm's long, dark hallway, careening as if it were the aisle on the commuter train. He can't stay centered, and he touches one cinder-block wall, which is both slick and prickly. In the effort to balance, the girl's name spills out of his head—he had it when he woke up, but just like that, he cannot come up with who is sleeping in his top bunk. And he'd thought *she* was a slut—what do they call guy sluts? Also, is he out to destroy his memory? He thinks about how electroshock works for some people by taking them back in time. He could return to being the anointed one rather than the middle child.

His bike shoes are an unfortunate combination of slippery, curved, and cleated. Walking in the Sidis is akin to tap-dancing on ice skates. It's not lost on him that this is the way his dad moves now.

He makes a lot of noise on his way to the overly air-conditioned bathroom, where the cleats could be ball bearings on the tile floor. He brings his bike in with him and rolls it right up to a stall. He sits down to pee and needs the handicap railing to propel himself out past his LeJeune to the sink. The water is so refreshing that he wedges his entire head under the faucet—he has to wave his hand in front of the photoelectric eye to keep the stream going. When he finally straightens up, his gut sloshes like his water bottle. He'll be fine, he tells himself, once his cleats meet the pedals.

Until then, there are doors and double doors and a flight of stairs. Without the bike or a hangover, he could parkour his way down the banisters and across the metal-edged steps, but the terrain is a death wish for a guy in his shoes. Anyone watching the security cam must be enjoying the show as he struggles toward the exit. And then, when he gets outside, the muggy air is a shock that brings on a sick sweat.

He keeps his bike close in; although he shouldn't be on the

street in his Sidis, it's easier to walk on the asphalt than in the dorm hallway. If his mother saw him now, she'd throw her hands in the air, and for good reason. The shoes have just developed the right amount of float, for one thing; for another, they are the most expensive things he owns, except for the LeJeune. Intelligent disobedience be damned! His cleats click on the sidewalk the way Sparky's nails used to skitter with eager happiness on their wooden floors at home, and remembering his former dog actually brings up the name again of the girl in the bunk bed. Cat. Her name is Cat, and someone said the stuff in last night's punch was *cat valium*. Kit Kat, they'd called it. He snorts and then has to walk through his own sour breath.

Will closes his eyes, squeezing them tightly shut until the burning dryness subsides. Momentarily blind, he can tell it's Sunday morning by the smell of coffee on either side, one trail from a café and the other from a tray full of cups carried by a high-heeled woman who's also carrying the smoky incense of Mass. Lox, diesel fumes from the tour buses outside the black church, dog shit in steamed-up plastic bags at the top of heaped trash containers that haven't been emptied for days. He is only breathing, but he may as well have swallowed the thick air— salmon and shit, exhalation and exhaust—that pushes whatever's in his gut up into his throat. He tastes the gush of saliva that precedes puking, and even though he wrenches fast to the left, a purple splash hits the top of his shoes.

He supposes this is rock bottom, and he's ashamed of himself. He rolls his bike along, tiptapping beside it until he can find a place to stop. He works his water bottle out of the pack's elastic crisscross. There are two kinds of high, and last night he went with obliteration. The fear of losing himself gave way to the joy of it, though he has no memory of getting to his room, let alone climbing the ladder and sleeping with Cat. Does sex you don't remember count? When Ricky used to call, Will had been the one to discern daring from reckless. Now he can't even tell existence from uniqueness. Such is the Kyra dilemma: Does he want a girl, every girl who exists, or uniquely Kyra? He thinks he wants to put all his chips on her, but then he thinks that if she's playing the wheel, she's also playing him. He takes a swig, spits, and takes another. He imagines his sweat bubbling up the color of Kool-Aid—or antifreeze, toxic runoff from the pills and tequila.

He reaches behind his jersey to the zippered pouch, which has the stiffness of a few bills, but he's forgotten both his wallet and his phone, not so smart on an urban ride. He can practically hear his mother ragging him about an ID and his phone; he's glad he's got his helmet.

The square is full of exuberant dogs running at full speed in a small pack and then making a beeline for a new arrival, who stands still while the group closes in to sniff his butt. Pissy as he is this morning, Will can't help but grin at all the wagging dogs rearing up and baring their teeth, jubilant at being off leash.

Me, too, he thinks. Downshifting to go uphill, he gets the headrush of being entirely on his own. He has lived the life of an Eagle Scout, watching out for Ricky, bringing home the As, playing jazz with a bunch of guys his parents' age. He'd volunteered at a senior citizens center. It doesn't make sense, the way he wants nothing but to be with Kyra, until she calls and he acts like an asshole. She has steadily offered to come to Philly, and each time, he has pissed her off enough to blow it. *I'm surprised, too*, he wants to tell her. I don't know I'm going to do it until I do.

Last week in lab, he'd been rewarded with the role of programming the arm they'd started during spring semester. It was something like brain surgery, tickling the circuitry by way of keystrokes, and he would have predicted that he'd be blissed-out. Instead, he ended up being dragged from the lab by Dr. Marzoni, still screaming at the stupid, useless limb, which he'd once seen as miraculous.

He could use a little more air in his tires to get that hovercraft feel, though the added muscle required to move along the pavement seems a reasonable character-building exercise. For a mile or two, he concentrates on the vectors of self-propulsion: as his right foot pushes through 180 degrees, his left pulls through the same arc, thereby doubling the force exerted on the pedals that drive the gear that bites into successive links of the chain to move the back tire. Mesmerized, he has a moment of relief from his internal combustion.

In fact, it is a gas to think he can bike all day or not. Some of the guys are getting together later to knock out a problem set, which is due tomorrow. Isolating the movement of his thigh (up and down) relative to his shin (semicircle) or foot (circle) is actually good practice for the physics they'll be working on. He could meet them or blow them off. He could show up late, hang, and hook up with some stuff and a girl, maybe two girls in one night. Kyra told him about a concert rave weekend she'd been to *in high school* where she'd messed around with three different guys, one of whom was in the band. He'd been saving himself for that?

A taxi sounds its horn right at his side, and startled, he very nearly steers into the asshole, who tosses off a friendly wave. Will gives him the finger. If he isn't careful, he could piss off a driver or slip on some gravel and go under the double tires of a Mack truck, end up bloated and dead by the side of the parkway like a maggoty deer. Or he could upshift and haul ass until he grabs the taxi's rear bumper for a thrill tow. Dangerous as he knows that is, it is very nearly irresistible. He could turn around, take a shower, and have a healthy lunch, listen to his voice mail, or throw his fucking phone at a wall. He can do anything he damn well pleases.

8

THE GREETING TABLE

Toni has to get herself to Back to School Night if she wants to honor a commitment she made last July. Before Owen's accident, working the Greeting Table seemed the least she could do; meanwhile, just leaving the house tonight will be a challenge. Her once-snug skirt practically falls to her hips—would it be hideous to appreciate losing ten pounds? But when she consults the mirror, what she sees instead of slim hips is her deflated face. Slight dewlaps have formed alongside her firm jaw, and her eyelids refuse to open completely, possibly saddened by the skunky stripe down her center part. There's barely been time to brush her teeth, let alone sit in a chair while Raoul paints her hair and wraps it in foil.

She leads Owen through an abbreviated bout of physical therapy and then situates him on his inflated doughnut, naked from the waist down, so that he's straddling the side of the bathtub, left foot under the spigot, right foot on the bathroom floor. She's looking forward to going out, even if it's to Fitzgerald High, and she's also grateful that Brooke is in public school, that being one bill they don't have to pay.

Owen taps her on the shoulder. "Is it a little hot? I don't have a heckuva lot of feeling down there."

Toni reaches under the faucet—it's scalding—and flings her hands up, spraying hot water across Owen's T-shirt. Like a film clip running in fast-forward and reverse, she swims through the air to twist both taps closed and flip the drain open, then windmills behind her to yank at a towel, whose bottom edge flicks the scissors off the counter. The skinny shears skitter across the tile floor as Toni sinks down alongside the tub. "God, I'm so sorry."

Owen points to the heat rising from the tub's smooth white belly. "I saw the smoke."

Steam, she wishes he'd said, but this is not the time to correct him. "You must have *some* feeling down there—or you did."

He pokes lightly at his shin, lobster red rather than the pink it was before the tub. "You know, it does sting! Pins and needles."

A breakthrough, then, and good thing, or she may have boiled him alive.

"Nerves grow back an inch a month," he says matter-of-factly, "though not always in the same places—I may have to scratch here when it itches there. You see it all the time: nerve endings get displaced by trauma."

From her spot on the floor, Toni is staring through her tears at Owen's rebuilt heel. "Displaced by trauma" seems an apt description of everything that's happened to them. The hinged flap of skin from the arch of his foot has nearly healed over the hollow crater of scorched flesh where the lightning left his body. For weeks, this sight turned her stomach. She supposes she is tougher now, but he is also healing, thank god. "Okay, start over?" she asks, but Owen blocks her with his good arm.

"Burn me once, shame on you; burn me twice, shame on me."

Toni snorts appreciatively—has anybody made a joke in the last three weeks? She pushes the towel and gauze closer to him, and his burn glove is right there, too. "Twenty minutes should be enough, honey." She sets the timer, allowing for the ten minutes of airing he gets after he's done rinsing foot, shin, hip, and hand. He really needs to bandage only his foot, but he doesn't like his shin and hip uncovered at night.

Downstairs, in the office alcove off the kitchen, she makes the checklist that will allow her to step away from the body—medications, doctors' phone numbers, cell phone—until fear cramps her hand. *One inch a month*—nerves growing at the rate her gray roots push through—and she may have just stunted his first month's growth. She snuffles up the weepiness that has begun its persistent drip. If he's capable of washing his own wounds, surely he's capable of spending an evening alone with Brooke.

Next to her list is an outdated *Post*, the front page covered with news of the Republican convention. You wouldn't think a presidential election could pass you by on the Washington, DC, border; however, Toni knows only what she's pieced together from headlines, close-captioned TV in waiting rooms, and radio snatches on the way to Owen's appointments. She can see by the picture that the vice-presidential hopeful might have once won beauty contests, but could the woman also have a Down's infant, a pregnant unmarried teenager, *and* be running for national office? While Toni's family drama has kept her from following the election, that woman may be running to escape her family drama.

And does the woman really shoot wolves, from helicopters, in Alaska? That has to have been from a dream or some parody. Maybe a few of those are rumors; in the photo, it's just the former pageant queen holding hands with the former POW. Toni tosses them into the kitchen's recycling bin, where they'll be in good company. As she sticks Owen's emergency numbers to the refrigerator and starts unloading dinner ingredients, she wonders who's making dinner for that woman's pregnant daughter tonight. In all likelihood, campaigning releases her from that level of detail.

In the middle of slicing leftover grilled tenderloin, Toni feels Mittsy mash herself against the backs of her legs. "Of course I'll feed you," she says affectionately, and stops what she's doing to fill Mittsy's bowls. Toni doesn't resent the cat for being a cat. Would she be more responsive to Owen if he wanted to be Owen? As Toni pops the can's top, Mittsy whirls trancelike at her feet, waiting for her to release the seafood-variety puck from its aspic-lined can. Mittsy lunges for the bowl, savagely biting at the dinner disk, and then halfway in, she freezes, her tail as straight and as fat as a bristle brush. She flees at the sound of Owen's thump-slide step coming into the kitchen.

"Mittsy," he calls, but she's gone.

Owen's wearing only his burn glove and loose black shorts, though he has certainly dressed his wounds; in fact, he appears to have wrapped himself in one continuous bandage from his left hip to his right foot. A white racing stripe comes out the right leg of his shorts and travels down his thigh to his shin, turbaned in gauze; from there, the bandage circles his ankle, crosses to his instep, and smothers his foot. A streamer trails from the bottom of his heel.

"Look at you," Toni says, borrowing the line her mother used on ugly babies.

"Got it covered," he replies, and that's putting it mildly. "The scissors disappeared, so I just finished the roll."

"Mmm," she sort of acknowledges. She's biting her lip, unexpectedly moved by his attempt to care for himself, and she makes a mental note to lay in a case of gauze on her way home.

Brooke clomps into the kitchen, too, laying Owen's inflatable doughnut like a wreath on his usual seat. In pajama pants, shearling boots, and a skintight camisole, she may be dressed for bed or a movie. "Is a salad afoot?" she asks.

"Of course not!" Owen says. "Why would you ask?"

Toni gestures toward the spinner on the counter, but she also leans to the left so he can see the tenderloin: there will be meat.

"Yes it is," Brooke says.

"Are you kidding? A salad is not a foot." Although Owen is plainly agitated, Brooke bickers the point with him a few times.

"Daddy, you're like Amelia Bedelia these days. Is a salad *afoot?*"

Toni wonders if Brooke remembers hating Amelia Bedelia and her antics. Toni blithely read and reread her daughter the stories about the literal maid who gives the bride a shower and dresses the chicken, until Will noticed that his little sister was upset. How could Toni have misinterpreted Brooke's flapping arms and moans as excitement? There was a lot going on that summer that Toni was missing.

"Dad." Brooke points to the refrigerator. "Is the door a jar? Is the dog a stray? Come on!"

"All right, already, cut me a little slack. I'm all assed up."

Brooke thinks that's hilarious, too. Not Toni, who's emotional about scalding him, about his gauzefest, about leaving him behind to go out into the world. His singed chest gleams above the table, tiny chest hairs sprouting in the center like a patch of sod.

"Would you please get your father a shirt?" Toni asks Brooke.

"I just got his doughnut," she protests.

"We don't want him to get cold."

"I'm not cold," Owen says. "I'm hot; it's hot in here. See, I'm sweating." He lifts his arm to reveal clumped wet hair beneath.

"Ew, Dad! All right, I'm going." She trudges as if her slipper boots were concrete blocks.

Toni remembers when her light-footed gymnast would bourrée across the kitchen floor in a tutu. Every memory being suddenly too dear, she focuses on tonight. Maybe he and Brooke will get out the Monopoly board the way they used to. Owen's the one who discovered that Brooke doesn't mind losing, as long as the rules are elastic; watching their games has given Toni glimpses of what he must be like as a therapist. Will he be able to play, and will he let her change the rules when the dice don't roll her way? Tears collect in the well Toni's glasses make against her cheek, and she pivots toward the counter self-protectively. She thought she'd tricked herself into dwelling on Monopoly, but every Owen question is the same, whether it's about tonight or six months from now—will he come back to them or not?

She sets a plate in front of Owen, who narrows his eyes at his salad.

Meanwhile, Brooke has already returned, and she's waving a shirt bearing the slogan *I psychoanalyze your honor student.* "How's this?" To her mother, she says, "Wait until you meet Ms. Mayhue—she's deranged."

Toni hands Brooke her plate. "*You're* Ms. Mayhue? Really, the hump on your back is hardly noticeable."

"Mom!"

"Don't worry," Toni says. "Is Madison's mother coming, do you know? Or Daisy's?" Maybe she'll have a drink with a few moms afterward.

"Which Madison?"

"Your Madison. I think her mom's last name is Waverly."

"There's Madison Windom—she has two moms. You probably mean Madison Calvert, but she's not really my Madison this year. And Daisy's only in French with me. I never see her." Brooke stabs once, twice at her lettuce and forks up a big chunk of steak, putting herself out of commission for follow-up questions.

How much has Toni missed in the wake of Owen's accident? She vaguely remembers Brooke complaining that most of the gymnasts wimped out of AP classes, but she hadn't heard that there is more than one Madison or that Brooke has shuffled friends. She says, "I'll check in around nine; some of us may grab a bite."

Mouth full, Brooke protests, "You can't do that!" Then, as something of an afterthought, "What if Daddy needs something?"

"I won't." Owen waves his gloved hand. "Go. Bite."

Toni points to the emergency list, which grows unreadable behind her ready tears. "There's all Dad's information. Love you both." And she gets herself out of the kitchen, through the living room, and out the front door, which she locks behind her. Her sinuses are racked from all her waterworks, yet at the sight of the van crookedly parked in the driveway, she unexpectedly swallows the lump in her throat. This anticipation is different from dread, different from the frustration she's been facing. What is this feeling called? She can't quite remember. Oh, yeah, *freedom*.

She clicks her key-chain button, still a relic from the future. Here is the activator for the getaway car. The tiny appliance has both a spy and a toy element built in, like her amazing phone, which is the size of a recommended dinner portion yet still manages to receive calls from down the street or across the ocean! She's not impressed by all gizmos—the TV remote, for instance, is no big deal—she isn't a simpleton. Nevertheless, when the van's lights flash, she is tickled anew by her "keyless entry." *Click*: she unlocks the van from ten feet away. If she wants to, she could *click*: open the sliding side door, or *click*: set off a blaring alarm. The spy side (honestly, she thinks this every single time she takes it out of her purse) is *click*: and she could blow it sky-high. *Click: kaboom!*

Of course, the van is more rolling rec room than sleek getaway car. When she unfolds the sun visor, a plastic bag blooms, dropping like an oxygen mask from the overhead compartment. Despite running late, Toni bags some car litter, the same way she's been e-mailing and texting the last few weeks in the two-minute intervals mothers are famous for. In fact, she's been singled out as resourceful for as long as she can remember, which makes her wonder how much we are the same at fifty as we are at five.

Come to think of it, that was the crux of Owen's summer reading. Is a brain scan a blueprint or an ever-developing photograph? She acted as if he were tearing through mystery novels rather than journals, because she has wanted to know the answer to that question for twenty-one years. "*Well?*" she kept asking, but none of the studies were about in utero results. Toni straightens the front wheels to reverse the van straight and fast down the driveway. When she was pregnant with the twins, their ultrasound technician saw lesions on Ricky's brain, while Will's brain was deemed "typical." Lesions on his brain—that can only mean deprivation and reduced aptitude, right? The radiologist had no idea; worse, he was excited about the discrepancy: "We just started seeing brain development at nineteen weeks! For all we know, this might be normal."

For all we know. Having seen that scan, Toni could never unsee it. Watching Ricky struggle to pick up a block, she'd visualize his pocked brain, puddled with lesions. Was Will rocketing past him developmentally? Would Ricky ever be able to grip, to bring thumb and forefinger together in such a way as to pluck a Cheerio off the tray of his high chair? Would he be dependent on her unto death? Her concern seems especially ridiculous in light of his heroics at the beach, but she's had his whole life to worry. She changes gear and peels off toward the high school, where the boys were equally successful, as if that hadn't been enough to convince her he was fine. And yet, what of those holes?

Which brings her to Owen's brain. What must it look like, every kink electrified for that brief, shining moment, a few bulbs no doubt burned out in the process? At Fitzgerald, in her book group, and on the neighborhood listserve, people have testified to Owen's steady wisdom and his listening ability, which is clearly impressive when you are paying him to listen. At the first traffic light she retrieves a Spoon CD from the van's side pocket and feeds it to the slot the way she spooned applesauce into her babies' mouths. Or into Owen's mouth, until he built up his strength. Thank god that didn't last long. Ditto for his blurting out obscenities or the unguarded truth.

Listening to her own music is a self-centered treat, as is hearing tunes from this century. Unlike the rest of her crew, she prefers what's current. She believes in moving forward. Music is tied to the headlines, to the calendar; even new covers usually sound better to her than the originals. Fresher. When a band she likes issues its greatest hits, she looks for a new band, and then she listens for the genetic material they've picked up from past generations. In the end, how many combinations can there possibly be? Eight notes in a scale as the building blocks for verse, chorus, verse, chorus. And for subject matter, the choices are love, loss, loss of love—it seems inevitable that a new person writes an old song every afternoon.

She's amusing herself. Apparently, she can't help it. A second earlier she was thinking that we might be delivered completely formed, temperament and tastewise, and now she is championing the flexibility of change and being open to newness. She supposes she wants to keep the definition of herself current, *just like Owen*. That thought and the sight of the school, literally in the spotlight, bring her to a halt.

Since she last visited, the façade has been treated to a flattering dose of outdoor lighting, no doubt a gift by some landscape-architect parent. Fitzgerald High School is the pride of Bethesda–Chevy Chase—woe be to those who leave out any part of that neighborhood name. There is a complicated pecking order among bordering regions: Kensington and Rockville have less cachet; Takoma Park is always described as "funky"; Potomac is pretentious; Silver Spring the poor cousin. Bethesda–Chevy Chase is just right. And it is, except for that attitude.

"Can you say *hypocrite*?" Brooke teases her. In some moods, Toni resists, defending her belief that kids need to clean bathrooms and rake leaves. Otherwise, she concedes. During Owen's hospital stay, for example, she used every lesson Bethesda–Chevy Chase ever taught her, from the scone and bagel offerings to nurse speak ("He says he's uncomfortable—what do *you* recommend?"). She should probably tuck thank-you notes beneath the wipers of the Jags and Tahoes, luminous cars from which radiant parents are stepping out.

Banners in the atrium advertise the school clubs, from Nerd-vana Tutoring and Home the Helpless to Gluten Free to Be You and Me. Ricky edited *Great Scott!*, the school's literary journal, with Mr. Holt, and he was in Infinite Jesters, a math club. Toni realizes that she hasn't heard any clarinet this fall and wonders if Brooke is still in orchestra—is that a club or a class? Will spent all his time with Bike Me, where he was exposed to the most expensive equipment, although he also learned bike repair and how to conserve energy by drafting behind another rider, which Toni adopted as her parenting style.

Tonight she feels more under these parents' wheels. Ricky and Will barreled through two at a time, providing her with a large peer group, but she hasn't cultivated many like-minded parents among Brooke's friends. It can be a tough crowd—fiercely successful in a high-achieving town. She dreads the way people ask, "How *is* Owen?" as if they're fishing for news rather than showing concern. There's added value in his being a shrink, because, like a spy, he keeps his confidences. Struck by lightning in a Rehoboth parking lot—really? Dr. Owen Lerner can't tell the twins apart—is that so?

Despite her misgivings, Toni is warmly received at the Greeting Table, where her station is the S–Z line. She thinks the Thompsons choose the M–R line over hers, but they're followed by Yvonne and Michael, whom she thanks again for the polenta casserole and brownies Yvonne made them. Betsy Bailey, who brought over chicken and dumplings one night, hugs Toni with her toned arms. "You're amazing," Betsy says, and that's nice. Betsy's nice.

Mostly, the night belongs to strangers, and she is cheered by every impersonal interaction. There must be a dozen twins, and two sets of triplets, in her section of the alphabet. Are people the world over reproducing in litters, or is it their zip code? "Just the one?" she asks the parent of a singleton. Eleanor, Saxy's mother, darts over to say hello and volunteers to drive Brooke to the weekend tournament, which Toni happily accepts. Basically, no one needs to know Toni's story, which turns the task she's been dreading into a respite. Peeling the last name tag from a slick page is a fulfilling show of progress. Cross off name, provide tag, say kind words, and wave good-bye. For this, she is considered a huge help.

Toward the end of Toni's shift, Charlotte Barnard and Pete Phillips come through the double doors without their spouses; they are laughing, and if Toni's not mistaken, making eyes at each other. After Owen's ordeal, Charlotte and her husband, Ken, sent a basket of flowers cut from fruit and stuck on skewers—the bizarre *edible arrangement*—but Peter and Marisol have not called once. She doesn't hold that against Marisol; it's Pete who's been AWOL. He and Owen coached the boys' soccer team together for years. At the M–R station, Pete deliberately fills out his name tag, affixing it as solemnly as if he were pledging allegiance. He's able-bodied and fully dressed, something Owen hasn't been in a while, and his stalling infuriates Toni. She imagines reaching into her purse to extract her magical key chain. *Click*: and what? She fantasizes sending a sonic boom into his phone earpiece or dropping him to his knees to beg for her forgiveness.

"Jesus, Toni, how *are* you?" Pete asks. "Is Owen up and around?"

"You should come see for yourself."

"Absolutely. We've been so worried, but you never know what hours someone is keeping. Marisol's in charge of the calendar, or I'd make a date right this minute."

Toni hears her own tongue cluck at his bold laziness.

Pete says, "Tell that husband of yours to pick up the phone and give me a call. Tell him not to be a stranger."

You are such a pussy, Toni nearly says, channeling that husband of hers. She considers enumerating Owen's surgeries, starting with the one that makes it hard for him to hold the phone. Instead, she promises to remember Pete to him, between his physical therapy and his neurotraumatist appointment.

Charlotte says, "We *miss* you guys. You were stuck in Rehoboth so long."

She makes it sound as if they sat in beach traffic, as opposed to a hospital room. "We've been home a couple weeks; well, you know, because you sent that nice fruit."

"Cute, right?" Charlotte says, and she explains to Pete: "They make these daisies from pineapple slices with melon balls in the center—"

"You eat them?" he asks.

No. Toni contains herself. *They shrivel on their skewers, swarming with fruit flies.*

"If there's anything we can do," Charlotte offers. "Anything."

Take my place. Clean my bathroom. She says, "I could use a glass of water."

Pete laughs. "Are you serious? Because I could find you some water."

She's not even sure she wants water, but it's satisfying to make him serve her. Charlotte takes off after him. Does Toni wish someone would take her place at home? A more considered response would be that she wishes Owen would take his place at home. Light-headed, she stacks papers, then name tags, then handouts. Maybe she should flee for home, she thinks, an instinct she forces herself to suppress. Flee, yes; home, *no.* And with this, she's stumbled on another reason not to go out: a person might very well decide to stay out. In the nearly empty hallway, a lone pair of high heels clack on the linoleum—the comforting sound of her mother in the grocery store aisles.

"Hello! I have caught you." A petite woman with a Latin accent click-clacks to her table. "You are Brooke's mother."

"Yes?" Toni says, then affirms her loyalty. "Yes. I am Brooke's mother."

"That is revealed in your concentration." The woman trails a hand across her own brow. "Brooke has your diligence about her."

Toni hasn't seen piping on a jacket in decades. Ditto for flipped-up black hair, which looks both classic and dated. The woman has a European Jackie Kennedy vibe, though she's curvier and less brittle; her name tag reads *Estrellita*.

"We finally meet, then." She kisses Toni on each cheek, an actual kiss of two lips pressing Toni's skin and Toni blushes with the sincerity of her affection. "I did not feel it was my place to call you until we met together first. For you it was the same, am I right?"

Toni has no context for this lovely woman, whom she wants by her side for the rest of the evening. Pete returns with her water. "Estrellita," he says. "A pleasure to see you. Will you give the ambassador my regards?"

"Certainly, Peter." Estrellita speaks with mock deference.

"Thanks, Pete." Toni snatches the cup from his hand. *We're busy here, pal.*

"How we enjoy your Brooke." Estrellita rolls Brooke's name to great effect. "Charming, agreeable child. Natalio kept promising to me, 'Wait until you meet her,' and he was right. After only one evening we had fallen for her. It is just as he said. Since then, I have come to tell her things my very daughters don't know! Can you believe it?"

"It's unbelievable," Toni says. Even as she laps up Estrellita's praise, she wonders if it's safe to drink. "I wish I knew Natalio."

Estrellita elegantly rests her manicured hands, rings of carnelian and filigreed gold, on the drab institutional table. "He is a good boy, I believe. A diplomat's family lives like nomads, but to leave São Paulo at seventeen for a new school . . . We ruined his life, he reminds us every day. Now he does well enough here, though I worry for his academics. He is not nearly as focused as Brooke is, that is one thing."

Toni tries to keep her water from sloshing over the sides. "You think Brooke's focused?"

"The way she spots herself, swinging around and around the bars. When she lets loose, I cover my eyes until I hear her feet hit the mat." Estrellita brings her bejeweled hand over her dark, heavily made-up eyes, and then peeks through to say, "Brooke and Natalio laugh at me."

Toni smiles. "Natalio's on the team," she deduces.

"It is a pity they don't share classes, though maybe your Brooke wants some time with her other friends, hmm? He has strong feelings for the women in his life, I know, I know."

What Toni doesn't know could fill an Olympic-size arena, perhaps the very one where Brooke and Natalio practice their routines. Regret burns her eyes, and she takes a drink of water to clear her throat. Could Natalio be her daughter's first serious boyfriend? Is he as elegant and polite as his mother? Is he as good a kisser? She wants to ask if Estrellita has a picture of her son, but it's too embarrassing to admit that she's never seen Natalio, never heard his name mentioned.

The school bell urges them to get going. Estrellita lays her hand atop Toni's, her rings cool against Toni's dry skin. "So I will go to meet all his teachers. That is what this evening is about. But I want to know the extent of your husband's healing. We will share meals and our stories soon. How could I presume to know Brooke when I did not yet know you?"

Toni wants to clutch Estrellita's arm. *Please take me by the hand and walk me through this pointless maze*, but Estrellita leaves for Natalio's class like the devoted mother she obviously is. Toni has no choice but to attend Brooke's first period, a poignant phrase when she's thinking about her baby girl. Being at school is standing in the way of talking with her only daughter about dating and sex, protection and love. Except that she is here for Brooke, here to learn something about what her daughter has been doing since school started.

First on the list is history, and duty alone carries her to the humanities wing. History, can't escape it. Geometry, sure. English literature and writing, of course. Tell me something I don't know. *Where is the gymnastics crowd?* Toni wonders. She moves at the sound of the bell, drafting behind the parents who stick their heads out, eager to question the teachers about rubrics and performance indices.

Estrellita's words burn in her brain as Mr. Holt yips about modernism, though he's kind enough to ask her afterward how Ricky's doing. "Tell him to come see me. Anytime he's home," he says, which sounds like a proposition, but maybe that's because she's anxious about Brooke's hidden life. She wants to set the clocks back so she can listen to her daughter tell her about the semester in real time. This new boy from Brazil, Natalio was his name-o, shiny black hair that looks wet in or out of the gym, invites her to his house for paella, puts his hand inside her blouse . . .

No, no, no. Toni shakes off her thoughts, realizing that as much as she is needed at home, home is also part of the problem. Owen's injuries may have levitated him, but they have nailed her feet to the ground. She's been stationary for so long she's forgotten how the world relentlessly rotates past. Getting out more would remind her of what husbands, daughters, grown married women do in the course of normal human events. Then she can return home, bringing a little of the world back with her.

When she gets to French class, Toni sees Mandy Berry, and she shoves empty desks aside to get to her irreverent friend. Maybe they're both victims of the youngest-child syndrome; during the twins' era, they would have known every parent in the room, and people would be guffawing at Mandy's take on parenthood and public education, Fitzgerald-style.

"Toni! Oh, Toni, I've been the crappiest friend on earth." Mandy steadies the travel mug on her desk and slips out of the chair to offer a hug. Toni holds in her surprise; maybe it's the magnification of her reading glasses, but Mandy looks downright aged.

"Sit right here. I was beginning to think I was invisible. Or odiferous."

Toni laughs. "Flash cards?"

"Shower curtain," Mandy says. "Have you seen it? Five hundred words to learn before mildew sets in. I'm ready for those tests if Daisy isn't."

Other parents give Mandy and Toni a wide berth. "How is Owen coming along? My god, you are way too thin. You must hate it when people say they've been worrying about you, but honest, I have. I should have stopped by with muffins—or tequila, for god's sake. I'm such a rat."

Mandy's candor wipes the slate clean. Toni says, "Thank you. You don't have any tequila on you now, do you?" Her friend's hardy laugh is a tonic. Whether or not they've sought each other out, the bond of prenatal classes, playdates, and nanny disasters holds fast. "How are Reg and Isaac? How's Daisy?"

"Reg is Reg," Mandy says, and they both smile. Toni hopes there will come a day when Owen is Owen.

"Daisy's good—this is the only class she has with Brooke. You don't think they had a falling-out, do you?"

"Not that I know of," Toni says. "And Isaac?"

"Isaac." Mandy says his name as a complete sentence. She lifts her travel mug to her mouth and, in so doing, transforms herself from thin to frail, folding into herself like an injured bird. "Up and down, I guess. He's always bushed, and it's impossible to get enough food in him. He starts round two next week."

Toni fixates on the word *bushed*, which is from her mother's era, to avoid interpreting Mandy's posture or all the other words she's spoken. Toni doesn't want to understand, but in fact, "round two" can only mean chemo.

Mandy says, "We hear lots of success stories, even though his strain is so rare. I don't have to tell you about odds; I mean, the odds of getting hit by lightning are meaningless if your husband gets hit. Am I right?"

"Jesus, where is it?"

Mandy pulls out a stack of tissues like a wad of bills, and she peels one off for each of them. "You haven't talked to a soul, have you? It's bone—they think they've saved his leg."

"I should have talked to you," Toni says. The two of them are alone in the center of the room, quarantined by misfortune. "When Isaac didn't coach swim team, I just figured he was done with all that, after a year at Oberlin."

"Oh, he didn't finish freshman year." Mandy hoists her travel mug to her lips. "Everything fell apart before finals, and we got the diagnosis within a few weeks. I'd give my right arm to see him swim again."

The eggnog smell of bourbon drifts toward Toni, who regrets asking for tequila. *We are each of us consumed by our own drama*, she thinks, with a penchant toward self-forgiveness. In June and July, there was work, Brooke, and the twins home from school. Although she'd missed Isaac at swim team, she hadn't gotten around to calling or thought to ask the boys. And then there was life since August. But the self-absorption of illness angers her, too. With Owen sitting around healing, requiring all her attention, she hasn't known that Mandy needed her, hasn't heard a word of Isaac's ordeal. "I hope you get good news soon."

"Me, too," Mandy says. "I'd kill myself, but who'd clean it up?"

"Don't say that. Why haven't we talked or something—aren't there a million ways to leave messages now? It's unbelievable." She hears the echo in her own voice. She'd said the same when Estrellita told her about Natalio and Brooke. "I am so, so sorry," she whispers to her friend. No matter what unfair hand has been dealt a spouse, god forbid the stricken child!

"*Bonsoir, chers parents*," a woman at the front greets them. Toni doesn't need to hear her voice to know she's the French teacher: swingy pleated skirt, tiny pearl-buttoned sweater, and knotted gauze scarf. This in September, though Mademoiselle probably doesn't sweat. Fluidly she writes her name on the board, then lifts the chalk to pepper it with a soupçon of accents. She turns to the parents and speaks in a low, purring voice, briefly touching on cell phones, the *plus-que-parfait*, and the children's *journal*, which she pronounces as if it were a perfume. Despite her Frenchified dignity, she radiates melancholy as well. Is she holding on to some private trauma, or has Toni's bitterness jaundiced her vision? If she and Mandy are suffering, are all of them? And if not, why not?

As soon as the bell rings, parents get in line to imprint themselves on Mademoiselle, who will have none of it, pivoting toward the door on her kitten heels. Toni admires the buttery leather satchel slung over the teacher's shoulder—her accessories have made more of an impression than her talk. Good thing Brooke comes to school and does her work.

She is fairly sure Brooke comes to school and does her work.

"I'll call you tomorrow," she tells Mandy, "unless you'd rather have a visitor."

"Come over around ten. Bring something."

She smiles. "I will. I'll surprise you."

Returning to the math-sci wing for physics, Toni tries to remember Brooke's beef against Ms. Mayhue. Maybe it's just that she's new and teaches physics. Toni takes a seat at a soapstone lab table, its familiar oiled sheen preserving every fingerprint. From the next table, Lazlo Hoerner gives her a friendly wave. She knows Lazlo from swim team, but not the older, pale man with him, who is tagged *Hans*. They don't look related, so she assumes they're together. Lazlo was with a different partner when his older daughter swam with the twins.

Unlike the twins, Brooke has never loved science, though she's good at it. When Toni sees the heavily plaided teacher, she suspects her daughter's aversion could be wardrobe-related. Ms. Mayhue introduces herself: MIT, Stanford, called to teach, inner-city Detroit, Fitzgerald High, and *your children*. She acts as if her feet have yet to touch the ground.

"We figure things out together in this class," she says. "The world isn't such a mystery. The physical world inspires questions that can be answered, and we puzzle through these as a team." She's staring at Toni, who disagrees so strongly she actually feels queasy. This woman and her delusions are making Toni sick.

Raising her tartan sleeve, Mayhue points to a flap of brown paper taped across the chalkboard. "Each Monday we have a question for the week, often a question one of *your children* has thought up. Applying physics to things that matter gives our Mondays a little thrill."

Ms. Mayhue whisks the brown paper from the chalkboard as carelessly as Toni has been ripping bandages off Owen. "Tonight's question is: How small can a full-length mirror be?" She turns to the parents, who must know that their children are not taken in by her. "In order to get a complete reflection, does the size depend on where you stand? Does it depend on the height of the viewer?"

It's not Mayhue's fault that when Toni hears "full-length mirror," she pictures the beautiful monstrosity she had inherited from her parents. The heavy oval mirror had seesawed in its oak stand in the master bedroom of whatever house they lived in. Way back in the twentieth century, before she thought to question everything, Toni had started her day marveling at her nude and pregnant self in that very glass, and then she'd left the twins quietly playing at its base while she wrapped herself in a robe and went to the basement for a load of laundry. Unsupervised for five crummy minutes, the toddlers managed to tilt the mirror flat and climb aboard on either end, and their makeshift teeter-totter apparently went up and down a few times before snapping in half. The explosion of glass sounded like a bomb going off, and Toni and her belly stumbled up the two flights of stairs to her boys, who howled in agony. It was a horrific scene of mirrored shards and blood: slices cut their forearms and their pudgy legs, which she had to pick clean of glass.

You want to talk about things that matter? Toni nearly sobs with all the tears she's swallowed today. How did those glass swords manage to miss a vein or an eye? Why do twenty-one-year-olds get cancer—why does anyone? Is her only baby girl sleeping with an older, foreign boy? Or how about this one, which is actually physics, Ms. Mayhue: What causes a cloud of electricity to ruin a family's life? Can anyone figure that out?

Agile as the field hockey players she coaches, Mayhue draws stick figures a foot apart, a tall rectangle surrounding one of them. Next, she dots a sight line between the eyes of both figures and then starts marking angles. As Toni sees it, here are the twins again, one on either side of the mirror and not quite identical, real and reflected. It's no wonder Brooke dreads physics, where they are doomed to figure everything out together. What the flux, indeed?

There's no calculation to explain instantaneous disaster: in the space between the real and the reflected, your children may be sliced to ribbons, your husband burned to a crisp. In the interval between the thunder and the lightning, your reflection could well disappear. Toni gropes for the tissue Mandy was kind enough to give her, but she's not fast enough for the first heavy tear, which finds a gap beneath her glasses and hits the black soapstone lab table with such force that a splash rises up around the droplet like a crown. A tremor shivers through her and then subsides. It happens again before Toni realizes that her phone is vibrating in her skirt pocket. She fumbles with the material and extracts the humming box; of course, it's home calling. "Hold on," she whispers into the receiver as she slips into the hallway. And then, "Yes?"

"Mommy. Are you all right?"

Toni looks around in little jerks, as if Brooke has been watching via a webcam or some other teen technology. "I'm still at school, sweetheart. What's up?"

"We're okay," Owen yells out in a jaunty tone that scares the hell out of her. "The bleeding's stopped."

"It's Daddy," Brooke says, her voice thinning to a squeak. "He didn't want me to call."

Now Toni is shaking so hard that the phone jiggles against her cheek. It doesn't take much to imagine the worst, and she clamps her molars together, trying to tamp them down so she can speak. "Brooke, what's going on?"

"He was on the roof! He's bleeding, Mommy, and he won't go to the hospital."

9

TWINS IN MYTHOLOGY

Last semester, before he saved his father's life, Richard was the one making appointments to see Professor Clifton.

"Come in, Ricky," Professor Clifton says. "Take a seat." She steps out from her desk to close the door, revealing a short black dress and an anklet that jingles like change in a tip jar—as if the circles slinking up and down her forearm aren't distracting enough. Those bracelets very nearly cost him his midterm last spring.

He says, "It's Richard now," but her phone rings just as he announces his new identity. Dashing back to her chair, she holds up one finger, and silver coils trill down her arm like a ringtone. He wonders who belled her, or if she did it to herself.

He used to spend hours speculating on Professor Clifton's behavior. Back in the spring, he would have read any number of messages into her decision to take this phone call. He'd exploited every legitimate reason to seek her out—paper topic, paper draft, paper comments—and he would sweat through his briefs just sitting across from her. He fantasized that someday they would move their discussions to her office couch.

Professor L. Clifton and her Exile in Dante and Ovid seminar had dominated his contact with Will back when they texted and talked about every little thing. Ricky would relay the week's Odysseus dis, because neither Dante nor Ovid considered cunning Odysseus much of a hero, the way they'd been drilled in Mr. Holt's class. He'd liked having Will's voice in his head as he moved through his day. That seems so juvenile now, like girl twins wearing identical outfits down to their hair ribbons and ruffled socks.

"Thanks for your help," the professor tells her caller. "My chair gave me your number because I had my doubts. He heard your presentation." Holding the phone to her ear, with her flexed arm and Hellenic hair, she resembles the archer Artemis.

He figures he should go invisible while she chats, and he concentrates on how her hair starts in small parallel waves close to her scalp before achieving liftoff. She reaches for her notepad, exposing a dark spot of sweat—a blacker semicircle on her black dress—which may mean she's nervous or the office is hot, but definitely means he's looking at her armpit. Where should he look? During lectures, he stares at her slender face and imagines her without her chunky glasses, but this doesn't seem the time to fixate on the asymmetry of her mouth or her weathered skin. She's in decent shape for her age, which he guesses to be mid-thirties.

He didn't bring a book, and he's not about to thumb through one of hers. When she leans on her forearm to write, her bracelets stand up in a line from elbow to wrist—she's a living Venn diagram: hoop earrings, ankle chain, low-slung belt, and those mesmerizing bracelets.

Richard distracts himself with his phone and sees that his mother has called. He should have returned one of her calls. Maybe that would get him out of his own head.

Last semester he found it unlikely that the Greeks actually believed their own mythology, but cosmic explanations are looking more plausible all the time. Especially since his dad walked out on the roof and fell on his chin; it's as if the man is marked for disaster. If his dad can't or won't recover, will Richard go back to being Ricky? He focuses on the framed photograph on Dr. Clifton's desk, the one with the thin, smirking man wrapping his arm around a woman's naked shoulder. While the guy's got full tux coverage, the woman's dress shows just about everything, from her jutting hip bones to her shoulder tattoo. Richard recognizes the woman as Dr. Clifton, but not quite. For one thing, she's younger; for another, the woman in the picture has a Monroe, though Abigail told him that the hole closes up pretty fast if you take out the stud.

He feels her watching him as she says to her caller, "I'm free later, actually."

When he finally got to school this fall, her class still had an opening—that seemed like fate right there—and while he's just as spellbound as before, he hasn't shown up for office hours once. Maybe his paper sucked, but maybe it was so good she wants him for a research assistant—he'd happily turn the pages as she reads. Maybe she and the smirky man need their lawn cut. For this meeting, he left his baseball cap in his room and put on an actual shirt, one that buttons. He's been doing stuff like that lately. He managed to ditch his annoying roommate, which he could have done with more finesse, and he even tried the town's Sri Lankan and Ethiopian restaurants.

"Right, right, right," she's saying. She touches her index finger to her upper lip, and he flinches to think of someone piercing her skin there. "Yes, that student is in my office."

Now he's "that student." He hasn't needed her constant coaching this semester the way he did last spring. Has that somehow offended her?

He's put some distance between himself and Will, too, though he imagines Will welcomes that. One of the problems with being a twin is the shadow factor. Ricky had to watch himself go through adolescence, webbed in braces and cratered with oozing pimples. For most of high school, Will was a train wreck Ricky couldn't stop staring at—Man, you're/I'm a goon! The paradox is that he also couldn't stop asking Will for reassurance about his own goonhood, even after they mercifully left that phase behind. Although Ricky wanted to be on his own, family dynamics being what they were, he also flattered himself by imagining that he kept Will in orbit with his pull on him. More Castor and Pollux than Artemis and Apollo, he's learned this semester.

Professor Clifton taught him that. He imagines pressing against her like the guy in the picture, both of them in shiny black, and then he imagines being between them, facing her with the guy at his back.

"Twenty minutes will work. Thank you so much." She finally hangs up. For a brief second she lightly rocks in her chair, eyes staring at her desk drawer, as if it held a bomb. He nearly laughs when all she retrieves from the dreaded drawer is a tan folder covered with circles, interlocking coffee rings that resemble the Olympics logo, another Venn diagram.

She says, "Before I talk, is there anything you want to tell me, Ricky?"

"Richard."

She opens the folder to reveal his paper inside. "Come on, now," she says. *Talk, or the paper gets it.*

"I guess I should tell you I'm a twin."

Dr. Clifton lets out a low grunt, as if he had said he was male. "Right. You and the rest of the class." She pauses, and her framed eyes have that oracle look. "Everyone in the seminar is a twin."

He knew Michelle and Tom were each twins—among kids his age, there is little novelty in that—but an entire class of them is something different. He wonders if the seminar is even more specialized than that. If, in fact, everyone is half an identical pair. Weirder still, maybe they are each the younger identical. Maybe that's who enrolls in Twins in Mythology and Literature; maybe that's why there'd been space in the class. The older twins make history and the younger ones are left blinking in a classroom, always watching and playing catch-up. It doesn't make sense, and yet there it is. Will is the firstborn, an only child for fifteen minutes. He and Ricky are not quite equals, and it isn't Will who has something to prove.

She lifts his paper by a corner, using her fingers like tweezers. "Is there anything you want to tell me about this?"

He would smile at her if she were smiling. She is obviously trying to lead him somewhere, and he'd confess to the long hours he spent or the massive research if that had been the case. "I gave it my best shot."

Now she lays the paper flat and pages through. There are red exclamation marks here and there, unlike the scrawl that usually filled his margins. "That's just it. Your best shot is alarmingly good."

"Thank you."

"Nothing like your writing last semester."

"Thank you?"

"Ricky," she says, closing the folder. *"Richard."*

Hearing her speak his full name, he has to cross his legs and put his hands in his lap. He'd barely ended up with a B in the spring, when his distractions ranged from the brain freeze that was differential calculus to his roommate, from the temptation of easy kegs to Professor Clifton and her musical jewelry. Life this fall seems preordained by comparison.

Each morning his feet hit the dorm carpeting with the sure knowledge that he brought his father back to life. What is linear algebra next to that? An abundance of confidence is his new familiar, and he can't believe he previously struggled with the reading lists of a few manageable classes coupled with home-work sets and a language lab. He resents how much time and energy his doubts sapped from him, though he is able even to compartmentalize the resentment. Now it strikes him as funny rather than pitiful to think of the motivational message his mother wove through the top bunk's bedsprings. Each night he'd stared at the Henry Ford quote, a little boost to help him rise from bottom to top bunk: "Whether you believe you can do a thing or not, you're right." *Believe it, baby*, he would say to Professor Clifton, if only she'd smile.

Meanwhile, since he wrote the paper she's waving around, life has taken a bizarre turn. His father thrown by a lightning bolt to the ground put him to the test, and he'd imagined sussing out myths on this topic. His father falling from the roof, though, and his not being there doesn't pack the same punch.

The professor takes a deep breath and speaks in the tone of an official. "The department has new software to check student work; I'm trying to give you a chance here." She begins doing her gesture of amazement, where she touches her finger to her upper lip. "What I'm trying to say is that this paper is too good."

This paper is too good. Like three equations in three variables, he plugs in her body language, her actual language, and her reference to "that student."

"You think I bought it somewhere," he says, having solved the matrix. "You didn't think I had this kind of reasoning in me."

Secretly, he's proud that she recognizes the great leap. He doesn't know how to tell her that he was a little afraid he'd plagiarized, too. The words came so easily, he wondered if he'd read something about Jacob and Esau and held on to the ideas, even the language.

"You required a bit of guidance last semester, and even then . . ."

"I'm not sure I required it," Richard says. "I *requested* guidance. Are you a twin, Professor?"

Startled, she jingles in alarm.

"Identical, too?" he asks. She ducks her head, and he knows the woman in the photograph is her twin, almost her, but not quite. When he'd googled her, there were mentions of a Professor L. Clifton teaching similar courses at Swarthmore. He'd just assumed that was an earlier appointment, but now he deduces the situation. "Your twin's an academic."

She places her hands far apart on her desk, and the pressure in the room gushes out. He feels he's opened her like a jar, even though she's the one who'd let on that the entire class is one of a pair. Maybe he has something of his father's knack for seeing through to a person's past; until now, he hasn't been able to see past himself.

"Lucy and Lacy," the professor says.

"You're not one and the same."

"No, Richard," she says testily. "Despite the fact that we look exactly alike, teach in small private colleges, and have come up with astonishingly similar courses."

He can't tell from her defensiveness whether she developed her course first or not. He points to the photograph on her desk. "Is that her?"

She laughs through her nose. "Yes, though he's mine. I mean, that's a picture of Daniel at our wedding."

Richard says, "But not a picture of you." Very possibly, no one else has noticed.

"Fair enough. She looks so much more relaxed than I do in all our wedding pictures."

"And yet everyone says you're identical." Who is she fooling, showing a stunt double in her own wedding snapshot? Surely *she* doesn't ever forget it's not her.

"You're only twenty, but you'll get to a point—or maybe you won't—where you finally say, 'Screw it! Can we at least share notes?'"

"I'm twenty-one," he says, hearing how that actually makes him sound younger rather than older. "Is that what you thought I'd done here? Is that why you're so upset?"

"I don't think so. I honestly thought you'd bought it. You had such difficulty asserting yourself last semester—there were all sorts of caveats and parentheticals in your papers. The first few pages were a justification for the topic you'd chosen. This paper never faltered, never apologized."

"Maybe I met someone," he says as a joke and a reckless show of bravado, especially for someone being accused of plagiarism. Loosey Lacy, lacy Lucy—at this point he's catapulted himself so far past Will, anything could happen. "Which one are you, Lucy or Lacy?"

She pivots the wedding picture away from him. Perhaps she's having a hard time seeing beyond herself as well. Richard can't tell if those are dark circles under her eyes or the shadow cast by her glasses.

"I'm Lucy," she says. Now she turns the wedding picture face-down, and he can hear her shake her foot under her desk, like a tambourine. "Basically, you're giving me your word that this is wholly your work."

"I suppose some of it's yours, if we're giving out credit. First of all, everything you taught us last spring finally seeped into my little pinhead. I knew I was apologizing all over the place, I knew the beginning of every paper was—what you called it, 'throat clearing'—but back then I was second in the race. Can you understand that?"

"Understand it? Honey, I wrote my thesis on it."

So she's Lucy, the younger. She's also from a generation when twins were less common—how might the literature change now that so many arrive two by two? What does it mean that mythology is populated with twins—Artemis and Apollo, Castor and

Pollux, Hunahpu and Xbalanque? He imagines her sister's scholarship revolves around the hero rather than the sidekick.

Richard says, "I wonder if everyone in the class is a second-born. As early as Genesis, you've got Jacob, favored by his mother but second in line. And he leapfrogs Esau to get both the birthright *and* his father's blessing. Meanwhile, he's not the 'ruddy hunter,' he's the gentle one, the one who 'dwelled in tents.' And meanwhile squared, Esau doesn't even want the birthright, because he knows that Abraham's descendants will be enslaved. The last shall be first restores order; that's the lesson, after what seems like deceit and duplicity."

"So you wrote," Professor Clifton says. She's practically panting. "And meanwhile cubed, are you going to tell me about your move to the forefront?"

"Well, that's fodder for a different discussion, I'm afraid," he says, not knowing if he is kidding or flirting. He's heard other students traffic in innuendo, but as second-born, that has not been his style. He would hate to announce *I saved my father's life* and have it sound like *I'm twenty-one and a half.*

Professor Clifton moves her glasses up the bridge of her nose, a Sisyphean task. "Then I look forward to a different discussion. What's your major—have you declared?"

"Mythology and applied math."

"Oh, math." She makes the sign of a cross with her two index fingers, and he can't help loving math a little less. "Well, the reason I ask is that on Sunday nights—not every Sunday, but this one coming up—we have a dinner at my house, and people bring whatever they can. It's informal, and we all pick each other's brains. Daniel does logic at UNC."

Daniel's sounding better all the time, and Richard wonders when his confidence will take him down that road. He squelches the urge to ask her, if her husband is a logician, why the hex on math? Instead, he relaxes back into the guest chair. *This is Will's default state. This is what it means to move through the world without constantly asking permission.* He wants an actual invitation from the very lips that called him here for an accusation. He wants to pick her brain.

She says, "I make the main course, and someone brings wine or a salad. We always think we're going to share abstracts—that's the plan before we start in on the wine. One time it was just vodka and brownies, until Daniel ordered pizzas. Are you interested?"

"Ye-es," he says, encouraging her to humbly request his presence.

"Well, all right, then," Professor Lucy Clifton says. "You know where I live, or should I draw you a map?"

10

REMEMBER ME?

Remember myth prof?
        I barely member u! Sup?
Accused me of buying essay & axed me to dinner
        Sweet
How's life @ home?
        BethChCh or Penn?
BCC
        ?
U havnt been? Wtf?
        U go!
Ur closer
        Not anymore
Ha ha
        And?
Roomie might be bi. Know anyone who's bi?
        As in polar?
No
        Then no
Me neither

I'M NOT A THERAPIST

On any given night, Owen is awakened by Toni's phone glowing or by her tiptapping away on it, leading him to believe that her office beckons. And yet, when he eventually opens his eyes in the morning light, she's there by his side. She stares at him as if he were a backed-up sink, flaking plaster, a leaking air conditioner—and they have people for those.

"You should get me someone," he suggests.

Toni's neck draws in toward her shoulders, hunching unbecomingly. "*Get* you someone?"

"Like a helper, a nurse. I'm a chore."

"No, you're not," she says. And then, softening, "Well, yes. Yes, you are."

So it goes. She's as contrary as a magnet: some days, she clings to his side, full of love and gratitude; others, she's repulsed by him. He manages to stretch his arm to the nightstand for the pill bottle. Breath and stretch are hell on his reinjured ribs, and pushing against the childproof cap hurts his reinjured collarbone so intensely he might have to take two painkillers, although once he gets the damn cap off, he shakes out a single Percocet to swallow with his own spit.

Toni hands him his water glass, an act that would have been considerate thirty seconds earlier. She says, "There's going to have to be some travel soon. So many colleges, every one of them with a president."

"Or without one. Which is where you come in."

"Where I need to come in. You wouldn't believe my e-mails, the chains are a mile long." Like a singer warming up, she sings, "Re: re: re:; re: re: re:; re: re: re:."

She's eyeing his chin, shorn and x'd with stitches, and annoyance prunes up her face.

Owen fingers the sharp threads that stick out like boar bristles. "This was a mistake."

"Climbing out the window or falling?"

What a relief it would be to have the stitches removed without her hovering. "I'll drive to the doctor on my own today, give you a break."

Toni rattles the bottle of painkillers maraca-style.

"I just took the one," he says, and holds up an index finger in his own defense. As if she'd called music into being with her shakey-shake of the pills, a clatter of salsa fills the room.

Toni lovingly strokes her phone, which quiets at her touch. "Selena," she says. Then the phone sings out in disco—"*Lookin' for some hot stuff baby this evenin'*"—and Toni soothes it back to silence again. "That's Levi—one always follows the other. They're a little unnerved because it's high season."

"Hunting season," Owen says.

"Headhunting season," she adds. "Aren't we the pair? You're the headshrinker and I'm the headhunter—"

He wishes she wouldn't call them that. He tries not to picture her wearing a necklace of wizened leathery heads, her own cheekbones striped with ash and a bone piercing her nostrils, but of course, trying not to picture something burns it into your brain. The lurid image Owen conjures up of his wife makes him catch his breath too quickly for his ragged ribs, and he yelps with pain. His skin goes clammy, as a shiver runs through him.

Toni's lips pucker like a stitched mouth on a shrunken head. She says, "I'm not a pharmacologist, but you might want to start cutting back on the meds again."

"I *am* a pharmacologist," Owen asserts. His fist closes with the muscle memory of unlatching his metal drug-sample cabinet. And then he hears himself say, "*Barbecue* could be from the French, where an animal was skewered *barbe à queue*, 'whiskers to tail.'"

"Give it a rest, Owen. I'm not a therapist either, but all this barbecue talk might be a diversion."

"Yeah, well, I *am* a therapist." He succumbed to an extra decade of school to expand heads, not shrink them. Meanwhile, he has little control over what comes into his own head these days. It's the same with his kids, whose unchecked imaginations make everyone nervous. "We should both go to work," he announces.

Toni asks him if he can go to the bathroom.

"Piece of cake," he says, and manages to sit up, stand, walk, piss, and return to his bedside. "May I have a piece of cake?" he asks his wife.

"Oh, brother," she says, and then more kindly, "I'll see what I can do." On her way out of the bedroom she thoughtfully lays his silver-lined glove and sock on the bed, the only dressings he needs anymore. The graft site along his hip as well as the second-degree burns on his chest and shin have all attained a high gloss, a polished pink. Tender and itchy as hell, they no longer require endless reapplications of gauze and unguents. Although his hand has healed pretty well, his foot still has that Chinese concubine look because they flipped the skin of his arch backward to cover his heel.

He is aware of saying all sorts of extraneous shit; he thinks it, too. And yet the glove and sock are noteworthy. *Healing is on hand*, Owen thinks. Healing is *afoot*, which returns him to the night a salad was afoot and he couldn't make sense of that phrase, the night Toni went to school and he went out the window. He and Brooke had stayed at the table for some time; she was particularly exercised about physics and a French quiz that had eaten her lunch. He'd reassured her that it wouldn't mean anything in a month, maybe in a week, and he'd shared the possible French origin of barbecue. She said that *chagrined* her. When the White Trash BBQ blog didn't lighten her mood, he took another tack. "Why do we hate Ms. Mayhue so much?"

"Mayhue's such a control freak, a total *oligarch*. From the start of school she makes me tutor this guy, and then as soon as we get to know each other, she wants me to stay away from him. I'm like, make up your mind already!"

Toni had told him about a Brazilian kid—whom Brooke has never mentioned. "Who's the guy?"

"He's new. We're on gym team, so I guess that's why Mayhue picked me to help. But she's just a teacher—she can't dictate who I should be with. That's up to him and me!"

"Now it's him and me?" he asked.

Brooke chipped away at her thumbnail. When she lifted her head, she had that rehearsed affect. "You know what I want to know? If it's too voodoo, you don't have to go there—but what happened when you got zapped?"

She'd purposely diverted him, he can see that now. She asked where he'd gone in those gravity-defying seconds, and he couldn't *not* go there. Perhaps inspired by her drama, he'd spread his hands wide in wonder, like a ringmaster in top hat and tails. *Children of all ages, prepare yourselves to be delighted and edified!* Here was his chance to communicate how, energized and uplifted, he'd treasured her birthmark as an exquisite flaw—more distinction than defect—and how he'd recognized her eagerness to please as potentially dangerous, albeit the source of her charm. Like previous visionaries, he'd risen high enough to witness the curvature of the earth, and . . . an eye on the horizon . . . the deal is . . . um, you know . . . what will be will be . . .

He couldn't eke out a sentence. His inarticulate, transcendent thoughts swelled and warped. They clumped together into a soggy and saturated pulp, like the pages of a book in bathwater.

If truth and beauty are so indescribable, if we are incomprehensible one to another, how could Brooke partake of his profound joy? Had Toni been home, he was convinced, she could have coaxed him toward sensibility. He could have ably explained how lightning, simultaneously hitting the trillions of synapses available in every cubic millimeter of the brain, had allowed him to *get it*. The very continuum of time, space, and purpose was illuminated—and unified—within the strobed spotlight. Frantic to share, he had scooted his tailbone off his doughnut, leading Brooke out the back door onto the patio, whose flagstones soothed the smarting arch of his left foot even beneath his wad of gauze.

A gibbous moon amid rounded clouds gave the September

night a bulging, portentous beauty. For real insight, they needed to be moon height. "Come with me." He beckoned to his one and only daughter. "Let's go to my bedroom." She followed him upstairs. In the master bedroom they sat on the bed for a minute, but it wasn't quite right. He took her by the hand, and they slid off together. Then he patted the window seat, and she climbed onto the cushion. Sitting crisscross applesauce, she looked out the second-story bay. Owen unlatched the large casement window and swung both halves wide open. "We need to be higher."

The dust he disturbed set Brooke to sneezing like a dog— *wuhf wuhf*. When she finished, she pointed at the bay and said, "The window is ajar."

"*Defenestration*," he responded, proud to have come up with one of her vocabulary words.

"That's being thrown out a window. Or throwing."

"Then not that," Owen self-corrected. "I guess I mean ascension, liberation." He had those words rather than the ones he needed to describe his plan, which was for them to go out on a limb. The oak had been planted too close to the house in preparation for this night. When he lifted his foot onto the window frame, the gauze running down his leg went slack, a definite safety issue; nonetheless, he stepped out, keeping one hand on the window trim until, sensing the nearly horizontal branch underfoot, he carefully transferred his weight to his legs. One foot was bandaged, and the other didn't *feel* right: patches of numbness tingled alongside hypersensitive stretches. "Here we go," he urged his daughter. "Let me show you."

"No, Daddy." Brooke was tugging on his thin shirt from her window-seat perch. "What are you doing? Mommy would want us to stay inside."

Wasn't it obvious that she had been trained for the purpose of this revelation? "Get out here!" he said, more harshly than he'd intended. She'd spent innumerable hours inching along a narrow wooden plank to be able to walk along their family tree. "Think of all those camps I paid for," he reminded her. "All those lessons." Owen took a breath, and in that pause he sensed her deciding against him. "Come on, already!" he commanded.

"I don't want to!" Brooke protested, holding fast to his shirt.

Owen stretched away from his mutinous daughter so she'd be pulled toward the open window. He'd never been a tyrant, which was all the more reason he expected her to follow his orders. But then his next step dislodged a cluster of brittle oak leaves, and the barbed tips raked the tender new skin along his calf. Pain seared his leg, which jerked into the air, and he would have lost his balance but for Brooke pulling his T-shirt taut. Unfortunately, when he did plant both his feet, the oak's buckled bark pricked the ball of his right foot as his bandaged left heel slipped against a smooth patch of limb.

There was nothing ecstatic in his two-story descent, only mortification that he'd bullied his baby girl, who nevertheless held fast to her father's shirt, slowing him in its stretchy sling until his weight ripped through the cocoon. Gauze streamed alongside Owen in a white flag of surrender as he headed toward the packed earth, and he landed on his chin, that vulnerable edge where the skin readily splits.

"Owen, Owen, Owen," Toni chanted in the emergency room. "That's two of your children who have saved your life."

Yeah, well, maybe Toni shouldn't have gone out that night— what could Brooke's teachers have been telling her that was more important than the three of them joining hearts and minds? He strokes his chin, and it occurs to him that he can remove his own damn stitches if he wants to.

Owen pads to the master bathroom on his tender feet. He snakes his neck to get a clear view of his chin's underside while preserving binocular vision, which takes some doing. The days of his pediatric residency were practically sutured together, and he remembers assuring terrified patients that this part didn't hurt. Ham-handedly he clips the crossed stitches and tweezes them from his puckered skin—in fact, it doesn't hurt, though the stretching and twisting required to capture them wrings him out. He leaves the eyelash-length threads on the bathroom counter as he pads back to bed, but to his surprise, he doesn't need a rest. Taking action has empowered him—cutting his own strings means one less specialist he has to face. *Healing is indeed afoot*, he thinks as he gingerly slides his silver sock over his mangled arch, whereupon he takes it up a notch. Putting on a sock can't be any harder than putting on his pants, one leg at a time, as they say.

•

In the kitchen, Toni wonders whether Owen really wants cake. Or if he'll even remember his request. Sometimes he gets fixated— the instant-read thermometer, for instance—while just as often, she'll fulfill his desire for green tea or gingersnaps and be met with his sincere surprise. Either way, his literalness is more creepy than endearing: back in the bedroom, he'd looked at her as if she were an actual headhunter. Going for cake approximation, she toasts a bagel and slathers both halves in cream cheese topped with blueberry jam.

The last time she left home, he climbed out a second-story window in front of their sixteen-year-old. There's the "disinhibitive behavior" every single one of his doctors warned her about— not to mention the fact that he may have dropped his inhibitions along with his pants months before his nerves were damaged. She tries not to credit the possibility of him and Kyra too much, lest she stir all his medication into one bubbling potion and pour it down his throat.

Toni is as impatient with herself as she is with him; she simply cannot believe how naïve she was about the extent of his recovery. These days, he's advanced to something of a flickering state, like a faulty connection, and she's never sure whether the light will come on behind his eyes or how long he'll stay lit. And honestly, he may burst into crazy at any moment. Is he really ready to be dispensing advice and drugs?

Everyone falls, Owen had said to her in the ambulance. And she fell once. Or she almost fell; she eagerly contemplated falling. She might have fallen that summer, except that the chance to fall fell away. There isn't even a verb tense to describe what happened, while Owen was at conferences around the world and the kids were all on swim team, and she fell for their coach like a horse off the high dive.

Seven years ago—no, *eight!*—and it still comes back with goose bumps. Owen calls it the Summer of Ritalin. When Dr. Owen

Lerner wasn't the keynote speaker in Little Rock or Lausanne, he was testifying before Congress. There were successes but also suicides he was called to answer for. Toni had the kids and his mother, which is to say strep and sprains, bedsores and bloated bowels, rides all over creation, including adult day care. And on top of that she was Owen's office manager. She mostly saw her husband on TV or in a magazine article, with his message of pharmacological empathy, and he was certainly deserving of the medical community's attention. But she deserved some attention, too.

The children's swim coach gave her that. He saw her, asked her how she was. In the middle of every hectic day, practice was a splashing good time. His daughter, Chloe, was on the team; she was between Brooke and the boys, and she swam an impressive butterfly. The look of pride and encouragement on his face when he cheered the kids on—Toni fell for that. She painted her toenails red, and he noticed. His palm on her waist, he ushered her to a spot poolside. "Watch the way Ricky comes up for air—that's a coach's dream." He ran that same palm over her biceps and said, "You should let me sculpt those arms," as if he were an artist who wanted to shape her from clay rather than assign her twenty reps of freestyle followed by ten of breaststroke and ten more with a buoy between her legs. All of which she did, growing stronger and more obligated. She bought a new swimsuit, one with a high-cut thigh.

He was less attractive than Owen, though far more fit. There was no time, and yet the summer stretched out, each afternoon a welcome oasis. Chloe said that her mother, a fair-skinned Brit named Jamilla, didn't show at meets because of "pool allergies." Toni's skin was itchy and her hair brittle from the chlorine. Eight years ago, she still had brown hair, which he urged her to keep long. His balding head looked the same wet or dry. He made the kids practice lugging each other the length of the pool. He certified them all in CPR—teaching them to chant between breaths, "Barbecue spareribs, barbecue spareribs."

There were meets and lotion and pizza and, because he thought of it, salads for the two of them. Mandy, whose kids were on the team then, saw the way he opened one packet of dressing for their two bowls. "Soon you'll be finishing each other's sentences," she'd said, and he flashed his chipped-tooth grin: "Already happening." She swam, the kids swam, he coached, and the season ended. That's almost all there was to it. When Owen returned, having preserved their August beach weeks, he admired her suit and announced, "You're tan," as if she'd sprayed herself brown rather than been out every single afternoon, including weekends, with her surrogate family.

Her coffee's no longer steaming when Owen finally marches into the kitchen wearing therapist regalia. Each shirt button is matched to its corresponding buttonhole; his wide-toothed comb tracks are visible through his plowed-down hair. His pants are tight—along with his summer weight, he's added another ten pounds in brisket and ribs, and the khaki fabric must be an irritant. He drapes a black blazer over the kitchen chair next to her. The lapel pin he's chosen says *Show Some Emotion*, although he's not showing any. His demeanor is almost military, like a retired officer stuffed into his old uniform, masking the extent of his war wounds. Her heart goes out to him. He's been so entranced with his experience that she rarely thinks of him as brave.

And then she points to the underside of his chin and gasps. "Your stitches!"

"Clippety-clip—that's all Wayne would have done."

"Well, yes, but—"

"You didn't think I had that in me, did you?"

No, not really. So complicated, this gray area they inhabit. Although she'd been looking for some independence on his part, self-surgery seems a little *too* independent. She wishes she knew which scissors he used or how he managed them with his gloved hand—if he wore his glove. Rather than ask, she slides his stacked and bedecked bagel halves down the table.

"Breakfast cake," he says, a short-term memory display that gives her hope until he points to the center hole. "Candle goes right there."

There's more of his flickering: half on, half off. Ditto when he eats, quietly growling as his chin nearly touches the plate, followed by the most civilized napkin dabbing to get the last bit of jelly from his lips. If he is half the doctor families claim he is, then half an Owen might be enough to hold office hours.

"I guess I should get ready, too," she says reluctantly.

"Isn't that what you want," Owen asks, "for everyone to get to work? God knows, we could use the eggs."

That ancient punch line is a relic of either long-term memory or marriage, which can deteriorate to a call-and-response of a couple's collected material. Because Owen often notes that people aim punch lines as directly as punches, Toni suspects that he's teasing her about her impatience with him and her money anxiety. But then she thinks she's giving him more credit than his flickering brain deserves.

"I can't win," she says.

"It's not a competition, darling." In his shrink clothes, he sure sounds like a shrink.

"You think I'm either holding you back or pushing you out the door. Let me know when you're ready to go back to work, will you?"

"I am ready," Owen asserts, though stomping his foot makes him flinch.

"Wash your hands—well, your hand," she reminds him. All it would take to undo her five weeks of meticulous, sterile wound management would be dirty hands.

He uses the soap and brush she keeps by each sink to scrub his ungloved hand and pulls a paper towel from the roll to dry it. Then he waves his car keys like a hypnotist's watch. She hopes he remembers all that driving entails. After all, he dressed and fed himself, his fly is zipped, and when he pivots and walks away, he puts his whole left foot down. He's missed two belt loops, where he usually overlooks just the one. Really, his only suspicious action is taking his plate and coffee cup to the sink, rinsing and loading them into the dishwasher before picking up his keys again. Silently, she offers the equivalent of a blessing: ready or not, here we come.

12

A MIGHTY HUNGER

While Owen is conscientious enough to be concerned for his patients, he doesn't feel so conscientious sitting in his gunmetal-gray office chair. He isn't even comfortable. His clothes are stiff and exceptionally scratchy against his new skin. Collared shirts seem practically Victorian, dating to a time when doctors treating his kind of patients prescribed bland food and sensory deprivation.

And also institutions, it occurs to him as his first patient, Constantine, maps the minefields in a typical school day, where the enforced conformity makes even neurotypicals long for anarchy! Owen's fears that his job might be too challenging seem unfounded. He has his well-thumbed *Physicians' Desk Reference* and a closetful of free samples. Kid presents as attention deficit hyperactivity disorder, you trot out the ADHD regimen, starting with Ritalin, Strattera, or Concerta once you consider the kid's age, weight, and drug tolerance. For this he went to med school? For bipolar or obsessive-compulsive, there's a different flowchart. For an autistic kid like Constantine, there are a dozen choices, some more sledgehammer than tweezer. Owen feels the most useful and the most useless with his severely autistic kids. With the siblings Helen and Robert, for example, he concocted drug combinations that helped lift the veil of their limitations. That's not the case for Constantine, who is just far enough along on the autistic spectrum to stay in public school but not necessarily to thrive there.

"What other options do you have?" Owen asks the teenager, whose bald spot catches the afternoon sun.

"I didn't even know it until my mom saw my scalp showing through. Maybe if you'd given a shit when school started, I wouldn't be pulling my hair out."

Owen's suit of armor covers nearly all his injuries, and sadly, his lightning flowers are gone, though they'd be mostly covered, too. If Constantine hasn't noticed the burn glove, he certainly won't catch on to the surgical sock. Owen says, "I always give a shit. Even when I can't get here."

"Shit, shit, shit," the teenager perseverates. "You missed our appointments! If I'd done that, you'd be all over me."

"Yes, I would," Owen agrees. "I had some health issues, and I couldn't get here." He can't in good conscience burden his kids with the details of his accident; instead, he lifts his chin to expose his recent scar. Constantine apparently misinterprets his nose in the air as a display of arrogance because his response is to give his doctor the finger.

Owen tries to communicate his enhanced empathy. "You and me, we should go out for barbecue some time. There's nothing like eating one of those big, messy sandwiches with your hands— everyone's a slob! You like white bread, don't you? And ketchup?"

The boy's smile shows a gap from the tooth he lost in a summer brawl. According to his mother, he didn't start it, and he gave as good as he got.

"I was sorry to hear about your fight," Owen says, "but I'm impressed that you stood up for yourself. There's something to be said for self-defense."

Constantine tugs at his bangs. "You wouldn't have been impressed pre-lightning."

"Touché," Owen says, and quickly turns the talk to Constantine's meds.

•

Alone in his office, Owen smacks himself on the forehead: just because he doesn't want to add to his kids' anxieties doesn't mean they don't know about his brush with death! The tics and hypersensitivities he's developed are their peanut butter and jelly, making them his most likely sympathetic audience.

Actually, fuck sympathy! That's not why Constantine's reveal threw him. And it wasn't because Constantine flipped him off. Just as most neurotypicals do, he'd underestimated Constantine, who had pointed out the very essence of Owen's divided self: from now on there will always be a pre- and post-lightning. Owen's dedication to mainstreaming the majority of his kids— pre-lightning. Post-lightning, not so much. Say Constantine is unable to sit still for six hours in a hot classroom with twelve high-pitched kids; maybe he should work on a farm instead and learn the math of the seasons, of seeds per plot and yield per acre and ears of corn per bushel. How outside the norm is acceptable and even possible, if you want a child to be independent but also a contributing member of society?

None of his kids comes to medication as a first resort. Mothers in particular will turn over hundreds of rocks before they say yes to drugs, and fathers are often willing to play unending card games or take yet another walk, years of one-on-one loving therapy compared with his pharmacological approach. Constantine went through sticker charts, tae kwon do, occupational therapy, and biofeedback. Later that day, Owen sees Alex, who tried flash cards, behavioral training, swimming, and fish oil before it was time for drugs. When Randy's mother hears that Owen is seeing patients again, she requests three sessions that week: before meds, Randy ran afoul of soccer, fencing, karate, and trampoline as well as B12 injections and diets devoid of sugar, dairy, wheat, gluten, and soy. The lists are endless and mostly serve to illustrate the amazing resourcefulness and optimism of mothers. As Toni likes to say, all help helps.

Medicine helps, unless it makes things worse. Usually it does both. Often he prescribes a drug hoping to ride the coattails of its side effects. Since the pathologies he treats are largely developmental disorders, a few kids simply grow out of their afflictions. He has counted them as successes. At every session Owen also reinforces the need for a schedule, regular exercise, and a diet with more variety and less sugar. He's seen that help, too.

"The art of family life is to not take it personally." That was his mentor's mantra, and Owen embraced it as his own, sooth-ing parents who feel responsible for their child's afflictions or take their kid's behavior as an affront. In fact, the majority of the help he offers has always been as a listener. Like a parking-lot time-stamp machine, he validates his kids. Frantic and detached, many need to park themselves in front of someone who's heard it all.

"What did you say to Constantine last week?" Margaret Hemp-hill asks Owen the next Monday. "He insisted that we go to Rock-lands three, four times. He tried shredded pork, chicken—he even ate ribs *off the bone!*"

"That's some good protein." Owen is proud of Constantine, who has shaved his head so kids can't see where he's pulled his hair out.

Margaret Hemphill's jaw audibly pops when she speaks. "He practically drinks the sauce, the sweeter the better, so it's hard to know how much benefit he got from it. But I was happy he tried some new things."

"We should all praise him for that," Owen says, writing "the sweeter the better" on his pad and tracing it over and over. Chew-ing meat and gristle might count as self-stimming behavior for his kids, not to mention for himself. He could use something to chew right now to distract him from Margaret Hemphill. She'd never unnerved him pre-lightning, but it's all he can do not to point out how aggravating her clicking jaw is, as is the way her layered hair and round white glasses make her look like an owl. As soon as the door closes behind her, he shucks his shirt over his head and steps out of his sweaty pants.

Sitting in his boxers, he reaches for the *PDR*, which likens lightning survivors to victims of post-traumatic stress disorder. His symptoms are poetically described as "a constellation of changes in personality and conduct," from erratic behavior to being easily startled. "Strike survivors have trouble with long-standing relationships and, in their paranoia, may make unfavor-able decisions." The great book has Owen joining the ranks of those he's been treating for years. Okay, he's a little jumpy, and he runs a temperature as a matter of course. But he would say he's full to bursting these days, as if there were a pinball machine behind his eyes—*ping! ping! ka-POW!* Perhaps he could write a *Diagnostic and Statistical Manual of Mental Health Orders* to match that of *Disorders* he regularly consulted, because unlike a combat victim or a trauma patient, he has not been brutalized. There's an electrical storm in his head, and despite the bad dreams and the physical discomfort, he can't escape feeling privileged by his experience. Rather than survivor's guilt, he would like to claim survivor's benefits.

To fuel all this, his is a mighty hunger. Toni, initially delighted by his increased appetites at the table and in bed, has started sighing at his mentions of their evening escapades, and she's getting stingy with the groceries. Last night she made a fist to demonstrate the recommended portion size. Owen defended himself—to arrive at medium rare, for example, requires a specific gravity of steak. "The boys aren't here," she said, and then, "We don't need all that extra food around." She means him—he doesn't need all that food. But he does. He's bulking up.

Having made it through an afternoon of appointments, he gets himself home for dinner. How far beyond the mainstream, off the grid, does he want to live? He asks himself this while working dry salt and ground chiles into a buffalo tenderloin, all of which he's ordered from Internet sites. Shipped to his porch packed in dry ice, the cut of meat was butchered to match a dotted line he drew on a computer screen. DNA extraction marked this steer as one of an original prairie herd, which is one way of getting back to the garden. Although Owen equates paradise with his primal urges—eat, roast, screw—he seems to be returning to Eden via Eden.com.

Who knows? Treating his kids, he may well stumble on the emetic that allows us one and all to regurgitate that first taste from the Tree of Knowledge. The way he sees it, barbecue shares a lot with psychopharmacology. Once you have your slab of meat, you season it with a palmful of this, a pinch of that. Sometimes you need $1/4$ c. of salt; sometimes $1/4$ tsp. puts the recipe over the edge. Same phenomenon as his Asperger boys: one can eat a bowl of Paxil for breakfast while the next can't stomach a fish-oil tablet.

Likewise for Owen's earliest attempts with turkey, brisket, and pork loin. He rubs and brines, he smokes and glazes. His yearning for a bigger playing field for his patients, he realizes, might be a projection of his big hunger: forget the fistful of meat, he wants to wrestle the whole bloody shank into a fire pit he himself plans to dig and brick in. He's not sure if this will prove something or show that he has nothing to prove; satisfying primal urges may well be the next therapeutic breakthrough.

"You're back in the saddle, then?" Toni asks toward the end of his second week. "You are a professional."

"No new patients. Just all the regulars." He doesn't mention the chickens, which will be delivered Friday along with their coop. "How about you?" he asks his wife.

" '*The pin-striped men of morning are coming for to dance,*' " she says, apparently quoting some song. "These guys have forty-page résumés; meanwhile, I throw them questions about classroom shootings and swine flu, firewalls, toxic drinking, neuroenhancers, and they just whine. We didn't even cover date rape or assaults by scholarship athletes."

Owen closes his eyes for a moment. His fevered brain sees a pimply student gunning down a professor, whose body jumps and jerks, and then it shows him a party scene of thick-necked athletes overpowering a drugged coed.

Toni taps her wineglass. "You asked me what my week was like."

"That I did. It's just—date rape, binge drinking—why does anyone want to be a college president?"

He serves up his question with a glass of Sauternes, which Toni receives as if it were an endowed chair. She says, "It would be an honor. Crap aside, they've got the brains and the funding in-house to tackle any problem they care to. Breast cancer, autism, you name it." She takes a long sip, watching him over her wineglass. "I hope you're not zoning out on your patients."

"I'm not," he assures her. "Though I have been thinking that their problems dealing with the world may be the world's fault. Institutions are so harsh."

"Nature is just as harsh, if you're thinking of returning to nature."

He will neither confirm nor deny that; instead, he refills her glass and relays Brooke's message that she has a ride home from practice. "A toast to nature," he offers.

"To wine," she says. "To dinner—what's on the slab?"

"Buffalo."

"To buffalo, then," she says. He sees her close her lids over her rolling eyes.

After all, she's probably thinking, he's back at the office. And most days he does go, stopping by the hardware store in Cabin John on the way home. There are picks and shovels to acquire, cement and flagstone. He draws more attention each visit, as news spreads and the hardware guys get increasingly excited about his big-ticket plans; one of them talked him into buying a nifty little chicken coop his brother-in-law's brood had outgrown—to sweeten the deal, he's throwing in a few starter chickens.

Neither his wife nor his daughter mentions the tarp-covered hills rising near the patio, so it's not much of a surprise when they don't notice the chickens either. The frightened hens barely leave their coop that first weekend. The few times Owen hears them, he initially mistakes their worried trills for the pond's pump. He's glad the rooster's coming later, but even so, Mittsy knows what's what; she spends her waking hours flat against the back window, her unblinking eyes aimed at the hutch, which is barely visible from inside. All Brooke or Toni would have to do is follow Mittsy's laser gaze, although Brooke probably thinks the cat is fixated on escape. Since Owen split open his chin that night, she's been eager to be out of the house. He's determined to cook up the answer to her question: what happened when he got zapped? The answer combines too many sensations to describe. He experienced a synesthesia of sorts. Smell that? That's where I went.

Owen thinks both girls are away when he puts his shovel to the dirt late Monday morning. His blade bouncing off the packed earth vindicates his hardware buddies, who'd said he would need more than sketches and supplies. He regrets ceding the shaded, loamy area beneath the tulip poplar to the chickens, who are not only acclimated but also prepared to defend their territory, shrieking and warbling in intimidating display.

Owen wields the shovel like a spatula, lifting a pancake of
earth in each hard-won scoop. The sun reflecting off the marble
table pockmarks his vision with bright squares, and he grunts
with the effort of every scrape. He should have soaked the ground
through the night and started digging at dawn. Hell, he should
have hired the hardware cronies to bring their bumper car–size
backhoes. Worn out by their objections, the noisy hens return to
their shady coop on this last day of September, which is as hot as
August in Rehoboth. Owen almost thinks he's delirious when he
sees Brooke running toward him with a bottle of water.

"Happy New Year, Daddy!"

"Happy New Year." He plays along. Maybe silliness and a
water offering mean he's in her good graces again. "What year
might this be?"

"Five thousand something. We got Rosh Hashanah off, and I
just woke up! Saxy might have a New Year's party."

He'd already been thinking of today as a fresh start, and the
concept of different faiths following different timelines appeals
to him. He could start a Post-Lightning calendar.

"I slept until Mom called. She kind of freaked that it was so
late, but Coach says sometimes it's a good idea—sleep when tired,
eat when hungry."

"Wise man," Owen says, and he takes another slug of water.
There's a lightness about her he hasn't seen since summer, which
makes him reluctant to introduce her to the chickens. "Do people
have Rosh Hashanah parties?"

"Saxy wants to. She's not Jewish, but she likes the food."
Brooke bends forward at the waist, lowering her elbows impossibly to the ground, and then she opens her body like a jackknife
until she's standing straight again. Next, she arches her back until
she's touching the grass behind her; from there she lifts first one
leg followed by the other, bringing herself into a handstand before flipping onto her feet in front of him. Her dark, shining hair
bounces to her shoulders as she lands.

In the presence of this nymph Owen feels like a gnarled and
dusty troll. He claps a hand against the sloshing water bottle, and
after a long draught he pours water directly on his head, which
cracks her up.

"Your lightning flowers came back," she says. Then she changes her tune, obviously recognizing the Sharpie that Toni uses for labeling her school and gym possessions. "Hey, that's marker!"

"I drew them," he admits. "With my left hand while looking at the pictures."

"Ambi-talented," Brooke says, a little warily. "Want to see something from floor?" She tugs her hair back, somehow tying it into a knot, and then lengthens her neck, as if she reached into her slouchy teenage body and pulled out a gold medalist. Elbows bent and knees lifted, she gets up considerable speed across the grass and leaps high enough to complete an airborne somersault with a twist before landing.

Owen recalls his time in the hospital during the Olympics coverage. Brooke has literally flown through the air with the greatest of ease. "How do you do that?"

"It's unbelievably hard," she says candidly. "There's like three months of practice in that sequence."

Getting an autistic kid to master a progression like getting ready for bed can take that long. Brushing teeth, for example, is broken down to discrete, rewardable steps, slowed way down, and eventually linked. Owen doesn't see how one could possibly apply that method to leaving the earth. "How do you learn a somersault in the air?"

"You don't. You learn it underwater. And on the tramp. Basically, you're tricking your own brain. You have to practice until you don't think about it, because if you think, you can't do it. How strange is that?"

"You're telling me." There are days when he can barely chew and swallow if he thinks about it.

Brooke hoists herself up on the terraced wall, settling her rump on the baked stones with a surprisingly graceless thump. She says, "Erstwhile, you're becoming a *naturist*."

Owen sighs. He's caught between her slang and her vocabulary drills, like a runner squeezed between bases. She points at a mound of clothes on the ground, his clothes, and so he looks down his bare white chest to his belly, which practically obscures his gym shorts. He has gone back to nature, digging a pit in the dirt to cook his meat. But naturist doesn't mean natural; in fact, seeing how sparsely dressed he is reminds him that it means nudist. He started out fully clothed this morning. He remembers being dressed in the mound of clothes near his feet; at some point he peeled off his shirt and left his shoes in the dirt. It's as if every day the lightning blew off his clothes anew. He's even removed his surgical sock, which he's not supposed to do. "It's warm out," he defends himself. "When I'm done with this, we can have cookouts here."

"Sadder but wiser, Dad: we do that on the grill."

"Big cookouts. Like roasting a goat overnight on a spit."

"You're going to roast a goat? That's so documentary," she says.

And he's lost her. Owen recognizes the sidelong glance from their recent trip to the emergency room, as if she cannot bear to look directly at him. Unfortunately, the chickens choose that moment to make their debut, three hens haughtily announcing themselves as they strut onto the patio.

Brooke's scream sends the birds straight up into the air, squawking like car horns. When they fall back to earth, they hit the ground at a trot. Scraping and fluttering, they bounce off one another in a spastic display of chicken gymnastics, and they unite to fight the swinging door flap until it lets them back into the coop. "Chickens!" Brooke yells.

"Yes," Owen confirms. "They got dropped off the other day," he says, as if he had nothing to do with it.

"Is that even legal?" she hisses, and then, in little-girl mode, "I'm telling Mom!"

"You said she was at the office."

"She left at noon—that's what she called to tell us." Brooke runs for cover, and Owen almost expects her to backflip across the lawn to the house.

When Toni comes home, she doesn't know where to start. Stepping onto the patio, she sees that sure enough, there's a hutch under the tulip poplar that wasn't there the last time she looked. Beaks and wattles are peaking out from a rubber flap of a door. Owen is practically naked, he's gripping the rusty shovel handle with his injured palm, and his arm is covered with jagged black lines. At least he's wearing his glove. That's something; however, he's standing, barefoot, in dirt even though the dressings just came off his foot in the last few weeks. He's already dug down some, though you're supposed to call the utility company before an undertaking such as this. She can't remember if the worry is of hitting a gas line or *getting shocked*. His actions aren't exactly surprising, as he's been going on and on endlessly about the joys of barbecuing in a pit. Unless she wants to have sex or talk about barbecue, she can't keep his attention. He's even mentioned the possibility of their buying a house with a larger, more level back-yard, one that would better accompany a stone-lined pit.

And now he's plowed ahead with his plans, undaunted by his inexperience with manual labor, not to mention cooking. He is wearing her out and, quite frankly, weirding her out. Last night, when he positioned himself on top of her, unsteady but deter-mined, she'd been regrettably reminded of Frankenstein's mon-ster, animated by a jolt from the blue.

He's supposed to be taking it easy, a directive the old Owen could have readily followed. Of the two of them, she is always encouraging improvement. Owen has been the one more accept-ing of status quo: families feud, paint peels, dogs (even the saintly Sparkle) chew—such is life. He didn't object to dog train-ing; however, he didn't consider inherent dogginess a strike against the dog or its owners. Maybe, she thinks, they should get a new dog.

She achingly misses the husband of August, taking his last outdoor shower of the beach season and singing "You Are My Sunshine" in the stall under their kitchen window.

A step closer reveals that he's drawn on himself with marker, and sweat drips off his face from his scarred chin. Every doctor's wife knows better than to lecture her husband about his health, especially within his specialty. Toni tries to adjust her demeanor from You Are a Mental Patient to You Are My Husband as she takes him all in. He is shirtless, almost certainly sunscreenless, though his skin is supposed to be well covered, and the crooked lines he's drawn along his shoulder resemble the electrical tattoo he got from the lightning strike. His white belly hangs down unbecomingly, tilting the elastic waist of his shorts forward.

"Hello there," Owen says, as if pleasantly surprised. His eyes burn bright, with pinpoint pupils; these days, he always has that crazy wandering-prophet look.

"It's only been six weeks," she points out.

"That's why I waited." He levers the shovel under a clump of hostas and puts them aside. "Since our water table's too high for a pit, we'll have a half-and-half, like your raised beds."

He lifts a tarp to show her the bags of cement and the trough for mixing it, leaning against a pyramid of stones. How could she have missed the mounting supplies? Every night she's passed him some hunk of dinner to grill. And chickens! The audacity of this endeavor is enough to blind her. She's known this man for twenty-three years as a laid-back shrink and for six weeks as practically an invalid. Who would have thought he was constructing a Trojan horse in their own backyard?

Showing more concern than alarm, she takes the shovel from his hands. He isn't on enough medication anymore to be oblivious to pain. "Does your foot hurt?"

It hadn't until she mentioned it. Usually his foot doesn't feel anything these days, but suddenly it's as if he's stepped on a fire ants' nest, what with the stinging and the burning. He looks at his wife suspiciously, not ready to discount her ability to bring on pain by suggesting it. Or guilt, the way she had by asking him about Kyra. "This takes my mind off things," he says, knowing that standing in pebbly dirt with exposed wounds is not technically considered physical therapy.

Toni reaches out to him and holds his hand the way a palm reader might. In their nearly half a lifetime together, she's had to talk Owen into all sorts of things. Another child so soon after her miscarriage. Setting up a private practice. This house. But she's never had to talk sense into him, and she doesn't know how to do it without talking down to him. She traces the welt of a rising blister on his good hand. "I wish I could take your mind off things."

Then why does she keep reminding him? Every conversation he starts about flavored salts or even buffalo meat, she steers toward amnesia, anxiety, aphasia, or seizures. She managed to bring up the numbness in his limbs as he was trying to share the latest thinking on how long to rest the meat before slicing into it.

Maybe he hasn't explained himself well enough. Rather than nailing his heart to a stop, the lightning changed its rhythm, a sensation that endured after his usual beat was restored. Speaking in this rhythm, which has the vocabulary and concerns of a new language, he says, "I don't even know if you like barbecue sauce or dry rub."

"Do you know how strange this is?" Toni asks.

Again, her pointing her finger seems to make it so, although Owen doesn't want to agree, for fear he'll be forced to abandon his project and be sent to bed with toast and tea. He sympathizes with Toni's predicament, even more so when she wipes her wrist beneath her nose and mashes her trembling lips together. He backs up against the dirt pile he has been making, opening his arms wide for balance, which Toni takes as an invitation to press her puckered seersucker against his sticky chest.

"Yes and no," he says.

13

WHOLE HOG

Ultimately, a crew of six burly men with earthmoving equipment, a cement truck, and two generations of stonemasonry skills builds Owen's barbecue pit. When everything has sufficiently cured, Owen stages a massive cookout for all the workers and their kin—wives, kids, and hangers-on bring the total past fifty. Toni gives her husband credit: what he doesn't know about construction he makes up for in grilling.

In the weeks that follow, Toni and Owen go through all their friends, serving up Owen's elaborate efforts. Toni can stomach his devotion to food and fire when the end result is sharing an exceptional feast around a backyard fire pit. Everyone says they're relieved to see Owen thriving, and if he can adapt, surely she can, too.

For guests, Owen trades the spandex bike pants he's been wearing for khakis, and he keeps his shirt on. Showcasing his obvious skills as a chef and a hospitable host, Owen is at his most civilized. Meanwhile, their guests are at their least! People tear chunks of meat apart more viciously than wolves. They lap up the sauce, with or without bread, with or without utensils. They relish the most arcane barbecue details. Either the fatty feast or the beers soften their starch enough that Marisol, a petite securities lawyer, starts a round of bawdy jokes, and then Reg, Mandy's usually reserved husband, stands up to sing a mournful ballad. Mandy weeps, and Toni throws her arm around her and weeps as well, which eventually leads to a good laugh. Chickens cluck in the twilight before settling down for the night. An evening that starts with the specter of skepticism—just how *is* Owen, after the accident—develops into an unexpected blast.

The intersection of Owen's obsession and everyone else's dinner is an oasis for Toni, who undoubtedly feels October's chill more keenly than her guests. To extend the season, she totes out lap blankets and extra sweatshirts from the back of the basement closet. This can't go on forever, but she's hopeful that it doesn't have to.

Meanwhile, Owen gives himself over to the fire. With the dedication he once brought to meds, he studies wood, twigs to trunks. From the strong flavors of hickory and mesquite, he moves on to the subtleties of mulberry and the delicate sweetness of alder. Wild cherry is delivered to his Bethesda backyard, followed by a truckload of red oak (no bark, only what the aficionados call the heart core). Aromatic grapevines, with their curling tendrils of surprising strength and elasticity, and, of course, the gnarled wood of the apple tree. When cast out of the garden, did Adam wrench a limb from the apple tree and burn it for fuel? What a poignant, bittersweet flavor that must have imparted!

He goes down the same rabbit hole for meat. He's already made buddies out of the UPS and FedEx drivers who deliver his Internet finds, and he gets cell phone calls from the butcher at Giant, who likes to talk shop. Organic, grass-fed, and aged meat leads Owen to the Farm Women's Coop in Bethesda and the Takoma Park Farmers Market before he's off to the farms themselves. Soon he thinks nothing of driving to Culpepper or Emmitsburg to visit Hedgeapple, Shagbark Mountain, or Fox Hollow Farm for a lamb. The new deep freezer in the garage is packed with white bundles wrapped and labeled like presents.

After meeting the right cow, he buys half of her.

He likens his single-mindedness to a ballplayer enduring endless batting sessions, hoping to preserve the feel of a homer. Come to think of it, he doesn't have to look beyond his own circle of friends for working habits that present as crazy. Steve has been traveling to Hong Kong all year for depositions and a trial, having just come off a trial in West Virginia. What is the point of that work, which Steve despairingly describes as taking place in generic office buildings and among chain restaurants that render Hong Kong and West Virginia indistinguishable? What is the point of the two-volume Herbert Hoover biography Betsy published, when it didn't even bring her tenure? Of course, another person might ask, what is the point of barbecue?

In the same way that a well-done sound track can evoke the flavor of its movie, the smell in Owen's barbecue pit occasionally matches the one in his head, when he felt a rapture he cannot help chasing. If a drug could replicate his electrified state, he would prescribe it for himself. He's heard about addicts leafing through reference books of medications looking for one word among the side effects: *euphoria.* They break those medications down into snortable doses.

"My god, you should open a restaurant," Lazlo compliments him, and his partner, Hans, says in his thick Swedish accent, "I could eat this every day of my life."

Folks clean their plates, pick their teeth, ask for doggie bags. Owen waves away their praise. Except for Yvonne, whose husband is their pediatrician and whose daughter is Brooke's age—when lovely, perceptive Yvonne takes a bite, she says, "Heaven smells like this." Owen kisses her tenderly on the cheek. He suspects his gratitude is a little too loving when he sees Toni share a sideways look with Yvonne's husband, Michael.

"Thank you for that," Owen says to Yvonne.

Long before shrinks studied the link between scent and memory, artists relied on it. Might these memories have preceded our time on earth or in this body? Innocence smells like a fresh-cut orange. And here's love, locked in the buttery aroma of pastry. The creosote odor of loss, the leaden trail of sadness and depression. Perhaps the fumes, like contrails, will send up a path he can follow across the sky to the horizon, where he once glimpsed everything at once. Why do shrinks say patients "suffer from" heightened sensitivity when sensitivity can transport you to such heights? He doesn't want to be recalibrated if it means being taken down a notch.

Owen and Toni decide to ask Natalio and his parents over for one of their feasts, although Brooke protests that the invitation is a breach of her privacy. Jorge is as charming as Estrellita, who arrives in a long-sleeved coral-colored dress and a white-fringed wrap. Jorge wears an off-white wool jacket that looks as soft and creamy as rising dough. Toni would love to touch it, but she doesn't dare. She worries that she left out some detail of "greasy backyard barbecue"; they may have thought she was exaggerating, or else they couldn't conceive of charred and crusty slabs as dinner-party fare. Natalio isn't much taller than Brooke, Toni notes, but he certainly has dark and handsome to his credit, though his unibrow could use some tweezing.

His light eyes are hypnotic: deep set in his olive-hued face beneath black hair in corkscrew curls, they shine with the knowing gaze of an oracle. All the mothers stare and stare; even Estrellita looks at her son in something like a swoon. Brooke does not. When Natalio puts his arm around her, she pulls her shoulders back slightly and expands her chest, as if she wants to break out from his embrace. He whispers harshly to her, and she bites her lower lip.

Dinner is another extravaganza of delicious excess, an entire pig Owen has been roasting since dawn. "I've gone whole hog," he remarks.

"Local?" Michael asks. He and Yvonne have become frequent guests.

Toni says, "Raised near Front Royal on buckwheat and clover." She winks at her daughter. "Never sick a day in his life, lived in a Mission-style barn with fresh air circulation and his own masseuse." She of the no-fixed-address childhood finds it especially strange to obsess about your meat's stable homelife. Instead of you are what you eat, they seem to be promoting you eat what you are.

"That must be so expensive," Michael sympathizes. "We should pass the hat."

And Owen says, "What's money to a pig?"

An old joke, although, honestly, Toni wouldn't mind following up on the hat passing. She's tempted to tell the guests how much bacon a pampered pig fetches. Also, there's so much food it's practically obscene. Despite their entertainment value, these dinners are going to send them to the poorhouse.

Jorge and Estrellita manage to eat rather than wear their dinner. Their gracious manner, which initially seemed formal, takes on a warm, expansive cast. They stay beyond the other guests, and in the flickering light, after a full meal and hard cider, Jorge yawns complimentarily. "What is it we know about our meat's effect on the brain?"

Owen says, "Pork has the same enzyme as turkey—tryptophan—which makes you sleepy."

"I think it's the prospect of cleaning up that's so exhausting," Toni says, and Estrellita eagerly agrees.

"This is what I am always telling Jorge! You have managed for the embassy staff to shop and cook for one hundred people, all of whom want to claim their coats and have their cars brought around! It is even this way with the staff. How many we hire to help us, and yet I end up alone in the kitchen."

"I'd help you, darling," Jorge says. "But you drug me with your feast. Am I right, Doctor?"

By Owen's side of the grill, Toni counts five empty beer bottles, which is three too many on his meds.

"Really, any big meal will do you in," Owen says. "This is more food and drink than we usually eat in an entire day. When all your blood goes to your gut, you get muzzy-headed."

"The medical term is *muzzy-headed*, is it?" Jorge says behind his upturned mustache.

"Papa!" Natalio calls out sternly, and Brooke flinches. "See how you embarrass Brooke. Mr. Lerner is a doctor and you are not."

Jorge deferentially waves toward Owen, who assures him no offense has been taken, and then Natalio's father reaches for Brooke's hand. "I would never willingly discomfit you," he pledges. Carefully, he lays her palm atop Natalio's. "Here, I came to pay my high respect to parents who could raise such a daughter. My dear, how did you learn to soar through the air the way you do?"

"Practice," Brooke says succinctly, and she offers a weak smile.

Toni knows a balancing act when she sees one. Brooke is taking steps that could be construed as submissive girlfriend, sassy teen, or respectful child. How much practice has this required?

"You may be onto something, Jorge," Owen says. "I should see if anyone's done brain scans on pork or beef consumption. Broiled, pan-fried, and barbecued trials."

"Do not forget the aroma," Estrellita says. "Like a lover, I think, the smell lights up your brain, you know?"

"Oh, I know," Owen says.

"Would anyone like coffee?" Toni quickly offers, bringing the Sunday evening to a close.

By the time Toni does the dishes and climbs into bed, Owen's already there. Despite the increasingly chilly nights, he's pushed the covers to her side so that he's under a single top sheet and she has a double dose of blankets and quilt.

"What did you think of Natalio?" Toni asks.

"As in?"

"No, you go first. Do you have an opinion?"

"Well, he seems rather cocksure."

An apt description, now that they have a rooster—he struts by with his pimpy swagger, always followed by one or two hens. "And Brooke?" she asks.

"Either in his thrall or cowed by him. It's too bad she's not dating Estrellita."

"I know, right?" Toni inches over to her husband's half of the bed and presses herself against his flat, hot rump. She's been his caretaker for so long, she's almost forgotten they're in this together. "He's beautiful, but tightly wound doesn't begin to describe him. The way he looks at Brooke!"

Owen agrees. "It's too proprietary. Do you think they're having sex?"

"She says they're not." Toni wonders why she hasn't shared this with him, let alone her fear that Natalio could well be a sociopath who has swept their sweet girl into his orbit. "Sixteen— how do I even feel about her having sex at sixteen? He acts like he has something on her. Brooke's just as strong a gymnast, and I know she's smarter than he is—"

"In English. The boy's lived all over the world. And for this move, they took him out of high school as a junior."

"Don't explain away what you saw. And please don't defend him against your daughter."

"I'm taking a case history."

Toni says, "Last time I talked to her about birth control, they'd just had condom races in health class. Can you imagine? A relay where each person has to run to the front of the gym, roll a condom on the banana, and then run back to their team!"

"So she knows how to put a condom on a banana," Owen says.

"I'll make her an appointment with Maureen—she'll listen to a doctor. Maybe even confide in her."

"Good idea."

Toni huddles closer against Owen, her mate. He's the one who knows teenagers, the one whose advice is so highly coveted. "What's your plan?" she asks.

"To fall deeply asleep." He's exhausted and gassy, and he wishes she'd stop talking. He overdid it on the pork, even nabbing the crackled skin others left behind, which he loves, but it upsets his stomach.

"And when you wake up?"

Her voice has the sound of an agenda, like a mosquito buzzing near his ear. Toni wants him to wake up as the practicing pediatric psychopharmacologist she has come to bank on, which is either about cash or cachet, maybe both. Surely she knows that what she considers a respectable specialty, he and a few others basically invented out of necessity.

Owen scoots away from Toni, and she pulls the quilt up under her chin. Her disembodied head above the covers reminds him of the jack-o'-lanterns in the toy store of his office building. It's a self-proclaimed Halloween Headquarters, though Halloween Free-for-All is more like it. They have a stockpile of costumes they allow kids to try on. Witch, firefighter, doctor, ninja—the kids run around shrieking in their new identities. Often, Owen lets elevators leave the lobby without him, just so he can linger over their jubilant role-playing. Maybe he should be dispensing costumes. Isn't that what the drugs are for, to mask whatever doesn't fit with our current attitudes of childhood?

"Owen." Toni speaks his name, so she's expecting an answer.

"I'm thinking of closing my practice," he says to the crack in the ceiling, which he can't see but he knows is there.

He hears Toni slap her hand over her mouth. Then she asks a muffled question that starts with why but degrades to a muttery whisper he knows isn't meant for him.

Show some emotion, he urges himself, *or some compassion, or at least some gumption here.* He has a dozen compelling reasons to close his shop, none he can bring himself to speak aloud. Lack of time, consumed as he is with splitting his own logs, growing and grinding his own spices. Lack of progress for his patients. Seeing those costumes has something to do with it— watching the ninja girl assume the poses to accompany her black suit and headgear, or hearing child after child in a firefighter suit sound the siren that beckons their kind. Each knows exactly what is expected of a person wearing a cape or wielding a stethoscope.

Or not. Just as clearly as he sees the need for individual children to play with notions of identity, he also knows that some kids are at the mercy of their brain chemistry. These kids require more than a hat and a hatchet to become a firefighter. And letting them be is no solution either, despite his current "I am what I am" phase. These kids have one lobe tied behind their back, and he wishes he had the wherewithal to help them release it. He has today's specialized knowledge, with all of today's limitations. Maybe he could stretch those limitations, of both expected behavior and treatment.

Toni's voice reaches an audible register. "You could treat adults. Would you prefer that?"

"God, no," he says. "I haven't lost interest in my kids."

"*My—kids.*" She stretches the words out. "I don't know about you, but two of *my kids* are in college, and the third one is caught up in something. Put that in your fucking pit and smoke it."

A painful twitch makes Owen flop like a fish, the sheet parachuting above him.

"Muscle spasm?" Toni asks, suddenly solicitous. Her hand

reaches through the dark and strokes his chin at scar level, turning her gesture into more of a reminder than a comfort. Climbing out the window seemed like a good idea, one that didn't pan out and ultimately cost him some credibility.

He hears his wife's long-suffering sigh. "All that cross wiring," she says. "Dr. Payne told me it takes at least six months for strike victims to be themselves again."

He considers what it would mean to be himself. Like the sheet that ballooned above his spasming body, he's expanded; he's taking more air into his lungs, more thoughts into his head. He says, "I'm just grateful my name's not Dr. Payne."

Toni says, "It's nothing new, being dissatisfied with what's out there. But you said every little bit helps those kids. You said, 'All help helps.'"

He'd thought that was her line; maybe she'd been quoting him all these years.

Toni wants both to be left alone and not to be left. What Dr. Payne had actually told her was that it takes strike victims six months to return to themselves, *if ever*. He'd also warned her that progress would be two steps forward, one step back.

Owen's insouciance hurts, that he could simply announce he is closing up shop. Didn't she help him through his residencies? Hadn't they, when you come right down to it, built his practice together? She rolls away from his side. He treats her own career with snideness, as if any birdbrain could be the president of a college. And he doesn't seem much interested in Brooke or the boys, either.

Ever since his accident he's become incredibly selfish. From what she's read, half the people recovering from situations like his walk away from their past commitments, and the other half double up. Essentially, there are two camps after major trauma: life is too short to live for others vs. life is too short to live only for yourself.

Toni had assumed that Owen's cooking for the neighborhood was an act of generosity. These dinners were about hospitality and socializing for her, because she wanted to rejoin their community in progress. She'd been giving Owen too much credit.

Probably he just wants to cook an entire lamb rather than a few chops, wants to stoke an all-day fire in preparation for whatever mission he's on. The feasts are beside the point, as are the guests, except as they get a taste of his transcendence.

Toni flips onto her back, so that she and Owen are now lying side by side, untouching on the queen-size bed. Although he'd no doubt disagree, he seems burned-out to her. The way he talks, he considers himself more alive than ever, positively glowing from within. *This is my pig, roasted for thee*—no, he's not in savior mode. He's more like Adam: clothing optional, as eager to fuck and light fires as if he invented both. Any day now, he'll probably start renaming the animals.

She imagines him staring into the darkness, light beaming from his hollow eyes like the spotlights that shine upward in memory of the Trade Centers towers, and she asks him, "Will you go on disability, then?"

"No, not disability. I'm getting a barbecue following."

Might as well declare bankruptcy and put the children up for adoption. "So it's time to buy a panel truck and sell pulled pork out on Route 301?"

"Could be," he says.

"For god's sake, Owen, I'm right here." Though they seem quite alone, the two of them more or less in separate beds, on separate meds in separate heads. Toni feels a perverse twinge of conceit—hadn't she suspected that he'd throw over his rewarding practice to smoke brisket all the day long? Of course, there's no joy in predicting this outcome. He'd turn his back on his life's work and, it seems, on his family.

Rather than buying into his barbecue shenanigans, she should have been basting him with praise; just because he shunned applause didn't mean she shouldn't have made a big deal of his reputation. Desperate for him to heal, she has nothing against him enjoying new hobbies—when all his spit-turning culminated in a greasy picnic, she adored his new hobby. So why does she want to smother him with a pillow?

"You act like you're a guru. 'Heaven smells like this'— Did it occur to you that what you smelled during the accident was your own burning flesh?"

"Of course," he says, having rejected that notion a dozen times. He's even found websites describing the way various body parts smell when burned or cooked; literature on the topic basically dates to the martyrdom of saints. "I'm not heading toward self-immolation, if that's what you're getting at."

"What are *you* getting at? You died in front of my eyes. Now you're beyond everything: me, *our* kids, the house, *working*. The old Owen would be the first one to explain what happened in medical terms—how endorphins kick in to compensate for pain and all that."

He is trying to remember how he used to feel in this kind of situation, but it's too much for him. She is right, and so what? Even if his mission is nothing more than a personal quest for medium rare, that's his business. It is a drag that she doesn't share his joy, but he isn't denouncing her, and he can't figure out why she's so judgmental. "You're incredibly angry. And fearful, for some reason."

"For some reason? Seven weeks ago, maybe eight—" She starts sputtering like fat on his precious grill. "I can't take it. You know how scary? Please, Owen." Any minute, she's going to start screaming obscenities like a Tourette's patient—she'll develop the very syndromes he's trained to treat. Frankly, she doesn't know if she is more afraid that he'll close his practice or go somewhere they aren't invited. He wants to break out the champagne, and all she can think about is the inevitable moving van.

He strokes the meaty part of her arm, and though he's showing it the same attention he would a tenderloin, it relaxes her a bit. Obviously, they've passed the point of going back to normal. What is the new goal, then? She thinks of alien abduction victims and remembers that Owen used to diagnose them as epileptics and their episodes as seizures—would he still say that? These people are allegedly fished from earth and reeled into the mother ship before being tossed back, gasping but not gutted, and they flounder with rejection on top of whatever the hell they claim to have witnessed or endured. Most of them would have willingly stayed with their captors.

Toni aims her words at the crack in the ceiling, the cleft that is visible only at night. "I am terrified," she says. "Aside from being abandoned and potentially penniless, I'm scared that after all this, you'll build yourself a metal platform to sprawl on during storms, hoping to be taken up by a lightning bolt."

"Then I don't have to explain it to you," he says. "You get it already."

14

THE PREMARITAL OOZE

"You know what's weird?" Owen asks at breakfast.

"No. What?" Toni appreciates how his frazzled attention span allows him to face the morning anew. She's grateful that they don't have to start in where they left off last night. For her, sleep came late and hard—she didn't hear Brooke leave for practice or Owen get up to cook.

"I'm asking you," he says. "I've lost weird. Some people lose weight or their keys. I've lost weird."

"It's right here." Toni scoots the assorted hot sauces and flavored salts, including both bacon salt and Himalayan pink salt, to the center of the kitchen table. She lifts up the plate of actual bacon, standard fare on many breakfast tables. Except that these strips—cooked outdoors over an open flame—are artisanal bacon, side cut, cured in a dry rub, and cold smoked over Maine hardwood and smoldering pecan shells before being shipped to their home. This bacon was dropped at their door by the FedEx guy, Ralph, who in addition to delivering much of Owen's food has twice joined them for dinner. Then there is the breakfast fruit plate, which she offers him. "First thing in the morning, you grilled the fruit. How weird is that?"

"I was cooking the bacon anyway," he says.

"Weird," Toni says.

"I thought I'd keep the chickens company."

This time she just bugs her eyes at him. Owen lifts a slab of grilled watermelon from the plate with a pair of tongs. He says,

"People eat stranger stuff than this. Deep-fried candy bars and mayonnaise sandwiches."

"Weird," she says again, relieved to say it out loud. She points to the stack of napkins held down by a fulgurite, one of the lightning collectibles he's bought off the Internet.

"It's weird that a lightning strike turns sand to glass tubes or it's weird that I bought the evidence?"

"Both, though neither is as weird as the food stuff." *We're having a conversation*, she thinks.

"Okay, only oatmeal and pasta for you," he decrees without rancor. He holds up an acrylic cube that has lightning feathered inside, a paperweight created by an electro-sculptor. "You know, researchers in Madison are doing some ear training with Asperger kids, like those tapes I made."

It's weird that he says this, considering that last night he announced he was giving up his practice. Staring at the measuring cup next to the coffeemaker, with its clear demarcations, Toni wonders if Owen's brain activity is like water sloshing above and below the desired measure. Maybe he'll settle down yet. "Are these the Chicago people you told me about, or is this another study?"

"Same one, I guess."

They have a moment of silence then, which Toni takes as a mutual acknowledgment of his compromised memory. He recalls tapes he made in the nineties, but not research he described last week or what he'd said last night. What else has been lost or garbled? Toni has a Kyra pang, and she wonders if he does, too. But, desperate to make new memories of life as usual, she willfully moves on. "I liked last week's pork loin—what did you rub it with?"

"Elbow grease."

"And butter?"

He smiles with his whole face. "After brining and drying. Butter with a fair amount of sea salt, ground orange peels, embedded garlic cloves and chipotles, raw honey, and more butter. I soaked corn husks and laid them on the coals."

"It was very good," she says simply, sometimes the highest

compliment of all. It's notable to her that they are making eye contact. On many days, she's been avoiding his or he hers.

Owen says, "Everything's so easy for you, so let me ask you this: Is it weird to think maybe I attracted the lightning?"

"By waving your quarter in the air?" she asks, though she knows he's going way beyond that.

"Maybe I'd been preparing for a strike. For twenty years, I've been studying neurological tics, medication to ease anxiety, brain chemistry of the oversensitive. Here I am with the symptoms I've been treating my entire professional life."

"Unless the lightning is a step toward empathy, so you can keep helping others."

Owen barks out a laugh. "That's what you want, I know."

Determined to take the high road, Toni ignores his scorn. She's trying to keep their ups and downs in perspective, something she learned from all the children's sports. Aside from teamwork, what soccer, swimming, gymnastics, and track each preached was the repetitive goodwill effort. If you set a new pool record or score the winning goal one day, you still have to start from scratch at the next meet. And if you fall off the beam or come in last, shake it off, because you get to start with a clean slate next time. Her generation didn't push girls to play sports, and so this practiced resiliency was a revelation to her. Toni wonders if men view marriage as a fifty-year series with winning and losing years. Or with slumps and streaks in any given year. Trying to get back in the game, she asks Owen what he wants.

He raises his sights beyond the back fence. "What do I want? I want a more fluid reality, one that allows for greater wisdom and tolerance."

"Me, too," she says, and she takes a bite of grilled watermelon to demonstrate her sincerity. "I want all that and money in the bank."

Owen draws his finger through the water drops on his juice glass. "Here's the rub: I haven't determined a reason that I was struck, but I can't seem to accept that there was no reason."

Toni nods at the need to make sense of things. "Welcome to hardship," she says. "Cancer, poverty, the loss of a child"—she crosses her fingers—"no good reason for any of those." Maybe that's what he has to heal from, the search for meaning. "When it comes to disaster," she asks, "which is more distressing—the random strike or the pointed attack? I'm wondering what your people advise."

"Random," he says. "Always random, when it comes to disaster, because the fear is that it could have been you. On the other hand, random kindness produces a ripple of goodwill on the same principle: this could have been you."

He can't possibly see what happened to him as a kindness, can he?

Owen says, "The truth is, you can't attract lightning until it's already on its way—so why have some people been hit five or six times?"

"Lucky, lucky, lucky," she says.

Owen helps himself to more bacon. "Have you heard the theory that enough volts can make you capable of universal comprehension?"

"Capable of," Toni repeats. She'd just read that there are a half billion synapses in every cubic millimeter of the brain, and lightning has the power to fire up *every single one simultaneously*. "Even if you were capable of universal comprehension, wouldn't you have to learn all there is to know? Lightning makes some people *think* they understand everything."

"Where'd you get that?"

"The Internet." Not until she got to work was there time to surf the Web. "Have *you* heard the theories that lightning may have produced the first amino acids—lightning may have started everything."

"I know. Like the stuff at the bottom of the pond," Owen reminds her.

"Ah, the premarital ooze," she says, and they laugh together.

Thoughts of Will both soften and harden her heart. Where have he and Richard been this fall? She says, "You're asking yourself what I ask about the kids. I didn't choose them, but are they arbitrary? Do we get the children we deserve? Or is each kid a fresh permutation of our genes?"

"Two of them are supposedly identical." Owen reaches for Toni's hips and lifts, standing her up from her chair. She lets him turn her around and pull her toward his lap, but she's reluctant to sit there. He says, "It's fine. Take a load off."

She relaxes her thighs so he is truly bearing her weight, and he hugs her around the ribs. This proves to be as comforting as their earlier eye contact, except that the kitchen clock reads 8:30. She has to leave in the next five minutes.

He says, "What do we do about this: I want to light the coals and feed the masses rather than sit on my butt and write prescriptions."

He had her at "we." She says, "Might there be therapeutic possibilities in barbecue? God knows, all your boys love fire."

"And sugar. You're thinking we should do a little group therapy."

"A Rocklands field trip," she says. "Most kids would be disgusted by the slabs of meat, but that might not be a problem with your boys."

"Oh, you squeamish neurotypicals," Owen says.

"Or you could start with the actual cows, like that autistic woman who designs entry chutes for slaughterhouses."

"Temple Grandin." He effortlessly supplies the woman's name. "Maybe we could come up with a wheatless, dairyless, *sugarless* approach to the greasy spoon."

Cooking hadn't occurred to Toni, but it isn't a bad idea. "They could make their parents a feast."

"They could make a living," Owen says.

"Talk about taking everything up a step—a restaurant?"

He says, "That would be so much work, wouldn't it? Maybe Hopkins or NIH would be interested."

"The Asperger Burger Shack," she suggests, and his belly shakes at her back while his ever-present erection presses the underside of her thigh.

He says, "What if we do it all ourselves, my kids and I: raise the hogs, slit their throats, split wood, light fires, make bread. Is that what you're talking about?"

"I don't know what I'm talking about," Toni confesses. "It's just refreshing to be back in their corner for a change." His patients need to practice their teamwork, not to mention standing near another person. "I miss knowing that you're out there trying. I miss your being in the world."

Owen takes a napkin from the table and reaches up under her armpit to dab at her cheeks. It is an echo of the silly story game he played with the children: one of the kids would sit in his lap with their hands behind their back, and he'd substitute his hands for theirs as the kid tried to recount "Little Red Riding Hood" or "Goldilocks." Owen indulged in elaborate shenanigans such as nose picking or head scratching, whatever was necessary to make them laugh hysterically.

"Soon it's just going to be the two of us," Toni says quietly.

With his two fists Owen rubs at her eyes. *Boo hoo.* Then he puts his palms against her cheeks. *Oh no.* He rocks her face back and forth a bit. Now he forks a piece of grilled pineapple from the dish in front of her, and he brings that to her mouth.

Toni obligingly takes the bite. Playing with him inspires genuine concern, which makes her rock forward until she's on her feet.

"What?" Owen asks.

"Your legs," she explains, patting his thighs. "Also, I have to leave. Would you really want them to kill a pig? I couldn't kill a pig."

"Just cooking with those boys would be quite an adventure."

She pictures those boys lobbing things toward the flames, attempting running leaps over a pit of smoldering coals. "Boys and fire—what is that about anyway?"

He snorts. "Let's just say it's primitive. We should call Ricky and ask him that question."

"Richard. Though I guess he'll always be Ricky to us." She kisses Owen soft and long, their lips tenderizing like meat. She feels the premarital ooze, as it were, but she has a whole day bearing down on her, too, and she loosens herself from his grip. "I have to put on stockings and get out of here. There's a lunch at Georgetown with a panel afterward."

"Starring you?"

"'Leadership in a New Economy.' Everyone's trying not to panic."

"Good luck," Owen says, and he moves in for another kiss. When she makes it clear that she's really going to suit up and leave, his ardor turns sour. "Everyone's trying not to panic, and only you're succeeding."

Toni pretends that he's annoyed with the college presidents rather than with her. "They thought they were hired to be adored and to spend their students' money."

"Meanwhile, Toni takes the new economy in stride. What are you going to tell them?"

Really, it's exhausting having to be the hard-core realist on a panel, in an office, in a household. Owen has never paid much attention to their accounts, and he's always enjoyed buying the children whatever they want, which is not how she was raised. God knows where *she* might have landed when the lightning struck, but she doubts it would have been on the other side of the rainbow. If she could, would she want to join Owen in the stratosphere? He is all over the place these days, much like the economy, and it isn't in anyone's best interest to pretend they aren't in for some serious hard times.

"I'll tell them to face the facts and get on with it," she says. "Same thing I tell everyone."

15

IRRATIONAL NUMBERS

Will is angry from whenever he wakes up, eyes bulging, to whenever he wrestles himself unconscious. He's pissed all the time, and what the hell for? It's not as if his dad were run over by a drunk driver or stabbed by one of his crazies. It's not as if he were screwed over by Mom—*cuckolded*, to use a Rickyesque word. And what is up with Ricky? Their whole life, Will has been whispering into his twin's earpiece so his twin could play at anchorman. Now the jerk's gotten used to being in front of the camera. The day Will decided not to talk him through every damn decision was the very day Ricky stopped asking for it, so he didn't even have the satisfaction of refusing. Don't think you're on your own, asshole.

Kyra's pissing him off, too. She wants them sharing a bunk, but if he's a no-show, she doesn't sit the weekend out. Not that she's currently talking to him either. Because he's been an ass—he knows that. It seems, however, just as asinine to be exclusive with her when she has years of fucking under her belt. He slides the bolt off his bike and swings his leg over her seat, fitting his cleats into her pedals and pushing off.

In spite of everything, he hasn't neglected his beloved LeJeune. It was smart to fit her with thick wheels for less bucking on Philadelphia streets. The worst bumps lift his backpack and drop it, so that it's weightless for a second and then seriously weightful, his laptop grinding his lock into his shoulder blade and a vertebra or two. Who's got his back? No one, that's who. Mom's busy with Dad; Dad maybe owes his life, such as it is, to Ricky; his girlfriend is not his girlfriend unless he gets over himself.

Fringed flyers flap in the breeze: every available surface, already papered with Obama propaganda, has been stapled over with Halloween announcements, and the campus is all whored up for the weekend festivities. These clowns will use any excuse for a party, though, god knows, Will is not getting his parents' money's worth out of this semester. He bikes past girls dressed like Disney princesses out to turn a trick, and he glimpses a girl— dressed from the waist up in a nude bodysuit and a long wig— who may be a mermaid or Lady Godiva. Do they plan to stay in costume until Halloween? Some guys are also wearing stuff, but only from the neck up: there's a sombrero and handlebar mustache, cowboy and wizard hats, a foam wedge of Swiss cheese. For a second, Will wishes he were wearing a loincloth and wielding a tomahawk that he could swing over his head as he rides screaming through campus.

He swerves into traffic to avoid getting doored and then leans back into the bike lane, barely missing a pothole so deep that cobblestones poke up like molars from the gummy bottom. It pays to pay attention—his fancy-ass bike can't ride itself to Linh's. Considering last time, "study date" is something of a ruse. He goes wide of a hubcap wobbling in the gutter, and he skirts the steel plates of a construction site. That's three disasters averted in one ride.

Used to be, thinking was this productive. There was pride in showing his work and arriving at clarity, the equivalent of biking a particularly challenging pass. And showing others, too, moving everyone along. Turns out, he doesn't really give a shit about explaining calculus to a bunch of nervous freshmen—why, indeed, do we take things to the limit? And why stop there?

He hops a curb to get to Linh's dorm and rides into a big puddle of dark. The isolated, unlit bike rack behind the building is a direct affront to campus safety obsessions. That pisses Will off, pissed off being his default setting this semester. He disconnects his cleats from his pedals and dismounts. Shallow breaths puff out of his mouth like empty speech balloons. The only food he's had all day is a package of crackers, but if he'd gone for takeout, it would be eleven.

He unzips his pack for the lock, wishing Linh would let him bring the LeJeune inside. "I don't even allow shoes in here," she'd said. Banning his bike is like banning his laptop. No, worse. His vintage bike is a far greater, purer specimen than he is. She is the best part of him, he thinks, but then he remembers that he thought that about Kyra once. He locks the bike to the rack and imagines shackling Kyra there for the time being as well. Where Kyra's binary, certain that he either wants to be with her or doesn't, he's more quantum. He both does and doesn't want to be with her.

He looks up at Linh's open window. If Linh took herself seriously, she'd be the whiz kid of the math department. She's younger than Will as well as smarter, and unburdened by experience. Will builds things, while Linh is strictly theoretical. Maybe they can take each other seriously, he thinks, maybe that's why he came, he thinks, until she opens her door and the strong, sappy dope she favors puffs out.

"I saved you some." She holds out the tiniest pipe he's ever seen. Her arm unfolds toward him, thin bones and tendons beneath skin like the travel umbrellas that used to entrance him, like the robotic arms he constructs. Is that it? She used to be a balance-beam gymnast like Brooke, though she's way smaller, stuck in that preadolescent size judges prefer.

He unbuckles his shoes, balls up his socks inside, and places them by the door.

She says, "These paradoxes were weirding me out. I wondered if the 'set of all elements that don't belong to sets' might make more sense in an altered state."

"If you don't get it sober, you're not going to get it stoned."

"I already get it," she says, her eyes nearly all pupil. She's obviously baked; she's a squab, a little delicacy.

He takes the pipe and inflates himself with smoke. Time stops for him to hold and exhale, probably part of the appeal. He'd do anything to stop time. He says, "When I was a kid, I was fascinated by those commercials where the guy's pointing to a TV showing the guy pointing to a TV . . ."

She says, "That's a simple recursion," and, of course, she's right. Then she says, "What if there were a TV, two screens in, that wasn't showing what was on all the other TVs? Maybe it was just showing a kid watching TV, but then on that one, there was the commercial again—"

She's way beyond him. He says, "Okay, how about this. I'd call my dad if he weren't my dad—paradox or recursion?"

"Call him and see," she says, further complicating the problem. Is that how she's smarter, braver than he is?

Will used to love going hypothetical. His favorite numbers used to be irrational numbers. But now, when he can't catch his breath and his heart does its flutter thing, he wants to know what the hell is wrong with him. His dad has a following for figuring out which drugs to give to whom: drugs to intensify, to vivify, and to obliterate. Will's latest approach is to take them all. He's starving, stoned, and lonely. Maybe Dad and all that's happened around Dad is what's wrong with him.

Linh reaches under his sweatshirt; she slides her cold hand against his sweaty skin, and his dick hardens.

"We haven't even cracked a book," he points out.

"True," she concurs. "Some people think I'm Vietnamese, but I'm only half."

Even when she hasn't been smoking, Linh speaks in non sequiturs, one of the things Will likes most about her. It would be great if the practice caught on and interpersonal communication aspired to one haphazard remark after another. "Which half?"

"Yes," she says. "I might ask you if that's an inclusive or exclusive disjunction. Which half, indeed?"

Linh has her window wide open this crisp night, as she has since school started in the heat of August, and they hear a rowdy herd snort and stomp into the courtyard below. Will reflexively checks on his bike, orienting himself to it as to a dot on a map: bike is here. Near the bike rack, frat guys in Kappa Alpha sweatshirts have helmets on with horns sticking out the sides and miner's lights strapped to the fronts. A few wear furry vests made from those bathroom rugs that wrap around a toilet. Will likes thinking about these bruisers crafting their own costumes, whatever they're supposed to be. They aim their beams into each other's eyes or cross them as if sword fighting. The better to see kegs with, Will imagines, though they're also packing croquet mallets. He likes that dissonance as well—burly guys out for a midnight croquet game. What they're probably up to are point-less feats of strength and drinking. How does his pointless be-havior compare to theirs?

He turns back to Linh, freshly surprised by her compactness. Her breasts are practically flat and yet they are breasts, her body is the size of a young boy's and yet she is a girl. When she pulls a shirt from beneath her pillow and, holding his fleece jacket away from his body, gently dries his back, his legs nearly buckle. He's been screwing his brains out since September, and this might be the first time since the first time that he's felt affection along-side his ruthless desire. A rare smile stretches his chapped lips as the two of them climb into her dwarfsize cot and he runs his fingers over her stomach. Maybe he's a stomach guy, he thinks, remembering the way Kyra's curls up like a cat on a pillow, stud-ded with its own jewel. In contrast, Linh's belly is a hammock suspended between jutting hip bones. Her veins crisscross just under the taut skin.

"You're practically translucent," he says. He marvels at the pulse that visibly beats beneath her navel. She seems too pure for his wastrel self. He peels away her membrane-thin leggings from her pale skin, and he's afraid a kiss might leave a bruise. Fearing for her excites him again, as if she were a real person in his life. I must care about something, because I don't want to leave a mark. Unless I just care about being undetectable . . . This saddens the hell out of him. He strokes her thigh; it's as smooth as a new eraser. Next to her, he's a sweaty muscle mass pocked with mos-quito bites, freckles, and pimples.

"Here you go." She offers him a condom the way she'd earlier handed him the pipe.

For the moment it's enough to move in and through her, to revel in her contortions and her strength. There's so much noise outside, he worries that they're being watched, but that could be the dope. Light zips at weird angles across the walls, and the voices get louder and more rhythmic. Someone affects a French accent to yell, "*Lay Toor duh Fronce*, my ass!" The maniacs raucously cheer, "Give it to her! Hit her hard!"

Linh guffaws, but then she picks up the refrain, speaking right into his ear: "Give it to her! Oh, yeah, you better give it to her hard!"

To Will, the gangbang vibe is disturbing. "Shh." He places his fingers on her lips, but it's just as creepy to be silencing her. He's vaguely queasy, sickened by his selfishness. He'll never catch up with Kyra, if that's his completely jerky intention; even jerkier, while Linh is moaning beneath him, he's worrying about his bike out there, unprotected.

A husky voice yells, "French piece of shit!" and then a bearish Kappa Alpha cheer is followed by the sound of clinking glass.

Goose bumps prickle his skin as he comes, one animal instinct supplanting another. Lust, danger, doom. Climbing out of bed and heading to the window, he peels off the condom, mentally adjusting what he saw earlier; for example, instead of croquet mallet, substitute weapon of destruction. And what he heard: several Tour de France decals adorn the LeJeune's willowy frame.

The clan has gathered in a circle; their massive shoulders touch and their fat headlights are aimed at the center, where they swing their mallets in surprisingly accurate arcs. Will registers the living geometry of their brutish exercise—their head beams divide the circle into pie slices; their blows are radii pumping up and down. Dozens of beer bottles litter the ground at their feet, but they aren't smashing glass; they're striking in turns where his bike should be. "Fuck you, Sarkozy!" "And Carla Bruni, too." Twisted metal tubes catch their headlights as they aim in dead earnest. Will sees a tire spinning and clutches his gut as if hammered himself.

"Stop!" he yells, leaning his naked torso out the window.

"Up yours, Lance Armstrong!"

Powered by alcohol and adrenaline, they've actually broken apart the steel bike rack. They've dragged the bike into their circle jerk and had their way with her. Her guaranteed indestructible lock is still intact around a piece of mangled frame and a freed spoke of the bike rack the demented musclemen snapped. A gang member extracts the chain Will greased earlier in the week and swings it over his head.

"You fucking Neanderthals!" Will screams. "Stop it!"

"We're not Neanderthals—we're Vikings!" they roar.

As Will leans farther out, the hissing radiator beneath the window ledge singes his thigh, and he jumps. The Kappa Alpha crew points and laughs.

A bathroom-rug Viking shrugs sheepishly. "Shouldn't leave stuff out, dude."

"Shouldn't leave your junk out!" the ringleader says, prompting another cheer. He gives Will the finger, and they all follow suit. One by one, their lights aim out into the night as they stumble away.

Will tosses his used condom through the open window, hoping to stick it to someone's horn. "I'll find you," he threatens lamely, because rage chokes his throat, which constricts with the grief of senseless loss. He flails with sorrow and fury as he bats his fleece to the floor. When Linh retrieves it for him, he accepts her help. Briefs, bike shorts, cleats—he prepares for battle.

"Let's call security," she says.

"Don't!" he moans. Security belongs to the rational set of talking and staying put and filling out forms. No way he's in that set.

Is he in *their* set, as in, is he really going to go up against a gang of thugs, each one twice his width, drunk, and armed? They pounded his bike frame flat, which is what each and every one of them deserves. It's not as if he's evolved much beyond Kappa Alpha this semester, leaning toward the primitive. Might as well live the life of a Viking: make fire, eat meat, fuck women, drink beer.

No. It's inexplicable that adultish, semi–college-educated guys would take down a hand-built transportation marvel—*with croquet mallets*—but it's also the culmination of everything that has been pounding at Will. His mangled bike makes no sense. Which is to say it makes as much sense as anything else in his life. More important, the cherished heap, rendered useless, embodies why he's so angry all the damn time. What you love can be damaged in an instant—*you* yourself can be taken down with a single blow. Or demoted, knocked off the firstborn pedestal. You can't prepare for it, and you may not be able to recover.

He can't do nothing. But what the hell he can do isn't clear. His dad has to live with this. And now him, too: When lightning strikes, how can you strike back?

He gulps air, trying to stem his fury, before he hoists his pack and runs downstairs, mindful of his bike shoes. There is precious little left of the LeJeune; Will pockets a snapped-off piece of the frame as a memento. Before he's even aware of where he's going, he has turned down Locust toward the Kappa Alpha house. Despite following in the frat boys' wake, he's stupefied by his lack of options. Campus police, frat council, rocks at their house or cars, a fucking handgun—as the saying goes, none of these will bring her back.

"It's only a bike," his mother will say, though she'd be stymied, too. No one abhors gratuitous destruction the way his mother does. His cleats clicking on the sidewalk actually sound like her in heels.

Will wonders what would have happened if he hadn't been stoned or screwing, if he'd interrupted the fatheads. Surely they wouldn't have pounded him with their mallets. Maybe if he'd begged them to put him out of his misery. He could probably accomplish that right now by pissing on the door of their house. The place appears to be empty. They may already be passed out inside, snoring in a heap like puppies after nursing. Those frat guys are always sleeping head to lap and wrapping themselves around each other, even as they freak about the gays. Tomorrow they'll stage some community-outreach event like Bikes for Tots or a Halloween party for underprivileged kids.

It's paradoxes such as these that are tearing Will apart. Everyone's illogic wears him down. He cases the Kappa Alpha house: near the cellar door, there's a pile of cardboard boxes and newspapers that would go up with a single match; an enormous TV flickers through the south window, the sound boosted through tiny Excalibur speakers that are practically begging to be stolen; there's a chain-link cage in the yard that houses two hulking dogs who could eat a poisoned steak if they're not careful. Will circles twice before stepping away from the frat house. He walks into the night, past rowdy parties and slobbering drunks, his bike cleats scratching at the sidewalk, until finally he walks home and climbs the ladder to sleep alone in his very own bunk bed.

LIGHTNING FLOWERS

The proprietor of Ink, Inc., looks every bit the part. Spaz has a shiny bald head and a gold hoop earring, and he stands like a strongman, his muscled, heavily tattooed arms folded across his white tank top. "Today's the day?" he asks Owen, who's sitting in his chair for the third time.

"Yes . . ." Owen says, palms out in front of his chest. "Though I did want to tell you an idea I had for my Asperger boys."

"In other words, not today," Spaz says.

Squinting to see the tattoo beneath the scrim of T-shirt, Owen makes out a sword-bearing demon with blood-dripping fangs before the tattoo artist faces him again.

"Fuck's sake, Doc, take a lesson from the book club ladies."

Spaz made him give up his chair the previous week, when those women chose their matching tattoos in the time it took his machine to swipe their credit cards and get their signatures. You didn't hear them asking about licensing or hygiene.

"They were a little impulsive, I thought," Owen says. "What did they pick?"

"An open book. Listen, if you're here to talk, I'm going to charge you by the hour."

"Let's do this," Owen says.

"It's only for the rest of your life," Spaz says, and smiles.

Owen isn't concerned about the permanence—he wants that—but he's finally on the other side of some serious pain. He should have taken something along with the prophylactic antibiotics he'd ingested before coming. When Spaz pulls his right arm forward, Owen tenses, anticipating a twinge from his collarbone; however, that fracture has healed, twice. Even the raggedy ends of his ribs have knit themselves together, allowing him to take deep breaths without consequence. His pain, in its covert form, has mostly dissipated, although he's left with numbness, abundant twitches, scars, scar tissue and sensitive patches, muscle damage, and fragile bones. His left foot still has a ways to go, and it may always.

"Fifty-year-old ladies, together since college," Spaz is saying. "The whole time, they're going on about *Wuthering Heights*."

"You've read it?" Owen asks.

"Love the Brontës. Hardy, too. Those ladies totally missed the references to Heathcliff as a vampire."

Owen laughs. "Sounds like someone was an English major."

"Is that germane?" Spaz says, the same thing he'd said when Owen asked about Spaz's own tattoos: *Is that germane?* A red crab darts up the man's left forearm, a koi swims down his right. In the bright light of the parlor, Owen can see the red-veined eyes of the ghoul that covers his muscled back.

What Owen really wants to know is how the women held up—is that germane? He's here because a tattoo is forever, but he's also a doctor, for heaven's sake, as well as a healing burn victim. His first visit had been for a tour of the autoclave, the hep B certificate, and evidence of a recent spore test. When Spaz kicked him out of the chair on his second visit, Owen had been showing him photographs of his lightning flowers for nearly an hour.

Spaz rolls Owen's short sleeve to the top of his shoulder and anchors it with a binder clip. He has to loosen the strap of the seat belt for Owen, whose gut rolls over the top of the stretchy bicycle pants he's taken to wearing. Spaz says, "You don't dress like a doctor," and thoughtfully tugs Owen's shirt to cover his belly so that the seat belt and buckle aren't touching bare skin. Finally he velcros Owen's right arm to an armrest, and he assures Owen, "We'll stay away from the new skin." Owen imagines soldiers come here from Walter Reed, outfitted with new skin and new limbs after a tour in Iraq. Talk about suffering.

Except for the restraints, the setup is similar to a dentist's. On the pole that would normally hold drills, brushes, or air hoses are various guns for lining or shading, and the sketch of lightning flowers is on a clipboard at the end of a gooseneck cable. Spaz peeks under Owen's glove but doesn't remove it.

"I've seen it all," Spaz says. He returns to the sink for a repeat of his hand-washing regimen. "You should have been here on Halloween—I had every chair filled. One guy wanted his leg and foot bones inked down his left side, some skeleton thing he had going. A woman I do, she has about ten tats, had me put a heart— not a valentine one, a real ventricle-aorta heart—on her chest. Breasts like those, that was challenging."

Spaz holds out a plastic bag for inspection. Sealed inside are a dozen or so needles, and when he slits the bag open, autoclave-scented air wafts out. He says, "Polls want to know which way the election's going. I'll tell you which way. Obama's got this thing in the bag. His face, his slogans—no one's paying to get McCain's ugly mug, not even vets."

Owen tightens his butt so he won't pass gas. He doesn't like being strapped in, but also his eagerness for Spaz to speak to him has been replaced by anxiety. He wants the tattoo artist to focus. Spaz hasn't given him any cause for concern. The man's hands are admirably steady; his fingernails clean and even. He'd already let Owen witness him breaking the tape seal on a new carton of Skin Scribes. He pulls on rubber gloves and clamps a needle into the liner gun, which is fitted with the black tubing Owen last saw on the skin peeler used for his surgery. Maybe that's what's making Owen nervous. The liner gun, however, looks more like a handheld sewing machine than the dermatome that sliced layers of skin off Owen's body as if he were a brick of cheese.

Spaz says, "No disrespect, but your whole appointment thing is fucked-up. Most people start bragging about their tats or goading each other on, they see my shingle, and they end up in my chair."

"Maybe shrinks should do it that way. We could offer walk-in hours near tattoo parlors."

Spaz pokes his index finger along Owen's upper arm, pushing hard. "You're a little thick, aren't you?"

Owen hopes he's referring to his skin.

Spaz says, "For head cases, calling for the appointment is part of the process, right? They have to pick up the phone, make a date, show up. *Fess* up." Spaz swabs Owen from shoulder to wrist with a microbiocide, blots the solution dry, and waves his hand above a can whose lid opens to receive the wipe.

"You're saying calling a therapist is therapeutic."

"Damn straight. I'm just a customs agent—someone comes through my gate, I stamp his passport. I verify, no questions asked. How much validation is each traveler willing to pay for?"

Owen uses the exact term, *validation*, for his clients—did he mention that to Spaz? As for himself, he passed through a portal and was tossed back; this tattoo will be the stamp of his singular trip.

"Moment of truth," Spaz says, and stretches out his bulging arms, angry crab over koi.

Owen offers the standard hospital line. " 'Some people feel a little discomfort'—that's what they say before surgery."

"This hurts, but unlike with surgery, you'll have something to show for it." With the marker, Spaz deftly re-creates Owen's Lichtenberg figures, and then he trades the felt-tip for his gun. His bulbous boot depresses the foot pedal that revs up the motorized needle. Owen thinks of the engraver his dad used for inscribing his tools so they'd find their way home.

"I don't hear you telling me to stop," Spaz says. The gruffness is gone from his voice, replaced by a dark, seductive quality. "Let me do what I do best now; just loosen up your muscles some. Relax, if that's possible." More creepy than comforting, his is the refrain you never want your daughter to hear, and Owen shivers to think about Brooke with her controlling boyfriend, who, come to think of it, has diplomatic immunity. Owen wishes he could take everything down a notch: the antiseptic and mechanical smells, the timbre of Spaz's comforting but also serpentlike voice, the gory beauty of tattooed bodies on display.

When the buzzing needle pierces Owen's skin, there is a pinch followed by a hot, stinging sensation. Is that pain or electricity? Owen tells himself what is happening: the motorized spike is puncturing through the epidermis to a deeper layer, where the ink will pool in a permanent subdermal channel. The needle extracts itself and plunges into the next millimeter of unbroken skin. Spaz repeatedly stabs, bringing on pain so intense that Owen's skin prickles with the clammy sweat that precedes throwing up or passing out. His scalp sweats, and he wonders if a customer has ever gone into cardiac arrest.

"Those first few inches are the worst." Spaz lifts a soft cloth to Owen's face and gently dabs his hairline and along his upper lip. "Try to unclench your jaw. You don't want to crack a molar."

Owen swallows and parts his teeth, imagining them falling from between his lips like kernels of corn. He knows to relax his muscles before getting an injection, but this is twenty long-needled shots per inch of skin. For each, the needle pushes his fat skin down until it punctures the surface. The hot scratching thrums, like a deep welt, separating the sensation from the actual tattooing, and he understands why this could be a rite of passage. God, it hurts, right up through his scalp and behind his eyeballs.

But the pain is a little exciting, too.

Spaz is talking fluidly in a smooth DJ voice. "You asked about the crab. My brother and I were tight, tighter than I've been with anyone before or since. We shared a pacifier, a bike—we just had the one dresser, and both wore whatever was in there. Sometimes he'd be talking and I'd think it was me, that I was speaking the words coming out of his mouth."

"Twins?" Owen asks.

"Irish twins," Spaz says. "Ten months apart. When we hit sixteen—he turned first—we started in on drugs. It was just one more adventure we were eager to share. Well, we hiked and climbed a lot, too. You okay?"

"Just barely."

"The endorphins will kick in soon, I promise."

Owen tries to smile. "That's my line."

"Listen, Doc, did you take any aspirin today?"

"You told me not to."

"It's just that you're bleeding a little more than I like. Aspirin can do that."

Spaz swabs off a dotted line of blood. Forget aspirin—Owen longs for the morphine drip from his hospital stay; one squeeze, maybe three, and he'd be feeling much better. "Your brother . . ." he feeds Spaz the thread.

"We'd scram on the weekends. There were four younger kids for our mother to worry about. Besides, she thought we were a couple of Boy Scouts. We were pretty good in the wilderness. But we also tried every goddamn thing we could get our hands on: beer, Scotch, dope, mushrooms, lots and lots of acid."

"Sixteen?"

"I know. And my dad just gave us his truck on the weekends. Billy Goat Trail was like our backyard—you ever been on that?"

He had, and it was no walk in the park.

"We got into rock climbing and rappelling—we were stoned the whole time, mind you, so my memory's churned. We'd be ripped on mushrooms or X and we'd free-climb up the side of a cliff and then—*zip*—practically free-fall down. My brother got the idea that maybe we didn't need the ropes."

"To climb?" Owen is having a hard time taking in Spaz's story, which is coming at him in great gusts. He holds on to particular words—*rappelling*, *churned*—as a pain-management tool.

"No, we free-climbed. He wanted to come down that way, too. Like I said, the whole thing's still cloudy, but you know how I said that sometimes when he talked, I thought it might be me? It's possible that I had the idea. It's also possible that as he told me about it, I was thinking I was saying it."

"I'm confused. That was the drugs?"

"No, it's just how we were. I assumed he was that way; we didn't really talk about it."

That part he's heard before, having tried to get Will and Ricky to articulate their twinness. But why is Spaz telling him this story? Owen watches the artist punch a line down an arm he knows to be his; the pain is causing no small amount of disassociation. After all the weird numbness he's felt since the accident, it's gratifying to know the pins-and-needles sensation he's feeling is pins and needles.

"We were scaling Carderock, and we'd been going up for the longest time. I remember the sun across my lats, then my traps, my neck, and finally baking my hair—" He puts his gloved hand in the air over his bald head. "That would take hours, right? But it was a lark. I was thinking that mushrooms made every fucking outcropping so vivid. Our climb was like walking and gliding up a long escalator, and we—or he, or I—said we could probably float to the bottom. Like a parachuter, but without a chute."

Owen is beginning to suspect that he might be going into shock. "You didn't rappel down?"

"We stepped off the ledge. Into thin air—we did it together. I broke a leg, a couple vertebrae. My brother snapped his spinal cord. I made my way over to him, scooting along on my butt, and I lifted him into my lap. He died in my arms."

The long and winding story ends there. Has Owen heard him right—his brother died? "I'm sorry," Owen says. He feels sad and disoriented. "You were experienced climbers at the top of a mountain . . ."

"He threw his shirt over first. That's weird how I forgot that. He threw it, and we watched it sail down and we laughed. Then we stepped off. All I can say is, right at that second, we were certain that the rules did not apply to us."

Owen, trained to respond to all kinds of grief and craziness, has nothing for Spaz. Fortunately, he feels sure that Spaz doesn't expect anything from him.

"He was a cancer," Spaz says.

"He was sick?"

"Born in Cancer, first of July. That's why I have the crab. He was my right arm, and I miss him."

Owen wants to mourn for Spaz—to lose a brother, your soul mate, under bizarre and horrible circumstances! Any other day, Owen would carve out some time to empathize. But just now it seems clear that the needle etching the fernlike fronds of his tattoo contains some measure of joy along with the ink, that he is being marked, much as his father's tools were announced to be the possession of his father. Soon Owen will bear the marks of belonging to the lightning.

"Hurts so fine, doesn't it?" Spaz says. He doesn't seem to mind that Owen has left him and his loss far behind.

Pain, rapturous pain. All the barbecuing he's been through to get a piece of this, and here he is, seated at the right hand of Spaz, the ink-spotted wonder of Dupont Circle, who is dispensing jubilation through an electrified needle. He begins to understand how a man can carve himself with his dead brother's zodiac. He begins to understand the allure of full-body tattoos, of ink along the groin, encircling nipples. He begins to understand everything, which is to say that he understands that everything is electrical: every thought that manages to send itself to memory or to the mouth for speaking it aloud or to the muscles for bending a knee to it; every pump of the heart, that reliable motor; every stimulation of the senses. He looks down at his legs, surprised to see them still, for he has a strong sensation of spiraling, like a kid on the Tilt-A-Whirl, spinning himself into some trance-like state.

"You should see your pupils, Doc. They are totally dilated."

That would explain the bright light streaming in. Now, what would explain the music? The pain raises him up until he's staring down at his own body in the chair. *Oh. My. Lord.* Great gobs of joy come in with each breath, and he's pretty sure he has an erection.

"Hold that thought." Spaz's voice comes through. "Wherever you are, I want to go there."

It is endless, this elation, because he's bought into such a lot of pricking down the length of his entire arm. It seems fitting that being marked with lightning returns him to his lightning state. He keeps expecting the scent of smoky ribs or basting sauce or his own charred skin, but he just gets whiffs of the buzzing appliance Spaz wields with such expertise. His cheeks hurt from grinning, and it seems funny that earlier he was clench-jawed and frightened.

How much of this Owen can take becomes moot because at some point he slips into a semiconscious pleasure pit, followed by a deep and restful sleep. Late in the afternoon he wakes up in a puddle of drool beneath the softest blanket on earth.

"How you doing, man?" Spaz's face has a look of pure absolution.

Owen can't begin to describe how he's doing.

"You are well on your way to a pain addiction, Doc. I haven't had anyone bliss out like that in a long time."

Has he been rewired to love pain? He'll think about that later, after doing something about his outrageous hunger. "Thanks for the cot," Owen says.

"Thank the day. Election eve, no one to push you out the door."

"Can we get a pizza up here?"

Spaz snorts in his face. "Sure, dude. Your treat."

Owen orders two from a place around the corner that knows how Spaz likes his pies. When they arrive, Owen has to remind himself that they're sharing; he even has to restrain from eating the crusts Spaz leaves behind. Yeast and cheese seem the stuff of life to him. One of the pies has black olives, which impart a musky fruitiness to the fennel-laced sausage surround; the other has roasted red peppers and thick, smoky pancetta.

Spaz says, "People don't hang around for dinner. You really worked up an appetite."

" 'Can we get a pizza up here?' That's what my wife said after childbirth. She was over the moon, holding on to our newborn daughter, and she looks up at me and says that." *His wife!* He hasn't uttered a word about his tattoo to her. So much for executive function. Not to mention the fact that giving birth isn't really analogous to getting a tattoo.

Spaz says, "Childbirth," with a surprising degree of awe. He flattens the empty boxes, stacks them, and neatly folds them over. "You couldn't pay me enough. And when all is said and done, you end up with clowns like us."

Owen nods gravely. Something like shame comes over him. It's as if Toni keeps disappearing into his blind spot.

Spaz says, "I'm always nagging people not to disturb their new tat for a few hours. With you I can rest easy because we started at two."

Owen is bewildered by the one-handed clock until the minute hand clicks forward so it's just past six-thirty—and the street outside flashes with the rainbow lights of restaurants and bars. He imagines Toni coming home to a dark, empty house, and then his coming home to her. His dread of facing her wells up into resentment. He'll take care of his tattoo, she doesn't have to lift a finger. It's his body after all.

Spaz is talking to him. "You didn't miss any head cases, did you?"

"Do you think I'd schedule psychiatric patients after this?"

"I never know what to think," Spaz says.

Neither does Owen. He can't get a grip on how strange the world, or his actions, might be. Since the lightning, he can barely make it through two appointments in a row, what with his twitches and wavering attention span. He's been bandage-free for only a month—he'll have the compression sock and glove until winter—and now he has an armful of white gauze. He has required hours of protracted care, constant supervision, doctor appointments, and therapy. What an ungrateful ass he is to pretend he's independent. "I'm not really supposed to be anywhere."

"Then you're in the right place," Spaz says kindly.

Owen remembers him gently swabbing his clammy face. "Thanks for babysitting."

"Shut up. Now keep it clean, man."

Spaz's unjudgmental concern touches Owen, who desperately wants to peel off his bandages. "I can't wait to see my arm." Part of him wishes he'd been duped, that when he uncovers his shoulder, the skin will be unmarked.

"You'll see it every day," Spaz says. He fans Owen's credit card receipt at the gallery on the wall. "When you're healed, I'll put you on the board—maybe you'll start a trend. Meanwhile, sign here. And feel free to tip, if you're so inclined."

17

SLIP SLIDING AWAY

The Zinfandel that Toni's pouring may have been intended to complement a rasher of ribs, perhaps from the half a cow wrapped in individual body parts in their freezer. She would have cleared her choice with Owen if he were home, but he must be pressing his nose against a meat locker somewhere. Toni sinks into the sofa and lifts her feet onto the ottoman, remembering the first morning she dropped Brooke off at preschool. The twins were in fourth grade and Owen was at the office, and when she returned home she filled a goblet with ice water and took the time to finish every drop. That was a miracle for its time, not only to drink from a breakable glass but also to do so without interruption. When Brooke leaves for college, the house will no doubt be too empty, although the boys may have moved back in by then.

She sniffs her wine, detecting hints of both black cherry and licorice, more reminders of the children. She'll catch up on the Brooke and Natalio story when she has coffee with Estrellita tomorrow. Maybe she and Brooke can go shopping afterward. She toasts Obama and—what the hell—McCain for giving her Election Day off. It's not necessary for her to drink this wine down like water, except that she just might. Here's to last week, while she's at it. Her job is more solid than ever; in addition to the retiring presidents are the ones who self-destruct or can't withstand the latest financial pressure. Some are such martyrs, acting as if they're running their campuses on five loaves of bread and two fishes. *Walk it off,* she was tempted to tell Cornell's president, pouting about his six-billion-dollar endowment. Instead, she'd pointed out that Afghanistan's GNP was around six billion, and left it at that.

The trick is to use her attitude sparingly, lest people think she's flip. That's what Owen said when she accused him of throwing his practice over for a pork shoulder, or maybe he called her glib. She's pragmatic; someone has to be. In fact, she and Owen had finally managed to have a conversation about his being both who he wants to be and who they need him to be. That strikes her as fair. A person should be able to change within reason, within the confines of his commitments. A certain amount of push and pull goes on in a family, allowing for shifts or subtle changes of direction but ultimately keeping each member inside the family's embrace.

Toni's ankles atop the ottoman are a stranger's ankles. They're puffy, and her swollen feet bear the imprint of her shoes. She's uncertain if pantyhose promote or cut off circulation. She should drink more water. Sitting up on a dais, she limits her intake so she can make it through an entire panel without running for the exit.

Acknowledging her own setbacks gives her hope that a portion of Owen's slippage is age-related as well. Last night, attempting to fend for himself, he'd put a potato in the microwave and then stood staring at the console as if it were a space shuttle dashboard. "What do I push?" he asked. She waited a beat before pointing out the button labeled *potato*.

Absurd, and yet friends are always telling stories about a husband bellowing for the toothpaste right next to his elbow or ranting about trying to find the very cell phone he's yelling into.

The hem of Toni's skirt reveals a few inches of thigh, and she pushes her thumb along the spiderwebby veins that ruin her for shorts. Where she crosses her legs, a dozen parallel threads of purple and red stripe her skin. They disappear when she presses on them. If she were one for plastic surgery, she'd be tempted to get them zapped or stripped, though she's sure she wouldn't be willing to spend whatever they charge. What might they charge? Her legs have always been one of her better features, as opposed to her midsection. Toni unbuttons the top of her skirt and watches the thin roll of fat, the thickness and color of pie dough, meet the flab beneath. She imagines tugging her skirt zipper down a few inches and watching her body gush out into a fleshy puddle, an exaggeration that strikes her as funny. Although she's actually lost weight, her muscles seem to be dissolving beneath her loosening skin. Things are slip sliding away: her waist, her bladder—sometimes she has to cross her legs before she sneezes. Lately, the shine seems to have slipped right off her hair.

When did she go up and over the hump? A key turns in the front door just then, and Toni relaxes more deeply into the couch now that she knows where Owen is. Starting on essentially level ground, they've made the most conventional of all climbs together: marriage, a house, more education, children. She thinks about couples who choose each other despite depression and drinking problems—for heaven's sake, prisoners on death row *get married*. Well, Owen had been divorced, which counted at the time but is barely a blip on the screen after their twenty-three years. And she had her own blip on the screen that one summer.

In any event, they have steadily risen together. Despite the fact that so many made the same climb, and that they had chosen to do it in a place defined by its competitive edge—half the town could be voted out in tomorrow's election—she doesn't think of keeping up with others. As long as they keep going up, which she realizes she's taken for granted. She wonders how many couples actually have a contingency plan for a setback as rare as theirs. Meanwhile, something crappy and unexpected eventually happens to everyone, doesn't it? For years, the phrase "family planning," meaning when and how many times to get pregnant, made Toni think of all the planning required to get three kids dressed, fed, and off to school daily with proper backpack fodder: permission slips, sports gear, homework, lunches. Add in flu season, cupcakes, her and Owen's jobs. Extend indefinitely, getting them to sports, music, camp, college.

What's taking Owen so long? As for her puddling body, she could get back on track with that, now that she doesn't have to be his nurse. Near the Metro, there are gyms on both sides of the street, rows of stationary bicyclists barely visible behind windows they've fogged. She pictures herself spinning her way back to miniskirts and muscled calves. Can exercise thin your ankles, or is she going to have to come to terms with their dimpled flesh?

Toni hears Owen's distinctive shuffle. "I'm in here," she calls out. "Honey?"

She swings her feet off the ottoman and, buttoning her waistband, pads toward the entry hall to see Owen scurry like a crab onto the landing and then sidle upstairs remarkably fast for him. Did he hear her? He seemed more lopsided than usual, and Toni worries that he is in pain he doesn't want to admit.

"Owen? Are you all right?"

"Fine," he barks. "You don't need to come up here."

If that isn't an invitation, she doesn't know what is. "Are you hungry?"

"I got a pizza. Thanks, anyway."

Did he actually remember that Brooke is at gymnastics until after eight? Toni was thinking they'd have a simple grilled fish for dinner, and she'd stopped by the fish store—the slab of tuna she bought should be gold-leafed for what they charged. She climbs a half dozen steps, thinks better of it, and returns to the landing. This is ridiculous; he's probably relishing a moment alone in his own bedroom, just as she was winding down after work. He's been so closely watched. On the other hand, where the hell *has* he been all afternoon, and why did he run past her without a word? With the kids, she tried to position herself midway between the poles of hovering and neglect, though it sometimes felt as if she were simply running to one pole, tagging it, and then running to the other.

Owen is not her child; he is not a child. Toni steps off the landing and walks back toward the couch until another equally valid line of logic loops through her brain. She would be irresponsible to ignore all the doctors' warnings of erratic behavior, especially considering Owen's erratic behavior. What's the proper response to "you don't need to come up here"? Tiptoe, she decides.

Toni makes her way upstairs, and it's habit rather than stealth that has her avoiding the creaky spots. However, when she faces their closed bedroom door, she has to decide whether to announce herself or not. In the end, knocking on their door seems more suspicious than respectful, and so she simply turns the knob.

"No!" Owen barks when the door swings open. He's standing in front of the dresser mirror, and for a man taken by surprise, he moves gracefully, twisting around to grab the corner of the quilt. He's stronger than she would have thought—he lifts the heavy coverlet clean off the bed, swirling the ersatz robe to settle around his shoulders. Despite Toni's certainty of bad juju, Owen strikes a regal pose there in his long hair and leggings, his gloved hand clutching the edges of the matelassé beneath his neck, the white quilt pooling on the bedroom floor into a kingly train.

He is shirtless beneath the makeshift robe, and a flapping bandage runs the length of his right arm, from clavicle to the edge of his burn glove.

Owen stares at her defiantly. "I said I didn't need you."

What he'd said, what she'd puzzled over, was "you don't need to come up here." That's different from "I don't need you." And far less hurtful. Toni sits down heavily on the bed, queasy inevitability now crawling up her legs like the spider up the waterspout. Eye level with the dresser top, she sees snapshots fanned out by the jewelry box, and she recognizes the pictures Ricky and Will took the first few days, those ghost images of electricity that flitted through his blood vessels. She remembers the Sharpie that Owen turned on himself after the marks had faded.

If he had cancer, she'd be right there next to him. If he'd been accused of malpractice. If he had early Alzheimer's. "You're still sick," she says. "You've got a long way to go."

"Don't talk to me like that."

"Why not?" she asks. "I have done a remarkable job—so many people have told me—of taking everything in stride. *Let him heal. Let his healing take its own course.* That's been my approach. Why are you making this so hard?"

"Because it is hard," he says. He's angry at his wife, who never got it to begin with. Jokes, love, faith—if you have to explain them, they evanesce, and yet each has the potential to be a shared experience. With the right person. If Toni had been to the mountaintop, he would try to meet her there. "Why can't you be happy for me?"

He's speaking from a deep well of confusion, for the tattoo that was meant to commemorate his glorious bolt of enlightenment has partially reconstituted it. The hot, tingling pain of the needles and his nervous system's compassionate reaction are eerily reminiscent of the euphoria he experienced that hot summer night. That's good. He's been allowed a brief return along with some understanding of the source. No, that's bad. He has a permanent reminder now of his potential delusion, the flash that perhaps not so much illuminated as fried him. Is he going to continue to chase euphoria with needles and burns and maybe shocks?

"I've been everything for you," Toni says, but there is a speck of truth in his accusation. She has not ever, starting the instant he was struck, been happy for him.

He holds the quilt edges together in one fist so he can thump on his chest with the other. "No one knows what it's like in here."

"Uhmmm," Toni moans, as if her jaw were wired shut. Why hadn't she stayed on the couch, where, having observed aspects of her life ebbing from her, she'd ably shored herself up. Here he was with his pile of rocks to take her under.

Six months, she tells herself, *six months to get back on track*. She's been at it nearly three; frankly, she isn't sure she has three more in her. His pronouncement that no one knows him seems especially absurd considering his profession. After all, he presumes to know for each patient what it's like in there. She is as desperate to slip the quilt from his shoulder as she is not to see beneath those bandages. She tries to reconstitute compassion any way she can. But honestly. Honestly. Even as they'd been having actual conversations, he'd been planning this. Unless he walked into a tattoo parlor this afternoon on a whim.

Ultimately, Toni points her long, accusatory finger at his shoulder. Speaking through clenched teeth, she asks, "Did they use sterile needles or do we have to worry about hepatitis now, too?"

Owen lets the quilt crumple to the bed, and he lifts the flap of bandage from his shoulder as if he were stretching out a wing. At the sight of his tattoo, Toni feels sick with hopelessness. Ten minutes earlier, she had just been hating the spiderweb veins on her legs and weighing the cost of having them removed. These thin red welts look as if her legs had run down his arms.

From his right forearm, past the crook of his elbow, and all the way up past his shoulder to his wrecked clavicle, he is inked with the veins and twiggy capillaries that truck his blood around his body. Through his puffy skin Toni sees the horrible artistry of the tattooist, whose work is as accurate as a medical illustration. There are the red branching lightning flowers, souvenir of his strike, which electricity first made visible and are now indelible.

Toni wants to reject what she has seen; failing that, she tries to rationalize: might getting this tattoo be part of his cure, as opposed to a descent into utter craziness? But staring at her husband's arm, all she can come up with is an elephant joke: What's gray on the inside and red on the outside? An inside-out elephant. She isn't sure she's prepared to live with an inside-out Owen. Hurt and hysteria have her gulping air like a fish. "To me. You. Couldn't. Even-mention-this?"

"You would have stopped me."

She's crying now, now that he's made it permanent. It is hard to breathe, the way she's sobbing. He's been cooking as if every meal were his last supper, maybe the Last Supper, and now he bears his stigmata. He's paid someone to etch him with a map, a target, which seems heartbreakingly apt. Of course she would have stopped him. She wraps her arms around herself, aware that he hasn't made any effort to comfort her. Her ears ring an alarm of light-headedness, and she coughs so she won't faint.

They are all of them in big trouble here.

"What have I ever stopped you from doing?" she moans. "What power have I ever had?"

"This has nothing to do with you," Owen says. There is some kind of tug-of-war between them, and he can't help but feel that she is bound to lose. *Go ahead and leave me*, he thinks impulsively. *I've been left before.*

She stops holding herself together, she is so stunned by his bluntness. What the hell did he see in that flash that outshines the life they've built together brick by brick? Toni covers her face with her hands and throws herself down on the bed. His capacity to hurt her knows no bounds.

She is as angry as she is envious. What a privilege, to do whatever the fuck you want. When she'd looked at her legs, she couldn't even bring herself to *imagine* paying someone to erase the veins. Meanwhile, a bright light and a blow to the head could be just the correction a person needed to get out of a rut. That's how she might see it if she wasn't the rut. Muffled by the pillows, Toni howls, "You don't even *want* to get better!"

Owen fans out his gloved hand, and he works the hinge of his wrist, still slightly tender from being thrown to the sidewalk. "I am better," he says quietly. "I'm not the same, if that's what you mean." It seems to him that if he's been one person for fifty-plus years and now is a different person, that is his prerogative. She acts as if his changing might make her disappear. But he is who he is—he's comfortable with that—and now he's been bumped up a bit. He wants to borrow the language of plastic surgeons— breast *augmentation*, figure *enhancement*. *You, only better!*

How can he remain in light? He can't even explain the message of the flash without alienating people. The energy, the heat did a number on him; however, his enlightenment doesn't negate who he had been. And it certainly doesn't cast Toni into shadow. But his one and only wife is suffering. He remembers the story he told about Toni when the pizzas arrived at the tattoo parlor. A shiny sphere of empathy rolls around his heart looking for a place to lodge, like the ball bearings in a children's puzzle that you gently tilt from side to side. His getting a tattoo is not about Toni, his rational mind tells him; however, the ball that rolls into its hollow makes him feel for her.

"Toni, sweetheart," Owen says. "What's the most profound experience you've ever had?"

She sits up to blow her nose, but she will not look him in the eye. Damn if she is going to say it was his rescue.

He waits, as if he really wants to know, as if she were his patient. Finally she says, "Childbirth. Well, not the first time—that was an ordeal." Because the twins' entrance was so chaotic, the university hospital room downright crowded, and she and the babies hooked up to every conceivable monitor, she hadn't been prepared for the intimacy of birth. But she had ushered her daughter into the world nearly by herself. Nothing she'd been through before or since holds a candle to that.

He says, "You were crazy in love. Blindsided."

You don't know the half of it, she thinks, wondering how many bridges, one to another, people can build. Despite herself, she has the first inkling into Owen's vision. Alongside the unthinkable pain and weirdness of childbirth, in which her own body opened itself from the inside, before she blinked the tears from her eyes or the nurse had fully wiped her newborn clean of blood and slime, Toni knew a love like no other. It seemed that Brooke *was* love. And a product of love and the embodiment of goodness that Toni had both sprouted from within and been implanted with, a love that had fed on her and grown so large, it was only natural to burst forth into the world, helpless and mewling but nonetheless complete, still dependent even as she was also independent, able to stretch her own nostrils and take in the smell of Toni's skin and breath, pucker her lips and taste milk Toni was already making for her, eventually a half pint gushing into each breast and leaving permanent marks of the skin stretching at the simple request of Brooke's cry, so that they could link their bodies together in a new way that showed their attachment and devotion to each other.

Brooke is something like Toni's living tattoo, herself turned inside out and visible to the rest of the world. Of course, her sweet teenager is far more than symbol, than inked homunculus, than inscribed stain. But she is evidence to Toni of a joyous mystery and of past lives and of lives to come. Had Owen glimpsed all that in the blaze that jetted him into the air and then dropped him on the sidewalk, melted to his shoes? Will he ever get over such rapture? Will they lose him in his attempt to sustain it?

18

AT THE BOTTOM OF A HOLE

Once Will's system crashes, there is no recovery. Halloween comes and goes while he's in his bunk. Linh is clearly spooked to find him in bed days later. "Do you feel sick?"

If he feels anything, it's expendable. He has nothing to contribute, and he makes no difference. A better, more useful version of him is already out there.

Linh wants the perpetrators brought to justice. "Those guys are brutes," she points out. "Their actions had nothing to do with you."

Exactly.

Henry, his helpful roommate, supplies him with food as well as drugs, and Will moves through his days as if through gel. Wrappers and yogurt containers litter his bunker. There are cords, phones, a laptop, and books—but he is bedfast. Bedridden.

Linh urges him to act. "People need to call them on their shit. If they had hurt me, you wouldn't let it go, would you?"

No.

A casement window of mullioned glass shows him the sky from his elevated cell. Despite climbing out to reload or relieve himself, he's still in his bunk come Election Day. It's the first presidential election he's old enough to vote in, if he could get out of his deep, deep hole. Instead, he spends that entire day watching the sunlight bend itself around corners to cross three of his four close walls, flushing pink before finally giving up. Shortly after dark, a worldwide party erupts. It's louder than a home game outside, and Will recognizes that history, his neme-sis, is being made without any contribution from him. The twi-light refrain of "Yes we can!" becomes "Yes we did!" Will sees the dandelion bursts of fireworks out the window and hears the booms that follow. Really, the booms were first and should be heard first. Even physics is unfair.

On what turns out to be her last visit, Linh leans against the ladder so she can shake him with her pale, spindly arms. "All the stuff they destroy in the name of fun—it's not funny."

You're way smarter than me, he wants to say. *Why don't you understand?*

Drs. Marzoni and Haverhill e-mail and text him. Although he's touched by the attention, the content is an insult: repeated links to freelist bikes and various Penn counselors. Which is more ludicrous—the idea that someone in his condition should see a social worker or that Will could possibly ride a rusty ten-speed?

Henry climbs the rungs to shine his phone in Will's face. "Gotta leave your bed, man," he says. "Come on, take a shower, and we'll go to Pasqually's." He turns the quilt down and cranks the window open. "Dude. Air this place out."

It feels good to wash his butt, which is pimpled with acne. Leaving the dorm, Will gives fair warning. "I'm dangerous. There's no telling what I'll do if we see any of them."

"Absolutely," Henry agrees. "There is no haven from your wrath."

"Have I said that?"

"Not today," Henry says. "Not yet."

Henry buys him a bright green salad and a stromboli, which hurts to chew, his teeth sore from grinding. It is heartening to sit at a table with his loyal friend.

But the uptick is short-lived; for the most part, Will stays abed. Haverhill sends a lab tech to the room bearing an actual basket of treats, little plastic bags of nuts and trail mix arranged on a nest of *excelsior*, a word he should text to Brooke but doesn't. Acing tests will only set her up for false expectations.

"Do you need more blankets?" his mother texts, and "Home for fall break?" which was in October, before he took to his bunk.

"R u effing there?" Kyra texts. Good effing question.

And then comes a clear November morning, as inexplicable as anything else, when Will wakes with a sense of urgency. How are his calculus kids making out? More to the point, why should they have to suffer in ignorance because of him? Paranoid that Henry has slipped him an incentive booster or an empathy stimulant, he welcomes caring. Is he entering whatever phase comes after demoralized? Perhaps he's sleepwalking. Slightly amazed that he can simply descend from his bunk to the floor, he robotically showers and dresses. There is a bag of pills on the desk of a handy size for slipping into his pocket, which he does after picking out two small Adderalls.

Downstairs in the smoothie line, he orders haltingly—he hasn't had to say anything like *mango whip* or *protein blast* in some time, let alone move himself along. A hairnetted woman adds a scoop of protein powder to his pulpy orange drink. "You look so pale, sugar," she says. The smoothie smells like the Fruit Roll-Ups he and Ricky used to beg for, what his mother called fruit roadkill because they looked like they had been run over. He feels bad about ignoring Kyra and his family, which is more than he's felt in two weeks. He walks like the Tin Man, all stiff knees and creaky joints. Not having a bike makes the trek from one end of the campus to the other unbearably long—as a mode of transportation, walking is seriously overrated. The scene in front of his eyes refuses to change. All the buildings obstinately hold their position, as if for the historic fucking record.

He's dressed for two weeks ago; meanwhile, winter has arrived. Wrappers blow between Philadelphia's architectural marvels and through the preserved fucking arches. The sheer posterity of the place mocks him. He checks his phone to make sure he hasn't missed the class just getting there, but time is as slow as he is. That's especially messed up, because he knows nothing endures.

Weak, confused, and freezing, he regrets leaving his room and is propelled for blocks by irritation alone. In this agitated state, he hears a bike behind him, a rattletrap with a loose chain. Stepping aside to let the moron pass, he sees a bruiser in a Kappa

Alpha shirt riding a dilapidated Schwinn. The dumbass doesn't even have a helmet! Will's revenge fantasies have been held in check by depression as well as Henry's meds; since the wilding, god knows how much sludge has settled in his bloodstream. This morning, however, he's had a double dose of Adderall and a smoothie.

His awakening is beginning to seem ordained. What are the odds that the day he finally rouses himself he also happens to come across a Kappa Alpha? He's grateful to the cafeteria lady for powering up his smoothie, just the boost he needs to fuel his twisted wishes. That and the adrenaline of anger. Will squeezes his fists in pulses, as if pumping the brakes of his dearly departed LeJeune.

The guy pedaling toward him is wearing stupid plaid shorts, and he has shins like caveman's clubs.

"Hey, Neanderthal!" Will yells.

"Dude!" the kid says, as if greeting a bro.

Will plants himself in the path of the Schwinn. Run me down, motherfucker.

"Whoa, Professor!" the kid yells, and swerves to the right.

Will wants to break his piggy frat-boy snout. "Don't call me professor!" There is some spark of recognition between them, before Will charges the kid.

Will juts out his lower jaw. "Grrr!" He growls in the kid's face and pulls him off his clunky Schwinn, throwing him to the ground. Will clutches the handlebars of the riderless bike and shoves it hard, as if to sail it off a cliff to a fiery crash. On the campus's level ground, the Schwinn merely veers sharply and falls over, hitting the dirt.

Will's ambush has fury and the element of surprise, but the frat boy has major mass on his side. Rearing up, he's the height of a grizzly bear. Will shoves a fist into his ribs, and then Will sees the kid's fist coming at his face and feels the knuckled mass crush his cheek. The sound of his own nose—*c-r-aaa-ck*—echoes between his ears as if his head were empty. A tooth jumps from the back of his mouth and arcs toward the ground in an inevitable gravitational trajectory. It's a wonder the rest of his teeth don't flee from the pain. Face throbbing, Will spits a clot of blood onto the pavement; meanwhile, the grizzly bends over as if to retrieve the molar. Will is furious. *Don't you touch my fucking tooth!*

Will shoves the brute, who staggers backward. The reeling, woozy frat boy trips on himself, and he cannot regain his balance. He looks directly at Will as if he is stumped by this problem. And then he falls down hard with all his weight. His unhelmeted pumpkin head actually bounces off the curb.

Will stares at his Goliath: the grizzled monster barely has a beard on his plump cheeks. As wide as a clock, his face is covered in sporadic stubble beneath his pushed-in nose, and his gapped front teeth are the size of Will's thumbs. His features are sickeningly familiar to Will, whose deductive powers kick in. Rather than his girth and his Kappa Alpha shirt, what Will recognizes is the face of a husky freshman from his calculus recitation. It's no coincidence that they were sharing the road; they were both heading to class, where Will was supposed to have guided him through the wonders of the unit circle. If either of them had made it there this morning, none of this would be happening.

Will doesn't know what to do, and any plan he hatches in his state of mind will hardly be state of the art. He can't use his own phone to call this in. If he could find a pay phone, he'd call 911 and get someone with real medical knowledge in on the action. *What's the number for 911?* he actually asks himself. Here's a better question: Are there any pay phones left on campus? He can't remember seeing any, but he's never needed one. He'll tell them a biker is down. Bikers bump their heads all the time; they get doored, hit a spill of gravel, go up over the roof of a car. That's what helmets are for, you stupid—*James!* Remorse takes Will's breath away, and blood gushes down his sweatshirt. This isn't some frat thug, it's James. Of course he has to call for help! He wishes he hadn't remembered the kid's name, and he feels a wave of crazy fondness for the goof, who was riding a yard-sale Schwinn to his early-morning tutorial for help.

Atop the powdery parking lot stones is a polished white nugget—a big chunk of Will's molar, the roots cracked off. He shrugs out of his sweatshirt, tugs his T-shirt over his swelling head, and slips his arms back through his sweatshirt. He could use his shirt to stop his bleeding, but he gives it over to pillow James's head.

If he gets himself to the emergency room, he'll have to explain his own injuries. Would you believe, fell off my bike? He wonders if they'll test his blood or piss for what all he's ingested. Desperate for support, he fishes out his cell phone and presses the side button. "Dad," he groans, and the phone obeys his command.

A girl answers in a know-it-all voice. "Hi, Will."

"Who is this?"

"Your sister, nimrod."

"Where's Dad?"

"He's letting me use his phone. I lost mine."

"Jesus Christ." Will wipes his bloody nose on the hem of his sweatshirt and slides to the ground, his back against a Dumpster. They are a sorry lot.

"Willy, I haven't lost a phone in months. You sound like you're calling from the bottom of a hole. Where are you?"

At the bottom of a hole. He's been determined to go it alone, to live as a free man, and to answer to no one. Well, he's certainly alone now, and apparently there is no one to answer. He wonders if they set noses and cheeks in jail or if they just throw you in as shark bait. Finally, he answers Brooke. "I'm at the bottom of a hole."

"Me, too," she says.

"What does that mean?"

"It means you don't have to live here," Brooke says. "You are golden."

Golden would be the other kid—*James*—coming to any minute, groggy and sore, unsure of what hit him.

"Brooksey, I can't talk."

"What else is new? You said you'd send me vocab, a couple new words every week, and then you're a ghost. Meanways, I'm stuck here all alone, with *them*. You know Dad fell off the roof, right?"

"The *roof?*" His dad seems determined to be a suicide. "I'll call later."

"You called Dad now," Brooke reminds him.

"That's because I need Dad now."

"I'm in my room but I know he's not home—he started to see his kids again. Maybe if I could cough up a hair ball of money, he'd listen to my problems. You should see what he's been grilling, entire animals, and—Oh. My. God.—you won't believe his arm! He—"

Will holds his phone out and chooses END.

How can he keep pretending that one thing leads to another, that he and his professors are inching their way up on all that had been previously unsolved? Artificial intelligence, ultimate data compression, information entropy—they imagine themselves closing in on the answers, smug bastards. When really, nothing makes any sense. Certainly not the things he keeps going over. His sister just told him that Dad *fell off the roof* but is treating patients. What kind of crazy is that? He swears that if he gets out of this jam intact, he will call his sister back. And meanwhile, why doesn't James wake up?

"Let's go, buddy." He gently rubs the kid's shoulder.

Will is through with thinking. He enjoyed it because he never had anything important or dangerous to work through, which reminds him that he has all kinds of illegal shit on him. *What would Henry do?* he asks himself, immediately rejecting the idea of sliding the stuff into James's pocket. It kills Will that he knows the kid's name.

He walks to the east side of the building, where a lone female ginkgo has not only evaded the university's ax but has also received a fresh blanket of mulch. The ammonia of the mulch competes with the dog vomit of slimed ginkgo fruit; whatever happened to his nose isn't affecting his sense of smell, and he gags. He scoops a divot in the mulch cone, spits, and empties the pills into the hole, imagining for a second that a thick psychedelic vine will sprout, the stem undulating upward and offering its leaves as ladders for him and his wounded giant to climb back into the sky. That's how he knows he's still full of shit.

His phone rings, and when he holds it out to check the number, his own bloodied hand so scares him that he flings the phone away, a hard and horizontal throw that crashes through a boxwood hedge. Still, his fucking indestructible phone continues to ring while he pokes through the bushes to find the thing. "What is it?"

"I lost you," Brooke says. "Do you want me to give Daddy a message?"

"My bike was wrecked."

"That so sucks! Your beautiful bike—was it an accident? Did you get hurt?"

"Look, it's kind of high pressure here. Don't tell anyone I called, okay?"

"That sounds *ominous.* You're scaring me, Willy."

"You and me both." His tears are making it even harder to breathe through his swelling nose. He searches his sweatshirt pocket for his tooth, which he must have buried with the meds at the base of the ginkgo tree. "I'd help if I could, but you're on your own."

"That's basically my problem," his sister says. "Maybe you should get the train home this weekend."

Brooke almost asks if he's in trouble. She has the phone smashed against her ear, but it seems that the problem is with her brother rather than his phone. The connection sounds blubbery, and she thinks he says "Take care of Mom and Dad" before they get cut off. He doesn't answer when she repeatedly calls back. Her dad's phone is so Amish, it won't even text. She's sure he'd been crying, and when she thinks of him telling her she's on her own, she clutches a stuffed parrot to her chest and cries, too.

She could use the guidance of a big brother or two. She's been so lonely all fall. She hates to sound like a complete brat, but both her parents have let go of her since summer. They don't seem to care whether she studies, goes to gym team, and practices her clarinet, or if she does stuff with Natalio and facebooks all night. Natalio was super-sympathetic at first, and what a rush to have a guy who looks like that come after her. But she's done stuff with him she didn't think people did until college. And he likes stuff that hurts, like coming in her butt. Saxy says you have to let them do stuff like that if you're committed. So how come she feels lonelier than ever? She hates the way he keeps her from her friends or, worse, tells them things that makes her sound mental. He's the one making her mental, like when he says that if she doesn't love him, then she must be a slut for hooking up.

Didn't her parents think he was sketchy? Her mom asked her like two questions after they met him, and then she totally let it drop. Dad has to heal from being nearly killed, so there's that. But it also feels as if her mom and dad are both of them done with kids. Neither has attended a single meet this season—you'd think an old guy who almost dies might start going to practices, maybe even ask her about her clarinet, whose case she hasn't un-buckled all fall. What started by accident continues out of something like spite. Evidently Dad's too busy turning weird (though there's always time for grilling). He wears tight bike shorts or leggings without a shirt, and his hair is curly and ponytail-long. With his round glasses and belly, he looks like the Tie-Dye King in the card game they played at the beach.

Will had promised to help her, and all he's done is send a link to a site where she can practice vocabulary and feed the poor *concurrently*. Supposedly, each correct answer prompts a spon-sor to send another twenty grains of rice to a food bank, if you buy that. She has no idea why a sponsor would contribute food in response to her choosing the right synonym, or *locution*, but she dutifully logs on each day and does a thousand grains. She pre-tends Will is quizzing her. While she's at it, she imagines herself graduating a year early and escaping to college.

Should she try to find Dad? Should she call Mom, interrupt-ing her at work with nothing more than a bad feeling? At the beach house, they'd been this TV family for maybe the first time ever, if you counted Kyra as one of their own. Both brothers had been willing to play pool with their little sister, umpteen games, and they didn't seem embarrassed to be with their parents either. It was her job to rack up the balls and, if they were playing stripes and solids, arrange them in order. She knew summer would come to an end, but still she blames the lightning for all that has happened. It hit her dad, and the whole family flew apart. The lightning knocked her into Natalio's arms.

For a fraction of a second she wishes the lightning had killed him. The rest of them would have stayed huddled together in their horrible shared tragedy that she shouldn't even be imagining. She would have worn her purple Lettie Gooch dress to the funeral. Makeup and mules, not just flip-flops. She would have written a poem to read at the service, or maybe played "You Are My Sunshine" on her clarinet, if she didn't break down in the middle of her presentation, her *eulogy*. That late in August, everyone would just be getting back from vacation, and the news would have made the Fitzgerald crowd uncomfortable, like baby poop in the neighborhood pool. Daisy would have been there and probably Madison, too. Brooke would have cried like crazy for her dad, maybe so hard Sebastian would have been moved to comfort her. His mom had died in a car crash back in sixth grade; maybe Sebastian's father would have put his arm around her mother and told her he was there for her. That's how selfish Brooke is and how cowardly. If she were as gutsy as Saxy, she could cut herself, rather than blaming everyone else for her pain.

19

WALKING ON HOT COALS

Dad must have forgotten he was supposed to pick her up after test prep. Ms. Mayhue's boarding-school pitch kept her late, but if her dad had shown, Brooke doesn't think he'd have given up and gone home without her. Probobably, a call is in order, though she doesn't want to be seen on his unsmart phone. She walks past the car-pool lane—the diplomatic limos make it look more like a valet lineup. There's even a Hummer, which must be handy for the blood sport, Brooke thinks, the *tauromachy*, of the Whole Foods parking lot. She disparages the Fitzgerald crowd even as she wishes she had a real phone and a ride. Or cab fare, which is so lush. There are bus stops every two blocks, except she's never taken a city bus home. What if she boards a 32 instead of a 23 or the driver takes a rogue turn and she's *jettisoned* to Anacostia? She doesn't think she'd be that passive, to sit there while the monuments clicked by and they crossed the river.

Talk about ovary action—she's pretty sure the blue Ride Ons can't even cross the DC border. She pictures the bus wheels locking, like the shopping carts that aren't allowed out of the parking lots. She'd ride the Metro, with its laid-down tracks, but the trail home from the station reeks of a slasher movie. Would she dare to walk solo through that dark, drippy tunnel? The effort of thinking herself home wears her down, *enervates* her, she thinks, and gives a nod to Ricky for teaching her the proper use of that word.

It's actually a relief not to see Dad out here in his spandex, unless she makes her way home only to open the front door and find him dead. She occasionally has this feeling, a *presentiment*, that he's going to do something nutso. Like the tattoo, which she knows, from the murmured arguments coming through the walls late at night, disgusts her mom. And him telling her to go out the window. He keeps scuffing himself up in his barbecue pit, and he's talked enough about walking on hot coals that she suspects he's tried it. When he makes those big fires, those *conflagrations*, the embers glow for about two days.

All she has to do is ask any driver if she's getting on the right bus—what is her problem? She'd have thought having a boy-friend would be a confidence booster, but now she second-guesses everything. Even Coach notices. If she weren't such an *inverte-brate*, she'd forget Will's request and tell Mom and Dad about his call. She could blame Mom's intelligent disobedience shtick, which seems more of a stretch with every repetition: just how *does* a people-pleasing dog get up the gumption to ignore a com-mand? She stretches out her arms, as if to prevent her brother from falling into an open manhole, from behaving *injudiciously*.

Maybe she's using Will as a human shield—she should go to Mom with her own problems. She doesn't trust Saxy not to share it all with Natalio, even though he says the three of them have such a great bond. She misses her phone—is it possible Natalio took it? To stave off paranoia, she spends her waiting time invent-ing vocabularic ways to ask her stupid question. "Do your *pere-grinations* include *immobilizing* this modern *charabanc* at Seneca Lane?"

The Ride On arrives, lowering itself to curb level with a heav-ing sigh, the way Sparkle used to collapse, and she imagines the bus turning a few circles before curling up in a parking space and dimming its headlights for the night, its eight puffy tires tucked underneath as the supermodels featured on the bus ad all snug-gle together in a puppy heap. But then the door unfolds to reveal a bus driver with yellow teeth and a braid of dreads as thick as the ropes on a whaling ship. Brooke imagines that he can tell that she's usually driven, belted into a heated seat, her ears plugged with the sounds of her custom playlist. "Do you, like, go to Seneca Lane?" she asks.

"Oh, Missy, I do," he says, and laughs. "Like it or not, I go there."

She hustles down the aisle to perch on the edge of a seat, mortified. On the other hand, she so did it. She's getting herself home on a roach coach that isn't nearly as skanky as she remembers. See, Ms. Mayhue, I have some independence; you're just jealous that I have a boyfriend. As she argues her point, the bus takes a sharp corner, nearly knocking her into the aisle, and it's almost as if Ms. Mayhue were shaking her by the shoulders. Something about being off-balance—a rare sensation for Brooke—and righting herself makes her realize that her teacher is paying attention rather than accusing her. "Use your good sense, Brooke," Mayhue had said last week, and then today she gave her the boarding-school brochure.

Shame and relief heat her up in equal measure. If she knew which bus to take back to school, she'd go looking for Ms. Mayhue; as it is, the bus is about to break a record getting to Seneca Lane. "You're next, Missy," the driver calls behind him. Who are all these strangers watching out for her? It's her parents' responsibility to make sure she's safe. When she unfolds the exit door, she still has to walk four blocks in the spitting rain, which suits her mood. It *aggrieves* her that no one at home nagged her to wear a raincoat. A standard puddle turns out to be a total foot soaker, which she so deserves. How shivery will she let herself get before she puts up the hood on her hoodie? A big icy drop falls on the back, the *nape*, of her neck and sluices down her spine all the way to her butt crack, an absurdity that would be funny if she had someone to share it with, to *commiserate* with. If she even said "butt crack" to Natalio, he'd be all over her, which is one more reason to feel sorry for herself.

She keeps coming back to Will's creepy pronouncement—"You are on your own"—which may be the meanest thing he's ever said to her. It used to be they'd horse around between swim practices—she'd flatten herself on the water so he could flip her pancake-style. She thinks of that sweet fun every time she sails off the beam, when she gets enough lift to flip and twist before planting her feet into the mat. The *whoosh* of a safe landing followed by the crowd's roar is like surfacing to Will's applause.

She wishes that both boys were home. Even if they just cranked up the stereo or ordered her around, she'd welcome the irritation, the *perturbation*. Not to mention the interaction. Dad is there, but he generally spends his time rearranging rocks or woodpiles. He's like those *tonsured* monks who rake patterns in their sand gardens all day.

Cold, dirty water seeps in, *permeates* her Converses; her wet toes rub against each other in pre-blister mode. Because of gym team, she has two nights' worth of homework, so she can honestly tell Natalio she's not ignoring him. Mud fills the construction site of yet another house tripling in size, despite everyone on TV bemoaning the end of money. Is that true for regular families, and if so, how expensive is boarding school? She knows how much jeans cost, not so much groceries or cable. The way she figures it, her parents already pay her room and board at home, so that money would just be aimed a different way.

On an occasional island of grass there is still a little cottage, a *bungalow* where a bent-over lady lives. Mom says she knew the economy had tanked when Mrs. Russell complained that real estate vultures no longer checked in on her. Mom said, "I guess even vultures are company," which Brooke thinks about a lot.

By the time she gets to her front door, she is so chilled that it hurts to wedge her fingers into her wet jeans pocket for her key. She unlocks the dead bolt but has to push against a stiff wind to get the door open. She drops her backpack on the marble floor as papers and mail swirl in the entry hall in a mini-twister. Okay, that's spooky. On a day like this one, you'd think the in-house pyro would have a big blaze going in the fireplace.

"Daddy?" she calls out. His doughnut is on the living-room couch, but he's not sitting on it. The back door is wide open, the screen door isn't locked, and all the kitchen windows have been hiked up—a breeze blows so strong that it has swept papers out from under refrigerator magnets. She sniffs, hoping there's been a minor kitchen fire or that her dad's airing out one of his experiments. Had he roasted peppers over the open burners again and forgotten them, again? The burners are all off, as is the oven. Surveying the kitchen, Brooke registers something through the keyhole office window and sees her dad slumped at Mom's computer. Ohmygod, ohmygod, what if he's dead? And if not, maybe she shouldn't be alone with him! He used to talk about people's wiring; meanways, his has been completely fried.

Years of gymnastics have turned fear into a pose, and Brooke freezes with her sternum raised and neck outstretched. Eventually she can detect that his chin resting on his bare chest is rising and falling. And so he isn't dead. She enters the alcove, nervous that except for the burn glove, he might be naked, but he's wearing his goofy bike shorts and one sock as well. The laptop shows a turkey splayed flat, and two disembodied hands massage the cavities with butter before trussing it with string as if corseted. Embarrassed, Brooke looks away from the cooking porn.

When will he turn back into her dad? She wants him to put on his khakis and black blazer bearing one of his lame lapel pins (*Dare to Care* or *You May Be Right*) and go to the office, where he is the wizard doctor with the long waiting list of kids who need his help. She doesn't exactly know what to do with him—is he sick or is this what he's going to be like?

"Daddy," she whispers near his face. "Maybe you want to take a nap."

"Time's up!" he says, startled. He passes the back of his hand across his drooly lips. "Don't sneak up on me like that. Jesus." Once he takes a look at her, he asks, "Are your clothes wet?"

"It's raining."

"I know that. Where's your ladybug coat?"

So his long-term memory's afoot. "I outgrew it," she says. She doesn't have the heart to tell him that the ladybug gear, complete with spotted boots and umbrella, was a kindergarten getup. "Meanways, everything's wide open."

He scoots himself away from the desk. "The house was stuffy." They spread out, sealing one window after the other. "It's better now. Fresher, don't you think?"

He would not want to hear what she thinks, which is that he left the windows up hoping for a full-blown lightning storm.

"Is *meanways* a word?" he asks.

"Probobably," she says.

He cups her palms together, keeping his gloved hand under his good one, and huffs hot breath onto her hands, as he did when they used to ice-skate at Cabin John. "This would have been a good day for an umbrella." He fetches the throw from the couch for her, ignoring or forgetting that the faux fur is for decoration. She used to be his Babbling Brooke, Brookeworm, his Little Slug. *Does he have those memories?* she wonders, and it makes her quivery to think what he may have lost.

A pile of papers splays at their feet. "Oops," he says. He bends over to shuffle them back together; then, when he has a semblance of a stack, he drops the whole lot on the floor.

Brooke laughs at the blatant anarchy. His way with board games used to blow her seven-year-old mind. He'd combine Candyland and Sorry or use the board as a roof for families of plastic pieces. "We can do that?" she'd ask, and he'd say, "It's a *game*, and we're *playing*!" Monopoly might become a village square, complete with a jail, four train stations, and a jewelry store. There was a lot going on in that box: money and deeds, green cabins and red McMansions, metal figurines: the thimble and hat were Mom and Dad; the dog was the dog; the race car and ship were the boys; the shoe was Brooke. That's not how Mom played.

Dad's recent rebellion has some of that charm, but there's an unsettling aspect, as if he's lost the rules rather than changed them. His shorts look like the men's old-timey bathing suits in the film Mr. Holt showed them of life along the Mississippi. Her dad isn't far from growing a big handlebar mustache and parting his hair down the middle, as if the lightning blew him back in time a hundred years or so.

He ushers her over to the Big Board. The cat is weaving in a figure eight around Brooke's legs, so she lifts Mittsy into her arms. The three of them stare at the board, where the family used to seek guidance. Back when Dad saw patients a couple of nights a week and Mom made an effort to get to their events, when Ricky (red) had swimming, soccer, and the magazine, while Will (green) had swimming, track, or music, and Brooke (purple) had swimming, sleepovers, and gymnastics, the Big Board ruled. Brooke looks at the blank squares—there isn't enough going on to confuse anyone. There is, in fact, one purple reminder on to-day's square: "Brooke @ 5:15!"

"I was supposed to meet you at school."

"The bus is right there."

"But I was, wasn't I?"

"Mom is sure I'll get abducted if I walk by the park," she says stupidly. Sure enough, he pulls the stole tight around her and the cat, who leaps to the floor. So he remembers Scarlett, the whole reason no girl walks alone in their neighborhood.

"I should have met you," he says. "I was ordering our turkeys, and I guess I fell asleep."

"You're not going to get a live one, are you?"

Owen laughs. "Can you imagine the neighbors? They called the cops on my rooster."

He's proud of that dinner, which she could barely eat. Why people have to know where their food comes from is beyond her. Brooke asks, "How many turkeys are you getting?"

"Just two. You have to order the fresh ones ahead of time. Some of the frozen ones are from last Thanksgiving! If you be-lieve the Whole Foods website."

"They're so preachy!" she whines. "People can't just buy eggs. They must have organic, free-range, hormone-free brown eggs."

"From happy chickens," he says, "with fulfilling hobbies and raincoats, like ours will have someday."

"You think everything there is stone-ground." She knows he's playing, but this isn't the kind of fun they used to have. "Sebas-tian's dad owns Whole Foods *stock*. So they're this huge corpo-ration, right? They act like they grow every morsel themselves, and their superiority complex is as bad as their fear factor: big farms poison people, white bread is worse than candy bars. Then when we shop, they have samples of steak and chocolate cake—"

"You gotta eat," he says.

"Eat *authentically* for Thanksgiving—as if the Indians taught the Pilgrims to buy organic."

Her dad is grinning like an idiot. Maybe he is an idiot now. He walks around practically naked, and he can't decide whether he's going to stay a shrink. He's become a specialist in cooking meat over fire, like a caveman or a Texan.

"All the cereals suck," she says, "and the breads weigh a ton."

"Bread with heft—you pay extra for that. If it's not stale in two days, it gets moldy."

"Well, now I'm sold."

"It's one of life's many paradoxes," he says, as if he's hit on a universal truth. "That rough, ripe flavor you guys complain about, that's what it's all about. Meanwhile, the way to make food last, which makes it cheaper, is to smooth it out or add handfuls of preservatives."

"This from the man who dispenses chemicals to children." Out of the corner of her eye, she checks on him, and the smile slides off his face. And yet she doesn't stop. She says, "'Eat your spelt-flour toast and wash your Ritalin down with fresh-squeezed mango juice.'"

Owen grips the kitchen table and falls into a chair, crying out when he hits the unpadded seat.

"Daddy!" Brooke drops the blanket in a heap. His face is as round and red as a cartoon thermometer. His nostrils flair.

"That was harsh," he says.

So he's pissed, as opposed to having a stroke. Brooke stands there, her elbows drawn to her sides like folded wings. She'd hug him, except she doesn't want to touch his tattoo or glove. She says, "I've got a lot of homework," and, grabbing her backpack, flees upstairs.

Even when she gets out of her clammy clothes and into her pajama pants, she is shivery and sad. One whole summer, her dad was on those split-screen news shows, pitted against opponents who attacked him for drugging children. She couldn't have said anything he hasn't heard before. Not to mention that he was totally provoking her. But what if she says the thing that sends him over the edge? Although she's grateful that he didn't die from the lightning, he isn't so alive to them these days. Except for their moment in the window seat and this one, he's been so damn content—so *impervious*—that he's like the yoga teacher up the street whose smug demeanor makes Brooke mental.

Owen retrieves the throw and sinks into the sofa on his doughnut. For the first time since his accident, he is cold. He's barely been aware of his daughter—he couldn't even bring himself to remember to pick her up at school—meanwhile, she has just laid bare the logical fallacy of his profession: he medicates children to help them act naturally.

How did he justify this, pre-lightning? Inattentive or socially inept kids used to get a kick in the pants to get them going. Plenty of them were also warehoused. He had been proud to pioneer more humane and effective treatments. But now he thinks of Constantine, whose morning regimen he's just expanded. A multivitamin as well as a fish-oil supplement, Zyrtec for his hives, Strattera for focus and hyperactivity, Zoloft for depression and obsessive-compulsive disorder, and, when the kid was flattened by peer pressure, the atypical antipsychotic Risperdal. How much can a brain take, no matter how challenged its chemistry?

Owen pictures Constantine, his palm full of pills, absent-mindedly manipulating a single tablet between his thumb and forefinger. Here is the gesture Owen remembers thinking had been lost, just before he flew into the air that late August afternoon. Peering into the parking meter as smooth as Constantine's shaved head and about the same height, Owen had spent a moment wondering whether he'd passed on the coin dexterity he'd learned feeding meters. Turns out, his professional legacy is teaching a generation of children even finer motor skills: the ability to pluck numerous pills, each smaller than any coin, and guide them into their own mouths.

His has been a quest to buy these kids time; otherwise, he would never have prescribed antipsychotics, amphetamines, tranquilizers. Time to focus, time to regroup, metered by a dosage he closely monitors. But every tenth kid slips a pill through his trusting lips and is thrown for a loop, tossed into an electrical brainstorm. How does Owen feel about this in light of what he's been through, in defense of what Brooke has pointed out?

"Mom, are you home?" a deep, wounded voice calls from the front of the house. "Dad? Brooke?"

Owen lets the faux fur fall from around his shoulders. He knows that voice, but not that uncertainty. "Willy?" he yells, pushing several times against the sofa cushions to get to his feet.

His son tentatively enters the living room. On this dark and rainy day, aviator sunglasses mask his face, and his bandaged nose is decidedly crooked. Will sets his duffel down as if it were an infant, and then he steps forward to tuck himself into his father, who holds on to him for a good long while. Will is trembling, *like an addict*, Owen instinctively thinks as he pulls him to his gut. He can feel ribs where there used to be muscles, and either rain or his son's own tears wet Owen's bare chest. Has it been only months? Will looks nothing like himself, nothing like his twin.

"You made it!" Brooke squeals from the landing, and she pumps her fist the way cheerleaders do. There are all sorts of things wrong with her brother, but he found his way back to them. His boxers are showing big-time over his droopy jeans, which look like they've been dragged behind a car. *Bedraggled*— she comprehends the word rather than just repeating it to herself. Also *dissipated*, because a part of him has disappeared, vanished. *Evanesced!* Terrible, appropriate words are coming together to describe this beloved wreck in their sacred home, *desecrating* it. Will points at her shirt, Penn, one of the ways she keeps him close, wearing her brother's proxy to keep him *proximate*. "Willy," she sighs.

This homecoming is more than Will deserves. He treasures their ignorance—*Sure, you're glad to see me now!*—and swallows his bitter reflux to taste their genuine, unrelenting love. His father has aged in a flabby, gone-to-seed way. His exposed foot and large patches of skin are shiny pink, and he's added another two inches to his gray hair, which falls in loose curls on his back.

"You look good," Will says. "It's good to see you." Then he points at the lightning inked from his dad's shoulder to his glove. "What the flux?"

His father leads him to the hallway mirror, where they stand side by side, Will nearly a head taller. Will removes his sunglasses to reveal yellow, red, and purple bruises, as if his eyes were two setting suns.

"What the flux yourself, Willy?"

"I screwed up," he says. "Big-time."

The compassion in his father's eyes about kills him, and that's just looking in the mirror. How will he be able to look either of his parents in the face? Will sees the new scar worming its way beneath his dad's chin, and the arm that isn't tattooed is badly mottled. Of the two of them, Will wonders, who is more damaged?

"Whatever happened, you're home now," his father says. "You're safe here with us."

20

BREAK YOUR MOTHER'S BACK

In the little office off the kitchen, Toni is staring at the laptop, her cell phone, and the landline. She could bring any one of them into focus, depending on which glasses she selects. She's trying to decide if she should wait to hear the whole story or start calling in favors. Penn's president is on her voice dial; if she speaks his name, her cell will take it from there. Did she use up her chits with him when Will got accepted? She'll simply confess to what she does and doesn't know, except that she'll be able to choose her words more carefully in writing. She exchanges her reading glasses for her computer ones only to switch back: e-mail leaves too much of a trail. She can keep it together for a phone call, and if she can't, the man has dealt with hysterical parents before. He's been one himself—she had coached him on how to manage that information in his job interviews.

She reverts to her regular glasses, which are for the big picture. Probably she should buy yet another pair, with lenses that incorporate all three distances: progressive lenses, they call them now, instead of the old-ladyish trifocals.

She sees bare trees out in the yard, evidence that seasons change, new presidents get elected, the stock market rises, falls, and tries to recover. All along the way, it rains on the just and the unjust. That's the big-picture view she should take rather than the narrow, petty one she's homing in on: Owen's stone pit, un-raked leaves, and *chickens*! She blames Owen's lightning round for everything falling apart, which may not be fair.

Theirs has been a charmed life, allowing her to draw from great reserves when she needed the strength to enter Owen's hospital room that cataclysmic night. Yesterday, when she tried to enter the living room after dinner, she wasn't even welcome. Will was leaning forward, earnestly talking to his father by the fire. From where she stood, she heard the tail end of a grocery list of drugs: Sarafem, Pristiq, Cymbalta. "My god, Willy," Owen said. "That combination could easily kill you guys."

"Actually, my friend is—" Will stopped mid-sentence. "Dad," he said, receding into the cushions.

Owen shifted protectively in front of Will. "How about you give us some time?" he asked Toni, although it wasn't actually a question.

Perhaps Owen's compromised state makes him a better confidant. They should all be under the kind of care he used to provide. Meanwhile, she's not sure which is more painful, Will's covertness or his contempt: although his nose is twisted like an S, he wouldn't even let her take him to the plastic surgeon. He's been sucked down a black hole, and Ricky's out of touch as well. For god's sake, they are a *family*. Which brings her full circle. She tells herself that whatever happened, she doesn't have to call Penn's president. It's a week until Thanksgiving, when so many college students crash and burn. Will's precious bike was vandalized, he got into a scuffle, and he came running home—these things happen.

As a mother, she knows Will overly well. People credit him with encouraging his twin, yet he was capable of encouraging Ricky into oncoming traffic: Check if the door's unlocked. Can the teacher see that far? You're only *borrowing* the computer. And she's also seen the ways Will outwits himself, arguing for two wrongs to make a right. Owen hasn't witnessed that firsthand. It occurs to her that she may have hit on the reason Will is avoiding her, as crushing as it is to be excluded. Toni tilts her glasses up off her cheek so her tear falls into her coffee mug, an odd but efficient move she's sure Ricky would appreciate.

What a fragile ecosystem a family is. That's the lesson to take from their ordeal. One kid is in another kid's shade, and either or both may flourish or suffer because of that; one parent nearly dies, and all hell breaks loose.

Toni leaves her little office for the kitchen. Out the back window, a spiderweb shines with dew, and she studies the web's center because Ricky once told her that every spider family weaves its telltale badge dead center, a unique pattern of identity. The outskirts of the web are woven for adaptability.

She hates to think they've lost this fall's tuition, that Will wasted it. They could buy a new car *every semester* for what college costs—she'll have to get over that so she can help him. *These things happen*, she repeats to herself to keep from mentally checking the price tag: a semester thrown away, and what else? Owen has already mentioned rehab and lawyer's fees, so there's plenty, and it's probably worse. Or not—for all she knows, the "friend" Will is purportedly worried about might actually exist. Maybe she's selling her son short, and he's come home after a self-sacrificing act of loyalty.

Although Toni heard the car-pool van around six, Brooke walks into the kitchen, still dressed in her robe and slippers. "What are you doing here?" Toni asks.

" 'Good morning, Brooke,' " her daughter prompts. " 'Sleep well?' "

"Good morning, sweetheart. I thought you had practice this morning."

"I'm exhausted."

Toni raises her coffee mug as if blessing Brooke with it; her daughter painted the mug for her years ago. "I was expecting your father. He usually shows up around now."

Brooke's eyes dart nervously around. "Where is he? And where's Willy?"

"Sleeping, I suppose." Toni touches Brooke's cheek and then her forehead. "Everything all right?" She wishes she'd rescheduled when Estrellita canceled their coffee date.

"My coach is psycho."

"They have to be," Toni says, though why on earth would she side with Coach Rayburn? He *is* psycho. "Even when he's being harsh to you, he goes on and on to me about your wonderful qualities: 'Her *balançoire* is coming along, and once we get more exemplitude on her Borden—' "

"More *amplitude* is what he said—last *year*. I had to get more amplitude on my Borden."

If not feverish, Brooke is obviously flustered; her birthmark is blotchy pink from her jaw all the way down the side of her neck. It reminds Toni of the weather-predicting knickknack she had as a girl, a crystal horse painted with something that changed from pink to purple when a storm was due.

"Is there a meet this weekend, honey? Maybe Daddy and I can both come."

"I guess," Brooke says. That's all she needs when she's supposed to be concentrating—her parents in the stands. Except that's what she's been wanting for months. Yet another example in her life of everything and its opposite being true at the same time. "Mommy?"

"Yes?"

What should Brooke say about Will's calls from last week? She's not sure if she's protecting him or withholding protection. That goes for her dad, too. She doesn't want to be part of her mother's daily disappointment and distrust. "Nothing."

"Okay. I'm right here," her mother says as she leaves. Typical, but it turns out she's just choosing a mug and a tea bag for Brooke; once she pours water from the kettle, she pulls up the chair next to her.

Since middle school, both parents have been eyeing her for gymnastics fallout like bulimia and coach abuse. Little do they know the spotlight is the least of their worries. In the spotlight, people *see* her, whereas, since August, she's been invisible. She was an easy target for Natalio, who plans to keep her invisible. He's wrong about Sebastian, anyway. They'd been comparing times, and then he'd just reached for her arm to take her pulse. It sped up as he took it, but she hadn't asked for his attention. Natalio says she has to prove her attachment to him, but she thinks the only thing doing it without a condom will prove is ignorance.

She looks out the windows, so clean they're transparent, and she hears herself say, "I found a boarding school in Rhode Island."

"For next summer?" her mother asks. "Not a circus camp, I hope, where they teach trapeze and dangling from ten-story ropes."

"For school. They take people midyear. The application's in my backpack, and Ms. Mayhue says she'll write me a recommendation letter."

"*The* Ms. Mayhue?" Her mother looks way down into her mug, as if she might dive in.

"It's too weird for me here, too competitive."

"Honey, you're doing great at Fitzgerald—your grades are good, you made the team last year as a sophomore."

You have a boyfriend, her mother doesn't say. Brooke goes from picking at her cuticles to peeling them. "Coach knows people there, too; he says the school might even offer scholarships."

"I'm not thinking about the money," her mother says, though Brooke can tell that she is now, the way she pushes her fingers along the surface of the table as if she's counting change. She says, "In two years, you'll be going to college. What's the hurry?"

Brooke wraps a paper napkin around her thumb. "You know on Back to School Night, when I was alone with Dad?"

"Yes." Cocking her head in suspicion sends a shooting pain up Toni's neck.

"Something kind of happened."

Kind of? Is it possible that Brooke thinks *home* is too weird, too competitive? Wherever this is going, Toni is sure they can't possibly afford boarding school. Money aside, she can't afford to let Brooke go.

"Well, you know what happened," Brooke says. "But something I haven't told you. I mean, in the end, it was kind of a lucky night, that Dad just cut his chin and all."

"Lucky." Toni sighs. Lucky the lightning didn't kill Owen, lucky he wasn't cooked from the inside out, lucky his brain is still responsive. But lucky is having three healthy kids who want to talk to you and keep in touch with one another. Lucky is loving your spouse after far too much familiarity, and your spouse giving it right back to you.

"After you left, I asked Daddy what happened to him at the

beach, and he couldn't really talk about it. I could tell he wanted to. But he said maybe he could show me."

"Show you what?" In the hope that she can mask the trembling in her hands, Toni presses them together.

"He said the experience was *ecstatic*, and he took me up to your bedroom. He asked me not to tell you this part, but I should, shouldn't I?"

"You can tell me anything." Toni inhales until her ribs widen with the effort. She's filling her lungs to capacity, the way infants do before screaming with all their might. She has never been so frightened in all her life. If, while ranting about his ecstatic experience, Owen made one lascivious step toward their daughter, if he unbuttoned a single button on her blouse, Toni will blow the roof off with her screaming. She'll scream to high holy heaven and then she will be forced to hunt him down and drive a stake through his heart.

Brooke says, "He talked about defenestration, too, and I even corrected him on that one. He kept saying he wanted me to feel for myself what he'd been through."

Guilt is seeping into Brooke like the water filling her sneakers when she walked home in the rain, like the blood from her chewed thumb soaking into the napkin. Her mother's hands are smashed together as if in prayer. She wants her mother to know that she kept her father out of trouble for a little while and that he yelled at her—he never did say he was sorry—but she also feels bad for using him as an excuse.

"He took you to our bedroom . . ." her mother prompts her.

"Yeah, we went upstairs. Before that, we were out on the patio, but Dad said the bedroom was better, your and his bedroom. We sat on the bed and he told me my birthmark was pretty." That part chokes her up.

"It's all right," her mother says.

Brooke wishes her mom had agreed with her dad's remark—she probably hates her birthmark as much as Brooke does. Since middle school, she's wanted to ask if she could have it removed or at least lightened.

"Honey." Her mother wags a finger in her face. "Daddy told you to keep a secret . . ."

"He just asked me not to tell," she says, hearing the difference between what she's trying to say and what her mother is hearing. It's like that moment in Ms. Mayhue's class when they have enough evidence to figure things out together, except the shock of discovery in this case is like an actual shock. *You've got the power in this relationship*, Ms. Mayhue had coached her, talking about Natalio.

Brooke is losing it. Her mother has expected so little of her lately, she doesn't want to disappoint her. It's her nature to please her mom—could that possibly be the right thing to do here? "We sat on the window seat, and we looked at the sky, but he said we needed to be higher." She feels as if she's wading into the water fully clothed, the way they used to in lifesaving.

"It's not your fault," her mother says through a tiny puckered mouth. Down the side of her forehead, a deep crease extends from her hairline to her unplucked eyebrow, almost like a gash.

"He said that what happened to him had to do with being above everything."

"What did he ask you to do, honey?"

Brooke pinches the fabric of her pajama pants and pulls it away from her thighs. *You can tell me anything*, her mother had said. Either way, she's going to be mad, though right now she sounds impatient, which is so familiar it's almost reassuring. Just then, a scratching, warbling protest is heard, followed by a testy rejoinder in the same garbled language. Brooke looks back toward the little office, as does her mom, before she realizes the squabble is taking place outside. She's trying to solve that puzzle—cats? construction workers?—when her mother shrieks.

"Fucking chickens!" she yells, and Brooke instinctively scolds, "Mom!" as one bird flaps into view above the windowsill and then another. She and her mom scoot their chairs far enough back to see the tussle outside, chickens squawking and slapping to beat the band. The birds can't get airborne. They can get just enough height to take turns flying into one another's faces. They're morons, and her father's affection for their simplemindedness reins her in.

"Oh, Mommy," she says. "He threw the window wide open and told me to go outside. He said if I did flips off the beams, I shouldn't be afraid of walking along the tree. I grabbed his shirt;

I think I even said it wasn't safe." Saved from lying, she bursts into tears.

"Let me get this straight." Her mom is crying, too. "That's what Daddy did—he tried to get you to climb onto the roof with him?"

She makes it sound as if it were nothing. "He *yelled* at me, Mommy—'Get out here!' But I wouldn't do it. Really, it seemed like a bad choice." She yips. "And it *was* bad—he fell! I'm sorry, Mommy."

Everyone falls. Toni hugs her darling daughter as they console each other. "It's not your fault, none of this is. You did all the right things. Oh, sweetheart, you've been all on your own." They cling together, weaving from side to side the way they used to when Brooke was little. Regret and relief seesaw within Toni: her poor girl is prepared to exile herself, having seen her father's crazy, dangerous behavior firsthand. That night they were alone, he walked out of the second story, and Brooke had to run downstairs and open the front door to whatever shape he was in. She had to call 911.

"You are such a star," Toni says. Brooke, who can turn one-handed cartwheels and vault herself into the air from the thin, sanded edge of a balance beam, chose not to listen to her beloved, imbalanced father. There's intelligent disobedience for you! What would Toni do if, in an effort to please, her only daughter had tiptoed along a rickety oak branch and, stepping on uneven and buckling bark, plummeted to the unforgiving earth below?

"She told you," Owen says, startling mother and daughter from their embrace.

Toni's still rocking in her chair, but as soon as Brooke is released, she makes a break for it.

"Hey, Daddy," she says on her way out.

"Bye-bye." Owen waves. He plops down on his doughnut-cushioned chair at the head of the table. "If you remember, I did say the whole thing was a mistake. I admitted to that."

"You're the one who can't remember shit," Toni hisses. "Do you remember telling our daughter to keep a secret from me? Do you know what mothers imagine in a case like that?" She grabs a tea towel and flicks her wrist. As she slaps it at her husband, the cotton towel cracks like a bullwhip. She hopes it hurts like that, too.

"Stop it!" He covers his face with his good arm. "What are you doing?"

Nimble as a bee, she stings his waist, his ribs, his arm— whipping up and down the length of his tattoo. She stands there with the limp towel, either stunned or preparing to start all over again.

In Toni's moment of hesitation Owen moves out of his chair and gets behind her. He wraps his arms across her chest, a technique he teaches parents for holding fast to their impulsive, dangerous children. "Toni, Toni, Toni," he clucks.

"You're lucky this isn't a skillet!" Well-pinned, she can barely flip the towel over her shoulder to hit his. For three months she's been coddling him—whether her heart has been in it or not—as he's been wielding a pick and a shovel, lugging stones and mortar, hewing an ax through a woodpile. She's been caregiving her ass off, struggling with his potential recklessness and deceit. She's been wondering if she could forgive him for fucking Will's girlfriend— but what if he kissed Brooke with his tongue, led her off the roof to a crippling fall, tried to indoctrinate her into his cult?

Owen's grip becomes a hug, and he rubs his cheek against her shoulder. "You'd beat me senseless?"

"You're already senseless! What sense have you made of anything? You asked her to keep a secret, Owen. She had to say, 'Daddy told me not to tell you, but—'"

"I was a little mixed up; my judgment was off." He releases her, and they both fall into their respective chairs.

"*The roof!*" Toni whines. "You opened a window and told your daughter to jump." She takes family life personally, unlike Owen—has that been her mistake? She's taken family life to her very heart, which every one of them has treated carelessly.

"She wasn't even tempted," Owen says. "She has your good sense. And her own."

Toni releases her hair as if giving up. She says, "She wants to go to boarding school. She wants to leave us."

"Go away?" Owen's eyebrows join together, as if to confer, and then he says, "No, that's not right. We need her here."

A thump sounds overhead, the thud of Will coming down from the top bunk to plant his big feet on the bedroom floor. The tiny earthquake rattles two goblets somewhere in the china cabinet, tremors that Toni feels deep in her chest.

"Dawn of a new day," Owen says. He rises and kisses the top of Toni's head, and she knows without a word that he's going to their son. All Owen has told her about Will's dilemma is that he's taken some alarming drugs this semester and that things got ugly—those are Owen's words: "Things got ugly."

Just this morning she'd been visualizing their family within a web, where each member weaves strong, supple connections one to another and out to the world. That seems wishful thinking in light of their trauma. She lifts the fulgurite that serves as their napkin holder. The ragged stick feels something like a thick piece of coral, as coarse as sand, because that's all it is, sand with a backbone of glass. It wasn't enough for a bolt of lightning to strike the earth; the spike had to keep going, driving itself into the sand to create this fragile sculpture in its own image. *And so it goes*, she thinks, with regard to her family—the lightning fused the five of them together, and what they've got here is a tenuous and brittle union. They've lost what give and elasticity had been theirs, so that any movement among them means snapping free. She's been devoted to Owen, who seems a little less likely to fracture the family—this week, anyway—and she would be relieved except that one, two, all three of her children are eager to break it, break another little piece of her heart now.

21

MOUNT OLYMPUS

Richard's been watching the clock for the official end of Dr. Clifton's office hours, after which he closes her big oaken door against any intruders. He'd sidle up to her if she weren't hiding way behind her enormous desk, but she is where she is, and so he sits across the room on the sofa. He wore his striped shirt today because once she'd noticed his abs in this shirt. "What about going to Turkey—have you ever spent Thanksgiving *in* Turkey?"

"Funny," Lucy Clifton says. "We'll be in Greece the entire spring—you and Daniel and I can do Turkey then. Aren't you needed at home?"

His feelings about home are even more mixed-up than his feelings about her. And her husband, Daniel. He slips off his shoes and, stretching the length of her couch, puts his long feet up on her armrest. He listens to the *whist, whist!* of her red pen, which used to bury his papers but now praises them. The freshman paper she's grading must be worse than most, because she's done with it so fast—she slaps the offensive paper facedown on the desk. With the next one, she settles in, allowing him time to figure out her shirt, whose inside-out and ripped features are finely tuned to get that fit. She moves a stack of books to block his view.

"You're distracting me," she says. "Go home and let them laud the hero in their midst."

He's pretty sure it won't play out that way. She's taught mythology long enough to know that there *are* no stories of sons reviving their fathers or twins sharing the gods' favors. Being home will no doubt return him to his tractable self, as set as his place at the kitchen table. "How about Thanksgiving in New York: you, me, Lacy, and Will? Independent codependent study."

"Daniel is bound to notice he's not on the guest list."

"It's about twins—Project Gemini. But if you feel that way, we can leave Lacy and Will off, too."

"You're becoming insufferable. Don't forget how many were brought down by pride."

"Daniel knows how I feel about him," he says, fishing.

"Mutual," Lucy says. "You should hear him, always: 'Should we call Richard? I'll get a ticket for Richard. Let's see if Richard's free.'"

"I'm free for Thanksgiving."

"I already told him you're going home. As your adviser, that's what I advise."

As his adviser, she's the queen of mixed messages. She's rubbed his shirtless shoulders, napped next to him (with Daniel on his other side), and has lately made a habit of kissing him on the cheek. Now she's sending him back to his family of origin.

The truth is, home hits him in waves. He feels heartless about being so out of touch. He's eager for details of his dad's progress, and he misses Mom. But when the waves pile on, they'll probably pound him into the ground. He'll be reduced to Ricky the meek, Ricky the sidekick.

"Speaking of independent study," Lucy says, "you and your brother should collaborate on something. Wish I'd done that with my twin."

"You practically teach the same damn course," he says, irritated.

"*Now* we do. You two have got that applied-math stuff going on, and he's computery, too. Put your heads together and invent the self-grading paper, why don't you?"

"We'll be immortal," he says.

"Forget immortal, you'll be rich. The self-grading paper—did I just make that up? God, you would change my life."

There is nothing he'd rather do. Surely she and Daniel know

that. They've summoned him to Mount Olympus, where he's enjoyed dinners, wine, dope. All he wants is to wedge himself into the rest of their lives.

"If Daniel and I had kids and we'd been through what your parents have, I'd be desperate to see you. Think of your mother."

He can't think of his mother in the same sentence as Lucy being desperate to see him. This is how she and Daniel operate, making overtures in otherwise wholesome contexts. Is that what sophistication is, a lewd undercurrent to social mores? She emerges from behind her desk and perches herself on the available armrest. In her artfully ripped T-shirt and leggings, she's got the rangy rock star–poet look going, complete with rings on her toes. She pulls her hair back the way his mom is always doing, but rather than twist and anchor it, Lucy just lets go. He wants to let loose as well—what would she do if he lifted her beringed foot from the cushion and brought it to his lips?

"How is your father?" Lucy asks.

Richard grunts. He gets his news from Mom's dwindling e-mails and Brooke's Facebook page, when he checks. "All over the place—one minute he's sweet and mystical, the next he's getting a full-body tattoo and hacking up a goat for dinner."

Lucy says, " 'Make a holiday feast of it and drink the bright wine recklessly.' " She pushes her glasses up her nose like a know-it-all.

But he knows it, too. Odysseus's son is freaking out because the suitors in the palace are helping themselves to goats and pigs and wine, the implication being that they're ready to help themselves to Odysseus's wife. "Book Two," he says, as if Homeric trivia will win him a place at her holiday feast.

Lucy slides down the armrest, planting herself on the couch. "Good one." She holds her hand just barely over his arm, hovering the way the puck does above the air hockey table. Electrified, the hair on his arm stands up to touch her palm.

"While we're talking mythology, your father's living it. That's richer than anything I have to offer."

"Make me an offer," he says. He can't help it.

"Your third paper is there for the taking. Write a little epic—what are those called?"

Epyllia, he remembers, but he says, "I don't remember." First, as the child they've never had and then as her student, she's put him in his place. He has to get out of there before he subjects himself to further humiliation. He steps into his shoes and raises himself to his full pomposity. "I suppose I shall be leaving then, Dr. Clifton. May I wish a very happy Thanksgiving to you and yours."

Still no offer comes, not even to watch a movie before he disembarks.

"We'll text you," she says, and then, goddamn it, she kisses him on both cheeks. "One for me, one for Daniel."

Richard sets off across campus, bitter certainly, but also befuddled and, despite himself, beguiled by those final kisses (the "one for Daniel" noticeably more smoochy). Lucy and Daniel are toying with him, which felt like an honor around midterms. He's worried that going home will break the spell they've cast, and then he can't believe he's in their stupid thrall.

On a frat lawn along the way is an opportune kegger, and Richard speaks the password to gain access: "What's up, dude?"

"Vacation, dude!" The guy fills an oversize cup to the brim.

"Thanks, man," Richard says. He wanders onto a private patch of grass, where he starts guzzling. Today Lucy acted as if he's their adoring pet who might embarrass them at their own Thanksgiving table. But she's the one jerking him around—there's no shame in wanting to mix all their texts together and write their own fucking epic! His dreams are full of three-ways—Lucy's breasts and Daniel's cock and then Daniel's lips and Lucy's pussy. Sometimes he dreams he's just watching them and jerking off, and that works, too.

Richard finishes off his sixteen-ounce cup before a kid with a Confederate flag on his baseball cap asks if he's a Sig Ep.

"Nope, just needed a beer," Richard says.

The kid pours him a refill. "No worries! You can be my community service."

Richard lets the guy help him, although if shame is his problem, another beer may not be the solution. Considerably slowed, he slogs to his room, the orderly den of a math and myth geek that is also home to a bi-curious sycophant at his lechy teacher's beck and call. The desk says it all: his hardcover partial diffy-q book sits next to a well-thumbed *Metamorphoses*, whose cover is a nineteenth-century French painting of a thick-lipped woman with ram's horns coming out of her head.

He feels both empty and full; pulling his computer from his backpack, he orders an extra-large pizza, hoping the smell might attract whoever's left in the dorm. He begins an e-mail to his mom with news that he's coming home. Does she even doubt it? So he cancels that and logs on to Brooke's Facebook page, which has taken a disturbing turn since last time he checked. Some guy he's never seen before has his arms wrapped octopus-like around his little sister, who is not smiling one bit. The picture is captioned "Save me!"

She's also left a message in his in-box with the subject line "locofoco." Richard clicks through and begins to read: "Our perturbation would be soothed should your peregrinations lead hither for the impending gratitudinous holiday. Provender for the peckish promises Tellicherry-seasoned forcemeat and the requisite fowl. Without equivocation, the enormity of your analogue's exploits requires kinship, as do I."

He wishes he'd stopped after the first beer. Another person might think she'd pushed the thesaurus button for every word, sometimes twice, but the slight dig of calling Will his "analogue" gives her away. Something is up—*Save me!*—and so he revisits her diction. She may be trying to exasperate an eavesdropper (Mom?), outlanguage someone (the swarthy boy wrapped around her?), or gobbledygook the message so it will seem too difficult (Dad?).

He burps, farts, goes to the head, and returns to his invitation to partake of forcemeat and fowl. Having spent the semester reading things into every word Lucy and Daniel say, he's primed for code. In the last sentence, her use of *enormity* to taint Will's exploits is notable: they'd had many conversations about misleading words, and she'd remember that *enormity* means wickedness, even monstrosity, as opposed to hugeness. If Mom is on Facebook, would she know the correct use of enormity? He no longer thinks she knows everything. Funny, they never felt that about Dad. What Dad knows (or knew) is a particular cluster, and his grasp exceeded just about anybody else's reach.

Richard clicks through a dozen websites, but he is so late making Thanksgiving plans that the planes are booked, except for a few seats in millionaire class. He sees flights to Wilmington, where he could get on the train, even if he has to stand all the way through Delaware and Maryland. There are buses from Wilmington to Rehoboth, too, where they sometimes celebrated Thanksgiving.

The intersection of Rehoboth, Wilmington, and his family is Kyra. *Kyra!* Will might have already invited her; she could be planning ways to get to their house right this minute. In that extended hypothesis, if he could get to her dorm, they could wend their way to Bethesda together.

Richard applies all sorts of math to convince himself that overshooting DC for Delaware makes sense. He figures into his calculations that Kyra, being practically kin, would provide just the buffer he's after. Her very presence would bring to mind the night that Richard rose to the occasion and, lest anyone forget: Saved. Dad's. Life. Her number's in his phone—more karma—and he dials before doubt sets in.

She answers on the first ring. "Hi there."

"Hey, Kyra, it's Richard Lerner. How you doing?"

"Ricky?"

He can practically feel his courage escaping, hissing out as if she were pushing a pin through his phone. He says, "I go by Richard now."

"That so. And how's your Willy?" She laughs like she's high.

"Never better, thank you. And how is yours?"

"Very funny, Richard." She pronounces his name as if he's turned French: Ri*shard*. "I guess the joke is indeed on me."

"Don't say that. I have no idea what I'm talking about." He can't afford to be a smart-ass if he wants her to accompany him. "Last thing I heard, Will was smitten. Are you guys still together?"

"Depends on which way the wind blows. He says he wants that, but he's kind of fucked-up, if you ask me."

"Yeah, well, you're talking to his clone."

"And which way is the wind blowing you these days?" Kyra asks.

"Every which way," he says, wondering if Abigail told her stuff. His palm is so slick with sweat he has to change hands. "I'm going to Greece next semester—my mythology professor invited me."

"Teacher's pet, eh?" Kyra teases, and then he hears her voice break. "Oh, Ricky! What has he said about us? We'd been friends for life, right, before we hooked up. Did I totally ruin it? God, I'd be pissed if I wasn't so hurt." She either blows her nose or flushes the toilet. "And I'm scared—he just dropped off the map . . . Are you still there?"

"I'm here," he assures her. "If it makes you feel any better, I haven't heard anything, either. You know—what I was thinking, why I called—"

"What—you've got me on the edge of my seat."

What the hell was he thinking? "I'm not sure what you're doing, for break and all, but we could go to DC together. If you want."

"Where are you?" she asks.

"Duke. I know you're out of the way. But there are still flights from here to Wilmington, and on the East Coast trains they sell tickets even if the seats are taken."

"Are you inviting me to the Lerner family Thanksgiving? Just out of the blue, *Rishard*, I'd say you're a little messed up, too."

Granted. Although he's promising her more of a freak show than a reunion with Will, he tries to be Rishard the Bold. "The food will be amazing—Dad cooks nonstop now. Maybe you were planning to see your parents—"

"Please. Mom sent me money, but I never bought a ticket. Is it terrible of me to avoid her, do you think?"

"No, no. I would never think that," he assures her. He wonders why we're all so scared of one another, especially of the people who mean the most to us. Is it because they know us so well, or is it that they're wedded to an early version of us and have stopped getting the updates?

She says, "You and Will are my only friends who still have their original parents, which is probably why you're so close. Is he all right, Ricky?"

He's just told her he has no idea what's going on with Will. He could probably tell her anything; hell, he could have called and pretended he *was* Will. But then he remembers Will propping him up all these years, and his sister's scrambled call for help makes its way through his own insecurities: *The enormity of your analogue's exploits requires kinship, as do I.* That's when he spots the star that has been eluding him, and he steps into its dusty beam. "Listen, if I said I had this weird feeling, call it a twin thing, that Will needs us, what would you say?"

Kyra moans. "I would say yes."

He holds the phone out from his ear as she yells, " 'Yes I said yes I will Yes!' " When he brings the phone back to his face, she sighs lustily, satisfied. "Jesus God, Ricky, I've been trying to say yes all semester."

22

NOBODY'S GOING ANYWHERE

"Talk to me, Willy," his mother begs. She can't see his eyes through his sunglasses, which he wears all the time, even inside, even drinking a cup of coffee at the kitchen table.

"I'm trying to understand what's what," she is saying. "You show up here, your tooth knocked out, your nose and cheek smashed. I'm spooked."

"Random happens, don't it, Mom?"

"It certainly do." Her phone scoots around the table, powered by candidates clamoring to lead campuses full of knuckleheads like him. "Tell me about your bike—it was wrecked?"

Now Will knows something that she doesn't know. He knows that Brooke spilled news of his call from ground zero, because his mother wouldn't say "wrecked." Dad's taking him to the lawyer again tomorrow, and he's promised to be more cooperative, as long as Mom isn't in the room. It's almost impossible not to beg for her mercy, and he wishes he had a cloaking device for his heart.

The back of her hand sweeps crumbs from the table into a pile. Tidying, always tidying. "I imagine you got to Delaware a few times this fall. How's Kyra?"

"Kyra gave up on me," he says, shame heating up his cheeks. He waits in silence for his mother to offer some sympathy; instead, she walks their empty mugs to the sink and tucks them into the dishwasher. Finally he says, "I'm sorry I cost you a semester of tuition. I'll pay you back somehow."

"I don't care about that," she says, resigned.

"Way to accept my apology, Mom."

"I didn't realize you were apologizing." Toni makes herself face her son, who's straddling the kitchen chair as if to shield himself from her. She cannot fathom how she's become the villain—it knocks the wind right out of her, just as when he and Ricky used to tussle beneath her rib cage. She says, "You obviously needed to come home."

"Obviously," he mocks. Though he is underweight, he is still a strapping young man. His muscles bulge as he raises his hands in the air, and he wiggles his fingers to signal air quotes: "Home is where, when you have to go there, they have to take you in."

"Nice," she says.

"I was paraphrasing Dad. It's his line."

"Well, he's channeling Robert Frost," she says, remembering Owen putting Dr. Payne in his place; she knew the poem when Owen quoted it, and she knows it better now. Will using the line against her is another kick in the ribs. It's a good thing she can't get her breath, or she might say, *Your father was scorched and paralyzed, he was spewing poetry and obscenities, and I took care of him around the clock. He couldn't remember his eye color or your middle names. And before all that, when he was allegedly in his right mind, he may have carried on with your girlfriend.*

Toni is cross with fatigue and their collusion. She wants to be sympathetic, goddamn it, but her son's derision is like water on a grease fire. Will has no idea that Frost's poem is a marital quarrel over sympathy itself. The boys are quoting what the husband says when he doesn't want to give their old hired man shelter—we don't have to take him in, because ours is not his home—but Toni remembers the wife's response, that home is *something you somehow haven't to deserve.*

Frost doesn't promise that there's a home for everyone or that family is family, an ever-present safety net. Neither does Toni. The truth as she sees it is that you choose to be in your family—or not. Every member is allowed to make that choice, even if their thrashing to escape ends up shredding the safety net. She's done what she can to keep the net up and in good repair. Maybe that's why she can so fiercely love her family and still want to wring Will's and Owen's necks.

Her silence has piqued Will's curiosity. "What?" he asks.

Rather than answer, Toni yells, "Owen! Owen, would you get down here?"

"Yep—coming!"

Will's pummeled face and the sound of Owen's telltale shuffling soften her fury. As Will's edges blur in her teary vision, she sees a child afraid of rejection—we must each of us, every day, choose and be chosen.

"Willy," she says to her son, "you think I am obsessed with money, that I keep a running tab on you. What you can't understand yet is that you are my investment. You and Ricky and Brooke." She has taken to breathing like a fish out of water, in little gaspy breaths. "I love you. My job, as a parent, is to take care of you, invent and discover you so that you can leave me."

He flinches before he allows her to stroke his unharmed cheek. But with her touch, something in him begins to crumble. By the time Owen makes his way to their son's side, Will is clutching the back of the chair and rocking like a little boy on a playground horse.

"Don't make me leave," he begs. "I can't do it."

"It's okay, buddy. You're staying put." Owen shoots Toni a harsh look.

"You, too!" Will howls. "You can't go yet. I'm not ready for you guys to go."

"Willy," Owen says, "nobody's going anywhere. We're all in this together."

Toni hears a presence in Owen's voice that has been sorely lacking.

"Nobody's going anywhere," Owen repeats. "You're staying put. We all are. Tomorrow, you and I will get some more legal advice; we'll see what's what. A friend of mine at Penn may be able to show me the brain scans. Think of the hit I took, a guy my age, and I've recovered. I'm recovering."

As Owen lays a floor beneath their son, assuring him that the earth will not open to swallow him up, Toni realizes how he may have become the preferred parent. Devoted father and gifted therapist, he knows to squat down to Will's level—not easy for him—and speak in a neutral voice—not easy for her. He's wearing his burn sock but not his glove, maybe because she screamed for him to get downstairs. He talks to Will with neither dismay nor condescension. "This week we'll cook Thanksgiving dinner. I'm getting two turkeys for us. You'll see, it will be a huge feast."

"I can't eat *Thanksgiving dinner*," Will says. "He's barely conscious!"

"He's eating," Owen says gently.

Will wipes his nose with his sleeve, balking at his own touch. "He's not feeding himself—that's not *eating*. I thought he was one of them; he had on their shirt. Well, he is one of them, and he might have been there that night."

"He wasn't there that night." Owen sets the record straight. "Everyone seems to agree on that."

Will is undone by what everyone seems to know. "He fell so hard—no helmet, the idiot! He lost his balance!"

Toni's lungs are constricted as if cinched by a corset. She wouldn't be surprised to hear that stress could suffocate a person. She prepares for the breath she'll be able to take when Owen says *everyone falls*.

But he doesn't say that. He says, "As bad as things are, I'd be more worried if you didn't feel remorse."

"*Now* I do," Will moans. "Nothing means anything—that's what I was thinking. Shit happens all the time and for no good reason. To stuff you care about. Shit happened to you, Dad, and my bike. Random shit. But what I did was different. I ruined everything for us, didn't I?"

Owen says, "We're here with you now. You're not as bruised today as you were yesterday."

"Yes I am, you just can't see it." He hangs over the top of the chair, as limp as a kitchen towel.

Owen rests his burned hand on the table, where Will can see it, and Toni admires how he lets Will know *I'm here* rather than patting him on the back—*There, there*. She sees the mangled healing of his glossy pink hand and the ragged lines of his stupid tattoo. It is a lot to see. Tugging a napkin free from beneath the fulgurite, Toni blows her nose so loudly that Will lifts his head, startled.

"It's okay," Owen says. "The thing to hang on to here is that people heal from all sorts of trauma. Young people especially. We'll go at it day by day. For now, why don't you take a nap, or maybe a bath and then a nap. Later, I'll make dinner. You'll see. We'll get some food in you, help you get your strength back."

"All right," Will says. "I'll take a bath."

"Good idea," Owen says, as if Will thought of it. After Will slinks away, Owen sits next to Toni, who is profoundly grateful not to be alone.

She watches her chirping phone shimmy up to her coffee cup, as if to consult with the mug. Toni's supposed to be working at home, but what she's facing at home can't be worked through. Her appliance, meanwhile, is taking care of business. Any minute now, it may pick itself up off the table, like the little gingerbread man off his cookie sheet, and make a run for it, fleeing from her with a goodly portion of her brain.

"Who's your friend at Penn?" she asks.

"Layton Roth. We did six or seven conferences that crazy summer, the Summer of Ritalin. We were in Geneva and Paris together, all over the West Coast."

She knows that summer well, though she just calls it *that summer*.

Owen tucks his long hair behind his ears. "We've had such an easy time of it with the kids, and it's a good thing, because I can barely stand this."

"You? I don't even know the whole story." Once she knows, she won't be able to unknow it. He mentioned brain scans, and she thinks about the lesions on Ricky's brain she has never been able to erase from her memory.

Owen says, "It's a wonder Willy made his way home. He could just as easily have jumped out a window, considering all the junk in his system."

Toni studies her ragged nails rather than comment on people jumping out of windows. "Tell me about the boy," she says.

"His name is James Westoff, and he's a freshman from Buffalo. Some guys in his fraternity trashed Will's bike." He reaches for the fulgurite on top of the napkins, turning the petrified lightning end over end as he explains. "With brain injuries, there's any number of potential calamities—even when it seems the worst has passed. The cognitive and emotional fallout is everything you've ever heard me talk about through the years, but there's also a slight chance of physical dangers. Blood clots, seizures—oh, honey."

She hasn't heard Owen speak so fluidly since his own injury, and she's sobbing at the cruel twist. She so badly wanted him to return to his pre-lightning guise; however, this may be more than she can bear, his cogently describing this boy's ordeal at the hands of their beloved son. Their family saga has become like the myths Ricky has always pored over, elaborate stories of favors granted at a brutal price.

"We'll see," Owen comforts her. "It's only been a week."

Her heart goes out to the boy and his family—to his *mother*!— who has no doubt been keeping vigil the entire week.

She asks, "How can I help?"

Owen waves the fulgurite through the air like a wand. He makes a few figure eights before pointing it at her. "Since you asked: I'm getting the impression that we're going to need a lot of money." He clears his throat. "I'm talking sell-the-beach-house money, second-mortgage-this-place money."

No one knows her the way Owen does: money for her has always been a measure of their life, how much they have and where the hell it all goes. What he's saying is both a warning and a call to arms. He's telling her without telling her that Will needs medical, legal, perhaps mental, help, and that's not even counting Will's responsibility to the injured boy. She follows the movement of Owen's hand as he replaces the petrified lightning on the stack of napkins, which are duly impressed with the relic.

Toni asked how she could help, and in return, he is asking her an essential question: How much is she in for? And the answer is everything. Of course, the answer is everything. That's how it is with your children.

Fully aware that the future will be different, she says to her husband, "Spend it all." Maybe this is why she's felt the need to pay such careful attention to their finances. Whatever she's been saving for is frivolous compared with what they'll have to face. That's one thought. The other is, she's been saving for this, saving to save Owen's life, hers, the children's. This is why it's called your life savings.

"My Antoinette." Owen kisses both her wet cheeks, and then he takes her hand between his good and bad ones. "Because Penn has its own security force, they'll decide whether or not to hand Will over to the city of Philadelphia. Frankly, they have a lot of leeway, lucky for us."

Lucky is back; maybe she can resurrect the benefit of the doubt, too. "James took a bad fall?" Toni leads Owen on.

"He did," Owen agrees. He squeezes her hand, but he may as well wring her out and hang her up to dry.

She's afraid to wish for anything else for fear of how it might come true. She saw Owen return to himself tonight—that's what she's wanted—but he did it to coax their feral, frightened son back toward them.

Owen feels Toni straighten her spine as she draws herself away from him and up to her imperious height. Tugging her blouse taut, she lengthens her neck and draws her shoulder blades down. "You told Will we're all in this together. You promised him nobody's leaving anybody."

"Will needs to hear that."

"Yeah, well, I could use a promise like that."

"Toni," Owen says a little impatiently. He's surprised that his ambivalence has been so evident. Still struggling with the randomness of his lightning strike, he's begun to contend with the randomness of healing, too. Despite himself, he is healing. He certainly hasn't worked toward any kind of recovery. Despite themselves, other people suffer and die. Even with proven mind-body connections, he should have known that who gets sick and who gets well carries a large element of chance. He's had patients determined to clobber diseases as well as those resigned to their fate. Neither fighting nor whining affects outcomes the way chance does.

What he says is, "I never said I was going anywhere."

"You thought it."

She's probably right about more than he's willing to admit. "Don't believe everything I think."

"I thought it, too, Owen." Her lower lip quivers.

He says, "I don't blame you for wanting that," and he holds her while the trembling subsides. He is conscious of what they've said and what they haven't. "If you go get Brooke," he suggests, "I'll figure dinner out."

"Okay," is all she can manage. When he releases his grip, she's glad to have an assignment, not to mention the right glasses. She picks up her key fob and clicks her way into the van, lit by the setting sun. The side mirror diminishes the long dent Will acquired scraping the principal's Prius. And she'd thought that was bad.

Desperate to forgive both him and Owen, she stumbles on her own past, when she stepped outside herself *that summer*. She starts the van, which was not the one she was driving then. Eight years ago, the swim coach didn't show up where they'd agreed to. The last swim meet was over: Ricky and Will had won first and fifth in All-State freestyle; his Chloe had done something in butterfly; Brooke was on a winning relay. All their time together had taken place surrounded by skinny kids in bathing suits. They'd never had dinner alone. When she thinks about it now, she wonders why they chose a hotel. Were they playing chicken with each other or taking some bold action that would catapult them out of their families?

To be away for one night, she had made elaborate arrangements for all her charges—her mother-in-law, the children, the *dog*—and then once she got to the hotel, exhausted with anxiety and the frenzied planning but also an hour early, she actually fell asleep in the luxurious white bed. And so she was groggy and disoriented when he called her, shouting over the noise of a crowded bar. "Toni? Toni, can you hear me?" They'd only ever spoken quietly, aiming below the rowdy kid chatter, or in adult code aimed over their heads. His drunken yelling voice made her cringe. He said, "I'm getting totally pissed. I took Jamilla to a pub—we're on our second bottle of wine. That's what I decided to do, Toni. I decided that was for the best." All she could say, as if he were one of her children checking in, was, "Thank you for calling."

Toni pulls off the road for a siren-blaring fire engine and then ingratiates her way back into the rush-hour lineup; meanwhile, Rufus Wainwright gently croons a Leonard Cohen hymn that U2 covered the very summer she's reliving. True to her nature, she prefers the newer version, which sends a ripple across her back as if he'd touched her there. How unfaithful she was is up to interpretation; maybe that's why Owen's limbo has been so disheartening. Although she's mostly satisfied that he has only fantasized about Kyra, how much we betray may be as hurtful as how much we're willing to.

When Owen says, "I don't blame you," could that be retroactive? After decades together, they could fill two volumes: the first with what they know about each other and the second with what they don't.

What happened after swim season that summer was that her family closed right back up around her, the way traffic does now. Pursued by a welcome display of flashing lights, she'd pulled off the road, but the emergency passed her right by. She was leaner than she'd ever been, and a little more vain; her wherewithal was both enhanced and shaken. *Nobody's going anywhere*—she hears it as comfort but also as lockdown.

In an earlier version of this van, listening to an earlier version of this song, she and Owen and their three lovely children got on the highway and drove to Rehoboth. She had the same life as before *that summer*, now with a tan and a flattering swimsuit! Owen took up his rightful place, too, including resting his palm on the small of her back and steering her toward the water. Toni joined the workforce in the fall; the following summer, Brooke told her that Chloe had moved to England. College kids coached swim team, and college kids also drove her children there and picked them up. Probably all the college kids hooked up after the endless laps and pizza parties. What had almost happened wasn't even history; it was just a feeling in the pit of her stomach of what she was capable of, once in a lifetime. Might this be a way for her to think about Will's cruelty, a terrible coincidence of urge and opportunity?

When Toni arrives at the gym, Brooke is sitting under a street-light on the sidewalk in a nest of towels and workout gear. She tosses load after load in the back of the van and then collapses, boneless, in the front seat. "I'm whipped. And starving. Coach wanted all our dirty stuff out of there. Will you wash it for me, please?"

"But of course. How much homework is waiting for you?"

Brooke has already plugged herself in to her music. Toni enters a rare jet stream of green lights and cooperative traffic to speed home, where Owen is preparing a standard everyday feast. White smoke billows down the driveway past the car as she and Brooke get out in the dark. Toni recognizes the smell as pecan wood, because more than most woods, burning pecan smells like a house on fire. Another person might worry that her house was on fire.

Brooke makes an exaggerated sniffing sound. "Dad's grilling— what a surprise." She closes her car door and heads to her room, empty-handed.

Toni hoists a bundle of Brooke's gym gear in each arm and walks around to where Owen and Will are sitting in the dark by the pit. Owen has put on actual pants and a long-sleeved polo shirt that covers his tattoo, making him look more like pre-lightning Owen. She longs to see the pre-lightning Will—darkness provides camouflage for his bruised cheeks but not his gaunt face. His ubiquitous sunglasses rest on the bridge of his mangled nose.

They're each holding a bottle of beer, and an empty on the patio table betrays Owen's telltale label-stripping. She doesn't think either one of them should be drinking. Will gives her a weak smile; whether genuine or guilt-inspired, his smile is the nicest thing that's happened in her long day.

He says, "You see the heat Dad gets out of this? It's a fucking inferno."

The chickens cluck and coo in the silence of Toni not remark-ing on Will's language. She doesn't even care, that's the truth, but it would bother Brooke if she were there. An uncut chunk of New York strip steak, maybe a four-pound slab, rests near the fire, as does a pan of squashes, carrots, and onions so tiny they look like marzipan miniatures. Every day, the meat is getting larger and the vegetables smaller.

Owen invites her to pull up a chair, and she drops Brooke's laundry on the patio chaise. He says, "We've been talking about your idea. If we figure out a way to get my kids together to cook, this could be a new kind of occupational group therapy. There's farmland in West Virginia where they could help raise the food."

"My idea was a field trip," Toni says.

"And a restaurant," Owen reminds her. "Not a residential facility, unless we got a school going. Wouldn't that be something? They could get their biology firsthand in the gardens and the barns, wear themselves out on the farm, but also learn how to care for animals—or carrots, if that's all they can manage."

"Or tractors," Will suggests.

"True," Owen agrees. "And then we'd have some sort of outlet, a food truck or catering."

Will says, "Maybe that would count as community service. Dad thinks I could even manage a farm or the restaurant part, after a while."

So they've been talking about more than cooking. She wants to remove Will's sunglasses to see if he looks contrite. Although he's always been clever, she doesn't want to think of him as conniving. Owen usually stands on the periphery of family chaos, keeping a bemused watch. Her place has been at the eye of the storm, which makes her expulsion especially painful, and the tenderness she feels is both that of affection and of an aching wound.

Will asks, "What do you think of the name the Pigpen? Do you know that code?"

"It's pretty obscure," Owen says.

Toni thinks Will is testing her. "The one you and Ricky used to write in?" She draws a tic-tac-toe grid in the air and then ticks off the squares, saying. "A-B-C; D-E-F; G-H-I. That's the first nine, anyway."

"Holy crap." Will is amazed. "I completely forgot—we wrote stuff in that code all through second grade, or maybe third. I should ask Ricky if he forgot, too."

Toni wonders if Owen is getting this. Not only that they're all harboring each other's memories but also Will's connection to his twin. His question for Ricky is like one of the boys' weird logic problems: Have you forgotten what I've forgotten?

Will says, "What I was thinking was that George Washington used the Pigpen Cipher, and it shows up in a video game that the boys might know. I completely forgot about Ricky and me—our logo could be in Pigpen!"

In Toni's opinion, robotics was a good fit for Will, directing his need for remote control. Code, substitutions, twin—they all overlap. She hopes school isn't entirely off the table, that he hasn't blown it. With the sun gone, the temperature drops. Owen sticks a fork into the meat slab and lays it across the grill. He's got a basket for the mini-vegetables lest they fall through the grate to a fiery death.

"Fifteen minutes," Owen announces.

Toni scoops up Brooke's dirty laundry. "I shall dress for dinner." She goes first to the basement washer and then upstairs to change clothes. Brooke is in her room talking on the phone. "He'll be here for a while," she says, falsely brave. There is a pause, and then her little girl says, "Well, maybe you should shit a brick, because he fucked up a frat guy pretty bad."

Toni stands outside Brooke's door, her mouth slightly ajar. She fakes a cough, then says, "Would you please set the table?"

"I have to go. My mom wants me right this minute."

Toni pushes the door open with her index finger, and Brooke rushes toward her, throwing herself at her mom as if she were six. They were just in the car together for a half hour and exchanged a sentence at the most. "What's going on, honey?"

"Nothing," Brooke says. "Crapulous day is all."

"You and me both," Toni agrees, though she bookmarks this moment for later. She says, "Crapulous to the max, abysmally heinous to the nth degree—"

"Mom, please. Must we?"

Apparently not. Toni glimpses a purplish circle just above the elastic of Brooke's pajama pants and has a moment of dread, thinking it's a tattoo before she recognizes the dark plum of a bruise. And then again with the dread as she tugs on Brooke's waist. "What happened to you?"

"Wipeout at practice," Brooke answers too readily. She stretches her camisole over her hips. "I'll go set the table," she says, and darts past her mother.

She's too fast for Toni, who could have stopped her in her tracks any other day and asked her some of the obvious troubling questions. In the master bathroom, Toni washes her face and changes into blue velveteen pants topped with a cream T-shirt and a soft gray cardigan. By the time she gets downstairs, Brooke has set the dining-room table all the way up to goblets and candles.

"Why so fancy?" Toni asks her.

"You got dressed up," Brooke says defensively.

"I did," Toni admits. There's all sorts of trouble about to rain down on them—might as well get out the good china. She fills a pitcher with water, which she pours into the goblets to preempt anyone filling them with wine. She appreciates that Brooke has given her the etched goblet that belonged to her mother. Toni lifts the Italian platter from its nail on the wall.

"What are you doing?" Brooke asks.

She carries the hand-decorated plate into the kitchen to rinse off the dust. "Daddy can serve us in style."

And that he does. Owen has managed to caramelize the vegetables in the smoky heat, and he's lightly crusted the steak with a salty rub of his own creation. There's sourdough bread with soft butter, into which he's mashed parsley and garlic, and he's also made a lemony slaw of crunchy broccoli with carrots. The children put away an astonishing amount of food, even more than Owen.

Helping himself to thirds, Will asks, "Why doesn't this get old? I've eaten this meal plenty of times."

"Maybe not this exact meal." Owen sounds a little put out.

Brooke says, "You know what he means."

Will nods toward his sister, acknowledging her support. "Meat, potatoes, bread—by now these foods should register as fuel. We eat to live. But I am wolfing this down."

"You're hungry," Owen says. "Good fuel is better than bad fuel."

"No, Dad. It's more than that. And a lot of times, we can't make ourselves stop—so it's more than fuel. Also, how can meat be so tasty when we know where it comes from?"

Brooke sighs. "I shouldn't eat it, but it smells so good. Even Saxy's a vegetarian now."

"Let's see her resist this," Will says. "The smell, the taste. I'm smacking my lips, acting like I've never eaten before. We've evolved some daily amnesia that wipes our brains clean."

Toni thinks he may have a point. Why is the first sip of coffee always a revelation?

Owen, however, disagrees. "It could be habit. Or pure animal instinct."

Will guffaws. "Are you invalidating our feelings? Things sure have changed around here."

"Of course not," Owen assures him. "But daily amnesia? Our pleasure could be the opposite—remembering how good this tastes."

"No. You're wrong," Will says. "I was hungry when I sat down, so at the beginning, yes. But second helping, third—I'm still enjoying the hell out of it."

Owen lowers his voice. "I'm glad you're enjoying it. I made it for you."

"Yeah? Well, this meal is not just dinner; it tastes like the First Supper. But you're saying I don't know mystical. We who have not been struck by lightning are somewhat limited in our understanding."

Dinner is turning into something of a turf war, and Toni's with Will. She, too, is weary of Owen cornering the market on insight. When Owen talks about looking down on them from above it sounds more like looking down his nose at them. Frankly, she's ready to hear tell of his grand tour.

"Okay, Odysseus," she asks, "where did you go?"

"Who?" Owen says.

She is staring at his tattoo. "You. In the flash. When the lightning hit, where did you go that was so amazing?"

Owen lifts his shirt and rubs his big belly, as if the question gives him indigestion. "That's the first time you've asked me that," he says. "Okay, here goes. You guys were messing around"—he points to Will and then to his daughter—"and you were practically naked."

Brooke presses her palm against his outstretched finger. "We're talking about you. Stay here, and tell us the crap you saw."

Will says, "She said 'crap.'"

"Sorry," Brooke says, and adds with a malicious grin, "Tell us what the flux happened to you."

What the flux, Owen thinks. Years ago, a fellow shrink told him that the one thing we can't handle is flux. That certainly seems to be the case here; all three of them are openly hostile when this should be his most receptive audience. "One second I had a handful of quarters—they don't buy what they used to, I was thinking—and then I was literally lifted off my feet."

"*Literally?*" Brooke asks.

Will says, "Did you feel the current?"

"It was more like getting slammed by a wave. You know how you're picked up and you ride the wave, but every so often you get pounded?" He closes his eyes and tips his head back. "I remember heat. And *pressure*: a white-hot wave was squeezing the daylights out of me but also transporting me."

"You went up in the air," Toni confirms.

"I'm talking ten, fifteen feet." As many times as he's relived the experience, he's never spoken it aloud, except for the night he tried and failed to tell Brooke. "I could grasp all sorts of impossible details. That the sandy cap of our sunscreen wasn't closed right and was oozing inside the pool bag. Toni, your roots were showing—I was over your head—and the color was flaking off your sandals. Your shapely ankles, they swelled so when you were pregnant with the boys, and then the boys were coming out of your swollen belly." Describing is sharpening his recall, and eagerness takes the place of his reluctance.

He says, "My mother was wrapping the twins like two burritos—that zigzag pattern of the white blankets she knitted them, the smile crinkles at the corner of her eyes, magnified by her glasses. No detail was unimportant, and everything was worthwhile." To his son's dear battered face, he says, "Even the scar on your chinny chin chin."

Words can't express all that he went through, but he's getting closer. He's conscious enough of his audience to leave his lust for Kyra out of this, as well as any love for his first wife. The truth is, his family memories are the most cherished, and recounting the microscopic clarity of their features and flaws reconstitutes some of the vivid joy he felt. Jumbled sensations and time travel allowed for a concentrated happiness. The trick, he's beginning to understand, is to be able to get some of that jolt on the ground, in the dilution of daily life—to taste the roasted beast in a suggested serving size.

To Brooke, he says, "The muscles on your back were like wings, and I finally got over your first competition."

"When I cracked my wrist?"

"Yes. Apparently, that has haunted me for years. From my height, I watched you go from somersaults in the yard to backflips and twists, and I could identify your mother in the way you carried yourself. Halloweens and birthday parties galore—the twins had an incident with a Batman piñata that went south. At the same time, my hand was on fire, which made a certain kind of sense: the pain was an element of our wonderful, terrible life."

He stops talking, and the three of them stare at him, their faces as blank as their empty plates.

"Really?" Will says. "That's all you've got for us?" He sounds like Ricky at his most sarcastic.

Toni is cynical as well. First of all, a hand on fire makes no sense; surely, Owen recognizes that. Just as obvious—to her, anyway—is that his great vision was one routine experience after another, lived right under his nose. When he saw what he saw that made him so outrageously goddamn happy, he was looking at a family with him in it. She says, "I'm glad it's not just about pain. Seems like trauma would be the most memorable."

Owen shrugs his shoulders, flipping both palms up. "What trauma?"

Toni drops her fork. How dare he disregard the scare he gave them and the chore of his care. Not to mention the collateral damage of his accident. *How about trauma as in Will; trauma as in Brooke?* A growl rises in Toni's throat, the anger of wanting to strangle the child who shows up unconcerned after a night of excruciating parental worry. It won't be long before she grinds her teeth to stumps. "Spare us," she says.

"I remember the Batman piñatas!" Will cries out.

Toni hears the dark tenor of self-loathing in his voice. He says, "I beat the shit out of mine and then 'accidentally' clocked Ricky with my bat. If your perfect-family film kept on rolling, you'd have gotten to the great reveal."

Owen inhales his son's anger and breathes out. "You wouldn't be the first four-year-old to lose control at his own birthday party."

"Stop protecting me!" Will yells. "Mom wants me to pour out my heart to her, but I did something heartless."

He pulls off his sunglasses, and she gasps at his bloodshot eyes, their lids and sockets still bruised the psychedelic colors of breakfast cereal: raspberry red, lemon yellow, orange orange.

Brooke's whispery sobs draw Will's genuine concern. "Brooksey," he says sympathetically, and then twists back toward Owen. "Get over yourself, why don't you? So your little mishap was Christmas: a multitude of angels gathered to give you one big blow job. Well, that's not what happened to *me*! To *us*!"

With the back of his hand, he bats first the salt and then the pepper grinder off the table to the dining-room floor. "That's what I think of all your precious rubs and *unguents*. I should have bought myself a souvenir at Rehoboth—*My dad got hit by lightning and all I got was this stupid T-shirt.* You only got electrocuted, but I got fried."

Toni nearly throws the Italian platter to the floor in solidarity with Will, but it would only make a mess. Instead, she reaches for her son's hand, and he turns on her.

"When you find out what I did, you won't want to touch me.

I thought nothing mattered—I acted on that assumption—and now I am truly fucked."

"Stop it, you guys!" Brooke pleads.

Toni says, "Willy, whatever you did, I'm your mother."

Owen scoots his chair around the table to his son, who falls against him, released into tears. Under the weight of Will's heavy head, Owen's collarbone throbs. He didn't mention the agony he daily endures—knives of pain through his muscles, shooting twinges that double him over, weakness, and seizing cramps. Uncushioned by his doughnut, his tailbone still jabs the vertebrae above it, and that pinches the nerve that runs the length of his left leg, which ends in the raw flap of his mangled heel. When he's tired or stressed, as in most of the time, his thin, shiny skin is crawling, and he has to scratch the top of his thigh to relieve an itch two inches lower, because the nerves have not yet and may never return to their original location.

He feels differently, it's as simple as that, a fact they'll have to grow accustomed to. The operative question, he's beginning to see, is not necessarily where did you go when lightning struck, but where might you land? Once he fell back to earth, he never did acknowledge the chaos and fear they were living with. Of all people, he should have paid attention to that. He should have comprehended that in a manner of speaking, they were all, that summer's eve, tossed into the air and forced to fend for themselves.

23

WHOLE FOODS

Dad is waiting for her as soon as she gets a ride home from her half day. He says, "Come on. You and I, we're on food patrol."

Brooke drops her anvil of a backpack and splays on the couch, knees over the armrest. "Daddy, break just started. I'm so tired, I want to stay right here until Monday. Where's Will?"

"Napping. He and I spent the morning at our lawyer's. If we go right now, we can get in and out before the stampede."

"I have to change."

"Not for me you don't," he says sweetly.

"Please," she says. "Did you know Ricky's bringing a friend? He texted me."

"Then we'd better stock the larder. Tomorrow will be a madhouse."

When she stands up, he hugs her, which is a little gross because he's not wearing a shirt and he's sweaty. He lifts his keys from their hook and slides his feet into lime-green rubber clogs. She's waiting for him to say he has to change, too; if he isn't embarrassed, you'd think he'd be cold. "You're not dressed."

He looks down at his belly. "Do I need long pants?"

"You need pants." Someone her father's shape shouldn't be allowed to buy spandex. His fat puffs out like cookie dough at the top and bottom. "And a shirt might be *apposite*."

"Apposite? If you say so." Then he hugs her again.

Is he going to start hugging them all the time; is that the next phase? Brooke follows his lumpy butt up the stairs. She throws on flannel pajama pants, a Duke sweatshirt, and shearling boots in a minute makeover, but her dad seems to be having some sort of wardrobe malfunction. She waits for him on the bottom step, wishing she could nap. When she's sleeping, she doesn't have to think about Natalio slashing Sebastian's backpack just because he told Saxy he'd be friends with Brooke if he wanted to. Doesn't Sebastian know you can't tell Saxy anything?

Dad returns in a T-shirt, and he's traded the bike shorts for plaid pants she's never seen before. "How am I doing?" He's apparently delighted to be joining the senior set.

"Medium-well," she says.

"That bad, huh?"

She grabs shopping bags from the kitchen, and they pile into the van. She waits until they're out on the road to say, "I didn't know we had a family lawyer."

"We do. Gloria and I kind of grew up together." Two squirrels chase each other into the street, and when her dad slows down, they freeze in the middle of the road. She can see the terror in their beady eyes; his tap on the horn prompts them to get going again, and they haul ass to safety. He says, "Glo was my first wife."

"Are you serious? Mom's okay with that?"

"Mom likes her. She's a good lawyer; well, I hope she's better than good."

"You people," Brooke says. As curious as she's been about *the first wife*, she'd never imagined her as local. The other night, half the stuff her dad told about his episode were just stories to Brooke; they'd already had a life before she came into their lives.

He says, "Your mother seems to respect Gloria for leaving me—go figure."

"Is Will going to go to jail?" She doesn't know where that came from, and she's shocked that she asked it. Worse, her father doesn't immediately deny it.

"The whole thing's a mess, really. Will's devastated; your mother and I are devastated. It's a blessing that James is home again."

She's never heard her father use the word *blessing*, so things must be pretty tragic. From what she's pieced together, the other kid's situation sounds like a text message of hurt; i.e., PT, OT, and TBI, which means physical and occupational therapy as a result of traumatic brain injury. That's not because Will pushed him, it's because he fell, although he fell because he and Will were fighting. Brooke's turning her stomach into a blender. She wipes her clammy palms on her pajama pants and punches the car player until one of her dad's songs comes on.

"*Troy*," he says, identifying the film score.

A woman croons an Indianish melody over a marching-band beat, and what do any of them know, maybe ancient Troy did have that music three *thousand* years ago. Her dad's a sucker for the sword-and-sandal flicks, with all the pageantry and honor flying; however, a movie of Troy seems like the opposite of an anachronism. Or maybe that's exactly what an anachronism is. Watching these movies, Brooke knows she's supposed to be worried about the hero taking a projectile to the heart, but she always gets derailed by the crowd scenes. How can a couple of guys with cameras manage a crowd in armor covered with dirt and blood—even if that's just makeup and costumes—running at one another with killer weapons?

Her father clears his throat as the emo sound track surges. First she has to tell him to get dressed, and now he's going to pieces over *Troy*. Why does everything happen to her? With Will, he's ready to be Dad and therapist, but every time he's alone with her, he reverts to basket case. "You doing all right?" she asks.

He gives her a wave with his tattooed arm. "We'll always have *Troy*," he says.

He's just a little choked up, as the sound track touches off Hector's love for his father and the cost of his brother's impetuous actions. The music is playing him, and he dials down the drums of war, the inconsolable women left behind. It used to be that while he was concentrating, he'd listen to sound tracks, which would in turn project the film against his thoughts. He didn't get worked up; the music and its implied movie were mazes his brain would run while he focused on issues more complex or dark. These days, when he can barely task, multitasking is out of the question.

When he passes Safeway, Brooke moans, "Oh, no. Do we have to?"

"They've got my turkeys, remember?" He drives on to Whole Foods, where there's already a backup in the parking structure. You don't have to be a teenager to see the disconnect in an organic, environmentally correct store hiring cops to keep the Land Rovers from hitting the Jaguars. They sit in the idling van.

"Hope all that freshness lasts until we get in there," Brooke wisecracks. "If the carbon monoxide doesn't take us down, we're ready to save the planet." Then, sincerely, she says, "Do you think Will would run with me when he wakes up?"

"You should ask him, though he's pretty out of shape."

Her eyes go to Owen's gut and back to his face. She shows mercy by withholding her comments.

"Your brother hasn't gotten out lately. He basically shut down when he lost his bike."

"He didn't lose his bike; it was trashed."

"True," Owen concurs. He wonders what Will has told his little sister, or what she imagines him capable of. According to Toni, she threatened to sic Will on that Brazilian boyfriend of hers. "Believe it or not," he tells her, "it never really struck me before, what you said about the drugs I prescribe—that I blithely dispense chemicals."

"I didn't say 'blithely,' I don't think."

"Maybe not. I was always on those kids to eat fewer preservatives and processed food, basically to try to get whatever nutrients they had coming to them." He rubs his cheeks, which sag without a smile to hold them up. "It's possible I haven't done enough to detox them—they're pretty sensitive."

She cringes at the memory of her snarky remark, which he nevertheless made a point of considering. That's something. And she's glad to hear him talking like a therapist. "You're obviously looking out for them," she says, which sounds like the false hope adults are always spreading around. *You did a great job. No one noticed. Your friends adore you.*

A cop waves them into a space so tight her dad steers himself into a sweat, twisting to see behind the van and backing up for another attempt. The mini-workout has him winded, and Brooke patiently gives him a moment to swab his brow.

"Come on, Daddy. Let's go get your birds." Once he's out of the van, he starts patting himself down. "Did you forget your wallet?" she asks.

"No, the list." He should have come yesterday or right when they opened. He gets rattled in crowds, and now he doesn't even have his list.

"Oh, Daddy. How hard can it be? It's Thanksgiving: turkey and all the fixings, pie stuff."

A no-brainer, then. Just how he's been behaving since August. All gut, no brain. Living by instinct, like a deluded moth flying toward the porch light. What exactly is he trying to recapture: heart-stopping, skin-charring, ozone-scented discharge of energy? He didn't realize until the other night how self-absorbed he's been; although, in his own defense, that may be how the body heals, by focusing entirely on itself.

Inside the sliding doors, toting their bag of bags, Brooke snags a cart gone astray, a *fortuitous* start. To the overpriced store's credit, they've organized the aisles with displays of the usual suspects. She puts evaporated milk in their basket because the cans are stacked next to the pumpkin filling. She'll figure out later what the two of them have to do with each other (and why "evaporated milk" is a can of liquid). She feels a little brainwashed; if the store arranged a display of prune juice and sardines, would they all be jostling to put them in their carts?

The idea of nearly all these people eating exactly the same meal on the same day strikes her as bizarre, as does her family eating the same meal they ate last year, when their lives are nothing like they were a year ago. Actually, their meal won't be identical, because her dad will undoubtedly be grilling the birds in his pit. Maybe he'll do the whole dinner out there, baking the pie on a pizza stone slid close to the coals. She watches him and she watches people watching him. He has this rubbery walk—his right elbow bent and his hand by his shoulder—that is kind of gay. He never used to move like that. Also, he's wearing *plaid pants* and *green clogs*. She knows it's heartless, but she wishes he weren't her responsibility, and in another first, she figures he's felt that way about her now and then.

Time slows way down in the produce section, which the adults treat like a candy counter, changing their minds a million times. The store fetishizes natural food in unnatural colors, and these people eat it up. They ogle golden beets, green zebra-striped tomatoes, polka-dot beans. "You think you know carrots," her dad says, "and then this." A glam Frenchwoman in a silver leather jacket and asymmetrical earrings picks up an iconic tomato, round and red, rejects it, selects a cluster of smaller tomatoes—still on the vine!—replaces those, and then starts pawing through the "heirlooms," which apparently means they date to another century. She chooses a gnarled mess of a tomato and makes a show of its smell, its *ambrosial* fragrance. Ultimately, this tomato is the chosen one. Brooke wonders if the woman has kids and what she might do if one of them disappointed her.

Her father picks a carrot bunch with the leafy greens attached, like cartoon carrots. Going on the offense, Brooke bags two heads of buttercrunch before her dad has to face the wall of lettuce, where he tends to go for pointy, bitter greens. He puts two whole pineapples in the cart and six mangoes that pass inspection. Then he inches along, making not nearly enough progress if they're planning to get out of the store before Thanksgiving. "*Capsicum* for us?" Brooke asks, pointing to the peppers. At the potatoes, she says, "Shall we *decorticate* them or leave the skins on this year?" But her dad just stares ahead with the pupils of a stoner. Speaking of which, the potato names sound like strains of weed: Peregrine Red, Purple Majesty, Allegheny, Adirondack White.

Brooke grabs a five-pound bag of Yukon Gold. "I got your tubers, Daddy." Cupping his elbow, she propels him and the cart toward the center of the store. "Let's move on to the poultry repository, the turkey *abattoir*."

It's a good thing Brooke's taking charge, because the vegetables nearly do Owen in. Everyone is dressed as if they're going directly to the opera after grocery shopping, and they all seem to be eyeing him. His own daughter is being just as formal and obtuse—does she have to practice her vocabulary here, when he can't even speak potato, for god's sake? People keep swerving too close to the basket, threatening his balance.

He's thrown as well by the dissonance of eggplant or Effexor, squash or Seroxat being good for what ails you. Will told him about the bowls of meds at Penn—he might well have died after one of those parties. Meanwhile, all the pills Owen has prescribed—laid end to end, would they reach the moon and back? Willy could do that math, or he used to be able to, which swings Owen's mood around. He wants to lash out at the crowd and their ridiculously high expectations. You may find the quintessential tomato and the purest cornmeal, untouched by chemicals and ground between two stones, and no matter how lovingly prepared, they may well be thrown back in your face. Owen focuses on the linoleum; he's become a living example of how overstimulation and an inability to read a situation lend themselves to paranoia, although everyone *is* staring at him, pointing and talking, too.

Brooke stays close by her dad's weaker side, mostly for support but also to block his tattoo from sight. Standing in the line for preordered turkeys turns out to be another time suck. He ordered *two*, and she has to wrestle the weighty, sweating bags into their basket without flattening all his still-life vegetables.

"Chesty bruisers," he says, which cracks her up.

"Gobblers run amok," she adds, relieved to see him smile.

People wheel through the aisles in pods. For each menu decision—fresh cranberries versus canned cranberry relish, kosher salt versus sea salt—Brooke trusts her first choice, a technique they're pushing in test prep. This serves her well until they get to the bakery, where all carts converge. Stuffing, bread, and dessert options abound. *Dare me to care*, she almost says to her father. But he's gotten away from her.

Brooke parks the cart in the homeopathic aisle, beneath herbal gut washes of zero interest to Thanksgiving shoppers. Most likely he's searching for grilling paraphernalia or making eyes at the meat. She watches the floor, remembering that this is how they find lost kids at Disneyland, and she locates his backless clogs in the oil aisle. He's dogging a boy whose loud voice draws stares, and she feels a twinge of jealousy at his interest in other people's kids.

Nine or maybe ten, the boy is too big to ride in the cart, and he's obviously got some issues. "I won't sit with Grandpa. He chews with his mouth open—and his beard is like dirty socks."

His mother speaks to him in a quiet, conspiratorial tone, as if to a special friend. Brooke admires the way she stays to the right, pushing their cart, and, with her left hand, covers his right hand on the grip, keeping him in the center as she holds on to him. Brooke wants to grab her father by his T-shirt, although the last time she did that, he still fell out the window.

"Not the cousins!" the boy says. "They all gang up on me. And I'm their relative!"

To Owen, the child's voice is a siren song, as familiar and soothing as it is grating. Although these kids have all sorts of noise sensitivities, they often talk too loud. A parade of faces begins appearing in his mind's eye: Constantine, Emil, the troubled siblings Helen and Robert, all his Asperger boys, and now Will. For whatever reason, these are his people. Maybe he's a borderline member of this peer group and has learned or stumbled on a few insights for living among the neurotypicals. Maybe he was in a rut before the accident, because as much as he wants to help them, he's desperate for a fresh start. He could join forces with a personal trainer, a nutritionist, and a biofeedback specialist in hopes of managing their stress and mood swings while he also pursues the ADD BBQ idea. He could see if anyone else has done ear training or voicework.

"No oysters and no chestnuts!" The boy is raging. "You will not catch me putting those in my mouth!"

And then boy spots man. Owen sees the kid's anxiety turn to excitement as he tugs on his mother's sleeve with his free hand. In a stage whisper as audible as his complaining, he says, "Mom, that man's arm! He's got Lichtenberg figures."

Busted, Owen lets out a loud laugh. The kid probably knows

the difference between lightning crawlers and a positive giant. He may have even seen a fulgurite.

"Of course you knew that," he says. "You're very smart. Are you twelve?"

"Ten," the boy says proudly, at the same time as his mother says, "Louis."

"It's okay, I'm a doctor," Owen says. "I work with kids." He could help Louis. Especially with a mother like that, who not only knows what's up with her son but is also doing a good job navigating a difficult mission.

In his megaphonic voice Louis asks, "Were you struck by lightning?"

"Yes, but this is a tattoo. Lichtenberg figures fade pretty fast."

"In two to five days," the boy confirms. "But tattoos are permanent. Mummies thousands of years old still have their tattoos. You'll have that even after you're *dead*."

At the mention of dead, Brooke and the mother each step forward to claim a corresponding arm. "Time to check out, Dad," Brooke says.

"I'm in the middle of a conversation here."

"To get a tattoo"—Louis speaks in park-ranger mode—"they punch your skin with a needle and squirt permanent pigments subdermally! Each dot of ink is another punch of the needle."

"That'll do," the mother says, and she makes eye contact with Owen for the first time.

Though she urges him forward, the boy resists. "Getting a tattoo is like getting a million shots. Do you know how much I hate getting shots? This much!" He throws his left arm wide, sweeping a pyramid of tea boxes from a display in the center of the aisle.

"Accident!" he screams. "Cleanup on aisle tea!"

In a bizarrely calm voice, his mother says, "Time to go."

"We're not leaving, are we? We haven't found my carob chips yet! You promised!"

"No. We'll leave," Brooke volunteers.

"Louis." Her father speaks the boy's name with quiet authority, and he responds as if hypnotized. "You're right about the tea—they shouldn't have things in the aisle like that. Maybe you and I can visit again in the future; would you like that?"

The mother's mouth is wide open. Brooke is taken aback as well. Her dad is creepier than Willy Wonka, or worse, some perv promising a puppy, and she yanks him by the crook of his arm, hoping to check out before the authorities show up.

Louis broadcasts his dismay as his mother moves him down the aisle. "You always want me to make friends. Is there a rule: Don't make friends with anyone who was *struck by lightning?*"

It's beginning to hit home that Brooke cannot rely on her parents. Just as Will predicted, she's on her own. And she's also a flaming hypocrite: the overdressed foodophiles she's been dissing are harmless shoppers, while her own father is a menace. They get in line to buy the stupid turkeys, and she gives thanks for Coach's crazy strength training. Each time her dad drifts toward a nearby display, she yanks him back to her side.

Her father says, "It's too bad he had to leave."

"You set him up, Dad. They were minding their own business, grocery shopping, before you got him going."

"It's hectic here," he defends himself. "I was drawing him out, but . . ." He looks into the distance, as if to assert his professionalism. "I could help that kid."

"You helped him fall apart," she says. He showed more interest in that kid than he's shown in her since August, though it's not as though he was professional about it. She's concerned that his slippage is about her, that she's not worth his keeping it together.

The grocery line moves slowly, until finally the woman in front of them places the recycled-plastic bar at the end of her groceries, clearing them for unloading. Brooke stands their bag of bags on the belt and starts pulling food out of their basket as rapidly as she can. In his own slo-mo way, her dad chips in. Brooke pries the olive oil away from him, lining it up with the other nonperishables, the way her mom does.

"If we were in my office," he specifies, "I could help him. He's like a lot of my kids."

"*My kids!*" Brooke shakes a pineapple at her father. "When

you say that, you know how that makes us feel? *My kids* should be Will and Ricky and me!"

Owen opens his arms to his daughter, and she gracefully pivots around into his embrace. Her head fits just under his chin. "My girl," he says, kissing the top of her beloved head. "My only baby girl." As paranoid as he was earlier, he doesn't give a shit if people stare or if he holds up the longest lines of the year to reassure her. When they're done, the carrots are still making their way down the gangplank. He and his daughter stand side by side watching the two recently slaughtered turkeys travel beyond them, followed by the golden crowned pineapples, like a king and queen processing down the conveyor belt.

Owen considers himself with the same level of detachment and self-awareness as his groceries. Beneath the frayed hem of his stained T-shirt are his mottled madras pants, the cuffs short enough to show the entirety of his ankles above lime-green clogs. His right arm is covered with an elaborate red-and-purple netting, a permanent, spooky representation of the blood and nerves animating him.

"Do you need validation?" the cashier asks, wielding her parking stamp.

"Very much so," he says.

He was certain he'd been to paradise, and maybe he had, but like Adam after his taste of knowledge, he feels naked and shabby and mortal—right up there, no doubt, with the rest of the shoppers in this joint. Father and husband, fire starter, working stiff, he is ready to end his vacation from himself.

24

OUT OF THE FRYING PAN

Owen wakes early to start on the turkeys. He'd turned in early, too—carting those chesty bruisers into their salt baths wore him out. He doesn't know if Ricky and his friend got in. Brooke thinks her brother's bringing a girl home, because he's being cagey about it, but Owen suspects the caginess might be about something else. He's unsure what the supportive parental response is these days to a bisexual college son, and he's a pediatric therapist! Romancewise, Owen hopes Ricky's having a better time of it than Will and Brooke.

He runs his tongue around his gooey mouth; he'll brush his teeth and put on some real clothes after he gets organized. Rejecting his ratty robe and his slick slippers as well, he makes his way down the stairs wearing only boxer shorts (mysteriously printed with red and black question marks), his burn glove, and his compression sock, which is nice and grippy on the bottom. In the entry hall near the lower landing is Ricky's—Richard's—big duffel, draped with a girl's coat and frilly scarf. Toni made up the bed in the basement, so they may both be down there. He'll be surprised to see any of the kids before eleven.

Owen plans to roast one turkey in his stone pit and deep-fry the other, despite having to run between the pit and the deep fryer at the far end of the patio. Last night he bathed the turkeys in the sink, just as he and Toni had done to the kids when they were infants, and then he eased the birds into the cool salted water of their respective coolers out on the patio. He gathered the accessories he'd be needing on a stainless-steel tray. Here are two thermometers, one for oil and one for meat, beside a cast-iron burner combo whose rubber tubing makes it look like a stethoscope. For the fryer, there's a lift hook and a massive syringe for juicing up its breasts and thighs, as well as extra-long silicon mitts for pulling a bird from either the oil basket or the pit. Altogether, the implements look like a doctor's tray of outlandish medical tools.

Owen is surprised by the force of the wintry wind at the back door. Leaves are regrouping, and the neighbor's spindly chair has blown over for a visit. The chickens are nowhere to be seen, and for good reason—the temperature must have dropped twenty degrees overnight. More worrisome is the wind. In these gusts, it won't be easy keeping four gallons of oil boiling over a propane flame. Although the websites are ablaze with *Caution!* and *¡Cuidado!* about never frying indoors, hundreds of men—they're always men—burn down their garages each Thanksgiving. Their defense sounds like the typical disaster joke: Did you see the ten warnings not to do this inside? No, I only saw three. That's the way his kids, his *patients* he should say, behave. They're either egged on by multiple warnings—*Oh, yeah?*—or they are undeterred, having learned that universal laws do not apply in their universe.

One touch of his bare foot on the flagstone patio and he hokeypokeys himself to the kitchen. Usually, every other chair is draped with a sweatshirt, but they were expecting company. Rummaging in the towel drawer, he finds a bibbed apron to tie over his belly and keep the breeze out of his shorts. Vegetables dance around a soup pot on his chest, where ruffles flutter on either side of his nipples. His bare, mismatched arms look weird, too. He remembers when things were steadily wondrous and plenty frightening, but nothing seemed weird. Toni had given him a tour of the breakfast table to show him how lightning had made everything strange. He'd shrugged it off and then subjected himself to a tattoo the length of his arm. Well, he's beginning to get it now, what with Will's debacle, Brooke's drama, and his wearing this getup to attend to two turkeys bathing in the yard. Weird is returning in waves.

He silences the coffeemaker, which beeps like a truck in reverse, and, swinging open the cabinet door for a mug, he dislodges the nesting measuring cups. They tumble from their shelf to the counter, where they upend his tray of gadgets. Everything scatters to the floor, a raucous clatter of plastic cups and turkey tools. Bending down to retrieve them, Owen smacks his funny bone against the counter's sharp corner and blurts out, "Cocksucking asshole!"—a pain reflex that surprises him. Tingling prickles shoot down his otherwise numb right arm, which he cradles in his left as wind through the weather stripping makes a slightly higher pitch than his moans.

After he drinks half a cup of coffee, the stinging in his arm subsides enough for him to pick his mitts up off the floor, but he leaves the rest. He'll retrieve them as he needs them. The thick silicone of the mitts is not very flexible, and they feel more like hand puppets he's animating. "Shall we?" one hand asks the other. "Yes, let's."

Out in the cold, he shrivels beneath his boxers. His twelve-pounder can pickle in its brine until a couple of hours before frying time—if fry he does. The wind whipping the apron against his thighs could easily gutter or spread an open flame. His fifteen-pounder is in a cooler of salt water to which he's added apple juice, star anise, and cloves. Okay, that's weird, too.

Plunging his arms into the cooler, he hoists the turkey to his sternum, as if he were going to bowl the slimy bird down the sidewalk. Gobbler brine soaks the bib of his apron and dribbles down his belly. His hands slip in the mitts; in fact, the whole setup is decidedly unstable. His best course of action seems to be making a half-assed run for the sink, and he backs himself into the kitchen, careful not to step on the spiky lift hook or the turkey thermometer, still on the kitchen floor. He hears footsteps coming up from downstairs, followed by the creaky basement door. In his question-mark boxer shorts, ruffled apron, and a single sock, barely holding a dripping turkey carcass aloft, Owen hears a familiar woman's voice behind him ask, "Dr. Lerner?"

He doesn't lose his tenuous grip; if anything, he clutches the turkey almost as if he were squeezing his brain. In the time it takes to turn around, he puts together the voice, being addressed as *Dr. Lerner*, and the fact that the person talking to him has come up from the guest room.

"Kyra," he says as a big glob of turkey brine runs down his leg. He feels his nipples hardening in his chilled state.

"Is everything all right?" She's wearing a T-shirt and underwear; there's a ring on one of her toes—it's no wonder she got lodged in his subconscious. "I heard this big crash."

"Yes," he says. "No, I'm fine."

A practiced waitress, she squats down to gather the strewn implements onto the metal platter. When she lifts the tray to the counter, the rounded top of her hip is exposed between her white shirt and yellow panties. "Dr. Lerner! Did you get a tattoo?"

"I did," he concurs. Owen instinctively sucks in his gut and revisits the thirty seconds he saved not brushing his teeth. The jewel in Kyra's nose catches the southern light through the kitchen windows; that same sun shines through her thin shirt, the shadows beneath completely showing her nooks and crannies. Plenty of his dreams feel this real, and as recently as a month earlier he'd be cupping her breast in his uninjured hands. But he smells coffee grounds and his own funk; his wet boxers are clinging to his thigh while turkey juice drips like semen down his calf. The skin on his arms is as dank and bumpy as that of the bird he's holding. In his experience, ordinary unpleasantries such as these are evidence of waking life.

That realization gives him a jolt, and he sloshes accordingly, swinging the bird out of range so Kyra will not be tainted. The ball of his good foot slips on what he's already spilled, putting him in serious danger of landing on his tailbone until Kyra darts deftly behind him and clutches the sides of his apron. Conga-line style, they walk past the kitchen island to the sink by the windows; she does not let go until he deposits the slobbery bird.

"Good thing I'm here," she says.

"You're the friend" is all he can manage. He's grateful that he didn't splash her thin white T-shirt, which nonetheless clings to her for dear life. He takes off the rubbery mitts and searches the towel drawer for another bibbed apron. Just then Kyra says, "Well, hello there," and even though he knows she's talking to the cat, she says it so suggestively that he has to turn his burning face away. "What a beauty you are," she tells Mittsy. In his peripheral vision he sees Kyra in her flimsy T-shirt bend over to scratch the cat, who escapes to the windowsill to watch the chicken channel.

The scene stinks of déjà vu, which is heartening because Kyra's never visited them here. May all his memories of their time together be so easily disproved. Woozy with confusion, Owen leans on the island in the middle of the kitchen; once Kyra ties her apron on, she leans as well. Now they're two people stranded on an island.

She says, "It's strange to think of this as your house. To me, your house is at the beach—bacon and toast and coffee going all the time. I don't even know you here."

"Yes, well, I barely know myself here, these days." He imagines the question marks on his silly boxers lifting into the air to circle around him. Why did Ricky bring Kyra home? Does Will know she's here? Did she sleep alone down in the basement? And, of course, the biggest question his boxers might ask: Did he ever violate the Dr. Lerner–Kyra trust?

Kyra says, "I'm really worried about Will."

"He's having a tough time," Owen says, pulling paper towels free from their roller to swab his face.

"Ricky thought he might need me here. I can't imagine what he's told you about us."

"Us?" Owen's heart pounds.

"Will and me," she says.

"You two are a couple," he clarifies.

"Seriously, he said that?" Her giant eyes are moist. "I wasn't sure he ever wanted to see me again."

Owen tugs a napkin from beneath the fulgurite for her. If she starts crying, he's a goner. Will's chaos may take them all down, this house and the beach house, too.

"Ricky called at the last minute," she says. "He said there'd be plenty of food and that you'd be cooking, but I can cook, too. Oh, Dr. Lerner." She leans forward and kisses him on the cheek. Then she says, "Excuse me?" except that her lips don't move and her voice sounds uncannily like Toni's.

In fact, it is Toni speaking.

"*She* kissed *me*," Owen says defensively.

"I can see that." She waves her hand through the air as if she were a conductor. "You're here for Thanksgiving?"

"Ricky and I came on the train together from Wilmington."

"Richard?" Toni asks.

Kyra grins her wide, bright smile. "I forgot. Ri*shard*—thank you so much for having me."

"You're welcome," Toni says. Owen volunteers to get her coffee, and though he's as wobbly as hell, she lets him do it for her. She reaches inside the basement door to lift a pair of fuzzy sweatpants and a T-shirt from a blurry hook. She thinks they're Owen's but she's not sure—in her hurry to get down there, she evidently grabbed the wrong pair of glasses from her nightstand.

Owen fills blue mugs with steaming coffee, which he manages to serve along with milk and sugar. Toni trades him the bundle of clothes for the sugar bowl. She settles gently on a stool but doesn't scoot in, wary as she is of causing a spark. She's a live wire; Owen's a leaky tank of propane; Kyra's a time bomb. With the slightest friction, the whole house might blow.

Kyra's coffee turns the color of her skin as it blooms with milk. She yawns extravagantly. "We didn't get in until around two. Thanks for making the bed for me."

"You're welcome," Toni says again.

"Pants," Owen declares, untying the apron. He steps into the sweats and pulls the shirt over his head.

Toni realizes that the racket Owen made would have sounded worse in the basement than it did from their bedroom—maybe their helpful guest rushed upstairs in her undies just as Toni rushed down. Maybe all those beach summers in bikinis have eroded Kyra's modesty in front of them. Maybe the air isn't actually vibrating, maybe only Toni is, wrestling with herself: she could beg Kyra for help getting through to Will, or she could smack her with the potato masher that's there on the island. It could go either way.

Kyra, meanwhile, has picked up a paperweight from the counter, a clear cube of lightning made in a lab. She brings it close to her face, as Toni has often done before.

"This looks like your arm," Kyra says of the lightning frond captured inside.

"It's part of my collection," Owen says.

Toni remembers the morning Owen knew he was getting his tattoo but didn't think to mention it, the morning he told her that he had lost weird—"the way some people lose car keys," he had said. Weird is becoming so common around here as to be ordinary. With his injuries, as well as his enlightenment, he's ruined normal for the rest of them.

Kyra puts the cube down and then stretches her neck unbecomingly. "I don't have my contacts in. I can't even quite figure out where you are."

"I'm right here," he says, misunderstanding.

"Have you diced all the stuffing stuff yet?" she asks. "I love stuffing, even more than mashed potatoes, I think. Or do you call it dressing? My dad calls it that. I'm glad I woke up early, so you can put me to work."

Toni knows jabbering when she hears it. Either Kyra's self-consciousness is coming to the fore or she's young enough that morning coffee still kicks in like a mule.

Kyra slides off the stool, tugging the bottom of her shirt past her bottom. She plants a kiss on Toni's cheek—a big, surprising *smooch*. "You're the best, Mrs. Lerner. My mom will be psyched that I'm here."

"Wait." Owen holds up a hand. "I hadn't planned to stuff either turkey. There'll be plenty of food, but no stuffing."

"Two turkeys, no stuffing. Is he serious?" Kyra asks Toni.

"Stuffing's always been my favorite," Toni says.

"Now you tell me," Owen says, though he knows this about Toni. On top of stuffing, she likes gravy, too, which neither grilled nor fried turkeys yield. He says, "One turkey, encased in a lovely fruit marinade, goes on the spit. And I'm deep-frying the other one, also outside."

"Oh, I get it." Kyra makes a show of finally understanding. "Your stove is broken."

"No, it's fine. The stove and oven are fine," Toni says, seeing their current life through Kyra's eyes but also wanting to turn herself toward Thanksgiving. "Owen, would you mind? I know this is your hoedown, but maybe we could cook one of them in here."

"I suppose that could be arranged. I'll fry, fry another day," he says, but only Kyra laughs.

Toni's already rummaging through the bread box, where half loaves and a bag of hamburger buns have considerately been drying themselves out. She plucks an onion and some garlic from the wire basket hanging in the corner. "Let's see what the fridge has to offer." Her approach to stuffing is to incorporate whatever's on hand. She brings forth the remaining carrots, still sporting their feathery greens. A few mushrooms, half a red pepper, some sausage, a carton of eggs, an apple, pecans: she brandishes each ingredient with the same flourish she exhibits extracting things from her magic purse. Then she visits her basket of glasses and trades her horn-rims for a bright orange pair set for middle distance.

Toni slaps a skillet on the stove, allowing the habit of stuffing to overtake her. Where Owen's on the lookout for the pinnacle of happiness, she finds solace in the everyday. She inspects the buns for mossy green or Swiss dots of mold and, satisfied, separates the round halves onto a cookie sheet that she slides into the oven. She's met people who insist on making stuffing from corn bread baked with organic stone-ground meal or sourdough leavened only by airborne yeast. The truth is, any bread will do. She wonders if Owen doesn't care for her results—which vary depending on the refrigerator's contents—or why her favorites don't merit his consideration.

"When did you want to eat?" Toni asks.

Owen strokes his bird's breast. "I was aiming for today."

He points to the pile of fruit intended for the marinade, and she and Kyra start in. As soon as Toni peels the first mango, Owen demonstrates how to cut the bottom flat and stand the slippery fruit on end to push a pitter through the orange flesh— the ingenious device slices along the oblong pit, yielding two halves of fruit. When it comes to the pineapple, he lops off its crown with a knife before unveiling another kitchen tool, which

he twists into the pineapple like a corkscrew to pull the core—
pop!—from its spiky shell. "Nicely done," Toni compliments
him, and Kyra agrees. "It looks like pineapple from a can!"

Kyra doesn't peel so much as shred her mangoes, which she
surrenders to Owen. "You guys. Before he wakes up, what do you
think is going on with Will?"

Neither Toni nor Owen looks up from their fruit.

"I want to respect his privacy—like, I don't want to tell *all*—
but he's been so dodgy this semester. He almost lost you, I get it.
But I'm talking some scary conduct."

If Toni's fingers weren't dripping with juice, she might very
well stick them in her ears. She's desperate to hear about Will
from Will, who would just as soon eat glass as reveal himself to
his mother.

"While Ricky and I were on the train—I'm sorry, *Richard*—I
started thinking that maybe Will's worked up because *he* wasn't
the one who did your CPR. Does that make any sense?"

"It might," Owen says.

All that really makes sense to Owen, Toni imagines, is what
kitchen gadget to use for what purpose. Inhaling the fruit mash,
for instance, does he recognize the beach scent he's stirring up? It
smells like their family vacation to her, and she lays her mango,
like a pulpy heart, on his cutting board.

Eager for small talk, she asks Kyra what she's majoring in.
She looks conspiratorially at Owen—*Psychology, am I right?*

"Postcolonial accounting," Kyra says. "My adviser rocks."

Toni, who is in contact with a dozen universities a day about
new programs and hot faculty prospects, has never even heard of
postcolonial accounting. Just below her right eye, her cheek
muscles begin a tiny tantrum she cannot control. When it comes
right down to it, what can she control? Not Owen, Brooke, or
Richard. Certainly not Will. She wishes she could keep her own
face in check, just as she wishes she could extend a little hospitality, a little credit, too, to Kyra, who has herself given Toni no
cause for suspicion. What's not to welcome about this voluptuous,
insightful, completely unguarded soul in her tension-riddled
home? Toni picks up the knife to dice the carrots and then

immediately sets it down. The only thing her hands would be good for right now is whisking.

"You probably want to take a shower," she urges Kyra. "You probably want to put on some clothes."

"As soon as we get the turkeys ready. Couldn't you guys use my help?"

"If you insist," Toni says, giving over the cutting board and letting her hands fall in her lap. "I suppose all help helps."

25

INTO THE FIRE

No matter how much wood he splits, Owen always needs more. Two of the braver chickens occasionally stick their beaks out the flap of their shingled shed, only to shriek every single time he swings the splitting maul. Their ridiculously impaired memory usually amuses him, but today he overidentifies, tortured by his lack of Kyra recall and the lust those nonexistent memories inspire. *Who wouldn't want to lift a skirt up over that plummy rump?* he thinks, before his conscience shrieks like the ridiculous chickens.

He has to concentrate lest he crush his foot. If he gets the fruit mash right, puts the bird in soon, and holds the temperature steady, the tom should become succulent bites beneath a hardened shell, something like a fifteen-pound candied apple. Childhood Thanksgivings were full of such ploys: marshmallows melted across the tops of sweet potato casseroles, maple syrup in the carrots, maraschino cherries on a ham. Kids love sweets, but sugar coatings may attract us for other reasons. He suspects that in his new incarnation, whatever it may be, food will supplement his behavioral theories. Perhaps he will go forth and preach the general theory of barbecue: keep your fires low and your dampers open.

Owen layers seasoned apple and pear wood atop his bed of cherry, which he has burned down to white-hot bones. He hears a commotion in the kitchen, where his turkey awaits him, and through the south windows he sees Toni hugging one of the boys. She steps back with a bounce, holds the boy's face in her hands, and hugs him again. That would be Ricky. She points out the window, and then she touches her chin and runs that hand down her right arm. That would be referring to him, he imagines. Ricky sweeps his own hand down his right arm, as if to corroborate what she's told him, and Owen can see the charades of their disbelief.

Next, Owen hears Brooke scream and sees her leap into the arms of her brother, who spins her around. Even through the windows and the wind, the sound of Ricky's teasing carries, as does his warmth for his sister. It's as if Owen is listening to a sound track—*a sound track!* For the first time, he makes the connection between the music he prefers and the profession he practices. His ear-training exercises aim to teach patients social cues with emotional sound tracks: maybe he should start with movie music. Do his patients hear the sigh of sorrow in the strings or the mounting suspense in the thundering timpani? Having a brand-new thought in his mixed-up head thrills him, but it also alerts him to the absence of the family sound track. Everyone's gone quiet for some reason.

Will is the reason. When he enters stage left, Toni elbows Ricky, who hooks his arm around his brother's neck in a half-hearted half nelson. Sound or no sound, Will's body language says it all: hands up in acknowledgment that shit does indeed happen; hands down and head down, bowed by the weight of his troubles. Both boys start talking like crazy, and a moment later, Kyra's name is blowing in the wind. Owen wonders where she is.

He is eavesdropping because he is outside preparing to cook their dinner. Of course, Toni's right there at the epicenter, listening in real time and space, and she's already cooking their dinner. She and Kyra got the first turkey stuffed and in the oven nearly an hour ago. He hefts two more logs onto the fire, followed by thinner splits, at the risk of smothering the flame or turning it into an inferno, which could well choke down to bitter smoke. He chooses getting to the kitchen over the patience he's bestowed on every meal this fall.

Ricky pulls him through the door with a hug. "Dad! The hero returns!"

"Who's the hero, you or me?" Owen squeezes his stinging eyes closed for a second and then claps his son on the shoulder. "You're looking pretty good."

He actually looks the way Will used to, the way they both used to. Ricky still has his swim-season brawn, though his tan has faded and his hair gone longer and darker. Neither boy has had a trim since summer, and their fluffy, thatched hair settles like a nest identically on each of their heads. With his sunken cheeks and deformed nose, Will is the shadow of his robust brother. He's not wearing his sunglasses.

"Happy Thanksgiving, Daddy," Brooke says.

Owen waves to the assembled. "That's right. Happy Thanksgiving, everybody."

"Not *everybody*," Will points out. "Someone's still downstairs, someone Ricky brought."

"You're welcome," Ricky says.

Owen folds his arms over his chest in a posture of sternness. "We've barely heard a word from you, *Richard*."

"I mentioned that," Toni agrees.

"Sorry," Ricky says. "I've got number theory, and my mythology class has been nuts. I missed you guys like crazy. I *did*," he insists to his mother. He pushes Owen's folded sleeve up his arm past his elbow. "This is the real deal."

"It's not a myth," Owen acknowledges, and then he says, "And we mythed you, too."

The kids moan, and Ricky—*Richard*—says, "Mom tells us you're doing great."

He is? Owen looks to Toni, who shrugs. She often nails it, but how he's doing, how she thinks he's doing, and how she might report on it to the kids are too many layers for him. He takes a bite of toast and chews deliberately. As he reaches for his mug, Brooke goes for it, too, and when they both touch the handle, she springs into the air as if he shocked her. The gang laughs at her gag.

"Sorry, Daddy. Anyway, I already *quaffed* that one. It's decaf."

Will mimes a spit take. "Decaf? No wonder I'm not buzzed."

"You've got regular," Toni clarifies. "God, you're all such grown-ups. And clowns. Okay, that's the last of the bread." She adds two slices to the tower before she moves from making toast to pie dough, slicing shortening into the flour with two butter knives.

"I'm in need of a turkey wrangler," Owen says.

"Allow me," Will volunteers. He hoists the big platter from the back counter. His own injured knuckles are swollen like marbles, making it hard to keep the bird level. The slick turkey slides to the dish's edge and beyond. Will tiptoes left before going right, until he centers the bird on the plate. It's not clear if he's horsing around or if he nearly drops the bird.

Brooke shakes her finger. "Wobble, wobble, wobble."

Will grins the way he used to. "Or, as Afghani turkeys say, Kabul, Kabul, Kabul!"

"And you wonder why I kept my distance?" Ricky asks his parents.

Owen nabs the orange mitts and turkey lifts and follows Will outside. It's not so easy to hook the lifts beneath the coated bird; however, it's impossible with his burned hand to muster the dexterity to lower a fifteen-pound turkey by a wire into a white-hot pit.

His son taps him on the shoulder. "I got it, old man," he says; in fact, he takes the silicone gloves from Owen and readily situates the fruit-slathered turkey on its pyre. Owen is grateful for Will's help and relieved that he doesn't have to manage the deep fryer.

After the bird is settled, Will stands barely out of range of the flames, which hiss with the wet, sugary pulp and drips of turkey fat. He seems grim and troubled as sweat beads up on his forehead. He says, "It's warm in Buffalo, above freezing. First Thanksgiving in years there won't be snow."

"They get more than their share," Owen says. He would like to offer an update on how James and his parents are doing, and although Gloria advised him against contacting the family, he wishes he'd overruled her legal concerns with his humane ones.

The fire pops and spits a shower of embers at Will, who merely cups his palm over the live sparks that land on his shorts and brushes away the ashes. He says, "I don't know about you, Dad, but I'm scared to death. Of everything." He speaks without affect, almost like a robot. "If Kyra breaks up with me, if she—deservedly—tells me to fuck off, that terrifies me. But if she gives me another chance? That's terrifying, too. What if James doesn't get better . . . What if I was the one who hit my head and you guys were standing around my bed? How can I live with myself if they don't send me to jail, except how would I survive in jail?"

Owen slings his arm around his son and they stand in front of the pit, staring into the fire. "You weren't the one who hit your head," he says, the only question of Will's he can refute. They'd lived a lovely, sheltered life nestled as a family until lightning cracked them open. All the security he gave his children seems to be oozing out of that crack. Once you've lost that innocence, Will wants to know, what does it take to get up each morning and face the day? "You have a say in more than you think," he tells his son. "When people get thrown for a loop, they can feel like victims. But you're the same intelligent, talented Will you were three months ago."

"I doubt it," Will says. "She and Ricky rode here on the train together—how whacked is that?—and you and Mom *cooked* with her this morning. I haven't even seen her yet."

Owen says, "All I know is that she's awfully worried about you."

"Aren't we all." Will elbows Owen, and it seems playful enough. "See you on the flip side," he says.

"Later," Owen confirms. He checks the temperature along with his wood reserves, which are both as expected. And then he walks down to the coop to feed and water his crazy chickens, who squabble and freak while somehow managing to stick together.

•

When Owen comes into the kitchen, Ricky and Brooke are watching Will scrub potatoes with a vengeance. Maybe he's trying to do something for Toni, who is coaxing her crumbly pie dough into a ball. It's so painful to see him grip the peeler in his wounded hands that Owen says, "You can leave the skins on."

"Taste or nutrition?" he says bitterly.

"Nutrition, I guess." Mercy, really, was the reason he'd suggested it.

Will leers. "And after they're mashed, do we sprinkle them with Zoloft?"

The vulnerability Will showed Owen by the fire has hardened, either out of embarrasment or sheer anxiety.

Ricky holds up the salt and pepper shakers, prominently marked *S* and *P*. "Strattera and Prozac, anyone?"

"Stay tuned for our next 'episode.'" Will makes air quotes for the doctors' euphemism. "Next week on *Owen Lerner, MD*, a poisonous snakebite allows him to predict the future."

Owen is accustomed to their teasing, but not their ridicule, and he feels the light drizzle of family dynamics turning to acid rain. He did urge people not to take family life personally, but he never said not to take it *seriously*. As for his "episode," Owen might struggle the rest of his life to metabolize what happened in those fateful milliseconds when he was taken out of himself, entertained, and plopped back into his gummy human shell. Who knows if he's up to rejoining the regularly scheduled programming, or if his family has regrouped without him?

Will flings his hands in the air. "The water turned hot. She must finally be out of the shower." He tosses a sponge at his brother. "Wish me luck, asshole."

"Good luck, asshole," Ricky obliges.

Owen tries his best not to picture the water dripping in a rivulet down Kyra's neck and between her breasts as Will clomps loudly down the stairs.

"He's sounding the alarm," Toni says. She shuts the basement door with her elbow. "Let's give them a little space. I'm covered in dough—can you turn the radio on?"

Brooke clicks on the radio, where an interview is in session. "It's news," she says, and immediately clicks it off.

Toni would welcome the certainty of news, she'd welcome the quavery voice of the public radio interviewer; on this Thanksgiving Day, she'd welcome a reading from the Puritans' diaries recounting their miseries and endurance. She wonders if Brooke is aware that there are other stations or how to find them, though Toni is hardly one to judge. Now that there are four remotes, she has to look at the cheat sheet to watch TV. It won't be long before turning on a light will be beyond them all. She feels years older this Thanksgiving than last; unfortunately, no wiser and much less secure. And yet she's survived a great deal, as has Owen, who is hovering nearby. She wants to ask him who these people are who emerge from adversity stronger and more determined. Instead, she tells him, "Your turn. Take a bath, if you want. There's time."

He braces himself for the fatigue his wife has already perceived. There was a phase after his accident when she possessed the power to exhaust him or make him feel pain. She would announce it, and then his body would comply. Now her anticipation is an act of compassion. This morning he's already struggled with two turkey carcasses in their tubs of brine, come face-to-face with Kyra, chopped fruit, and chopped wood. That doesn't even count being the brunt of his children's humor. He sips his coffee, and there it is: he could use a long bath.

Owen goes upstairs, and he doesn't stop at bathing. He brushes his teeth and flosses; he shaves and clips his fingernails; he trims his nose hairs. He thinks of Rip Van Winkle, come to after twenty years, and of Odysseus finally returning to Ithaca, ten years of war in Troy and ten more on the high seas. Rip Van Winkle just slept; Odysseus slept around, fathering a few more kids and losing his entire crew along the way. Both of them missed a lifetime at home.

In his closet, Owen reaches beyond the leggings for a pair of gray dress pants and a striped, long-sleeved shirt; it's not as if they'll be playing touch football. He gets himself buttoned and zipped and belted. Since his accident, he hasn't worn shoes with laces, and they feel a bit funereal. He tucks a hand towel into his waist to go downstairs and out the front door to the yard, where his turkey is beautifully browning. After its early-morning stunts, the wind has calmed down. Owen returns a tarp that blew off the flagstone remnants and checks on the chickens again—*What? We're fine*—stepping gingerly in his lace-up shoes so he doesn't slide on wet leaves. Might as well visit the koi and give them their Thanksgiving kibble.

From the kitchen table, Will sees his dad tiptoe around the yard, and he wonders how much pain the man is in. At the same time, he's watching Kyra encourage Brooke to talk about the possessive Brazilian shit she's dating. Horribly grateful for Brooke's lousy boyfriend, he also wants to kick the guy's ass.

"Has he ever hurt you?" Kyra's asking her.

"No. Well, kind of, yes," Brooke says. "He tells me over and over he loves me—"

"He can't hurt you," Ricky interrupts. "It doesn't matter what he says, even about love. Why do you stay with him?"

"Because he hurts me," Brooke says.

"Okay, well, that's not love," Richard says.

Will moans in protest. "Who are we to judge?" he asks. Feeling as desolate as the day he came home, he pours himself another glass of vodka. Kyra's still there, which seems a Thanksgiving miracle, if there is such a thing. But despite how happy he is to see her, he wonders why she should stay with him. And as much as he loves his parents, he's only bringing them pain.

Richard says, "Here's what we *can* judge: it's a little early for that. Seriously, Will."

There must have been some reason why his dad locked away the medications but left the liquor in the cabinet above the refrigerator. In a mock whisper, Will asks, "Brooksey, are you guys having sex?"

"Did Mom say that? Does she know?"

Kyra slaps his hand. "He's just guessing. Don't worry, you don't look different or anything."

"But it is different," Brooke says, her voice turned babyish through her tears.

"Please don't cry. I'm being a dick," Will says. "Ask Kyra what a dick I can be."

Kyra spills Will's vodka into the island's sink behind her without even disturbing the cat in her lap.

"Hey!" he protests, but Kyra swivels farther away from him. She asks Brooke, "Different how?"

Brooke says, "He was so funny, so sexy, and he thought I was those things. Now he's mad all the time, unless we're doing something. When we're at practice, he's like an owl turning his head all the way around to watch me every second. I'm like, 'Nothing is going to happen at practice.'"

"I know the type," Kyra says, and when Mittsy chimes in— *mrowr*—even Will laughs. Kyra lifts the cat in the air. "Ask yourself, what would Mittsy do?"

Richard answers, "No idea. We were raised on the dog model."

"I'm talking to Brooke, you guys." Kyra turns Mittsy to face Brooke. "Would she ignore him—cats are great at that—or would she claw his eyes out?"

Will says, "Those aren't her only options. Or yours." Kyra hands Mittsy off to him, and he hopes she sees how gently he pets her.

"You heard your sister," Kyra says. "These guys who charm you into choosing them and then panic when you're not in a room together. Why are they like that?"

Would that Will could cover for the stupid, primitive boys of the world. He says, "I blame the parents."

What else is new? Toni thinks, walking in on the conversation. Already the kitchen is infused with butter and onions, carrots and garlic, celery and sage. Seems a waste to cook outdoors when you can fill a home with these aromas. Brooke is wiping her swollen eyes, and Toni wonders who has been told what and, when she sees the open bottles of vodka and wine, who has been drinking what.

"This doesn't seem wise," she says, and Kyra and Ricky both glare at Will. "Everything all right?" she asks Brooke, who nods meekly. "Honey, here's Selena's pie recipe for the filling; my crust should be ready to roll."

Owen arrives just then, dressed to the hilt. He takes both bottles off the table. "You know what this 2006 Woodenhead Vineyard Pinot Noir would be good with? Turkey."

Richard says, "If it lasts that long."

Will clears his throat and begins reading from the pie recipe. "Canned pumpkin filling, canned evaporated milk, 'pumpkin pie' spice—not very *artisanal*, guys."

"Knock yourself out," Toni says, and she takes the ball of dough to the far end of the island. "There's a nutmeg grater in there, if you're so inclined. Hell, you can pulverize whole cloves with the mortar and pestle."

"She said 'hell,'" Will mocks, and an exasperated Kyra says, "You're acting like a child."

Looking down the table, Toni has a hard time imagining that they don't consider themselves children. In fact, Kyra looks younger than usual today in her abbreviated cardigan over a Peter Pan–collared blouse.

"The other night?" Brooke says to Kyra. "Before you and Ricky got home, Daddy tried to describe his episode. It was more like a scrapbook than anything else—sorry, Dad."

"I guess you had to be there," Owen says.

Ricky says, "We *were* there."

Owen sees Ricky sit up straighter, pushing his shoulders down his back just the way Toni does when she's about to deliver a verbal blow. "I've been meaning to tell you," his son says, "the smell in your nostrils, all this grilling—I think that's from me."

"I smelled it," Owen says. "When I was hit, I can practically tell you the recipe."

"Maybe you heard it," Ricky suggests. "That coach who drilled CPR into us, he made us count that way: breathe, then chant 'barbecue spareribs, barbecue spareribs,' then breathe. That's how I brought you back."

Toni, who's rolling out the piecrust, bears down at the mention of that coach. The night of the accident, she'd swooned when Ricky recited his incantation.

Ricky says, "That summer was a trip. You remember that bald coach, don't you, Mom, how *intense* he was?"

"I do," she says, and it's a good thing she answers right away, because Ricky's attentiveness swells up in her throat and behind her eyes. Because of a blurry scan in utero, she's watched him his whole life for signs of brain damage; meanwhile, his whole life, he's been watching her, too, just as closely. How does what they know of each other compare with what they suspect?

"No, no, no," Owen says, confused by his own certitude. He doesn't want to be ungrateful, but he needs to set the record straight. "First of all, they don't think I stopped breathing—I may not have required CPR. While you and Will were messing around, I remember seeing your stringy neck muscles before you sprang off that bike rack. So I was conscious. And I smelled barbecue cooking. I could smell the exact sauce."

"*You* were cooking, Dad," Ricky says, not unkindly.

Owen has already admitted to himself that it could very well have been his own flesh he smelled in the tropical marinade of suntan lotion and sweat. These days, he likes to be out in his pit with the fruity smoke of the wood and the heat radiating back at him from the stones. The fragrant meat is stirring, too. But it hasn't smelled like heaven for a while. For all he knows, everyone in hell is sniffing the air, their own skin crackling in the flames, and saying, "Ummm! When do we eat?"

But he went somewhere and saw some things. He unbuttons his cuff and begins rolling his sleeve up his right arm. It is not the arm it was last July. "I'd think you'd want to hear my whole story before you reject it." He is more gentle with himself as he rolls the left sleeve past new skin. "Where've you been all semester?"

Toni isn't sure whether to rein in Owen or Ricky; after all, Ricky's bullying both her and Owen, rubbing their noses in his superior knowledge. Sometimes, family life is like a game of tag: one person corners another—*you're it!*—and then runs away, off the hook for the time being. Just like tag, it can turn from playful to painful in an instant, *someone's going to get hurt*, and alliances can change just as quickly. Where the hell *has* Ricky been all semester? Neither boy made an effort to visit, and it saddens her to think she's raised selfish children who sit in judgment of them. God knows, she's been eager to get that crazy glint out of Owen's eyes, but there are aspects of this Owen that she doesn't want to lose.

Brooke, who has poured pie filling and milk into a bowl and

is now whisking in the eggs, says, "Mom, you're down to the counter."

Toni has made a complete hash of her piecrust. She pushes the dough back together in hopes it will give her another chance.

Owen says, "Man punished and elevated at the whim of the gods; shape-changing, time-traveling quests. Maybe your professors would be interested in me as a case study."

"You should be so chosen," Ricky says, his shoulders rounding protectively.

Will says, "Hanging with Dr. Clifton again—is that how you know so much about love?"

Ricky stands and retrieves the peeler from the counter. He feels his mother's eyes on the back of his head as he lifts the top from the stockpot, where the potatoes are waiting to be boiled. Selecting one of the potatoes Will scrubbed clean, he begins to peel, separating a thin, unbroken ribbon of brown from the white flesh. The others look to the pleasing spiral he creates in the air, the freestanding thin skin orbiting the potato. "Don't forget applied math," he says, as if he's been spending all his time on, say, polygon-inclusion and enclosure problems. But he learned to peel potatoes in Lucy Clifton's kitchen.

Will is on his feet, in his face. "Leave the skins on! Dad said leave them on." He swipes the naked potato from his brother and drops it—*plop!*—into the pot of water with the others.

Ricky says, "He suggested it. I happen to prefer them off. You don't mind, do you, Dad?"

What Owen minds is Ricky baiting and Will biting the hook.

Will says, "I'm telling you: Leave. The skins. On!"

"Look at yourself." Richard is disgusted. "One more drink and you'll pass out before dinner."

Will takes a step back, scanning his brother from head to toe. "I am looking at myself, and it makes me sick." Even as he's wondering what the hell he's doing, Will snatches the fulgurite from on top of the napkins and raises the glass wand like a fencer wielding a sword. *This is the way a robotic arm works in real time*, he thinks, commanding his fingers to grip and his elbow to bend, yet it might take him another semester of programming and lab work to get this half second of movement. Is he messing around? Is he drunk? Is he out of his mind? *When it comes right down to it*, he thinks, *artificial intelligence is the only kind we have.*

Ricky grips the stockpot lid by its black knob and extends it like a shield in front of himself, but no blow comes his way. Changing up the game, he flips the lid into cymbal mode and strikes its fat lip with the potato peeler once, twice, three times. The dinging could be the signal for a boxing round or a call to meditation. Will's nostrils flare, and he snorts through his bent nose. It's hard for Ricky to tell whether his twin is more eager to commit suicide or fratricide. There's so much twin lore in Ricky's head, including a wild twin civilized by his brother's friendship and, always, Cain slaying Abel, whose past tense, *slew*, also means to rotate around an axis. That's how his mind works, and he'd guess it's the same for Will. So much wisdom to choose from, yet as the clanging subsides, Ricky blurts out, "Dad fooled around with your girlfriend!"

"What?" Kyra says. "Who *told* you that?" Her dark skin turns wine dark.

From where Toni is standing, she sees Ricky's distorted reflection in the polished stainless steel of the pot lid. On the other side of the makeshift mirror is Will's wrecked visage, mouth wide open, giving her full view of the space left by the molar he lost in his brawl, a permanent tooth. Of course at his age it's permanent.

Ricky tilts the lid toward Owen. "Dad told me—in the hospital."

Toni's palm on the counter raises a cloud of flour. "Oh, for god's sake. He said a lot of things in the hospital. Remember the dancing girls every night? He roasted Sparkle on a spit!"

But that just makes it worse for Will, who cannot bear one more word about his father's episode. His own looping memories replay endless games of sock ball with Ricky on their bunk beds, laughing until their cheeks ached, or texting him one hundred times in a single day. Also, Kyra reaching into Ricky's dresser drawer to get the condoms they needed, and the woozy, wounded James spiraling toward the curb. Kyra won't stick with him after this weekend—how could anyone? That thought alone propels him to strike against his brother's stupid lid. Ricky's quick on the upswing, but Will has a drummer's wrist. He flicks the lightning rod hard against the hi-hat, and the ragged stick shatters, explodes really, cracking like gunshot. The surprise, the blow, the noise all take Ricky down with it. He hits the floor between the kitchen table and the island.

It is Owen who is by Ricky's side in a heartbeat, swabbing blood from Ricky's lip, which he bit hard as he fell. When Owen looks around for his other son, Toni is hugging the boy, though she might actually have him pinned. And Kyra is shielding Brooke, complete with her hands over Brooke's eyes.

Owen takes the pot lid from Ricky, who returns his father's loving gaze with his own. The boy's eyes are steady, his pupils of equal size and not markedly dilated. He doesn't seem to have hit his head, though his split, swollen lip looks like a chicken liver.

"Missed me," Ricky says to Will.

"No, I didn't," Will objects. He's pushed his mother aside and is crunching on ground glass to get to his twin. "I was aiming at the lid. Jesus, I must really be a monster."

"You're not," Kyra says. "Well, you *are*. But you weren't. You didn't used to be."

There is powdered glass, like grains of sand, all over the kitchen. There is glass floating in the bowl of Brooke's pie filling, sparkling shards dusting the ball of dough. Owen feels grit back between his molars—is that even possible?—and glittering silt lines the folds of his rolled sleeves. He's grateful to have tied on real shoes when he got dressed earlier.

"Stay put," he says. "I'll be right back."

He goes to the basement to retrieve the broom. Downstairs he walks past Kyra's suitcase, blooming with bras and soft sweaters. Everyone is guilty and everyone is loved here, even if the extent of the guilt isn't known. Owen thinks of patients he has ferried through ordeals such as this. The palliatives he prescribes allow them to endure, as does his listening and counsel. Gathering his courage, he pauses on the bottom step, where the smell of their roasting turkey reaches down to meet him.

Ricky is at the table pressing a freezer pack to his lip, and Will is dusting him off with the brush they use to clean out the coffee grinder. "All of you, go downstairs and come up again," Owen says. "You won't believe it."

The five of them allow Owen to herd them into the stairwell, all the way down to the laundry room, whereupon he bids them to turn around and follow him. As they ascend a dozen steps to the kitchen they have just left, they begin to moan with the savory smell of the crackling skin and fat in the pan, the roasted browning bird, and the custardy dressing within. They are back where they started around the table, inhaling and exhaling like swimmers pulled from the cold, dark deep.

Owen sweeps the floor. Eventually Toni says, "We lost the pie."

Owen turns the doorknob, and the back door swings in. "Then we'll have turkey for dessert."

Grilled pineapple and smoke come in on that breeze, mingling with the traditional indoor fare. Toni reaches into the drawer beneath the towels for a fresh pair of candles. Against all odds, they will sit at the table and give their peculiar version of thanks. Brooke will mourn the loss of the pie, or maybe the kids will pitch in and put one in the oven to be ready for them after the feast. *This is how family life will be from here on out*, Toni thinks. By any means necessary, they will have to take turns saving one another's lives.

While the wind blowing into the overheated kitchen is too cold to be refreshing, the breeze permits Owen to smell the charring sweet flesh of the turkey in the pit along with the succulent butter-basted one at hand. His intention, as he sees it, is to keep a foot in each world, sustaining the strike even as he lives in the day-to-day. He pulls a towel from the rack on the oven door to blot the tears spilling down his wife's cheeks. Her glasses make a ledge for a waterfall, which is strange given that she's also smiling. But then he thinks of their daughter, who can ignore gravity when it suits her, or their sons, one of whom shifts between math and myth and the other—may he earn a second chance—who tries to teach machines to think.

They will have to forgive him for being struck by lightning, and he will have to forgive them for being grounded that blustery night. As Toni wordlessly offers him the candles in trade for the tea towel, Owen sees his outstretched arm in another light. The innocuous glove he wears masks the ropy welts of his grafts; however, his arm is etched with fault lines marking the lightning's path, cracks in his mortal shell. With less clarity than he had when he was above them all, he has an inkling of how they might move ahead.

There will be plenty of struggles to come, he imagines, and we may well come apart before we're parted. But in the meantime, let us dish up a feast and give thanks for what we have weathered.

ACKNOWLEDGMENTS

Decades of loving thanks to Gary Zizka for his attentive care, to Theo Zizka for his creativity and nonconformity, and to Eliza Zizka, heart- and book-smart, for noticing everything. There is no better company. Thanks, too, for letting me use your great lines.

With deep affection to Jonathan Galassi. Sarah Burnes quoted me poetry, and Donna Oetzel provided daily affirmation. I thank these three up one side and down the other.

A bouquet of long-stemmed thanks to Susan Campbell and Margaret Talbot for friendship extraordinaire. Michelle Brafman and Maureen Taft-Morales get family business like no one else, except maybe Catherine Batza and Bridget Bean. To Kate Blackwell and Deborah Galyan, and to Terence Winch, who has my back. I cherish them all. I'm indebted to Karen Sagstetter for her love of barbecue and for reading a primitive draft, along with Mandy Berry, Carolyn Parkhurst, and Erica Perl. The early enthusiasm of Jane Hamilton, Aimee Bender, and Laurie Foos was invaluable.

Joyful praise to the DC Women Writers and their dinners. Thanks be to the talent, guts, and grace of Susan Shreve. And to the PEN/Faulkner Foundation for spreading the gospel of literary activism and the redemptive power of the imagination.

I'm grateful to Linda Hopkins for explaining my dreams to me and to Lance Clawson and Howard Bennett for their compassionate concern.

Virginia Center for the Creative Arts provided a haven, as did the quiet room at the Little Falls Library of Montgomery County. Gib and Camilla Durfee handed over the keys to their house when I was a stranger to them, and Sally Kux offered the keys to hers, knowing me as well as she does. The folks at Modern Times Coffeehouse and Politics & Prose Bookstore helped me every single day.

At FSG, Miranda Popkey and Christopher Richards were a joy to work with, and Jeff Seroy, Nick Courage, Kathy Daneman, and especially Lottchen Shivers helped spread the word, all for the love of books.